An OPUS book

Science Fiction in the Twentieth Century

Dr Edward James is Senior Lecturer in the Department of
History and Director of the Centre for Medieval Studies at York
University. He is the editor of *Foundation: The Review of
Science Fiction*, and co-editor of the book *The Profession of
Science Fiction: SF Writers on their Craft and Ideas.*

D0168657

Science Fiction in the Twentieth Century

EDWARD JAMES

Oxford   New York

OXFORD UNIVERSITY PRESS

1994

Oxford University Press, Walton Street, Oxford OX2 6DP

Oxford New York Toronto
Delhi Bombay Calcutta Madras Karachi
Kuala Lumpur Singapore Hong Kong Tokyo
Nairobi Dar es Salaam Cape Town
Melbourne Auckland Madrid

and associated companies in
Berlin Ibadan

Oxford is a trade mark of Oxford University Press

British Library Cataloguing in Publication Data
Data available

Library of Congress Cataloging in Publication Data
James, Edward, 1947–
Science fiction in the 20th century / Edward James.
    p.   cm.
"An Opus book."
Includes bibliographical references.
1. Science fiction—20th century—History and criticism.
I. Title.
PN3433.8.J36 1994   809.3'8762—dc20   93–47106
ISBN 0–19–289244–4 (Pbk.)

10 9 8 7 6 5 4 3 2 1

Typeset by Graphicraft Typesetters Ltd., Hong Kong
Printed in Great Britain
by Biddles Ltd
Guildford & King's Lynn

To Frank Hampson (1917–1985),

who introduced me to science fiction

Preface

Near the beginning of Gene Wolfe's immense five-volume *The Book of the New Sun*, one of the masterpieces of modern science fiction, Severian comes across an old man in the Citadel's art-gallery.

The picture he was cleaning showed an armored figure standing in a desolate landscape. It had no weapon, but held a staff bearing a strange stiff banner. The visor of this figure's helmet was entirely of gold, without eye slits or ventilation; in its polished surface the deathly desert could be seen in reflection, and nothing more.

A later conversation makes clear to Severian, and perhaps the reader, what the image is:

'See how nice it's brightening up? There's your blue Urth coming over his shoulder again, fresh as the Autarch's fish' . . .
   'Is that the moon? I have been told it is more fertile.'
   'Now it is. This was done before they got it irrigated. See that gray-brown? In those times that's what you'd see if you looked up at her. Not green like she is now.'[1]

The picture on the wall is of an American astronaut standing on the Moon, near the end of the twentieth century of the Christian era. It is from thousands or millions of years in Severian's past.
   This particular image of Earth viewed from another world—a photograph familiar to us from countless reproductions—stands as a complex symbol for different aspects of science fiction in the twentieth century, and therefore for this book. Through science fiction, writers have allowed the problems of humans and of the Earth to be viewed from a distance, as if from another world, or by aliens. This may serve a satiric purpose; much more often, however, this deliberate distancing is intended

to offer the reader a refreshingly different, perhaps more 'scientific', perspective on the human species and the world it inhabits, just as the passage from Wolfe cited above allows us to see a familiar image in a startlingly new way. This distanced perspective gives science fiction readers an experience very similar to (but much cheaper than) that gained by some American astronauts and Soviet cosmonauts, who have returned to Earth musing on the effects which the sight of Earth from space has had upon their attitudes to nationalism, human conflict, the environment, and the fragility of human achievement when placed in the infinite vastness of galactic space. In addition, this image illustrates the way in which science fiction in this century has prefigured many of the technological advances of the century. In some sense, indeed, science fiction made this image possible: a high proportion of the NASA scientists and engineers involved in the first manned voyage to the Moon were readers of science fiction, and had been inspired by its vision, particularly prevalent in their youth in the 1940s and 1950s, of the conquest of space. Science fiction, through most of this century, has been dominated by American writers; it was American scientists who solved the myriad technological problems which lie behind the taking of that photograph (with a Japanese camera). At the beginning of the twentieth century, that picture would have been science fiction; now, twenty years after the image was captured on film, and after the conquest of space has dwindled to the launching of satellites for commercial, military, or (occasionally) scientific purposes, it is history—and it seems almost as unreal as it had seemed before. The placing of men on the Moon encapsulates the immense scientific and technological changes of this century which have been a major impetus behind the development of science fiction; science fiction has been, above all, the literature which has realized the social and historical importance of those changes and the way in which they will affect the future development of the human race.

This book is an introduction to science fiction (henceforth usually 'sf'), intended primarily for those who know little about it. It attempts to be as much a cultural history as a literary history. Indeed, sf is no longer simply a collection of texts which can be analysed by a literary critic. Its ideas and icons have permeated the imagery of cinema, television, rock music, and advertising; have come to dominate the world of play, from Ninja Turtles and transformer robots to comics and computer games; and have helped to create religions (like scientology) and popular delusions (like flying saucers). Nor is sf just a collection of texts to many of those who read it; it offers a different way of looking at the world, a substitute for, or complement to, religion and, like religion, a sense of community and of purpose.

The book is about the sf *of* the twentieth century (without excluding a brief discussion of the origins of sf, and reckoning the twentieth century to begin in 1895 with H. G. Wells's *The Time Machine*), looked at from a literary point of view, with an analysis of a selection of key texts. But it is also about the historical relationship *in* the twentieth century between the growth of sf (and its community of writers and readers) and general cultural, political, and scientific developments. One of its constant concerns is the difference between sf in the United States and in the rest of the world; the history of sf in the latter part of the twentieth century is much involved with the interaction between American and other cultures. The main other culture discussed is that of the United Kingdom. The focus is sf in the English-speaking world, for various reasons: world sf remains dominated by Anglo-American sf; other traditions of sf have been much less studied by sf scholars; and, except for French-language sf, it is largely unfamiliar to me. The main underlying thesis of the book is that sf is a major cultural phenomenon, an understanding of which is essential if one wants to comprehend the ways in which Western societies have come to terms with the rapid change and uncertainty which have characterized our century. Another possible title for the book —drawn from a remark of Doris Lessing's—would have been 'Science Fiction: A Dialect for Our Times'.

If any new insights are forthcoming in what follows, they are likely to arise from the oddity of my background as compared with the backgrounds of other authors of other single-volume introductions to the subject. I am not an sf writer (like Brian W. Aldiss or Lester del Rey) or a full-time sf academic (like

Eric S. Rabkin or Robert Scholes), let alone both (like James Gunn); most of my professional work has been as an early medievalist. But I have been reading sf now for just over forty years. My earliest reading memory of any kind is of the 27 June 1952 issue of the *Eagle*, with the first episode of *Marooned on Mercury*—the third graphic novel, as it would now be called, to feature Dan Dare, Pilot of the Future (hence the dedication of this book to Frank Hampson, Dan Dare's creator). I joined the British Science Fiction Association ten years later, and became involved in the world of sf fandom: heady experiences for a teenager from the sheltered background of a minor British public school. Even today, I still float on the margins of fandom, go to the odd sf convention, review sf for a number of publications, publish academic articles on the history of sf, and belong to the Science Fiction Research Association (US). Since 1986 I have edited, on behalf of the Science Fiction Foundation (based until 1993 at the Polytechnic of East London, now at the University of Liverpool), *Foundation: The Review of Science Fiction*. This journal, the only academic journal outside North America devoted to the history and criticism of sf, publishes some 400 pages of articles, reviews, and debates each year; through it, I have been privileged to get to know some of the most knowledgeable and perceptive critics of sf on three continents. Over the years I have found much valuable material in the extensive collection of the Science Fiction Foundation.

As an early medievalist, I am used to approaching literary texts as historical documents; I am hardened to making wild generalizations backed by the minimum of data; I have, like many early medievalists, become a cultural historian almost without knowing it. And, most important, I stand outside the mainstream of sf academia, which has been not only strongly North American, but also firmly based within departments of English. Attitudes have certainly changed over the last decade, as the discipline of literary studies has begun to welcome specialists in popular literature as well as film and other non-print media; but hostility towards sf is still frequently to be found in departments of English. This is one reason why sf academics normally feel constrained to justify their existence by defending sf as 'high literature'. Authors who can be considered respect-able, like J. G. Ballard, Philip K. Dick, or Ursula K. Le Guin, have thereby achieved a position in the canon out of all relation to their actual importance in the history of sf as a whole. A cultural historian has none of these worries: for her, Hendrik Dahl's 'Monsters of Neptune' has just as much potential inter-est as Samuel R. Delany's 'Time Considered as a Helix of Semi-Precious Stones', and she may not even share the unconscious privileging of print over other manifestations of the science-fictional imagination.

I should like to thank friends and scholars on both sides of the Atlantic—Marleen Barr, John Clute, Graham Ford, Colin Greenland, Eric Rabkin, Brian Stableford, James Walvin, and Gary Westfahl—who looked through the final draft of this book and made innumerable valuable corrections and suggestions. Some of their advice I have ignored; much of it I have accepted, sometimes regretfully, such as the near-unanimous opinion that I should not use 'she' and 'her' as the generic term for authors and critics (as at the end of the previous paragraph), because it is inappropriate when women remain in the minority in both professions. I should like to thank John Clute for his willing-ness to share his encyclopaedic knowledge of the field over the telephone and for the timely arrival of John Clute and Peter Nicholls (eds.), *The Encyclopedia of Science Fiction* (London, 1993) just as I was finishing my book. It is not only by far the best reference book on sf, but one of the best reference books I know. I have tried to follow its lead on matters of spelling and chronology, and if readers of this book want to follow up any-thing I have discussed, there is a wealth of information and cross-reference in Clute and Nicholls. Last of all, I offer special thanks to Farah Mendlesohn, for examining draft after draft of the text without complaint, and for offering me perceptive and informed advice, as well as much-valued encouragement and support. Numerous ideas in this book have emerged in discussions with her, and I hope that this acknowledgement gives her sufficient credit.

Contents

Introduction

This book is an attempt to define science fiction, while recognizing that a proper definition can be achieved only by understanding what authors are trying to do, or have tried to do throughout the century; how readers approach the books; how the market works; how critics have approached and redefined the field; and how sf itself (and its readers, markets, and critics) has changed throughout the last hundred years. I will certainly not make the mistake of trying to begin, or conclude, with a simple definition. Attempts at definition usually seem to imply a belief in a Platonic idea of 'science fiction', rather than a bundle of perceptions about what constitutes sf—a bundle whose contents are constantly changing, from decade to decade, from critic to critic, and from country to country. Attempts at definitions, in other words, frequently appear to be laying down rules about what sf *ought* to be like, rather than offering some kind of all-embracing description of the great range and wide variety of texts which have been, and are, recognized as making up the body of sf. Definitions are thus frequently closely linked to the desire of sf critics to defend their interests in the face of hostile attacks by emphasizing one element of sf at the expense of others. A cartoon by MacNelly expresses the distance between the high-flown claims of some defenders of sf and the reality of the average ephemeral sf paperback. Shoe sees his friend reading a book and comments, 'Not that dumb science fiction junk again . . .' 'Dumb? Obviously your pathetic little pea brain cannot comprehend the intricacy of modern science fiction, Shoe . . . [And here Shoe's friend moves into determined professor mode.] Science fiction not only allows us to escape our assigned space and time and step into other dimensions. It lets us examine our mundane, earthbound problems from a fresh, original viewpoint. This isn't comic book stuff here, Shoe! This is PHILOSOPHY! Mind-expanding, heavy *philosophy*!!' Shoe looks at the book: '*The Feast of the Khroobles*?' The shame-faced response: 'It's about these creatures made of meatloaf who eat Toledo.' Shoe stares speechlessly, but meaningfully, at the reader.[1]

'Sf' is a label that can be applied to everything from heavy philosophy to invading meatloaf. Moreover, sf today is certainly very different from sf in 1970, let alone 1930. To understand sf, therefore, one is forced to be a historian. It is with history that I shall begin, looking not only at how sf developed in the first half of the century and how it emerged as a distinct genre in the United States, but also at how definitions of sf changed as sf itself changed; the development of sf as a literary category is bound up with attempts to define it and with attempts by writers to live up to those definitions.

But, first of all, a practical experiment.

Browsing through the Categories

Go into any bookshop or bookstore, and look at the section marked 'SF' or 'Sci-Fi'. Often, to confuse you, the section will actually be called 'SF and Fantasy', or even 'Science Fiction, Fantasy, and Horror'. In most cases the cover will leave the casual browser in little doubt as to which of those three possible categories a particular book belongs, at least in the mind of its publisher. A horror novel will bear skulls, teeth, gore, rotten flesh, and creeping things; a fantasy novel will display dragons, elves, wizards, and heroes (or heroines) with swords, mighty thews, and not very many clothes; an sf book can draw on a more varied range of images, but will often feature spaceships, futuristic machinery or architecture, robots, weird alien landscapes, and alien creatures. Sometimes covers may hint at a crossing of category boundaries by portraying an alien's head with its teeth dripping gore, for instance, or a dragon flying across an alien landscape. But most of the covers represent the core of what each genre is ostensibly *about*, and may suggest to you some possible differences between genres. Horror calls on, plays on, and perhaps exorcizes innate fears of pain, death, and the unknowable; fantasy draws its inspiration from mythology and folklore and from popular images of medieval or pre-industrial society, and often appeals to nostalgia and conservative values; much sf is concerned with the future and with the possibilities presented by scientific and technological change. And all three are clearly distinguished by their covers from what appears elsewhere nearby, in the sections devoted to popular fiction: corpses with daggers in their backs, men in battledress aiming bazookas, bejewelled women with fancy cars and other symbols of life among the rich and powerful, horsemen in check shirts chasing Indians, haughty Regency-clad gentlemen striding away from tearful women. Not one of these books, of course, is dealing with the real world; but only sf and fantasy seem to renounce the real world openly, and deal with imaginative alternatives to it. You, the casual browser, might think of all these brands of popular fiction as escapism, and might think that sf and fantasy were the most escapist of all; but if you did a careful comparative study of these books, you might note that only on sf shelves are there serious fictional discussions of the possibilities of survival after nuclear warfare or the consequences of the greenhouse effect or of overpopulation or of the possible dire consequences of genetic engineering. And if you thought about it, you might see that sf (and, to a lesser extent, fantasy), because they deal with imaginative alternatives to the real world, also frequently offer criticism of that world—and thus may, in short, be much more subversive than anything else that is marketed as 'popular fiction'. Frank Cioffi, who has looked at early sf as 'formula fiction', has argued that the subversive qualities of sf and its estranging 'other worldly' qualities distinguish it from popular fiction; Farah Mendlesohn has argued that it is rather more useful to think of sf as a form of élite fiction, the élite being of a technocratic, rather than a literary, intelligentsia.[2]

Sf is what is marketed as sf: that is a beginning, but no more. Almost everything which is labelled 'sf' *is* sf, but there is a great deal which is not so labelled which, in terms of approach and content, seems to belong to the same category. Move away from the 'SF' section, and go to general fiction. Pick up Michael Crichton's *Jurassic Park* (1990). It would seem to be about the extraction of DNA from fossils and the re-creation of living dinosaurs for display in a theme park some time in the near future. It is a subject that has been treated before, by sf writers. Those in the know will be aware that Crichton has written other sf books, as well as being the director of several successful sf films, such as *Westworld* and *Coma*. But the book is not marketed as sf; Crichton and his publishers know that his book will sell to a wider readership if it is marketed as a thriller. The label 'sf', however proudly worn by many sf authors, is one that repels readers as frequently as it attracts.

There are two categories of sf book in particular which escape the label 'sf'. The first are those books produced by sf authors who actually have ambitions at literary quality and at recognition by the critics who review 'serious' fiction in the weekly reviews or the Sunday review sections; they know the repellent characteristics of sf very well, and publishers are happy to conspire with them. A paperback original clearly labelled 'sf' has no chance of being taken seriously by literary reviewers; a hardback labelled 'sf' will usually be distributed only to specialist bookshops (a major non-specialist bookshop in New York solemnly assured Samuel R. Delany once that Isaac Asimov's latest hardback couldn't possibly be sf, because they stocked it[3]); a soberly presented hardback which avoids the letters 'sf' anywhere on its dust-jacket has some real chance of success. Pick up the UK hardback of George Turner's *The Sea and Summer* (Faber and Faber, 1987; sadly, it is out of print, but this is an imaginary bookshop). The back cover tells us that it is set in the twenty-first century, as the greenhouse effect raises the sea-level and begins to drown Melbourne. But it is George Turner's new 'novel—marked as is all his work not only by compelling imagination but by powerful intelligence', not his new sf novel. The inside back flap reveals that Turner is 'one of Australia's leading novelists', and mentions his other novels, without saying that all but one are sf, or that Turner is also one of Australia's leading sf critics. Turn to J. G. Ballard's most recent collection of short stories, *War Fever* (Collins, 1990).

Again, the dust-jacket, with its biography of the writer, avoids all use of the terrible phrase 'science fiction', the only hint being the remark that Ballard's first short story was published in *New Worlds* (the initiated will know that this was the most celebrated of the British sf magazines). Yet the stories, several of which were first published in genre sf magazines in the 1980s, are all, save one, sf, and very much more traditional sf than Ballard was writing in the early 1970s. But since *Empire of the Sun* (1984), Ballard has been lionized by the British literary establishment, and therefore cannot be an sf writer.

The second category is the situation in reverse. Every now and then authors who have made their names outside the field (and often without knowledge of the field) will produce a novel which every sf reader will recognize as sf—even if the author sometimes does not deal with the problems of subtly presenting an unfamiliar world to the reader as deftly as most professional sf writers do today. These authors will be indignant if the work is treated as sf; their loyal non-sf readers will be equally indignant if the book is classed in the despised category. I am thinking of *The Handmaid's Tale* (1985) by the Canadian poet and novelist Margaret Atwood and *The Children of Men* (1992) by the British writer of detective stories, P. D. James, but there are numerous others.

In some ways this refusal to ghettoize by slapping the label 'sf' on a book is healthy, both for the reading public and for the author. More readers are, perhaps, introduced to the science-fictional imagination (even if they may not realize that is what it is). Authors have the literary recognition that would be denied to them within the ghetto, and may feel that they do not have the literary constraints that writing within the narrow confines of the sf genre would impose. Motifs and themes from sf are thus drawn into the world of contemporary fiction, fostering a cross-fertilization that enriches both sf and the wider field of literature. In the 1960s both Kurt Vonnegut, jun., and John Wyndham (John Beynon Harris) managed to escape the sf label, even if they may have refused ghettoization for commercial rather than artistic reasons, and thereby achieved a much wider readership than they would have received in the ghetto.

Ghettos are often culturally rich, of course, and their culture may well be destroyed by the breaking down of the ghetto walls. But for society as a whole, ghettoization, in any sense, can only be a cultural impoverishment, an exclusion, a refusal to admit the validity of different ideas or standards; and bringing a few names out of the ghetto does nothing to break down the walls or to help make sf better appreciated in the literary community. The standard reaction is: 'This is good; therefore it cannot be science fiction.' The cultural reasons behind the common prejudice against sf, both among apparently informed readers and critics and also among the general reading public, will be examined later. Publishers have had an impact upon this prejudice, however. The popular image of sf is expressed in those spaceships, robots, or aliens on the covers of paperbacks which publishers have decided express the essence of the field; no matter that a spaceship may appear on the cover of an sf book which in fact deals with a pre-industrial and non-technological culture (a misrepresentation which, admittedly, was more common in the 1970s than now, and more so in the UK than the USA). Most publishers appear to want to define sf as no more than another genre of popular fiction, like westerns or romances; they believe it will help the many readers who want to be led quickly to the only type of fiction which they are prepared to read (even if it also discourages those with untested prejudices from ever venturing into new areas). Publishers treat sf as a genre: that is, a body of writing which has a consciousness of a shared range of conventions and approaches and themes. I have been suggesting above that there are works of sf which are produced and published outside the genre. But it is important to note that there are many writers, readers, critics, and academics who are prepared to accept this narrow publishers' definition, and who thus effectively recognize as sf only those works which are consciously written as contributions to the genre, normally by writers who think of themselves primarily as sf writers. Sf was first named, and first became a genre, in the sf magazines published in the United States before the Second World War; not surprisingly, it has thus tended to be American readers and critics who narrow the definition of sf in this way. Not surprisingly also, their image of sf is dominated by American sf, and primarily American sf after 1926 (the year the first specialist sf magazine, *Amazing Stories*, was published). The history of the development of the genre, which is also the history of the establishment of the ghetto walls, is certainly an extremely important part of the history of sf, and we shall examine it in the first chapter; it runs alongside the history of labels, the topic of the next section. But to exclude from the study of sf works which have avoided the label, either because they were written before the label's invention or because they were deliberately written and published outside the ghetto, would be to distort the subject. It would devalue the contribution made by non-American writers: not only Jules Verne and H. G. Wells, but also Karel Čapek, Olaf Stapledon, Doris Lessing, and many others. It would also deny sf—the child of Gothic horror, of utopian tract, of travellers' tale, of scientific prognostication—some of its considerable variety. Perhaps even more seriously, it would deny the student of sf any opportunity to examine those writers who, in much more recent years, have written works which may well be sf, and certainly have much in common with it, who would never be found in our imaginary bookstore alongside the so-called big three, Isaac Asimov, Arthur C. Clarke, and Robert A. Heinlein: writers such as Peter Ackroyd, Donald Barthelme, Jorge Luis Borges, William Burroughs, Angela Carter, Don DeLillo, Thomas Pynchon, and many others.

Sf is a genre, therefore; and genre sf (now produced all over the world and not just in the USA) stands at the core of the subject and of this book. But it does not constitute the whole of sf. And this is the nub of the problem of definition. We might agree on a definition of genre sf (though no one has, so far); but there have always been problems on the fringes, and there always will be, as long as there are some writers who refuse to write work which can be readily labelled.

Labels

The phrase 'science fiction' first appears in 1851, in a treatise on the poetry of science by the English writer William Wilson:

Campbell [the Scottish poet Thomas Campbell] says that 'Fiction in Poetry is not the reverse of truth, but her soft and enchanting resemblance'. Now this applies especially to Science Fiction, in which the revealed truths of Science may be given, interwoven with a pleasing story which may itself be poetical and *true*—thus circulating a knowledge of the Poetry of Science, clothed in a garb of the Poetry of Life.[4]

Wilson marvels at the poetry lying behind the wonders of creation—the fact that a tear-drop 'holds locked in its transparent cells an amount of electric fire equal to that which is discharged during a storm from a thunder-cloud', or that 'minute insects have built whole islands of coral reefs up into light from the low deep bed of the vast ocean'; his musings have a close relationship to the 'sense of wonder' which sf critics have discerned as one of the major pleasures of the genre (see below, p. 103). Wilson also finds poetry in current technological change, as no doubt did others in that year of the Great Exhibition: 'The modern discoveries and applications of Science throw deeply into the shade the old romances and fanciful legends of our boyhood.' And stories and poetry about science, replacing the old romances, will in future be a means of instruction for children.

Except for an editorial response to a 1927 letter to *Amazing Stories: The Magazine of Scientifiction*,[5] no one used the phrase 'science fiction' again until 1929, when the New York publisher Hugo Gernsback, who had just lost control of *Amazing Stories*, decided to replace his own coinage 'scientifiction' by a less cumbersome term for his new magazine *Science Wonder Stories*. And, by an odd coincidence (for William Wilson had been long forgotten), Gernsback's own prospectus for sf was not that different from Wilson's:

Not only is science fiction an idea of tremendous import, but it is to be an important factor in making the world a better place to live in, through educating the public to the possibilities of science and the influence of science on life . . . If every man, woman, boy and girl, could be induced to read science fiction right along, there would certainly be a great resulting benefit to the community . . . Science fiction would make people happier, give them a broader understanding of the world, make them more tolerant.[6]

Gernsback, arguably, not only invented the term for sf but also invented it as a self-conscious genre. But most modern commentators are happy to use the phrase 'science fiction' for the very considerable number of stories of the same kind which pre-dated Gernsback, not only those by Verne and Wells (or, earlier, Mary Shelley and Edward Bulwer-Lytton), but also those by a host of other authors; the modern bibliographer Everett F. Bleiler lists over 3,000 sf stories and novels published in English before 1930. There was no generally accepted contemporary terminology for these stories of adventures in space or time, of amazing inventions, or of romances on other planets. The stories of Jules Verne, published as *voyages extraordinaires* in France, were published as 'scientific romances' in Britain, and Wells was using that term informally to describe his 'sf' as early as 1897; he sometimes referred to his less plausible stories as 'scientific fantasies'. In Britain 'sf' books were often subtitled 'A Romance' or 'A Romance of the Future'. There was more variety in the United States. 'Romance' was used, and, as early as 1876, 'scientific fiction'. The prolific American publisher of dime novels, Frank Tousey, used the phrase 'invention stories' in the 1880s. Frank Munsey, publisher of the magazine *Argosy*, used phrases like 'off-trail stories' and 'impossible stories'. The most frequent label was simply 'different stories'; this continued until the 1920s, when it was replaced by 'pseudo-scientific stories'. Gernsback's *Science and Invention* magazine published some fiction, and after 1922 this was referred to as 'scientific fiction'; *Argosy* itself started using the term in the late 1920s.[7] The triumph of the term 'science fiction', after its introduction in 1929, was rapid in the United States, at least among readers and publishers of sf magazines. The first fan magazine, *The Planet*, which started in 1930, from the beginning favoured 'science fiction', even though it continued to use 'scientific fiction' and 'scientifiction' (and sometimes used all three terms in one paragraph). *Amazing* shifted definitively to 'science fiction' at the end of 1932. By then there were few opponents to the new term within the field in the United States; the only disagreement was about whether the two words should be hyphenated or not. The outside world was somewhat slower to recognize the term. The US librarians' *Readers' Guide to Periodical Literature* used 'pseudo-scientific stories' as a heading right through the 1930s and 1940s, and only in 1949 introduced 'science fiction: see pseudo-scientific stories'. 'Pseudo-scientific' disappeared from the *Readers' Guide* altogether only in 1961.

By then 'science fiction' had become firmly established not only in the United States and Britain, but in much of the rest of the world as well. The importation of American sf magazines into Britain and, from August 1939, the publication of *Astounding Science-Fiction* in a British edition introduced British readers to the term; 'scientific romance' disappeared as the American market began to dominate. 'Science fiction' neatly transferred into French and into countries where English terms were readily accepted, such as Sweden and Holland. 'Science fiction' was eventually accepted in Germany, after a long struggle with *utopische Romane*. It is not the same in all languages, many of which have adopted some translation of 'science fantasy': this is true in Chinese and Italian (*fantascienza*), while the Russian *nauchnaia fantastika* (or just *fantastika*) has been the standard term since the 1920s. The Japanese just call it SF, 'blithely adding the English acronym to their melange of Chinese characters and homegrown syllabaries'.[8]

Even as 'science fiction' was established, it became common to abbreviate it: stf (originating as an abbreviation of 'scientifiction', pronounced stef), sf (or SF or S-F, pronounced essef), and sci-fi (rhyming with its model, hi-fi). Stf reached its peak in the early 1940s, and has since faded away. The other two abbreviations have become something of a shibboleth, with those who use 'sci-fi' being dismissed as neophytes or outsiders by the initiates, who sometimes pronounce it 'skiffy' and use it to mean low-grade mass-market science fiction (like the film *Star Wars*, for instance), reserving 'sf' for science fiction of (to them) greater value. 'Sci-fi' has become common within film and television circles, however; it is not going to die out.

The move towards 'sf' was not just a move to a shortened

form; its use became more widespread because of dissatisfaction with the term 'science fiction' itself. As we shall see in the following chapters, when the boundaries of science fiction grew, and as the aims of science fiction writers changed, particularly from the late 1940s, 'science fiction' began increasingly to seem an unhelpful label. 'Sf' had the advantage that it could be translated as 'speculative fiction' (by Robert Heinlein first, but by many others, particularly in the late 1960s and early 1970s) or 'science fantasy', 'speculative fantasy' (Alexei and Cory Panshin), 'scientific fantasy', 'science fable' (Judith Merril), or, most recently, 'structural fabulation' (Robert Scholes). This freedom suited some people's concepts of what the genre had become, or should be, much better than the old 'science fiction', with what many people saw as its off-putting technological and often technophilic associations. One could even begin to revel in the oxymoronic properties of a phrase, 'science fiction', which brought into union two incompatible concepts, 'science' and 'fiction': 'basically, SF is a developed oxymoron, a realistic irreality, with humanized nonhumans, this-worldly Other Worlds, and so forth.'[9]

The establishment of a near-universal label (or labels) and discussions about the relative merits of 'science fiction' and 'sf' were closely tied up with the emergence of sf as a genre, and hence with a concern to determine what the genre actually was and what its boundaries were. That there is no generally agreed definition of sf is, of course, largely a result of the fact that since 1929 sf has been in a state of constant change.

1 The Development of a Genre
1895–1940

SF in 1895

This study of sf in the twentieth century begins not in 1900, but in 1895: the publication date of one of the greatest of all science fiction tales, and one of the earliest and best its author ever wrote—*The Time Machine* by H. G. Wells. Wells has sometimes been called the Father of Science Fiction. He was certainly prominent in the field and immensely influential; but the force of this section is to show that he was mining what had become quite a familiar literary node, and that although he was the best, he was by no means the only contributor to the field in 1895. What would later be called sf was in fact in the middle of its first important boom when *The Time Machine* was published. Fifty-two items of sf were published in English in that year, twenty-seven by British authors, twenty-two by Americans, one by an Australian, and two translated from French.[1] Among them the stories represent most of the categories which we might recognize as sf, even though our problems of definition create disagreements concerning the boundaries. E. F. Bleiler, for instance, denies 'prehistoric fiction' the status of sf that other critics would allow, but accepts the 'lost race' story, which Darko Suvin would deny is 'sf' at all (see below, p. 109). The most important thing to remember, however, is that no one in 1895 would have thought that all these works belonged to a single branch of fiction at all: all that they possess in common is their similarity to works which, by the second half of the twentieth century, would be known as science fiction.

It is useful to divide these fifty-two items, and the rest of nineteenth-century sf, into a number of categories based on subject-matter; it was subject-matter, as much as objective or mode of narrative, which later determined membership of the genre. There was the extraordinary voyage (within which we might place the lost race story); the tale of the future (including utopias, tales of future war, and what Stableford calls 'eschatological fantasies', like *The Time Machine* itself[2]); and the tale of science (notably concerned with marvellous inventions). But, as our 1895 sample shows, there are numerous cases of overlap: the extraordinary voyage often ends with the discovery of a utopia, for instance, or it may be dependent on a marvellous invention as a means of travel; while tales of future war may sometimes be about the impact of new inventions upon warfare, or have utopian elements. Moreover, there are some stories from 1895 which cannot be placed in categories, even though they may be seen as prefiguring twentieth-century categories. Thus, Castello N. Holford's *Aristopia* (US) can hardly be seen as a standard utopian novel, in that his fictional utopia was founded in seventeenth-century America, according to Thomas More's principles, in an alternative history framework which was to see the state of Aristopia take over all North America at the time of the Revolution in 1776. Alternative history is now a flourishing sub-genre within sf, but in 1895 this work stood alone. Despite the success of Mark Twain's *A Connecticut Yankee in King Arthur's Court* (1889; UK: *A Connecticut Yankee at the Court of King Arthur*, 1889), there is no category of time-travel; Grant Allen's *The British Barbarians* (UK), in which a time-traveller from the twenty-fifth century comments unfavourably on the barbaric customs of the British in 1895, is instead part of the strong satirical tradition in sf. As long as we are aware of the problems, some examination of the main categories may be helpful, above all, in establishing something of the ancestry of twentieth-century sf.

1. *The Extraordinary Voyage*

Of the three main categories, the extraordinary voyage has probably the oldest history. The medieval tales about the voyages of Sir John Mandeville, much reprinted in the post-Caxton era, were, during the age of Columbus and the discoveries, to develop into the full-blown genre of the imaginary voyage. Much early utopian writing, such as Thomas More's *Utopia*, Sir Francis Bacon's *New Atlantis*, or Tommaso Campanella's *The City of the Sun*, fits very neatly into this genre, and utopian comment was indeed a frequent element of these imaginary voyages. There were at least 215 stories of imaginary voyages published in Western Europe and America in the eighteenth century,[3] of which Swift's *Gulliver's Travels* (1726) is undoubtedly the best known. Most of the stories of imaginary voyages written in the nineteenth century continued to be about the discovery of marvellous or mysterious people and places in the remoter parts of the world; it was not, after all, until the present century that the globe became too well known for people seriously to imagine that marvels still awaited discovery. There are nineteenth-century tales of imaginary voyages which discover lost races in every conceivable corner of the Earth's surface, as well as a large sub-genre which finds them inside a hollow Earth, following the once fashionable theories of John Cleves Symmes (d. 1829).[4] Voyagers inside the hollow Earth found whole solar systems, the Garden of Eden, dog-headed humans, utopian societies, and prehistoric monsters. In one of the most interesting and impressive nineteenth-century examples, Mary E. Bradley Lane's feminist *Mizora* (US, 1890), the heroine, Vera Zarovitch, found an all-female society, lacking not only men, but also crime, religion, class, disease, domestic animals, and brunettes (brunettes were considered troublesome).

In 1895 seventeen examples of the extraordinary voyage were published. Charles Dixon's *Fifteen Hundred Miles An Hour* (UK) was a boys' story about a German inventor who took some young friends with him to Mars, to meet Martians. Gustavus Pope's sequel to his *Journey to Mars* (1894), *Journey to Venus* (US), was an early example of what became a cliché, that Venus was the jungle home of prehistoric monsters and cavemen. Not all the travel was by spaceship: Edgar Fawcett's *The Ghost of Guy Thyrle* (US) had a drug which allowed a scientist to roam at will in his astral body, to the Moon and the stars; while Tremlett Carter's *The People of the Moon* (UK) used the occult device of astral projection in order to explore the

Moon, and Willis Mitchell's *The Inhabitants of Mars* (US) had his protagonist study the utopian society of Mars under hypnosis. Earth had lost races galore: Howard De Vere's *A Trip to the Center of the Earth* (US) found one underground; Henry Clay Fairman's *The Third World* (US) found it underground, at the North Pole; André Laurie's *The Crystal City under the Sea* (translated from French) found Atlantis and the Atlanteans under the sea; A. S. Morton's *Beyond the Palaeocrystic Sea* (US) found a lost race of Vikings beyond the polar sea; and Rider Haggard's *Heart of the World* (UK) found his lost race in Central America. Some of the lost race stories were making very obvious points: both R. D. Chetwode's *The Marble City* (UK) and Paul Haedicke's *The Equalities of Para-Para* (US) parody and attack socialism, while in *The Mysterious Mirage*, a 'Frank Reade, Jr.' dime novel (US), the members of the lost race were blond, blue-eyed Hebrews, preserved in their original form, because their remoteness had prevented any inter-marriage with inferior races. Other 'Frank Reade, Jr.' dime novels of 1895—*The Chase of a Comet*, *The Electric Island*, and *Lost in a Comet's Tail*, one of the very first stories of space rescue—were extraordinary voyages concerned much more with adventure and marvellous machines.

It ought to be obvious from these brief descriptions that some writers found inspiration in a contemporary writer who had made his living out of 'extraordinary voyages': Jules Verne. 'Voyages extraordinaires' was the general title of the series of books which Verne wrote for the publisher Jules Hetzel: one or two a year for over forty years following, the first novel in 1863. Verne's voyages took him and his many readers all over the globe, from South America to Antarctica and to the centre of the Earth, from under the seas to the Moon and around it, and beyond into the further reaches of the solar system. Less than a quarter of his sixty-four novels (the later ones written with, or by, his son Michel) could be counted as sf, but it is notable that those were among the most widely read when they were first published, and have remained so. Verne, particularly in his early career, was an enthusiastic prophet of scientific progress, and saw his own 'Voyages extraordinaires'—subtitled *Les Mondes*

connus et inconnus (*Known and Unknown Worlds*)—as a didactic work in many volumes which shows his readers how the
universe was 'forcibly linked to the idea of progress, . . . a
universe where the line between the conquests already achieved
by science, and those which have not yet been achieved, [was]
constantly moving'. Verne was not interested in speculation or
in using science to develop his fiction; for this reason, a distinction would be made by some critics between Verne's *scientific*
fiction and genuine sf.[5]

Verne and Wells have frequently been thought of as the
pioneers of the tale of the extraordinary voyage into outer space,
the most typical of all science-fictional themes. Stories of travel
to the Moon have a venerable ancestry, going back to Lucian
(second century CE), Francis Godwin (*The Man in the Moone*,
1638), and Cyrano de Bergerac (*L'Autre Monde*, 1657). But
the popular impression has been that Verne and Wells were
the first to raise this fable to the status of scientific prophecy.
There are two points to be made about this. First, one might
argue that neither Verne nor Wells took their space travel
stories very seriously; both Verne's *Hector Servadac* (*cadavres*
backwards) and Wells's *The First Men in the Moon* have far more
than their authors' normal ration of humour and satire in them.
Second, and more to the point, by the time of Verne and Wells,
tales of interplanetary and even interstellar travel had, in lesser
hands, become familiar, if not commonplace. Nor should modern
readers find it surprising that fictional travellers to other planets
in the nineteenth century found life, intelligent and otherwise;
many scientists in the eighteenth and nineteenth centuries were
convinced that such life could, and did, exist.[6] (Although, in one
of those information lags of which several instances can be found
in the history of sf, writers were elaborating the theme at the
precise point, in the late nineteenth century, when more and
more scientists were beginning to doubt the possibility of intelligent life, at least in our solar system.) One of the most
interesting early tales of interplanetary travel was Percy Greg's
Across the Zodiac (1880), which is in many ways an astonishing
prefiguration of twentieth-century sf. The English hero builds a
spaceship, and deals with the problem of maintaining an air

supply by taking plants along with him to provide the oxygen. He travels to Mars, where he finds that the Martialists [*sic*] have established a high-technology utopia, the details of which, including not only social arrangements but even language and proverbs, are worked out by Greg with considerable care.

If Verne was not the only early writer of stories of extraordinary voyages, there is no doubt that he had an enormous influence upon sf. His major science-fictional 'Voyages extraordinaires' were translated into English soon after publication: *A Journey to the Centre of the Earth* (1863) appeared in London in 1872 and New York in 1874; *From the Earth to the Moon* (1865) was published in Newark, New Jersey, in 1869 and with its sequel *Round the Moon* (1869) in London in 1873 and New York in 1874; *Twenty Thousand Leagues under the Sea* (1870) was published in London and New York in 1873; and so on. He was also very widely imitated, in Europe and in the United States, and was an influence on the earliest American magazine sf some fifty years after his greatest works appeared (nearly all in the 1860s and 1870s). From its first issue in 1926 and for years thereafter, *Amazing Stories* had a drawing of Jules Verne's tomb at Amiens on its title-page, the immortal Verne in the act of raising the lid of his tombstone to peer into his own future.

2. *The Tale of the Future*

Verne almost invariably set his science-fictional tales in the present or in a future indistinguishable from the present; he wanted to show his readers that scientific and technological changes were occurring in their own society, and that more were imminent. There is nothing in Verne of that vision of the far future which was to be found in *The Time Machine*. Wells was in a worthy tradition, one which went back, arguably, to Jewish apocalyptic writings like the book of Daniel and the New Testament book of Revelation: the prophecy of the end of all things, but seen in a secular, post-Darwinian, guise. An important predecessor, 'an event of high significance in the history of secular eschatology, and in the history of the secularization of Western consciousness itself',[7] was Mary

Shelley's *The Last Man* (1826). Taking her cue from the cholera epidemic of the 1820s and inspired also by Cousin de Grandville's *Le Dernier Homme* (1805), Shelley described the course of a plague, how it destroyed a Europe on the brink of utopia at the end of the twenty-first century, and how her romantic hero, Verney, wandered in vain through Europe searching for other survivors, until, at last, having reached St Peter's in Rome, he plans to carry his search to other continents. Musings upon the future death of civilization were to have a long history within sf: Richard Jefferies' *After London* (1885) is the most distinguished nineteenth-century successor to Shelley, but the entire sub-genre of sf concerned with the destruction of civilization by nuclear holocaust or other disaster and the numerous sf magazine illustrations of drowned, mutilated, or toppled Statues of Liberty are in the same tradition. Sf writers have derived from the Gothic fiction of Shelley and her contemporaries a fascinated and appalled delight in the contemplation of death and destruction on a large scale: a considered reaction to complacency in the face of a dangerous universe.

When Mary Shelley wrote, tales of the future had not themselves had a very long history. There are two texts from the mid-seventeenth century and two from the mid-eighteenth century, and that is all until Louis-Sébastien Mercier's *L'An 2440* (1771) (published in English as *Memoirs of the Year Two Thousand Five Hundred*, 1772). In this story, the narrator falls asleep and wakes up some 750 years later, to find himself in a utopian society (utopia on French Enlightenment lines, naturally, in which women were placed more firmly under their husbands' control than in Mercier's own France). 'Rip Van Winkle' (or, much earlier, 'The Seven Sleepers of Ephesus') is a literary device to be repeated often, right into the twentieth century, through Edward Bellamy's *Looking Backward* and Wells's *When the Sleeper Wakes*. Mercier's story is the first utopia ever set in the future. From his time the utopian tale increasingly becomes a 'tale of the future' rather than an imaginary voyage: a shift, in the terminology of some utopian specialists, from *eutopia* ('good place') to *euchronia* ('good time'). The change, of course, is linked to a realization that the past was very different from the present (an idea that only slowly gained currency from the sixteenth century onwards) and that the future was going to be very different, too. When linked to the idea of progress, which became more and more a part of nineteenth-century thought, the tale of the future almost inevitably had utopian overtones; very frequently, that utopianism was heavily tinged with socialism, an increasingly influential nineteenth-century political philosophy and one of the first to dream deliberately of better futures.

Paul Alkon has unearthed an early text by Félix Bodin which, astonishingly, laments how the tale of the future has fallen victim to the utopia and the apocalypse: why can't we have *novels* set in the future, he asks in his *Le Roman de l'avenir* (1834)?

If ever anyone succeeds in creating the novel, the epic of the future, he will have tapped a vast source of the marvelous, and of a marvelous entirely in accord with verisimilitude . . . which will dignify reason instead of shocking it or deprecating it as all the marvelous epic machinery conventionally employed up to now has done. In suggesting perfectibility through a picturesque, narrative, and dramatic form, he will have found a method of seizing, of moving the imagination and of hastening the progress of humanity in a manner very much more effective than the best expositions of systems presented with even the highest eloquence.[8]

Bodin is calling for sf as a tool for education in similar terms to those used by Hugo Gernsback a century later.

His plea for something more than utopia was not heeded (indeed, his whole treatise had no discernible influence at all). There are still utopian tales of the future in our 1895 sample. There is Amelia Garland Mears's *Mercia, the Astronomer Royal* (UK), which depicts Britain in 2002, where women are emancipated and can become astronomers-royal, like Mercia, and in which solar power, psychic science, a world tribunal, and (it is delicately implied) a rigid system of birth control have combined to produce a near perfect world. Other utopian futures include Edward Bellamy, 'Christmas in the Year 2000' (US), reflections on (and criticisms of) nineteenth-century Christmas by someone writing in 2000; Titus Smith, *Altruria* (US); and Albert Chavannes, *In Brighter Climes, or, Life in*

Socioland. None of these would have been written had it not been for the tremendous success of another book: Edward Bellamy's *Looking Backward, 2000–1887* (US, 1888), the most influential of all nineteenth-century utopias. Bellamy's own 1895 piece was one of several postscripts to his own novel; the novels by Smith and Chavannes were two of the fifty or so utopian novels inspired by *Looking Backward*, both supporting and countering Bellamy's arguments. The most famous of them was English: William Morris's *News from Nowhere* (serialized, 1890; published as a book 1890, US, and 1891, UK), a utopian vision of a post-revolutionary England which itself inspired generations of British socialists. Reaction to Bellamy's book today (as I learn each year from students) usually includes boredom with the lecturing style of Dr Leete and irritation at the coquettishness of his heroine daughter, Edith; in the United States, one might add also hostility to its state socialism and its attacks on free market capitalism. But the reaction in the nineteenth century was mostly much more positive. There can be few sf books which have become such enormous best-sellers; there are certainly none which, within two years of publication, inspired the founding of 162 political clubs (Bellamy clubs) in twenty-seven states and the creation of political magazines like the *Nationalist* and the *New Nation* and of a political movement, a specifically American version of socialism called, confusingly, Nationalism.

From our present point of view it is worth underlining that *Looking Backward* is indeed sf, by most definitions. The means by which Julian West was transported from 1887 to 2000 are perhaps not plausible even by nineteenth-century scientific standards; since West had insomnia, he was mesmerized each night, in an air-tight, sound-proof room underneath his Boston home, when one night a fire destroyed the house, and he slept on, until woken by Dr Leete in the year 2000. But thereafter the logic is maintained, and the standard nineteenth-century device whereby it is all discovered to be a dream at the end is neatly turned on its head: he 'awakes' near the end to find himself in his nightmarish capitalist Boston of 1887—but then discovers that *this* is a dream, and that, to his relief, he is still in 2000 with his beloved Edith. Most of the novel is taken up with his exploration of the social system in 2000, through the lengthy disquisitions of Dr Leete. It is a society that has shaken off the injustices and inequalities of the capitalist system (the few pages at the beginning which describe life under capitalism are the most passionate and memorable of the whole book); all adults have the same wage, which cannot be accumulated year by year or passed on to heirs; all alike must work in the industrial army until retirement at the age of 45; the efficiency of the large scale (a few large department stores rather than large numbers of small-scale enterprises) ensures a high degree of prosperity for all. It is a middle-class utopia, and one that has arisen not out of revolution, but natural evolution: Bellamy extrapolated his future from current trends with as much care as any later writer of sf. And his middle-class utopia had considerable appeal for Americans in the 1890s. The huge readership it thus won for itself has importance as far as we are concerned, an importance which is rarely stressed in histories of sf. More than any other book, above all in the United States, it accustomed people to think about the future as something that could be rationally extrapolated, that could even be planned for, and, perhaps above all, that could serve as a setting for entertaining and instructive fiction.

The second main type of the tale of the future in the nineteenth century was even more popular than the utopian novel: the future war story. This sub-genre was essentially created by Lieutenant-Colonel Sir George Tomkyns Chesney, when he published (anonymously, in *Blackwood's Magazine* for May 1871), *The Battle of Dorking: Reminiscences of a Volunteer*. An old man tells his grandchildren about the collapse of the British Empire fifty years earlier (presumably around 1871). The British Army had been poorly prepared, and thinly stretched; a German invasion caught Britain unawares, and took over the entire country. Britain became a pauper nation; Ireland, India, and Australia achieved independence. The book came in the aftermath of the collapse of France in the Franco-Prussian War, which raised the spectre of the Paris Commune and the realization of the vulnerability of Britain. Its publication caused a furore, and it was rapidly translated into French, Italian, Dutch, Spanish—and German. Imitations followed equally rapidly; *The Victory of Tunbridge Wells*, *After the Battle of Dorking*, and *The Commune of London* all appeared before the year was out. There were not only direct imitations; there were also scores of other warnings of future war disguised as fiction which appeared between 1871 and 1914.[9] Wells himself contributed *The War in the Air* (1908).

The future war story took different forms, according to historical circumstance and the anxieties of the moment. As is so often the case in the history of sf, works of fiction purporting to be set in the future are actually ways of clarifying the mind about contemporary issues. Thus, in the 1880s a spate of British stories warned about the poor state of the British Navy; in France stories expressed not only fear of the Germans, but, in such stories as *La Prise de Londres au XXe siècle* (1891) and *Mort aux Anglais* (1892), an ill-disguised delight in the thought that Chesney might be right about Germany's plans for England. The view from America was rather more global (and, arguably, more racial); there, stories of future invasion concerned the Chinese and Japanese, 'the Yellow Peril'. In Ireland, on the other hand, the genre of future war concerned itself with the possibilities of Home Rule (the first Bill was introduced by Gladstone in 1886), and, from the Protestant point of view, the consequent breakup of the Empire and the victory of Papism in Ireland. Most of them were written by Protestants, and, naturally, relate how good honest Orangemen invade southern Ireland, defeat the Catholic rabble, and restore law and order and British values to the misguided Irish.[10]

In 1895 this sub-genre was represented by a number of examples. The Australian writer Kenneth Mackay published in London *The Yellow Wave: A Romance of the Asiatic Invasion of Australia*, a yellow peril story of the type which was, in the twentieth century, to be more characteristic of the United States. Fred Jane (of *Jane's Fighting Ships*) published *Blake of the 'Rattlesnake', Or the Man Who Saved England* (UK), which stressed the significance of naval torpedos, and told of the dangers of the French and the Russians and of striking workers in

England; James Eastwick published *The New Centurion* (UK), in which an advanced battleship sinks a large proportion of the French Navy; and George Griffith published *The Outlaws of the Air* (UK), in which air warfare, between anarchists and utopians, plays a major role, and in which the huge air fleet of the utopians establishes world peace (in scenes which startlingly prefigure those filmed by Alexander Korda for Wells's *Things to Come*, 1936).

The decade before the Great War saw another spate of warnings of war, of which the most delightful is undoubtedly P. G. Wodehouse's *The Swoop! or How Clarence Saved England* (1909), in which a Boy Scout saved the day against the Germans, Russians, Swiss, and Chinese and the combined troops of the Mad Mullah and the Prince of Monaco. It stands out in an otherwise largely humourless sub-genre, and one singularly lacking in literary merit. Future war stories tended to be written by Army officers or journalists, who produced fictionalized polemics rather than novels. They are no doubt marginal as sf (and some would not include them in the category at all); but again, they are important in the growth of acceptance of the future as a setting for fiction. And with them we see the birth of the tale of the future as warning, a form of fiction that may be as much propaganda as entertainment. It has had many descendants in the twentieth century, in novels which are not just warnings about wars—above all nuclear war—but warnings about other modern plagues: pollution, over-population, and so on. The function of the sf novel as warning has had a long career which shows no signs of ending. It may be noted here that it was a common theme in the British scientific romances of the period after the First World War, the two greatest examples being Aldous Huxley's *Brave New World* (1932) and George Orwell's *Nineteen Eighty-Four* (1949), perhaps the only novels of warning which had such influence that, it could be argued, their message had the required effect.

3. *The Tale of Science*

The third category of sf represented in 1895, like the other two, has had a vast twentieth-century progeny: the tale of science, of the marvellous invention, of scientists at work. William Livingston Alden gave us 'The Purple Death' (UK), with its mad scientist and his plague virus; Robert Cromie's *The Crack of Doom* (UK) has a mad scientist who is prevented from detonating the world; while in Robert Barr's 'The New Explosive' (UK), a French minister blows up an inventor rather than allow armies to get hold of his new explosive. Mullett Ellis's *Zalma* (UK) has an aristocratic woman anarchist who plans to sow anthrax bacilli from balloons over the capitals of Europe. Roy Rockwood's *The Wizard of the Sea* imitates Verne, introducing Captain Vindax and his submarine; Verne himself published 'An Express of the Future', a dream of an undersea railway to America, in *The Strand*. Robert W. Chambers's 'The Mask' (US) is about a liquid that petrifies bodies; Alice Fuller's 'A Wife Manufactured to Order' is a short story in which a husband tries living with a 'robot' wife (forerunner of numerous twentieth-century tales); while Charles Hinton's *Stella*, about an invisible woman, treats the same theme as does Wells in *The Invisible Man*, published two years later. No fewer than three of the 1895 publications—George Griffith's *The Romance of Golden Star* (UK), Grant Allen's 'The Dead Man Speaks' (UK), and Frank Moore's *The Secret of the Court* (UK)—deal with scientific attempts to revive the dead, a variant of *Frankenstein*.

Mary Shelley's *Frankenstein* is indeed right at the start of this sub-genre, and colours its subsequent development. There was never a time in the history of sf when the scientist appeared unambiguously as the hero and the herald of progress. The scientist has always had the capacity to wreak evil, often consciously, sometimes by accident, as well as to bring good. Frankenstein stands in a line which includes R. L. Stevenson's Dr Jekyll and Wells's Dr Moreau. Indeed, Dr Moreau is Wells's comment on Frankenstein. Frankenstein succeeded in his experiment to create life and a soul, even if he suffered isolation and despair as a consequence; Moreau failed, and in his failure shows the inhumanity of his desire, which resulted only in pain and madness. If Moreau is in a line begun by Frankenstein, then he in turn is at the head of a long line of fictional mad scientists, who always forget what every B-movie fan knows by heart, that there are things with which man is not meant to meddle. It can be seen from the plot descriptions in the previous paragraph that all our 1895 stories present science as something to be wary of and something that can be, and will be, abused; mad scientists were already commonplace in 1895.

Most sf, in the nineteenth century and subsequently, concentrated its attention much less upon the scientist himself than upon his creations, his discoveries and inventions. Verne is a much better instance of this than Wells. Wells always had his eye upon the human impact of his fiction, but in some of Verne's stories it is the machine that is the hero: the submarine *Nautilus* in *Twenty Thousand Leagues under the Sea*; the steam house pulled by its steam-driven elephant in *The Steam House*; the flying machine *Albatross* in *The Clipper of the Clouds*; the huge paddle-wheel liner in *The Floating City*; even the spaceship in *From the Earth to the Moon*. Extraordinary voyages were carried out in extraordinary vehicles; one of the most extraordinary is to be found in Edward Everett Hale's novella 'The Brick Moon' (US, 1869), about the world's first artificial satellite (and if brick seems an odd material, one may note that the American space shuttle has an exterior covering of ceramic tiles).

People at the end of the nineteenth century, seeing their world changed out of all recognition from earlier times by the steam-engine, by the mechanized factory, by gas and increasingly by electricity, were fascinated by machines and gadgets, and fully conscious that the lives of their children, even more than their own, were going to be transformed by them. A set of fifty cigarette cards produced by Armand Gervais of Lyons in 1899[11] shows the range of expected wonders: personal flying apparatus, helicopters, children being taught via electric head-sets and news coming through a superphonograph, mechanized house cleaning and farming, and so on. The most extensive fictional manifestation of this fascination was the Frank Reade, jun., stories, most of them written by Luis Philip Senarens under the pseudonym 'Noname'.[12] He was born in 1863, and by 1877 had already written the first of around 1500 dime novels (forty million words, claims Moskowitz) which he produced in just over thirty years, using at least twenty-seven pseudonyms, according to the hazy memories of Senarens himself. In 1879 the publisher Frank Tousey called him in to put some life into Harry Enton's series of dime novels about a mechanical man, the Steam Man of the Plains (itself a shameless plagiarization of Edward F. Ellis's *The Steam Man of the Prairies*, 1868). Sixteen-year-old Lu Senarens retired Enton's hero Frank Reade, and replaced him by his son, Frank Reade, jun., who for some years had adventures over the whole world with his steam carriage, electric boat, helicopter, submarine, and other miraculous contrivances. So successful was 'the American Jules Verne' that in 1892 Tousey founded a weekly, called the *Frank Reade Library*, to be devoted entirely to 'invention stories'.[13] Senarens wrote the better part of the 179 stories issued between 1892 and 1898: stories of electric and steam robots, submarines, armoured cars and tanks, and 'more about the possibility of air flight, projecting regular winged planes and dirigibles as well as helicopters, than all the rest of American writers up to his time combined'.[14]

In many ways Senarens's work typified the dime novel at its worst, with weak or no plotting, repetitiousness, bad writing, deliberate lowering of level, sloppy research into background, jingoism, sadism, and outrageous racial prejudice focused on blacks, Mexicans, and Jews.[15]

Indeed, it was 'invention stories', above all by Senarens himself, that helped give dime novels a bad name, and which in the 1890s drew down the wrath of the moralists and reformers upon the whole category.

Dime novels came to an end; but 'invention stories' continued to be a major element in early sf, particularly in the United States. Hugo Gernsback's *Ralph 124C 41+* (magazine publication 1911–12, book 1925) is the classic example of the sf novel written to extol the role of the gadget in creating a future utopia; its inventor/hero Ralph (One-to-Foresee-for-One) is just one of many similar figures from the sf of the first decades of the century. Just as Robinson Crusoe gave his name to the Robinsonade (the story of a lone individual trying to survive on a desert island or alien planet), so John Clute has recently taken the American inventor Thomas Edison's name to dub the prolific sub-genre featuring the inventor hero the 'Edisonade': 'Any story which features a young US male inventor hero who uses his ingenuity to extricate himself from tight spots and who, by so doing, saves himself from defeat and corruption and his friends and nation from foreign oppressors.'[16] Robinsonades are frequently conservative in their effect, since the hero is trying to reproduce his home environment in a supposedly alien land; Edisonades are frequently progressive and radical, since these inventions inevitably change the home environment.[17]

The interest in 'invention stories' is part of what Neil Harris has called the 'operational aesthetic'; he has suggested that it is a particular manifestation of American culture in the nineteenth century. Ordinary Americans were disturbed by beauty, significance, spiritual values, but were fascinated by the absorption of knowledge; museums were much more popular than art galleries. 'This was an aesthetic of the operational, a delight in observing process and examining for literal truth.'[18] It is a significant element in the growth of sf. Readers then (as, frequently, younger readers today) had insatiable appetites for learning about the universe, and the lengthy disquisitions about science which were to be found in early sf stories were not then seen, by most of their readers, as literary flaws, but as an essential part of their reading pleasure.

Herbert George Wells

Four publications of 1895 were not mentioned above: those written by H. G. Wells. 'The Remarkable Case of Davidson's Eyes' is a short story about a man who discovers that he can see in the fourth dimension; 'The Argonauts of the Air' tells of the fatal crash of a new flying machine; *The Stolen Bacillus* is a collection of sf stories, mostly published first in 1894; and *The Time Machine* is one of that tiny number of nineteenth-century sf stories (most of them also by Wells) which can still be read with unalloyed pleasure today. Wells was 29, still at the beginning of his career, and moving into what, for sf readers, was to be the most productive decade of his life.

The influence of H. G. Wells himself upon the development of sf was enormous. In his early short stories and novels as well as in numerous short essays on the future, Wells not only reached and impressed a very large number of people—preparing an audience for sf—but also set the agenda in subject-matter and tone for much of the sf to come. In Wells's *œuvre* are to be found stories of time-travel (*The Time Machine*), the creation of new forms of life (*The Island of Dr Moreau*, 1896), alien invasion (*The War of the Worlds*, 1898), space travel (*The First Men in the Moon*, 1901), utopia (*A Modern Utopia*, 1905, and *Men Like Gods*, 1923), dystopia (*When the Sleeper Wakes*, 1899), future warfare ('The Land Ironclads', 1903, and *The War in the Air*, 1908), and cosmic events ('The Star', 1897, and *In the Days of the Comet*, 1906), and numerous tales of future scientific inventions, plausible and implausible, with unforeseen human consequences: invisibility (*The Invisible Man*, 1897), a drug to speed up human motion ('The New Accelerator', 1901), new food to boost animal growth (*The Food of the Gods*, 1904), and so on. In terms of subject-matter, the subsequent history of sf almost seems like a series of footnotes to Wells.

The strength of his influence certainly has something to do with the complexities and uncertainties of his own mind. He was a great believer in the power of science to improve the lot of humanity, but was well aware of science's potential for bringing destruction or despotism. He was the greatest utopian writer of the twentieth century, yet wrote enduring dystopias as well. His Fabian socialism persuaded him to think in utopian terms about the future, but his innate pessimism inclined him to think the worst. Above all, perhaps, he was a believer in the power of science to change the world, but—crucially for his development as a writer of 'scientific romances'—saw science not as the creator of certainties and unveiler of mysteries, but as the great purveyor of mystery and wonder, just as religion had been in its time. He expresses this at the end of one of his early essays. 'The Rediscovery of the Unique' (1891), in an image which reflects the scene where the Time Traveller uses his matches to see in the world of the Morlocks:

Science is a match that man has just got alight. He thought he was in a room—in moments of devotion, a temple—and that his light would be reflected from and display walls inscribed with wonderful secrets and pillars carved with philosophical systems wrought into harmony. It is a curious sensation, now that the preliminary splutter is over and the flame burns up clear, to see his hands lit and just a glimpse of himself and the patch he stands on visible, and around him, in place of all that human comfort and beauty he anticipated—darkness still.[19]

Some writers have seen Wells's writing career in terms of his growing pessimism about man's future, summed up in the title of his last work (*Mind at the End of its Tether*, 1945) or in the epitaph he suggested for himself in a conversation with Sir Ernest Barker in 1939: 'God damn you all—I told you so.'[20] But that passage from 'The Rediscovery of the Unique' suggests that a bleak vision of the universe was with him from the beginning of his career, and his earliest and greatest scientific romance, *The Time Machine*, confirms the suspicion. The Time Traveller himself 'thought but cheerlessly of the Advancement of Mankind, and saw in the growing pile of civilization only a foolish heaping that must inevitably fall back upon and destroy its makers in the end'. The narrator of the tale sees some hope for the future in the two withered flowers which had been given to the Traveller by the Eloi girl from AD 802,701, 'to witness that even when mind and strength had gone, gratitude and a mutual tenderness still lived on in the heart of man'.[21] But the future revealed by the Traveller encompassed not only the evolution of humanity into two degenerate races, the Eloi and the Morlocks (the final result, perhaps, of the capitalist division of labour), but, ultimately, the dying of the Sun and the disappearance of all life on Earth:

I travelled, stopping ever and again, in great strides of a thousand years or more, drawn on by the mystery of the Earth's fate, watching with a strange fascination the sun grow larger and duller in the westward sky, and the life of the old Earth ebb away. At last, more than thirty million years hence, the huge red-hot dome of the sun had come to obscure nearly a tenth part of the darkling heavens. . . . I saw nothing moving, in earth or sky or sea. The green slime on the rocks alone testified that life was not extinct . . . The darkness grew apace; a cold wind began to blow in freshening gusts from the east, and the showering white flakes in the air increased in number. From the edge of the sea came a ripple and whisper. Beyond these lifeless sounds the world was silent. Silent? It would be hard to convey the stillness of it. All the sounds of man, the bleating of sheep, the cries of birds, the hum of insects, the stir that makes the background of our lives—all that was over.[22]

This description of the end of the world is contained in some of the greatest pages in all sf, which have hardly been surpassed in their visionary majesty.

Wells's understanding of the poetry and mystery of science, his realization of the puny nature of humans in the face of a cold and indifferent universe and of humanity at the whim of cold and indifferent processes such as evolution, his fascination with the future: all these things, manifested in *The Time Machine* as clearly as in anything else he wrote, have seemed to many to make Wells the obvious Father of Science Fiction. This is so even if he himself, in mature life, derided his scientific romances as slight juvenilia. Wells had an immense influence on the development of sf in the present century, not only in England (where the tradition of scientific romance was dominated by the memory of Wells well into the 1950s, and where sf was not infrequently called 'that Wells stuff'), but in the United States too, where, for instance, the first specialist sf magazine, *Amazing*, published twenty-six of his novels and stories in its first five years, between 1926 and 1930. But, as we have seen, he was by no means the only writer of sf in the 1890s, when most of his greatest sf was written; he stood out from the rest more for his intelligence and his literary ability than for his originality.

SF in Britain and America: Publishing History

The 1890s was in fact a decade in which many writers began to express their thoughts about the future in fictional terms. The figures drawn from Bleiler's study *Science Fiction: The Early Years* speak for themselves: between 1848 and 1859 there were 23 works of sf in English; in the 1860s there were also 23; in the 1870s, 91; in the 1880s, 215; and in the 1890s, 551.

What are the reasons for this? No doubt the increased speed of technological change, together with the *fin de siècle* feeling that one age was over and another about to begin, led people to speculate more about the future. There was much anticipation of the coming twentieth century not only in fiction, but also in non-fictional essays and popular journalism. Familiarity with the idea of a fictional future, thanks to Verne, Bellamy, and others, clearly encouraged people to express their hopes and fears in those terms: the phrase 'literature of ideas' was current in the 1890s, and much of British sf in the 1890s was part of that. When the Fabian socialist Beatrice Webb was working on her history of trade unionism in 1895, for instance, it seemed to her perfectly natural to think of writing a novel called *Sixty Years Hence*. This would not be a utopia, she hastened to tell her diary (that is, not another *News from Nowhere*), but a tale of life in the future 'if we go on "evoluting" in our humdrum way': a collectivist future, and one in which 'the fully-fledged woman engaged in a great career should be pictured just as we should now picture a man'.[23] She never wrote it, but others did.

General trends in fiction may also have helped prepare the ground for the scientific romance, in Britain at least. Elaine Showalter has recently argued that in the Britain of the 1880s there was a conscious move away from the realistic novel, as epitomized by women writers like George Eliot, concerned with domestic matters, love, marriage, and relationships between people, towards new forms of romance. Romance dealt with adventure, with Empire, with the deeds of men among men. Rider Haggard dedicated *King Solomon's Mines* (1885) 'to all the big and little boys who read'. Women were largely excluded from this world, as protagonists, as writers, and as potential readers. 'If the critic is a woman', Walter Besant wrote to Haggard after the publication of *She* (1886), 'she will put down this book with the remark that it is impossible—almost all women have this feeling towards the marvellous.'[24] R. L. Stevenson, G. A. Henty, Haggard, and Kipling all wrote stories in which male friendships are much more important than female relationships and in which the imperial quest is also a flight from domesticity and marriage. The almost exclusively male writers of British 'scientific romance' in the period up to the First World War fit neatly into this trend.

The differences between sf in the United States and Britain—marked in the nineteenth century and even more so in the early twentieth, and continuing until the victory of American sf in the 1950s—are important for the history of sf, and are a matter for discussion throughout this book. These differences concern not just the different political and cultural histories of the two countries, but also the different history of book publishing and the different ways in which both publishers and authors treated sf.

In Britain, as is well known, the three-volume novel, the 'three-decker', dominated the respectable novel-writing scene in the nineteenth century, and there was an enormous unfilled gap in both price and quality between these and the penny dreadful market. Because three-deckers were so expensive, circulating libraries were established, which in turn dominated the field, fixing prices and causing writers to self-censor themselves in order to achieve publication. Sf was outside this system. In Suvin's list of 360 items of Victorian sf, only 11 are three-deckers.[25] Even if the circulating libraries had been interested in such material on a large scale, the three-decker form simply did not lend itself to sf; the kind of detailed description and analysis required to fill hundreds of pages was very difficult to apply to scientific romance. At the other end of the scale, the penny dreadful (the English equivalent of the Senarens dime novel) did not adopt sf themes either; for different reasons, it too preferred the familiar.

Sf as it existed in Victorian Britain therefore mostly survived outside the generally accepted forms: as novelettes published in magazines like *Blackwood's*, as pamphlets, or as single-volume publications intended for boys (like the translations of Verne). But the situation changed radically in the 1890s, not only because the circulating libraries turned against the three-decker in favour of single-volume novels, but also because of the great expansion of middle-brow periodicals. The *Strand*, home of Sherlock Holmes from 1891 and of various sf short stories (including some by Doyle himself), is well known; but there were many others. These weeklies and monthlies published much of the sf of the 1890s and 1900s. *Pearson's Weekly* serialized George Griffith's *The Angel of the Revolution* from January 1893, the most imaginative yet in the 'future war' mould. (Griffith established himself as the best-known writer of sf in Britain in the early 1890s, and Wells, wanting to be taken seriously, always fumed at the obvious comparisons made between him and the popular Griffith.) Wells himself had his short stories published by the *Pall Mall Gazette* and others, while his novels were serialized in the magazines before book publication: *Pearson's Weekly* took his *The Invisible Man*, for instance, and *Pearson's Magazine* published *The War of the Worlds*.

The proliferation of markets for imaginative romances was not just a British phenomenon. Magazines like the *Strand* and *Pearson's Magazine* both had American editions, which helped introduce some of these British sf writers to a much larger readership, while American magazines of a similar type were created. There were all-fiction magazines too, like the *Argosy* (monthly from 1896) and *All-Story Magazine* (1905); there was also a smaller-circulation fiction magazine, published in Boston between 1895 and 1919, called the *Black Cat*, which specialized in fantasy fiction. These magazines allowed a large number of writers to establish themselves and to reach a very large number of readers; at its peak in 1907 the *Argosy* was offering some 135,000 words of fiction on coarse pulp paper, at a cost of 10 cents, to around 500,000 readers each month.

In the United States the increasing number of popular magazines had not had the profound effect upon the kind of fiction produced that it had had in Britain. The three-decker had never been important, and the huge gap between 'literature' and the penny dreadful which existed in Britain until the 1890s had in the United States been filled by a wide variety of 'popular' literature. In the United States romance had never been so marginalized by the realistic novel as it had been, earlier in the century, in Britain. Throughout the century, most of the respected (male) writers of fiction in the United States had dabbled in what we could call sf; Edgar Allan Poe is the most obvious example, but there are also Charles Brockden Brown,

Washington Irving, Nathaniel Hawthorne, James Fenimore Cooper, Fitz James O'Brien, Oliver Wendell Holmes, as well as, somewhat later, Mark Twain, Herman Melville, Henry James, and Ambrose Bierce.

The American public was introduced to Wells and other English writers through these new periodicals, which also allowed the republication of older material and the appearance of some newer American writers, such as George Allan England and Garrett P. Serviss. On the whole in this period, British writers had more of an impact on the American market than Americans on the British, but there was considerable cross-fertilization, even if there were differences in taste. Our sampling of the publications of 1895 suggested that the theme of utopia was more popular in the United States, the future war story in Britain, and that fiction aimed at a semi-literate readership was more common in the former (in the form of dime novels). But the two markets also had a lot in common, and by the early part of the twentieth century it looked very much as if British and American markets and readerships had converged, and were destined to follow a similar evolution.

By 1910, however, much had changed. In Britain, many of the periodicals disappeared with the rise of the popular daily press, and those that were left, like the *Strand* and the *Pall Mall Gazette*, were yearning for respectability, and became reluctant to publish anything like the quantity of speculative fiction which they had done before. The fad for scientific romance declined. Interplanetary tales virtually disappeared from the scene until Olaf Stapledon in the 1930s; when such stories *were* written, they tended to be published as 'boys' books'. Before the First World War, and particularly just after it, when scientific romance was written in Britain, it was published not in magazines, but in book form. It rarely appeared in a cheap hardback series, like Collins Shilling Fiction Library or Newnes's Sevenpenny Series, just as, immediately before and after the Second World War, it very rarely appeared in paperback format, since scientific romance was regarded as unlikely to achieve mass-market interest. Moreover, British scientific romance tended to be published in full-length novel form, not in the short story form which dominated

American sf until the 1950s. Brian Stableford (whose excellent and indispensable *Scientific Romance in Britain, 1890–1950* is the otherwise unacknowledged source for much of this section) sees a highpoint in the production of scientific romance in Britain in 1898, with a steady decline thereafter to the trough of 1918, and only a slow recovery to a new phase of popularity and a new generation of writers at the beginning of the 1930s.

Publishing in the United States took a totally different direction. Books had been cheap even before the 1890s, and widespread pirating of foreign books helped to keep prices down. The boom in periodicals, which the United States shared with Britain, continued long after the decline in Britain, and publishers deliberately aimed their publications at a wider public than in Britain. There had been considerable indignation at the low literary level of such dime novels as the *Frank Reade Library*, but the result was the replacement of the dime novel by almost equally low-grade fiction magazines aimed at almost the same public—'the pulps'. The average pulp was a magazine measuring 10 by 7 inches, printed on thick coarse paper; it was the development of the technique of producing cheap paper from wood-pulp, in the 1880s, that created the possibility of mass production of cheap magazines as well as the name by which they became known. The pulps often had ragged untrimmed pages and, later in their history, covers printed with cheap lurid coal-tar dyes. Now, yellowing and fragile, they are expensive collectors' items; but when published, they were the kind of thing that respectable readers shunned, or kept hidden. The publishers of the more up-market middle-class magazines (printed on better quality, shinier paper, and hence known as 'the slicks') came to see the fast-paced adventure stories to be found in the pulps (which included sf) as tainted by their low-grade associations, and they stopped printing them. While sf in Britain, when it was published, came out regularly in hardback, in America it was largely restricted to the pulps.

Publishers of dime novels had realized that there were readers who liked only one kind of fiction—westerns, perhaps, or detective novels—and eventually the pulps began to specialize as well. *Thrill Book* (which began and ended in 1919) was the first pulp to specialize in fantastic fiction; *Amazing Stories* (1926 to the present, in different guises) was the first 'scientifiction' pulp. In the 1920s specialization reached spectacular heights: 'there were magazines specialising in railroad stories, sea stories, yellow peril stories, the exploits of crime-fighting superheroes, and even a short-lived pulp called *Zeppelin Adventures.*'[26] Tradition has it that the most famous of all the pulps, originally called *Astounding Stories of Super-Science*, came into existence almost by accident as the result of the pulp publishers' specialization. William Clayton published some thirteen adventure magazines of different types. But his garishly coloured covers were printed on a large sheet of glossy paper with sixteen spaces on it. Looking around for three new titles so that he could do the colour printing most economically, he was advised by one of his editors, Harry Bates, to produce an imitation of Hugo Gernsback's *Amazing Stories*: thus was *Astounding* born.[27] *Astounding* has had an unbroken run into the 1990s, although in 1960 it changed its name to *Analog* in a final effort to disown its pulp past. The success of *Amazing* inspired not only *Astounding*, but numerous other sf pulps. Although general fiction pulps like *Argosy* and *All-Story* continued to publish sf (the two merged in the 1920s), most American sf in the 1930s was published in the specialist pulps, and little ever reached book form.

It is clear that the different publishing histories of sf in Britain and the United States has had a profound effect on the subsequent development of the genre in those two countries. The differences between American and British sf (and indeed between American and other European sf traditions), which had always existed, became much more marked, thanks to the pulps. As we shall see below, scientific romance in Britain inherited from Wells a seriousness that concerned itself with the future of humanity and with philosophical, as well as scientific, questions; the various visionary works by the philosopher Olaf Stapledon may stand as the epitome of this tradition. In the United States, sf before the Second World War was often fast-moving adventure and colourful romance, with rather more suspense and thrills than philosophy; Edgar Rice Burroughs is the typical example. Sf in the United States suffered profoundly from its restriction to the pulps; it reached a wide public, but denied itself any sort of respectability. It is true that in Britain scientific romance remained a minority interest, but it was one which, thanks largely to Wells, was accepted in some way as legitimate. Well-known writers and novelists in the United States could never have dabbled in the field in the 1920s and 1930s— or would never have thought of doing so—in the way that Aldous Huxley, Julian Huxley, C. S. Lewis, and J. B. Priestley did in Britain.

SF between the Wars outside North America

The history of American sf between the wars has often been written as if it were the history of a movement: a collective urge to produce sf which was given expression in magazines like *Amazing* and which culminated, at the beginning of the Second World War, in the inevitable emergence of modern sf, with the great names like Asimov and Heinlein. By the 1940s, as we shall see in Chapter 4, American sf fans had acquired a strong collective feeling; they helped give American sf writers the sense of being the spokespersons for an entire community and begin to construct the past history of the movement. Many of them viewed sf as a way of life and a way of thought as much as a type of popular literature, and they were often fervent missionaries for the cause. Sf writers were often drawn from this group of readers, and even if their background was different, they wrote for those readers in the manner which those readers preferred. A genre emerged.

If this collective vision of the development of sf is a possible way of viewing developments in the United States, it certainly does not hold true anywhere else. Some authors in Europe no doubt had the feeling that they belonged to a tradition; but for many of them that tradition was dominated by the two great figures upon whose shoulders they perched, like pygmies: Jules Verne and H. G. Wells. Otherwise, authors wrote in isolation from one another, and usually wrote what we may call 'sf' as only part of their output; the type of market provided by the

American pulps, by the 1930s at least, simply did not exist in Europe, except perhaps in the former Soviet Union, where, according to Patrick L. McGuire, there were full-time writers of sf by the 1920s.[28]

The influence of Wells and Verne was dominant in Britain and France, respectively, right up to the Second World War, even though Verne had died in 1905, and by 1905 Wells had published nearly all his great scientific romances (although he continued writing occasional examples right into the 1930s). Their influence extended, via translation, far beyond their own countries and continents. Wells has been estimated to be second in popularity only to Shakespeare among Western writers in Japan in the early years of the twentieth century, while the Vernian inspiration for Oshikawa Shunro's best-selling *The Undersea Warship* (1900) is fairly obvious; Verne had indeed been the first Western writer to have been translated into Japanese, and was published from as early as the 1870s. At the very end of this period, in 1940, when the world's first weekly sf magazine was founded, in Sweden, it was given the title *Jules Verne-Magasinet*.

To harp on the contributions of Verne and Wells, however, as has so often been done, is to underestimate the strength of various national traditions of sf writing before the Second World War. If in this book (and most previous studies of sf) the Anglo-American tradition predominates, that is partly because the Anglo-American tradition has indeed dominated the publishing of sf throughout the world since the Second World War. But before 1939 sf was much more diverse. The true extent and importance of the national traditions of, say, Russia, Japan, or France have yet to be properly assessed in the English-speaking world. Translations are few, and, when available, tend to extract the individual work from its proper context, and distort its significance; often those works are remembered for quite extraneous reasons. Thus, Yevgeny Zamyatin's *We* (1922), a powerful attack on the dehumanizing tendencies of totalitarian systems, is well known partly because of its influence on George Orwell's *Nineteen Eighty-Four*; Karel Čapek's *R.U.R.* (1920) is familiar as the work which introduced the word 'robot' into the English language; and Thea von Harbou's *Metropolis* (1926) and *Frau im Mond* (1928) are remembered as the books of her husband Fritz Lang's films. Very few other Russian, Czech, or German works from before 1940 are known outside their countries of origin. Indeed, even the pre-war British sf tradition is very little known by today's readers, once Wells himself is discounted. Huxley's *Brave New World* and possibly various works by Olaf Stapledon are almost all that various reprintings have preserved from that period in the recollection of the average reader of sf today.

It is in the former Soviet Union, particularly during the 1920s, that sf appears to have had a stronger presence and identity than anywhere else outside the United States. It received its name, *nauchnaia fantastika*, perhaps as early as the 1890s, and the name was certainly well established in the 1920s, before 'science fiction' had been invented in the United States. The subtitle of the state-owned periodical *World Pathfinder*, founded in 1925, was 'Travel, Adventure, Science Fiction'. However, the bulk of Soviet (or specifically Russian) sf was published outside the state system in the 1920s, by those private publishers that were allowed to survive, and the authors were more independent then than they were later on, using sf not simply to show the inevitability of the Communist world state. The novel *Beyond the Planet Earth* (1920) by the pioneer theorist of space travel, Konstantin Tsiolkowski, was an inspiration to a number of writers and, indeed, to the post-war Soviet space programme. But the experience of the best-known writer of the 1920s and early 1930s, Alexander Belyaev, shows some of the problems faced by the Soviet sf writer. He wanted to set *The Struggle in Space* (1928) in an era of worldwide communism, and consulted various authorities, including even the commissar of education, as to how he could bring dramatic conflict into his novel in a future in which war, crime, capitalism, and class conflict would all have been eliminated. In the end he gave up, and put some capitalists in his future; by the early 1950s he would never have been allowed to do so. In 1931, Ian Larri's *The Land of the Happy* solved the problem by having a conflict, in his utopian state, between supporters and opponents of the space programme. With the disappearance of independent publishers at the end of the 1920s, there was a brief hiatus in the production of sf, and some of the writers of the 1920s were sent to the labour camps. But sf continued to be published, although often the novels were merely rather obvious fictionalizations of current state policy initiatives; future war stories were particularly current in the late 1930s.

Sf was in just as strong a position in Germany, even if it did not have the same sense of identity. Germany had its equivalents of the *Frank Reade Library*: *Kapitän Mors* appeared weekly between 1909 and 1913, for instance, featuring a Captain Nemo of outer space and achieving a circulation of something up to 100,000; in the 1930s there were the 150 issues of *Sun Koh, the Heir of Atlantis* and the 120 issues of *Jan Mayen, Lord of Atomic Power*. At the other literary extreme, there were, as in Britain, occasional forays into sf by distinguished novelists, such as Bernhard Kellermann and Alfred Döblin, and there were also a number of prolific sf writers, the most successful of whom was Hans Dominik, who published sf novels throughout the 1920s and 1930s. He was not untouched by the political climate any more than his colleagues in the Soviet Union, and his novels became increasingly nationalistic. Other writers were straightforwardly racist, like Edmund Kiss, whose tetralogy about Atlantis is a celebration of Aryanism. On the other hand, just as some Russians were inspired by the work of Konstantin Tsiolkovsky, so in Germany the pioneering work of Hermann Oberth and other members of the Society for Space Travel inspired attempts at prophecy such as Otto Willi Gail's *The Shot into Infinity* (1925).

In France too, sf was never relegated to the ghetto of the pulps, and established authors often dabbled successfully in the field. André Maurois' *The Weigher of Souls* (1931) and *The Thought-Reading Machine* (1937), for instance, are distinguished contributions to the genre. Verne's influence remained strong, and one of the first generation of his Francophone followers, J.-H. Rosny aîné (1856–1940), a Belgian, was still publishing in France between the wars. In its treatment of aliens, his *Navigators of the Infinite* (1925), the story of a human expedition to Mars and its attempts to save the Martians from their evolutionary successors, is far in advance of anything being published in the English-speaking world at the time. But there were a number of other important novelists in France, and even a short-lived sf publishing label, Hypermondes, founded in 1935. Of the other romance-language areas, Italy and Romania had the best-developed sf traditions; elsewhere in Europe, sf novels appeared only sporadically. The early appearance of sf in Japan likewise had few repercussions in the inter-war period, with the Japanese version of the pulps publishing sf stories only occasionally, and Unno Jūza being one of the few significant figures. In most of these countries, the Second World War brought the publishing of sf virtually to a halt, for political as well as economic reasons. When publishing resumed, American sf was to begin its domination everywhere outside Eastern Europe.

The contribution of Britain to the sf world between the wars was considerable, and its achievements, together with the still enduring prestige of Wells, allowed it to retain an individual voice after the Second World War, while the slow redevelopment of paperback publishing after that war enabled British writers to develop without being swamped immediately by reprints of American sf. In Britain, as elsewhere in Europe, the First World War had a very pronounced effect on the development of sf. Gung-ho tales of future war, which had poured from the presses before 1914, turned into sombre stories of the deaths of civilizations once the realities of modern warfare had become apparent. Edward Shanks's *The People of the Ruins* (1918), which envisaged a Britain returning to barbarism after war, was the first of many; by the 1930s they were beginning to be replaced by novels which looked forward to the future horrors of high-technology warfare. S. Fowler Wright's trilogy began with *Prelude to Prague* (1935), the story of a second world war beginning with a German invasion of Czechoslovakia, continued with a German airborne invasion of Britain (published 1936), and concluded (1937) with the arrival of Americans in the war. The standard (and still current) characterization by Americans of the downbeat, depressing character of British sf, as opposed to the striving optimism of American sf, had its origins in the very different experiences of the two nations in the First World War; the successes of American sf (and more particularly of British sf adopting the American idiom) in the Britain of the late 1940s and early 1950s had at least something to do with the invigorating and lively tone of the American writers, which contrasted so strongly with the rather staid and more literary tradition of British 'scientific romance'.

As we have seen already, those 'scientific romances' were generally of novel length, and in hardback form. Only in 1937 was the first British sf magazine founded, *Tales of Wonder*, and that soon turned to the reprinting of American pulp sf. Before 1937 there had been no regular outlet for British sf in short form, and the unfettered speculation about the future which had become common in American sf remained largely absent: sf adventure and space exploration could find publication only as boys' fiction. As a result, therefore, and because of the continuing dominance of Wells—by now a political guru as much as an sf novelist—British sf had a predominantly earnest tone: even the satires of John Gloag, like *The New Pleasure* (1933) or *Winter's Youth* (1934), had their serious side. The only major figures to publish utopian sf in this period were Wells himself, with novels such as *Men Like Gods* (1922) and *The Shape of Things to Come* (1933), and George Bernard Shaw, with *Back to Methuselah* (1921). The tone of the period was caught much better with Aldous Huxley's *Brave New World* (1932), in which Huxley unloaded all his élitist, snobbish, Oxonian, anti-American spleen on to a large and appreciative audience. His book was also, of course, an attack both on Wellsian utopianism and on what Huxley saw as the modern slide into hedonism and mass consumerism; those bogey figures who represent Huxley's view of the wrong turns the world was making all appear in the book, mostly in the names chosen for the characters. Apart from Wells himself (of whom Huxley said, 'I don't know him at all well; but he has always struck me as a rather horrid, vulgar little man'[29]), there were (in alphabetical order) the atheist Charles Bradlaugh, Diesel, Engels, Hoover, Lenin, Alfred Mond (founder of ICI), Marx, Mussolini, Pavlov, Primo de Rivera, Jean-Jacques Rousseau, Shaw, Trotsky, and, of course, the 'gods' of this atheist future, Our Ford and Our Freud. It is a witty and skilful work, as well as a bitter and conservative one, and it is not surprising that it has emerged as the best-known work of British sf from between the wars: works which mock the very idea of looking into the future and which ultimately present the reader with no solutions whatsoever often seem to have more appeal than serious sf.

As Brian Stableford has pointed out, however, serious speculation about the future was much more firmly established and influential on contemporary thought in Britain than it was in the United States. Between 1925 and 1935 there was quite a boom in 'futurology'; in particular, more than 100 pamphlets were issued in a series called 'Today & Tomorrow', which looked at the future of every conceivable institution and aspect of life. The first was the most distinguished and influential of all, J. B. S. Haldane's *Daedalus; or, Science and the Future* (1924); other contributors included people like Sylvia Pankhurst, Vera Brittain, and Sir James Jeans, as well as a number of people who, before or after, contributed to the field of sf as well: André Maurois, J. Leslie Mitchell, A. M. Low, John Gloag, Bertrand Russell, and Haldane himself. J. D. Bernal's *The World, The Flesh and the Devil* (1929) had almost as much impact as Haldane's *Daedalus*. These two pamphlets provided (and could still provide) sf writers with innumerable possible plot lines. But Bernal and Haldane were also two significant influences on a part-time Liverpool philosopher called Olaf Stapledon, the most individual and visionary of all early British sf writers.

Stapledon wrote over twenty works of philosophy and sf, but he is primarily remembered for just four: *Last and First Men* (1930), *Odd John* (1935), *Star Maker* (1937), and *Sirius* (1944). *Odd John* and *Sirius* are striking and often moving novels about highly intelligent beings who are isolated outcasts in their worlds, Odd John because he is a super-child in a world of ordinary humans and Sirius because he is a dog, artificially endowed with high intelligence. *Last and First Men* and *Star Maker* defy easy categorization. They are not novels. The first is cast in the form of history—the history of the human race, as it evolves through two billion years, from one new human species to

another, until the last, the 'eighteenth men'. The second is more
like a travelogue, roaming through the entire history of the
cosmos and looking at its habitats and its myriad life-forms,
until finally the star maker himself is glimpsed. It is as if
Stapledon had looked at H. G. Wells's advice to the writer of
sf, to content himself with one marvel ('Nothing remains interesting where anything can happen'[30]), and turned it on its head.
No sf before or since has been so prodigious of marvels, so
fertile in imagination, and so bold in speculation. Because of
their form, they remain oddities. But they also remain inspi-
rations to sf writers. For Moskowitz, they are enough to rank
Stapledon among the sf immortals (alongside Shelley, Poe,
Verne, and Wells); Brian Aldiss called *Star Maker* 'the one great
grey holy book of science fiction', ranking him alongside Wells;
while Eric Rabkin and Robert Scholes reckoned Stapledon to
be 'the most distinguished writer of science fiction in English
between the first and second World War' and 'one of the most
influential to write in any language'.[31] Stapledon, of course, did
not consider himself an sf writer, but said that he was writing
'romances of the future', 'myth', or 'fantastic fiction of a semi-
philosophical kind'. In 1937 Eric Frank Russell placed in his
hands a number of American pulp sf magazines (including
Astounding, in which Russell's own first story had appeared),
and Stapledon was polite, but far from impressed.[32] European
sf, by 1937, had begun to make a respectable place for itself as
a branch, if a minor branch, of literature, and could be taken
seriously by intellectuals and even literary critics. One glance at
the gaudy, crude covers of American pulps, at their cheap paper
and production, and at their adverts for denture fixatives, trusses,
acne cream, and lucky red lodestones was probably all that
Stapledon needed.

SF in the American Pulps

The creation of specialist sf pulps after 1926 may have been a
significant fact in the publishing history of sf and in the foundation of the sf community (see Chapter 4), but it did not have
an immediate impact on the type of sf being written, nor did it

create a new generation of authors overnight. Many of the important names in the early sf magazines had already written sf for several years in the general fiction pulps. Murray Leinster, for instance, who continued publishing sf up to 1969 (he died in 1975), made his début in *All-Story Weekly* in 1917, and published his imaginative story 'The Mad Planet' in *Argosy* in 1920. But probably the most influential of the writers who began in the pulps was Edgar Rice Burroughs, whose 'Under the Moons of Mars' started as a serial in *All-Story* in February 1912.

Brian Aldiss has taken Wells and Burroughs as being at the two poles of sf; it is an illuminating idea, and helps to explain some of the complexities of modern sf. He takes two novels published in 1923, Wells's *Men Like Gods* and Burroughs's *Pellucidar*, originally serialized in *All-Story Cavalier Weekly* in 1915 and appearing in book form in 1923. In the Wells book Mr Barnstaple finds himself in a fourth-dimension utopia, and struggles to defend it against more worldly travellers from Earth. In Burroughs, the hero searches for his love in a primitive world inside a hollow Earth.

Which of the two is the 'better' book? If the question has any meaning, my answer would be that *Pellucidar* is the better. If one's choice of company lies between a fatigued schoolmaster and an inspired anecdotalist, the better bet is the anecdotalist.

Burroughs, in this novel, writes about as well as he can write, not well but serviceably, while his fertile imagination pours out lavishly the details of his preposterous world. Wells appears constipated beside him. Wells's novel is laborious, and, whatever it was in 1923, takes an effort to read now. With Burroughs you can have (moderate) fun. Wells here gives off what Kingsley Amis categorises as 'a soporific whiff of left-wing crankiness'.

So why does one obstinately respect Wells the more? It must be because, whatever else his failings, Wells is trying to grapple with what he sees as the real world. Burroughs, however expertly, is dishing out daydreams. . . .

Wells is teaching us to think. Burroughs and his lesser imitators are teaching us not to think.

Of course, Burroughs is teaching us to wonder. The sense of wonder is in essence a religious state, blanketing out criticism. Wells was always a critic, even in his most romantic and wondrous tales.

For Aldiss, Wells and Burroughs represent the thinking and the dreaming poles of sf. 'At the thinking pole stand great figures, although it is easy to write badly. At the dreaming pole stand no great figures—though there are monstrous figures—and it is difficult to write well. In the eighties the dreaming pole is in the ascendant.'[33]

And, one might add, for Aldiss, Mary Shelley stands near the equator, in that ideal state of balance between thinking and dreaming which marks the perfect sf writing.

The dreaming pole was in the ascendant in the American pulps as well. There was little or no pretence at scientific correctness in Burroughs. If his Mars (which natives call Barsoom) is not too unlike the dry, canal-scored planet of late nineteenth-century astronomers, John Carter does not get there by spaceship but, literally, by wishful thinking. And what he finds is an exact prefiguration of what scores of writers in the dreaming 1980s created in various fantasy and science-fictional worlds: an exotic mélange of different races and cultures, almost all fixed in a pre-technological and pseudo-feudal epoch, almost all with a warrior ethic and hence with plentiful opportunity for exciting sword-fights, and offering scope for endless expansion into as many volumes as the readers can afford. The continual reprinting of Burroughs's novels right up to the present day—not only the series set on Mars and Venus and in Pellucidar (inside the hollow Earth), but also his more celebrated Tarzan adventures—suggests that, despite the very evident racism and sexism, readers can still find excitement, or escapism, there. Burroughs was published in Britain not long after he appeared in book form in the United States; the 1912 serial appeared as a book called *A Princess of Mars* in 1917 in the United States and 1919 in Britain. Significantly, like Verne before him, he was published in Britain as a writer of stories for boys; tales of interplanetary derring-do were suitable for boys and Americans, but not for British adults. And, it is fair to say, those intrigued by Burroughs's brand of romance tend to be captured young: few young males can resist riding in their imagination on a six-legged thoat across Barsoom's dry sea-beds, underneath its hurtling moons, and alongside John Carter, helping him search (once more) for his beautiful (and generally nude) wife, Dejah Thoris.

Another key writer who came to prominence in the pulps (although, unlike Burroughs, exclusively in the specialist sf specialist pulps), and one far removed from the thinking pole, was E. E. Smith, usually known as E. E. Smith, Ph.D., or E. E. 'Doc' Smith. (Real scientists, even scientists who specialized in the chemistry of doughnut mixes, were rare enough among writers of sf for the editers of the pulps to trumpet the fact.) His first novel, *The Skylark of Space*, was in fact written in 1915, not long after Burroughs's *A Princess of Mars*, although it was not published until *Amazing* took it in 1928, in the same issue that introduced Philip Nowlan's space hero Buck Rogers, in 'Armageddon—2419 A.D.' Smith too wrote series, notably the 'Skylark' and 'Lensman' series, and he too appealed, and still appeals, to adolescents. He wrote about super-science rather than sword-wielding primitives; but his super-scientists, invariably of awe-inspiring intellect, had the comforting habit of speaking and behaving like American adolescents of around 1930. Yet, behind the awkward prose and embarrassing dialogue, lurks an ability to inspire awe and wonder. Smith knew that tremendous size and power were the key to awe; he thought of the tremendous, and doubled it. His plots span billions of years and millions of light-years; his massive spaceships, piloted in the Lensman series by beings whose mental powers have been magnified many times by the lenses they wear, travel at unimaginable speeds and lash out at their enemies with incredibly powerful force-beams. The type of preposterous galaxy-spanning adventures in which he specialized have been christened 'space operas' (the term invented by Wilson Tucker in 1941, by analogy with 'soap opera'), and they still flourish. George Lucas's *Star Wars* films are directly descended from Smith's space sagas. The crudeness of the original is hidden by the sophistication available to a modern film studio, but has the same power to thrill and awe the young (and not so young) mind.

Smith was only one, though perhaps the most prominent, of those who experimented with stories of super-science in the American pulps of the 1930s. There are innumerable genius inventors, like Richard Seaton of *Skylark* fame, or heroes with super-powers, like Kimball Kinnison, the First Lensman. The Earth, or the human species itself, was saved from appalling perils every month in one pulp after another by men such as these. The pulps indeed spawned the comic-strip super-heroes of the 1930s, who have succeeded in surviving through several changes of fashion right into the 1990s; Buck Rogers, Flash Gordon, Superman, and Batman all made their appearance in the decade before 1939, and all achieved cult status again, with the help of lavish Hollywood budgets, in the 1970s and 1980s.

The super-hero, in fact, was one of the most prominent creations of the pulp era, and continued to play an important part in American sf long after the pulps died. He (and even, latterly, she) was largely an American product; when British writers took up the theme, as Olaf Stapledon did in 1935 with *Odd John*, it was generally treated in a more reflective and critical way. The inherently anti-democratic tendencies of the super-hero have been savagely dissected in Norman Spinrad's *The Iron Dream* (1972); this novel purports to have the original title of *Lord of the Swastika*, and to be written in an alternative world in which its author, Adolf Hitler, came to the United States to make his living illustrating and writing pulp sf, rather than staying in Germany to found the National Socialist Party. More recently, Batman and the whole super-hero theme have received a similar critical treatment in the sophisticated comic books or graphic novels of the late 1980s, notably *The Dark Knight Returns* (1986) by Frank Miller and *Watchmen* (1987) by Alan Moore and Dave Gibbons.

The American pulps may have bequeathed a largely unfortunate heritage to sf in the second half of the twentieth century. Their concentration on action not thought, on power rather than responsibility, on aggression not introspection, on wish fulfilment not reality, has survived into much contemporary sf. 'By far the great part of pulp fiction from the time of Wells till now', wrote Thomas M. Disch in his embarrassingly accurate 'The Embarrassments of Science Fiction', 'was written to provide a semi-literate audience with compensatory fantasies.'[34] Yet this judgement conceals some of the successes of the pulps of the period before the Second World War. They were what inspired the writers of the classic sf of the 1940s and 1950s to pursue their careers; they were schools in which some of the writers of the 1940s and later learned their craft; and they sometimes saw the publication of fiction that was far from clichéd and run of the mill.

Part of the credit for this originality should go to the second editor of *Astounding*, F. Orlin Tremaine, and his assistant, Desmond Hall. Starting in December 1933, Tremaine tried to publish in each issue at least one story that he called a 'thought variant': a story whose driving force was a speculative idea, rather than a gadget or a sequence of cliff-hangers. The first such story was Nat Schachner's 'Ancestral Voices', in which a time-traveller kills a barbarian who is sacking Rome and discovers that this has resulted in the disappearance of thousands of his twentieth-century contemporaries—including a caricature of Adolf Hitler and the time-traveller himself. Schachner uses the story to satirize the idea of racial characteristics; readers seem mostly to have been intrigued by the time paradoxes involved. As Albert Berger has commented, 'As prepared as were some writers and editors for such social and political speculation [about race], the SF community revealed a distinct preference for the intellectual games of extrapolation rather than for real issues and real lives.'[35] Tremaine and Hall emphasized speculation rather than endless action, and placed more stress too on characterization, even of aliens, and on mood; they were laying the foundations for the more speculative and 'modern' sf which was to emerge from the pulps at the very end of the 1930s, in which 'idea' would be hero. As examples we may take two Don A. Stuart stories from *Astounding*: 'Forgetfulness' (1937) and 'Who Goes There?' (1938).[36]

'Forgetfulness' concerns a colonizing expedition which arrived on the planet Rhth, near a place called N'yor, some ten million years in the future. The colonists found cities whose builders had clearly been masters of technology, including the technology of space flight; their archaeologists discovered that, in the far distant past, their own civilization had been founded by these space travellers. But the cities were deserted; the only inhabitants of Rhth lived simple lives, in small settlements in the countryside, and had forgotten all about the technology that had created the cities. The colonizers plan to put these people in reservations, and take over the planet to learn about the forgotten knowledge. But suddenly they find themselves and their ships six light-years away, in orbit around their own star; they have been removed by the mental power of the people of Rhth, who were not the simple degenerates they had imagined, but had moved beyond the need for material technology. They had forgotten the details of technology, just as the colonizers had forgotten how savages make fire with two sticks. The story is about human evolution (the planet is, of course, Earth, the place New York); about the possibility of moving beyond dependence on the machine; about the latent potentialities of the human mind. It puts the problems of twentieth-century humans into the longest possible historical perspective (from 'savagery' to god-like status), and, unlike Stapledon's *Last and First Men*, offers hope and optimism about the human condition. Its themes would be taken up by the next generation of writers, not least by Arthur C. Clarke.

'Who Goes There?' has been filmed twice, as *The Thing*, and in both 1951 and 1982 the emphasis was on the story's horror elements. This emphasis overlooked the qualities which made it one of the most significant stories of the 1930s. A spaceship which had crashed into the Antarctic millions of years ago is detected and uncovered by a team of scientists, who find its horrifically alien pilot frozen. When the pilot thaws, it comes to life and escapes. The scientists eventually realize that it is able to take the form of other living things, and perfectly able to mimic one of their own number; their problem is to discover the alien in their midst before it escapes to civilization and uses its obviously enormous powers to destroy or conquer the planet. That plot was relatively standard pulp, but the treatment was not. Apart from the fact that the author provided a grittily realistic setting, with a highly effective sense of tension and suspense, the crux of the story was the premise which was to fuel much modern sf: that the laws of science are universal, and that problems can be solved by using the logic of science. What gives the actual story a twist was that the scientist who enunciates this principle was himself one of the clones of the Thing; the first reaction of one of the unmistakably human scientists to the problem had been 'I—I guess Earthly laws don't apply'.[37] A belief in the problem-solving properties of science and in the plot potential that such problems offered was to become commonplace in the next generation of American sf.

Defining the Genre

Those who had written or published scientific romance, invention stories, 'different stories', or scientific fiction before the advent of Hugo Gernsback do not seem to have spent time wondering about how to define the genre within which they were writing. If there were no attempts to define the genre, then arguably the writers were not conscious that they were writing within a genre, and therefore were *not* writing within a genre. A genre requires a consciousness of appropriate conventions, a certain aesthetic, and even a certain ideology, as well as readers who have particular expectations. It is more than a publishing category, because it assumes some bond or imaginary contract between writer and reader. Sf is what sf writers write for sf readers.

In the course of the 1930s sf fandom became an organized voice for the sf reader, and began, through regular sf conventions, to establish the close link between writers and readers which was to have such a pronounced, and unique, effect on the history of the genre. Nevertheless, some kind of self-consciousness, and hence perhaps some feeling of a genre, can be found even before the 1930s. In the first quarter of the century, there were readers who had clear ideas of what they wanted, and searched diligently for scientific stories or invention stories in books and periodicals. The editor of *All-Story Weekly* noted on 20 April 1920 that there were a large number of vociferous and discriminating readers of 'different stories'; Gernsback himself noted as early as his third issue of *Amazing* that there were a lot of people (whom he called 'fans') whose hobby was collecting and listing 'scientifiction' stories in English and other languages.[38] Sf fans existed before sf itself was named: in a sense readers had created a genre before publishers, or even writers, were clear what that genre was.

The creation of specialist sf magazines was a recognition of the existence of a genre, and once that genre was named, in the late 1920s—first as 'scientifiction', and then as 'science fiction'—we get our first attempts at definition. It is no coincidence that the first definitions came with the coiner of those names, Hugo Gernsback. He produced various formulations, in the editorials of the various magazines he edited in the late 1920s and early 1930s, of which 'the Jules Verne, H. G. Wells and Edgar Allan Poe type of story—a charming romance intermingled with scientific fact and prophetic vision' is one of the more significant. Gernsback knew the ancestry of his type of fiction. As we have seen (above, p. 8), he was a firm believer in its educational importance: it was a means of introducing a scientifically illiterate public to the discoveries of modern science, via the sugared pill of 'charming romance'. He even specified the thickness of the sugar coating at one point: 'the ideal proportion . . . should be seventy-five per cent literature interwoven with twenty-five per cent science.' It should be romance (drawing no doubt on the still current phrase 'scientific romance'), a dictionary definition of which is 'a narrative work dealing with events and characters remote from ordinary life'. And finally, it ought to contain 'prophetic vision': it was a common expectation among early sf writers and readers that sf writers had the potential to generate ideas of future technological and scientific advance that would actually influence scientists and inventors and thereby ultimately change the world. The slogan of *Amazing Stories* was 'Extravagant Fiction Today—Cold Fact Tomorrow'. Gernsback had a lively sense of the importance of sf. He even suggested that sf writers ought to be able to patent their own ideas, so that they might benefit from them when they happened to be adopted by some practical engineer and brought into production. For him, sf was to be a conscious spur to scientific progress and the consequent betterment of humanity. It is interesting that in 1931 Gernsback reacted strongly against those stories submitted to him which depicted the possibility that science might lead to domination of human beings by machines or by scientist-tyrants: '*Wonder Stories* will not, in the future, publish propaganda of this sort which intends to inflame an unreasoning public against scientific progress, against useful machines, and against inventions in general.'[39] Sf was not merely entertainment: it had a mission. From the late 1930s the most prominent of the evangelizers on the mission trail was John W. Campbell, jun., who had published a number of 'Doc' Smith-style space operas in the early 1930s under his own name, and who, under the pseudonym Don A. Stuart, had written the two stories discussed above, 'Forgetfulness' and 'Who Goes There?', and a dozen other stories which gave pointers to the direction the 'Campbell Revolution' would take.

By the end of the 1930s, the genre of sf had been fully recognized in the United States. It had its own specialist magazines and its own specialist readership, and by 1940, the stage was set for many of those readers to become writers themselves, to close the circle and help create American sf as an inward-looking self-referential ghettoized genre. Since sf in the United States was largely restricted to the pulps, it enjoyed none of the literary prestige that was grudgingly bestowed on some sf in Europe. Sf in most of the world would only become a recognizable genre once it had succumbed in large measure to the ideals and conventions of the newly self-conscious world of American sf. This development belongs largely to the postwar period.

2 The Victory of American SF
1940–1960

Campbell and New Definitions of Sf

During the 1940s and 1950s American sf developed in maturity and complexity, and above all in sheer quantity. But the changes affecting American sf in this period were as nothing compared with the changes which affected sf in the rest of the world. In 1940, sf in most countries was not a genre at all, but merely, as we can now see, a collection of texts which can retrospectively be gathered together into a literary category. By 1960, science fiction was known in many parts of the world, often under that very name; and the genre could be perceived as part of the Americanization of the non-Communist world. It was not a small part, either; it offered some help to people trying to understand other aspects of the new world order, including technological progress and the bomb, and it featured prominently in such features of exported American culture as the Hollywood movie and the comic. Sf had become a recognized entity, and one that had a very specific image, although sf readers and non-readers had very different ideas of what that image was. In Britain, at least, 'That's just science fiction' had become a common dismissive phrase for an implausible technological speculation; but at the same time there was the strong feeling, particularly since the launching of the first orbiting satellite in 1957, that the real world was rapidly catching up with the world of sf. The future British Prime Minister Harold Wilson, in his famous 'white heat of the scientific revolution' speech in 1963, said: 'It is, of course, a cliché that we are living at a time of such rapid scientific change that our children are accepting as part of their everyday life things which would have been dismissed as

science fiction a few years ago.'[1] Sf was not becoming respectable—it was still something to be 'dismissed'—but at least it
was becoming significant; sf writers were beginning to be regarded as what some of them claimed themselves to be, the
gurus of the future.

We shall look at some of the reasons for this development
later in the chapter; first, however, we need to understand how
American sf itself developed during what readers have come to
call the 'golden age'. It has been said that the golden age of sf,
for any particular reader, is when that reader was 14, but the
traditionally accepted beginning of the golden age is 1938, when
some of the great writers of modern American sf began to
appear, when new ideas about what sf actually should be began
to emerge, when new motifs and ideas which were to dominate
sf for a long time began to be explored in detail, when standards of writing began to improve, when the level of scientific
accuracy increased, and when John W. Campbell, jun., became
editor of *Astounding*.

The mythology of *Astounding*, and of Campbell himself, has
been a powerful one for most of those who have written about
sf, and it is not easy to untangle the historical truth. By 1940
Campbell had already transformed his magazine into the leader
in the field; though whether that was because of his own editorial policy or because of the already high prestige of the magazine—and the fact that he was able to offer the highest rates—is
debatable.[2] He continued as editor of *Astounding* (later re-
named *Analog*) until his death in 1971, but it was in the early
1940s that his influence on American sf—and subsequently on
the history of sf throughout the world—was, for better or worse,
most marked. Under Campbell's editorship *Astounding* became
closely linked with the writers who brought some maturity to
American sf and set the parameters for its development right
through into the 1960s. Robert A. Heinlein started his writing
career there in August 1939; throughout the 1940s Isaac Asimov
and the Canadian A. E. Van Vogt both published in Campbell's
magazine almost all the stories that were to make them famous;
and L. Ron Hubbard, from July 1938, was to be found largely
in *Astounding* or in Campbell's other magazine, *Unknown*. These

four writers set much of the tone for *Astounding* in the 1940s, but behind them was Campbell himself, who, through his editing and his editorials, played a much more prominent role in the magazine and in the development of sf than most other editors in the history of the field. No reader would fail to note the changed look of the magazine soon after Campbell took over, which itself symbolized the changing direction of sf. Campbell avoided the garish cartoon-like covers of predecessors and rivals, showing bug-eyed monsters (BEMs in the terminology of sf fans) chasing women in metal bras or mad scientists placing scantily clad maidens inside fiendish-looking machinery or implausible spaceships slicing each other apart with gaily coloured death-rays. The new *Astounding* was sombre in colour, with slick modernistic machinery, plausible human beings, and sometimes with realistic astronomical paintings which illustrated the theme of the human conquest of the solar system rather than a particular story. He changed the title from *Astounding Stories* to *Astounding Science-Fiction*, and would have dropped the pulpish word 'Astounding' altogether had not a new magazine emerged in 1939 which pre-empted the title *Science Fiction*. Campbell had plans for sf.

Campbell helped to create modern sf, and he did it in part through having clear ideas of what sf was and what it should do. In some ways his ideas about sf were not very different from those of Gernsback.[3] Entertainment, instruction, and prophecy were all emphasized by Campbell, as by Gernsback. 'Basically, science fiction is an effort to predict the future on the basis of known facts, culled largely from present-day laboratories', written by Campbell in 1948, could have come from Gernsback nearly twenty years earlier. Campbell adds, however, 'There are many different species, types and families of story material.'[4] 'Charming romance' is only one possibility: 'the gadget story, the concept story and the character story' are three others he mentions in the same 1948 essay, and he adds that 'science-fiction is the freest, least formalized of any literary medium'. Moreover its subject-matter was almost infinite, compared with conventional mimetic literature (which sf critics have come to call 'mainstream literature'):

That group of writings which is usually referred to as 'mainstream literature' is, actually, a special subgroup of the field of science fiction— for science fiction deals with all places in the Universe, and all times in Eternity, so the literature of here-and-now is, truly, a subset of science fiction.[5]

In descending from such grandiose (and blinkered) formulations to the level of practical editing, however, Campbell modified Gernsback's ideas in other crucial ways. Stories should not be about machines and great ideas, but about how those machines or great ideas affected individuals and society as a whole. There should be no scientific lectures clumsily placed in the story: authors should present the background and the scientific information seamlessly woven into their stories. The science that sf writers should concern themselves with need not be just physics and engineering, but could include sociology, psychology (and, notoriously with Campbell, parapsychology), and even—as in Asimov's 'Foundation' series, developed in close co-operation with Campbell—historical science. Indeed, one of the main themes of sf should be future historical change; Campbell himself said that sf was the history that had not yet happened, and the most important of his writers in the early 1940s, Robert A. Heinlein, stressed the importance of recognizing historical change in his guest-of-honour speech to the Third World Science Fiction Convention in Denver in July 1941:

There won't always be an England—nor a Germany, nor a United States, nor a Baptist Church, nor monogamy, nor the Democratic Party, nor the modesty tabu, nor the superiority of the white race, nor aeroplanes—they will go—nor automobiles—they'll be gone, we'll see them go. Any custom, technique, institution, belief, or social structure that we see around us today will change, will pass, and most of them we will *see* change and pass.[6]

This call to arms, a challenge to imagine very different futures, would have seemed revolutionary to many of the old guard of sf writers. It not only brought into question and threatened with subversion all the values of their own society, but suggested to them that the conservative sf they were writing was the sf of the past. The new sf would be interested not so much in amazing inventions and heroic scientists as in the societies and cultures of the future. Heinlein himself spent the next forty years of his writing career presenting disturbing and subversive alternatives to his readers: only a year after his speech, he published *Beyond this Horizon* (serialized in *Astounding* 1942), with its male executives who compare their shades of nail polish, surprise their wives by staying the night with them twice in a row, and sleep on water-beds (the latter being the first of Heinlein's contributions to real-life American culture).

Campbell the editor insisted upon scientific accuracy, whether the science concerned was social, physical, or parapsychological. How else could the readers of his magazine—many of them scientists and engineers, as he always noted with pride—be inspired by fiction to expand the boundaries of their own science? Sf and science, for Campbell, should be two facets of the same intellectual endeavour: using human imagination and ingenuity to explore the universe. In sf, writers (including scientists themselves) could speculate about all aspects of human knowledge, about the effects of scientific change on human society, and about possible futures: they could use stories not only to argue with each other, but to argue with Campbell himself (although, rather more frequently and diplomatically, they drew on his ideas and put them in fictional form). Like Gernsback, Campbell believed that this enterprise could actually have an impact upon the development of human history—indeed, that it had already done so. In the 1940s Campbell noted how there were a large number of subscribers to *Astounding* at Los Alamos during the development of the atomic bomb, and during the 1960s remarked that *Analog* was favourite reading among employees of NASA.

Campbell's ideas about sf's educative and missionary role remained alive up to and beyond Campbell's death in 1971, although their influence declined. Even in the 1940s, Campbell's own writers were prepared to share his vision of sf, and yet modify it. In 1947, for instance, Robert A. Heinlein (whose own very original sf between 1938 and 1942 may well have influenced Campbell's thinking) looked at the question of defining sf much more from the point of view of the writer.[7] He pointed out that there are basically only three plots: boy meets girl, the little tailor, and the man who learned better. Sf needs to have one of these plots, in their myriad variations: it cannot (meaning 'should not') be a fictionalized essay. He sums up: an sf story should follow five precepts:

1. The conditions must be, in some respect, different from here-and-now, although the difference may lie only in an invention made in the course of the story.
2. The new conditions must be an essential part of the story.
3. The problem itself—the 'plot'—must be a *human* problem.
4. The human problem must be one which is created by, or indispensably affected by, the new conditions.
5. And lastly, no established fact shall be violated, and, furthermore, when the story requires that a theory contrary to present accepted theory be used, the new theory should be rendered reasonably plausible and it must include and explain established facts as satisfactorily as the one the author saw fit to junk. It may be far-fetched, it may seem fantastic, but it must *not* be at variance with observed facts, i.e., if you are going to assume that the human race descended from Martians, then you've *got* to explain our apparent close relationship to terrestrial anthropoid apes as well.[8]

When Ronald Knox offered his ten rules for writers of detective stories in 1929, writers immediately set about subverting them, and the reaction to Heinlein's precepts was similar. Even Heinlein added, on the following page, 'Don't write to me to point out how I have violated my own rules in this story or that. I've violated all of them.'[9] Nevertheless, Heinlein's idea of what constituted an sf story has remained in the minds of many or most sf writers ever since. Precept 1 certainly defines the field rather broadly; many thrillers of the 1980s or 1990s, which revolve around, say, a Russian secret weapon or a new biological discovery threatening environmental destruction, would thereby count as sf. Precept 2 emphasizes that the plot should not be set arbitrarily in the future or on another planet or in another dimension, when it 'could just as well have happened on Fifth Avenue, in 1947', as Heinlein said. Precept 3 suggests that even if the characters are alien, the problem with which the story deals should at least be recognizable as relevant to the reader, and that the story should not (as in some stories of the 1930s) basically be about machines or gadgets. Precept 4, less easily followed in detail, is essentially an extrapolation of precept 2. But of all the precepts, the fifth is probably the most important, and has come to be accepted as a major element of sf criticism. Even today, sf critics will turn on an sf writer for violating the laws of science and/or extrapolative probability—that is, for violating Heinlein's fifth precept—while a reviewer of a novel in the mimetic tradition is very unlikely to pick on an author's grasp of social or economic theory.

Heinlein's formulation suggests a profound change from the earlier days of sf. It could all have been written by Campbell, and yet it is Campbell shorn of missionary zeal, setting forth sf as entertainment and intellectual game, rather than as instruction and prophecy. Few subsequent definitions of sf deviate far from Heinlein's, although they are phrased in formal terms rather than as a series of instructions to writers. Some examples of attempts at formal definitions of sf may serve as an illustration. The major British anthologist Edmund Crispin proposed that 'A science-fiction story is one which presupposes a technology, or an effect of technology, or a disturbance in the natural order, such as humanity, up to the time of writing, has not in fact experienced.'[10] Shortly afterwards, novelist Kingsley Amis published a set of lectures he had given at Princeton as *New Maps of Hell*, and offered his own variation:

With the 'fiction' part we are on reasonably secure ground; the 'science' part raises several kinds of difficulty, one of which is that science fiction is not necessarily fiction about science or scientists, nor is science necessarily important in it. Prolonged cogitation, however, would lead one to something like this: science fiction is that class of prose narrative treating of a situation that could not arise in the world we know, but which is hypothesized on the basis of some innovation in science or technology, or pseudo-science or pseudo-technology, whether human or extra-terrestrial in origin.[11]

Even the writer Miriam Allen DeFord, in her lapidary formulation—'Science fiction deals with improbable possibilities, fantasy with plausible impossibilities'[12]—offers a similar view, and expresses what the other definitions leave unspoken: that these definitions are in part an attempt to distinguish sf from fantasy. Sf deals with what is possible, in the present or plausible future state of scientific knowledge; it is concerned with the universe as we know it, or can conceive it, even if it is not concerned with the world that we currently live in. Fantasy, on the other hand, deliberately ignores the laws of science, operating (mostly) in a world of magic and mythology. It should be noted that sf writers frequently write excellent fantasy, and that they often approach it in a science-fictional spirit, inventing a universe of magic operating strictly according its own internal logic, its own 'science'; but when they do this, they are very aware that they are writing something quite different from sf. And stern physicists who write sf as a hobby may declare that since faster-than-light space travel, or travel back in time, are both irredeemably contrary to the laws of science, they belong to fantasy rather than to sf. Yet such hypotheses may be justified with suitably scientific terminology, and Amis is, historically, quite right to include 'pseudo-science or pseudo-technology' within his definition.

These early definitions all place a heavy emphasis upon science, even when, as we see in the extract from Amis's *New Maps of Hell*, there is a recognition that science is not necessarily important in it at all. Brian Aldiss has commented that sf is no more written for scientists than ghost stories are written for ghosts. But in the era of Gernsback and Campbell there was a strong feeling that sf *should* be written for scientists, and indeed that sf was part of the scientific discourse which would remake the world, quite as much as the experiments in the laboratories; sf offered the opportunity for innumerable thought experiments, and was also in effect a training course in avoiding the worst effects of 'future shock'. Science, of course, had high prestige in the 1930s and 1940s, and there was general optimism about the possibilities of technological solutions to problems, even to social and political problems. In the nineteenth century the American belief in progress depended in part on the expanding frontiers in the West; in the twentieth century it was the expanding frontiers of science and space which offered the possibilities for optimism.

By the 1950s that attitude towards science seemed outdated to some, and the very formulation 'science fiction' was questioned. Even if it was, ironically, Heinlein who first proposed that 'science fiction' be replaced by 'speculative fiction', the move towards new definitions came with a generation who wanted to move the genre away from Campbell and Heinlein— and, perhaps, towards greater literary respectability. The newer definitions do not offer prescriptions to writers, as we shall see in Chapter 3; rather, they attempt to link sf with the history of literature in general. Campbell himself did not worry about sf's status; he believed that sf performed a social function quite different from that of 'mainstream' literature, and was content for it to find its own literary level. And throughout the 'classic' years of sf, from the end of the 1930s until the early 1960s, Campbell's idea of sf was the dominant one.

Astounding in the 1940s

Astounding was not the only English-language sf magazine during the 1940s, but it is generally agreed that it set the standards, in Britain as well as the United States. It was only at the very end of the decade that magazines were founded—*The Magazine of Fantasy and Science Fiction* in Autumn 1949 and *Galaxy* in Spring 1950—which rivalled *Astounding* in quality and ambition, and whose philosophies were different enough to challenge the style of sf that *Astounding* had made its own. Not that *Astounding* had a monolithic style; Campbell was perfectly capable of accepting serious speculation from Heinlein, broad humour from Henry Kuttner or Eric Frank Russell, and straight space opera from E. E. Smith. But *Astounding* in that period certainly had a unique feel to it, and it is reasonable to conclude that it was largely because of the personality of the editor, perceived both directly, through his editorials, and indirectly, through his writers. If it should seem odd that one magazine should dominate the entire genre (even if that magazine paid more than the others), it must be remembered that sf during the 1940s very rarely achieved book publication, either in the United States or in Britain. Sf was magazine fiction, and thus very largely short fiction. Novels serialized in magazines often found publication in book form only at the very end of the decade or, more usually, in the 1950s, but these were the exceptions. Halfway between the short story and the serialized novel were series of several linked short stories. A number of significant 'novels' to be published in the early 1950s were in fact linked short stories or novellas of the 1940s stitched together into book form: Asimov's 'Foundation' trilogy and Clifford D. Simak's *City* are probably the best examples. A. E. Van Vogt, himself a master of this form of publishing, called it a 'fix-up', a term that has come to be used widely by critics today.

The question of Campbell's influence upon sf, like that of Gernsback's influence, is a controversial one among sf scholars. It is a two-pronged problem: was Campbell really so influential in the development of sf, and, if he was, was it a good thing?

It must first be recognized that Campbell came at a crucial time in the development of sf. Many of the most highly regarded writers of the 1940s, the ones most receptive to Campbell's ideas, were new to the field and young. The stalwarts of the pulps continued to write as before—E. E. Smith's *Grey Lensman* was serialized in *Astounding*—and others adapted themselves to the new ways. Among the more adaptable were Jack Williamson (who had published his first story in 1928, at the age of 20); Clifford D. Simak, who published some sf stories in the early 1930s, and was then inspired to return to sf because of Campbell's revival of *Astounding*; Henry Kuttner, who had begun in 1936 (aged 22); and Catherine L. Moore, who as C. L. Moore—it was necessary to hide one's gender in the sf pulps—published first in 1933 (also aged 22). (Kuttner married Moore in 1940, and thereafter their collaboration was so close that it is impossible to distinguish their individual input; most critics agree that Moore was the finer writer, and suspect that she was behind some of the stories published under the single Kuttner by-line.) But there was also a distinct new generation. Isaac Asimov was 19 when first published, in 1939; Ray Bradbury was 21 when he was first published, in 1941; James Blish was 19 in 1940, when his first story came out; Lester Del Rey (who published almost exclusively with Campbell until the 1950s) started in 1938, at the age of 20; Frederik Pohl started editing *Astonishing Stories* and *Super Science Stories* (and selling his own stories) in 1940, aged 20; some of Pohl's early stories were in collaboration with Cyril Kornbluth, who had started publishing solo stories in 1940, at the age of 17; Damon Knight was 19 when he first published in 1940; Robert A. Lowndes was 24 when he first published, in 1941, and a year later he was editing an sf magazine; Theodore Sturgeon published first, in *Astounding*, in 1939, at the age of 21. And so on.

There was a new generation, therefore, and a generation with a difference. They had grown up reading the sf pulps, and many of them had been involved with sf fandom before they started writing. As we shall see in Chapter 4, fandom had been developing throughout the 1930s; but by the end of the decade it was becoming organized and, at least in centres like New York, a forcing-house for new ideas. Of the writers named above, Asimov, Blish, Knight, Kornbluth, Lowndes, and Pohl were all in the New York sf group called the Futurians, best known, perhaps, for its left-wing politics (fostered by a hatred of fascism). Because of their politics, they had broken away from other less radical New York fans, led by Sam Moskowitz, in 1938, and were excluded from the Moskowitz-organized and grandly named First World Science Fiction Convention, which took place in New York in July 1939. Asimov, by then an Author and thus a figure of importance, attended; the rest of the Futurians skulked in an automat across the street. The Futurians acted as a small-scale self-help group, publishing each other's stories and working on collaborations; but above all, they discussed and argued and worked for the improvement of sf.

With all these imaginative, highly intelligent, but inexperienced young men coming into the field, it is perhaps not surprising that it was Robert A. Heinlein who emerged as the most mature, forceful, and influential of the new writers. By the time of his first publication in 1939 he had graduated from the US Naval Academy, served for five years as an artillery officer on board destroyers and the world's first modern aircraft carrier, been retired because of TB, studied physics and mathematics at UCLA, and stood for the California State Assembly.

Heinlein was indeed probably the most influential figure in the history of sf. The critic and writer Samuel R. Delany, while recognizing this fact, recalled André Gide's reply when asked who was the greatest poet in the French language: 'Victor Hugo, alas!'[13] Heinlein's role in the history of sf will be overshadowed, for some, by the meandering and self-indulgent novels of his later years (an unkind wag has suggested dividing his work into 'classics', 'juveniles', and 'seniles'), and, for others, by his strenuous support of the rights of the individual over those of the community, and hence his vocal opposition to many fashionable liberal causes. But the face of modern sf would be quite different today without the novels and short stories which Heinlein produced between the late 1930s and the early 1960s, and the impact of the stories written for Campbell was enormous. Heinlein published twenty-eight stories between August 1938 and October 1942, and all but four appeared in Campbell's two magazines. In 1942 he started war work, along with Campbell writers Asimov and Sprague de Camp, in the Naval Air Experimental Station in Philadelphia: he worked on the design of a high-altitude pressure suit—a prototype spacesuit. He returned to writing after the war, and almost immediately sold four sf stories to the *Saturday Evening Post*, the first sf writer to place stories with the highest paying short fiction outlet, and starting selling a series of highly influential 'juveniles' (aimed at the teenage market) to the publishers Scribner's. His brief apprenticeship with Campbell was over, but it had had a considerable effect upon the field.

For many of the new generation of writers Campbell was a domineering father-figure. He was 28 when he became editor of *Astounding*, older than many of his writers. And if the ripe old age of 28 was not enough to give him authority, then his scientific training, his overbearing manner, and his forcefully and lengthily expressed opinions all allowed him, usually, to get his way. Even Heinlein—as forceful and opinionated as Campbell himself—was in the first year of his writing career forced to rewrite stories to conform to Campbell's particular vision of the genre. But it took scarcely more than a year before Heinlein was producing exactly what Campbell wanted:

stories of a future whose plausibility was established not only by some hard-headed extrapolation but also by a carefully realized social and cultural context, with a 'lived-in' feel. Heinlein was able to increase the depth and resonance of his short stories by linking them together and by gradually building up a picture of a single, varied, complex, and, above all, plausible future. It was in 1940 that Heinlein realized the possibilities of this approach: he fitted eight of his previously published stories into a time-chart covering the next few hundred years of human history, and then set about writing stories which would fill in some of the gaps. Campbell published the time-chart in the May 1941 issue of *Astounding*, and tried to communicate his own enthusiasm in an editorial; it was here that he declared that sf novels were 'historical novels laid against a background of a history that hasn't happened yet'. It is tempting to see Campbell's understanding of sf changing in response to Heinlein's own development as a writer, more than Heinlein adapting to Campbell's ideas. Heinlein's idea of a future history, inspired in part by Stapledon's time-charts and in part by Sinclair Lewis's meticulous historical preparation for his novels, was to become a staple of sf writers thereafter. There are still writers in the 1990s producing work set within their own future histories—C. J. Cherryh provides the outstanding example—while many other writers understand that to give their imagined futures some solidity and depth may require the writing of many pages of background 'history' never intended for publication.

Whether we see the firm leading hand of Campbell or the creation of a collective approach by contributors, it is certainly possible to determine a number of attitudes emerging within *Astounding* during the 1940s which are of great interest to the cultural historian, and which help us place some of the crucial texts of the period in their context. I shall concentrate on attitudes to history, democracy, and psychology.[14]

Ideas about history are best discerned in Isaac Asimov's 'Foundation' series. This epic, ultimately 'fixed-up' into three books which were published between 1951 and 1953 (and expanded by the addition of several large volumes between 1982 and 1993, the year after Asimov's death), has the science of psychohistory as its hero. Devised by Hari Seldon, thousands of years in the future, this science brings together mathematics, sociology, psychology, and history in order to be able to predict the future course of human action. With the help of psycho-history, Seldon hopes to rescue learning and civilization after the inevitable collapse of the Galactic Empire and to preserve it through the Dark Ages: Seldon's Foundation and Second Foundation were to play something of the role of monasteries after the collapse of the Roman Empire. The parallels with the history of the Roman Empire were deliberate, and reveal Asimov's belief that no changes in technology or environment are going to change the basic characteristics of human nature. History is predetermined by the rules of science in much the same way as chemical reactions are; given the same circumstances, the same results will emerge. This notion derives in part from Toynbee's ideas about cyclical history, and from writers as different as Marx and Spengler. In the course of writing his series of short stories, Asimov himself became worried by the simplification involved, while Campbell became concerned at its determinism. Seldon's Plan was designed to break the cyclical pattern; but it seemed as deterministic as cyclical history itself. Campbell persuaded Asimov to subvert Seldon's Plan, by introducing the Mule, a genetic freak whose psychology could not have been anticipated by the laws of psychohistory. What happened was the end of Seldon's First Foundation, based on rational planning, and the start of the Second, based on psychology and the use of mental power.

Asimov's change of plan while writing ('The Mule' came over three years after the first 'Foundation' story) does not necessarily mean that some of his basic assumptions changed. It seems clear, for instance, that he believed that constant effort and struggle were required in order to keep the level of civilization steady, let alone enable it to progress. The second law of thermodynamics—all systems tend to deteriorate, in the process of entropy—held sway for him in history as well as in physics. This is an idea he seems to have shared with more than one *Astounding* writer, including Campbell in his own early stories 'Twilight' (1934) and 'Night' (1935). A. E. Van Vogt's memorable 'Black Destroyer' (1939) has a spaceship's crew meet a bloodthirsty alien in their steel corridors (one progenitor of the 1979 film *Alien*) who is the survivor of one of these degenerate civilizations: the last lines are: ' "It was history, honorable Mr Smith, our knowledge of history that defeated him," said the Japanese archaeologist, reverting to the ancient politeness of his race.' This theory is recalled in many modern science-fictional utopias. Utopia, in American sf from Campbell to *Star Trek*, is generally to be avoided not because it is inherently totalitarian, but because it is static, has ceased to struggle and to progress, and hence is doomed to decay. It has often been suggested that America, in the nineteenth century, flourished because the existence of a frontier encouraged growth, experimentation, and change; travel into 'Space, The Final Frontier' (in *Star Trek*'s phrase) was, and remains for many American sf writers, the ultimate way of avoiding society's stasis and degeneration.

How else could this degeneration be avoided? Not, clearly, in the minds of *Astounding* authors (even the liberal Asimov), by entrusting one's society to a democratic government. *Astounding* seems almost wholly committed to the idea of government by a technocratic élite. In the light of Asimov's more recent very public contests with fundamentalists and pseudo-scientists, it is interesting that his first *Astounding* story, 'Trends' (1939), puts the point very clearly. The people are becoming more and more wedded to religion and superstition; they have to be led in the right direction by a scientific élite. In the story the mob destroys the first moon rocket and hunts down its makers; Congress acts to stem scientific research. But a rocket is built in secret, and successfully reaches the moon; and this stunt wins the fickle public back to science. In the 'Foundation' stories too we have the idea of the necessity of a learned élite which can guide the masses. Psychohistory works only because the masses are unaware of it and of Seldon's Plan; the masses are variously described as 'blind mobs', 'fanatic hordes', 'a Galaxy of stubborn and stupid human beings'. The Second Foundation is made up of an élite group of psychologists with considerable mental powers who secretly manipulate the government and people of the galaxy. In Van Vogt's *Slan* (serialized in 1940) a group of telepathic superhumans called slans—the next step up from *Homo sapiens*—is being persecuted by a tyrannical government; at the end, the young hero learns that the government itself is being manipulated and controlled by an inner group of slans, who are struggling to avoid the worst of the human attack upon the telepaths: 'What is more natural than that we should insinuate our way to control of the human government? Are we not the most intelligent beings on the face of the Earth?' The idea of an irrational and emotional mob which has to be controlled by a hard-headed (and preferably scientifically trained) élite is common also in stories written by Heinlein throughout his long career. The title of his May 1941 story, 'Solution Unsatisfactory', suggests that Heinlein (or possibly Campbell, who often imposed his own titles on stories) does not actually approve of the protagonist, who brings world peace by means of atomic warfare and an imposed military dictatorship; but, as Berger has argued, 'there is more zest for authoritarianism than is covered by the disclaimer'.[15] Finally, L. Ron Hubbard's 1947 serial *The End is Not Yet* has democratic scientists opposing a corrupt conspiracy of businessmen; they take power, but come to realize that their only chance of maintaining order is to act much as their tyrannical predecessors did, only more efficiently. It is perhaps worth remarking that of all those young left-wing sf writers who belonged to the Futurians, only the politically naïve Isaac Asimov became an *Astounding* writer. Writers like Pohl and Kornbluth, whose criticism of current political structures came from the Left and who were to become the masters of satirical sf, were not generally published by Campbell. The *Astounding* tendency is still alive in American sf. A study of fifty-two sf films between 1970 and 1982 noted that not one depicted a functioning democratic future.[16]

The main problem with the human condition, for *Astounding* writers, was the basic irrationality, ignorance, and emotionalism of the ordinary human being; it could almost be said that they stood for the principles that were generally thought to be masculine, against those most commonly associated with women.

For them, one possible way out of this problem, in the future, would be the development of the human mind. This could be either a specific philosophy of mind training or else an expansion of the mind's potential into the area of telepathy, psychokinesis, and other mental powers, known together either as ESP (extra-sensory perception) or psi. It was a common idea among sf writers, derived from J. B. Rhine of Duke University (one of whose volunteers for ESP experiments, in the mid-1930s, had been John W. Campbell), that normal mental activity occupied only one-tenth of the brain; this potentially left the rest free for paranormal activity, or at least for exploitation by sf writers.

ESP was a fairly common topic for *Astounding* writers, although Campbell and the rest of sf would be much more obsessed by it in the 1950s than in the 1940s. Van Vogt's *Slan* set the pattern for a whole series of stories about persecuted telepaths, whose ultimate victory will mean a new stage in the evolution of humanity; one later version of this scenario, John Wyndham's *The Chrysalids*, will be discussed in the next section. 'Fans are slans!' became a fan slogan; sf fans naturally identified themselves with a minority who saw the world more clearly than their fellows, who represented the future, and yet were despised and persecuted by the establishment. More common than ESP in the *Astounding* of the 1940s, however, were stories which looked at different ways in which the ordinary human brain might be trained and expanded. These ideas owed a debt to Alfred Korzybski, the originator of General Semantics, whose *Science and Sanity* was published in 1933. To simplify drastically, he argued that by training oneself to use words clearly and to think logically, one could attain a greater level of sanity and intelligence. In Heinlein's future history, the 'Crazy Years' were effectively ended by the application of something closely resembling General Semantics. Clifford D. Simak's *City* (a 1952 fix-up of a series beginning in 1944) had a Martian philosopher called Juwain who had developed a system whereby people understood the deepest semantic meaning of everything that others said; it gave a comprehension and empathy comparable to telepathy, ending all conflict—and, perhaps, the ambition and drive which result from ruthless egotism. In Van Vogt's

The World of Ā, whose serialization began in the month of Hiroshima, Korzybski's idea of non-Aristotelian logic (Ā or Null-A), was seen as a way of giving individuals enormous mental powers and allowing communities to live in harmony without conventional social organizations: the hero, Gosseyn ('go-sane'), has mind and body perfectly integrated and logic so highly developed that, in effect, he is a superman. One fan suggested to Campbell in 1948 that dealing with the ideas of non-Aristotelian logic in a series of articles in his magazine would be the only possible way to avoid destruction by nuclear war.

L. Ron Hubbard is probably the sf writer who has brought more change to the lives of more people on Earth than any other. (A much more beneficent contender for this position is Arthur C. Clarke, whose ideas for communications satellites lie behind the communications revolution of the last two decades of the century.) Hubbard had been a prodigious pulp writer since the 1930s, and, a favourite of Campbell for both *Astounding* and *Unknown*. He was inspired by the fear of nuclear war to write a long article for *Astounding*. 'Dianetics: A New Science of the Mind' was published in May 1950; it was the origin of Hubbard's huge best-seller *Dianetics* and of his science-fictional religion scientology (of which more in Chapter 4). 'Dianetics' adopted many of the ideas which had been common in sf, and attempted to make them into a practical course for psychological improvement. When individuals got rid of all their harmful 'engrams' (psychological traumas dating from the time in the womb) by means of 'auditing', they would become 'clears': real-life equivalents of the superman Gosseyn. By August 1950, over 500 auditing groups had been set up in the United States; Van Vogt gave up writing, and became a full-time auditor. For a year Campbell, through his editorials, was a vocal supporter of dianetics. Many saw this as the first of his forays into the 'lunatic fringe', which was, during the next two decades, drastically to diminish his credibility and influence. It was not, however, the first time that sf had given rise, to the embarrassment of many of its readers, to a cult which was to attract many non-sf readers and bring sf itself into some disrepute. Flying saucers had made their appearance three years earlier.

American Sf and the Rest of the World

By the 1930s, as we have seen, a number of countries had a tradition of publishing sf. Some differences between the publication of sf in the United States and the rest of the world were apparent. In the former, sf had become a recognized publishing category, although it had a low literary reputation. Most sf was published in short-story form; it hardly existed in book form. Outside the United States, book publication was much more common, and that in itself gave individual books and authors more literary prestige. But production was sporadic, and in most countries sf had not acquired any sort of tradition; nor were most writers aware that they were writing within a genre. Only in the former Soviet Union had this inchoate form been graced with a generally accepted genre name, and only in Britain, by the end of the 1930s, was there a regular sf magazine (and that was inspired by the American example), and was American sf beginning to be read and imitated.

By the 1950s, however, American sf was being reprinted all over the world, in the original and in translation. American sf was widely imitated. Publishers in West Germany, Italy, and Spain gave their local authors American-sounding pseudonyms so that they might be accepted. Science fiction (a term which, in its local variants, became rapidly accepted as a genre label in many parts of the world) had become identified as an American product.

There are many reasons for this dramatic development, most of them fairly obvious. In general terms, the victory of American sf was just one facet of the post-war cultural supremacy of the United States. The dominance of Hollywood, of jazz and American popular music, and of American fashion styles was already being established, in Western Europe at least, before the Second World War. But American cultural influence was much more widespread after the war, as a result of American economic predominance, the new high profile that the United States took in world affairs, the prestige that it won for itself in its struggle against the Axis and, subsequently, against communism, and the physical presence of ordinary American citizens in every part of the world except the Eastern bloc. The cultural victory of the United States was more than just a corollary of political and economic preponderance; it was also a natural result of the vigour and originality of American culture, which offered an apparently democratic alternative to people whose own cultures had often been élitist and dismissive of popular culture.

Other factors probably played a significant role within the field of publishing, and sf publishing in particular. The hiatus which the war brought to many local publishing industries was clearly significant; it brought local sf publishing to an end, leaving a vacuum which could be filled by American sf. Had it not been for the war, the influence of American sf would no doubt have started much earlier. In France, for instance, *Conquêtes*, founded in 1939, was reprinting the British magazine *Tales of Wonder*, and thus translating American as well as British writers. However, it had only reached issue no. 2 when the war forced it to close. It was very different in one of the very few neutral countries in Europe: Sweden. There *Jules Verne-Magasinet* began publication in 1940. It was, astonishingly, a weekly magazine, and had reached issue no. 331 by the time of its closure in 1947. It published a considerable quantity of Anglo-American sf, with the British John Russell Fearn and the American Edmond Hamilton as major contributors, the latter with all his juvenile *Captain Future* stories; it also ran reprints of *Batman* and *Superman* comics and, bizarrely, non-fiction articles on boxing and athletics. But few European countries were as favourably placed as the neutral Sweden. Elsewhere, outside Britain, circumstances such as the Nazi occupation, the political impossibility of importing American sf, and paper shortages all contributed to the complete hiatus of production, and thus broke the continuity of the tradition of sf writing. The economic and political conditions for mass publishing only slowly returned in most European countries. And when they did, arguably the events of the immediate post-war period—in particular, the emergence of the cold war and the threat of nuclear war—were favourable for the importation of American sf; they made people more interested in a fiction which looked to the future, and to a future which increasingly looked as if it was going to be an American one.

The victory of American sf assumed different forms and chronologies in different countries. When French sf re-emerged, in the early 1950s, it owed more to figures like Boris Vian, an enthusiast of American jazz and film as well as of sf, than it did to memories of Jules Verne. The series 'Le Rayon fantastique' got started in 1951, which was to publish translations of many Anglo-American works, as well as a few new French writers; the writers for 'Fleuve Noir', also founded in 1951, were largely French, but produced low-grade and pseudonymous sf inspired by the American pulps. In 1954 'Présence du Futur' was created, again featuring French as well as American writers; it has continued to the present day. In 1953 two sf magazines were started, *Galaxie* and *Fiction*, which were, in origin, translations of the new American magazines *Galaxy* and *Magazine of Fantasy and Science Fiction*. *Fiction* in particular matured and lasted, becoming a major outlet for French writers, as well as continuing to publish translations of American stories. In Italy too there were versions of these two American magazines. Both *Fantascienza* and *Fantasia e Fantascienza* were short-lived publications (1954–5 and 1966–7 respectively), but *Galaxy* lasted for seventy issues between 1958 and 1964. Much more important, however, was the series 'I Romanzi di Urania', whose issues had the appearance of magazines but were actually novels, mostly translated from English (and often in abbreviated form); this began in 1951, and still flourishes, more than 800 novels later. Italy had rather more home-grown magazines than France in the 1950s, mostly republishing Anglo-American sf. But sf was considered American, and to succeed as sf writers, Italians had to have American-sounding names. Of 114 Italian sf novels published between 1954 and 1967, only 11 were published with the real names of their authors—and of those, several looked non-Italian anyway.[17]

In West Germany the first American sf novels began to appear in hardback in 1951, and Pabel's series *Utopia-Grossband*, which began in 1954, consisted mostly of translations of American novels. The first proper sf magazine in Germany, *Utopia-*

Magazin, was also filled largely with translations of Anglo-American writers. The German writers who were inspired to write sf tended to write imitation American space opera, and to be published in pulp paperback series, often of very poor production quality (so-called *Hefte*). The most successful of the paperback series was started in 1961, featuring the space hero Perry Rhodan; Rhodan's career continues, more than 1600 adventures later, and it is estimated that one billion copies of this series have been sold in West Germany. In East Germany, of course, sf developed along very different lines. American sf was, officially, unknown; when sf was published at all, it had to demonstrate the correct ideological commitment. By the 1960s only some half-dozen sf books by GDR writers were published each year and about the same number of reprints; translations were of works from the rest of the Socialist bloc.[18] In the Soviet Union, too, strict control was maintained. Writers of sf were expected to follow the rules for 'socialist realism', like all writers; but they also had to obey a 'near-target rule' according to which sf should deal only with innovations already at laboratory stage. Anything visionary or imaginative was liable to be denounced as 'mystic' or 'cosmopolitan'. As a result, perhaps, little sf appears to have been published. The break, and the beginning of a boom, came only in 1957: in that year *Technology for Youth* published what was probably the first translation of a post-Wellsian sf story from the West, one by the American writer Edmond Hamilton; and the launching of Sputnik showed to Russians, as well as Americans, that the speculations of sf writers were not so fantastic after all. A boom began, but it was, of course, an entirely home-grown boom; American sf had no chance of having the same impact on the Communist world as it had on the West.

The situation in Britain was more complex than elsewhere, mainly because the use of English not only enabled American sf to be imported or cheaply reprinted, but allowed British writers direct access to publication in American magazines or paperbacks. The impact of American pulp magazines on British sf began, as we have seen, before the Second World War. The first issue of *Tales of Wonder*, the first British sf magazine, came out in 1937, with stories by a variety of British authors, including John Russell Fearn, Eric Frank Russell, and John Beynon Harris (later better known under the pseudonym John Wyndham). The following year the magazine carried the first story by William F. Temple and the first professional sale by Arthur C. Clarke (an article on the planets). The editor, Walter Gillings, did reprint American stories, and even published new stories by American writers, although he always intended it to be primarily a vehicle for British writers. But those British writers were of quite a different generation from the writers of 'scientific romance' in the 1930s; they had been brought up on the American pulps which had made their way across the Atlantic. Arthur C. Clarke saw his first *Amazing* (which belonged to a neighbour in Somerset) in 1928, when he was 11; a photograph of the teenage Clarke shows him in his room at home, sitting in front of shelves filled with runs of *Amazing*, *Astounding*, and *Wonder Stories*.[19] *Tales of Wonder*, a British imitation of an American pulp, managed to publish each quarter down to Spring 1942; but much more significant in terms of the introduction of American sf to the British readership was the British reprint of *Astounding*, which first appeared in 1939. It was usually only sixty-four pages in size, corresponding to an individual American issue, but habitually dated two or three months later, entirely reset, and with one or two stories dropped to fit the page count. This was the only sf magazine to appear in Britain throughout the war (the reprint continued until August 1963, after which the original US editions were distributed in the UK); during the 1940s British readers (and later, presumably, Americans stationed in Europe) could read the latest Heinlein or Asimov not long after the first publication.

Those British writers who were inspired by the American pulps to take up a writing career soon found that those pulps offered them a better market than anything in Britain. Wyndham was the earliest to break into the American market; his first American publication was in *Wonder Stories* in May 1931, and he published thirteen stories in the American pulps during the 1930s. John Russell Fearn was much more prolific; he published fast-paced, imaginative, and poorly written stories by the yard in the American pulps during the same decade. Much more distinguished were William F. Temple, who published two stories in *Amazing* in 1938, and Eric Frank Russell, who published seven stories in *Astounding* between 1937 and 1942. As Malcolm Edwards has said of Russell: 'He developed a racy, wise-cracking style in most of his stories [for Campbell's *Astounding*]; often it made his stories seem more quintessentially American than those of any American contributor to the magazine.'[20] His Jay Score series featuring a humanoid robot (which began publication in *Astounding* in May 1941, a few months before Asimov's much more famous robot series began) was very popular with American readers, few of whom realized he was British. Campbell himself thought highly of Russell; it was the receipt of the typescript of his novel *Sinister Barrier* that helped solidify Campbell's plans for *Astounding*'s sister magazine, *Unknown*, and the novel featured in its first issue (March 1939).

The cross-fertilization continued after the war. Russell and Temple went on publishing in the United States, and Arthur C. Clarke had a number of stories in *Astounding*, beginning in May 1946, and in other American magazines. But more significant was the foundation of several British sf magazines, which encouraged the development of British writers, as well as providing another point of entry for American writers into the British market. E. J. Carnell, after some false starts, successfully launched *New Worlds* in 1949, and this was shortly followed by a sister magazine, *Science Fantasy*. Both were to continue under his editorship until 1964. Writers such as Brian W. Aldiss and J. G. Ballard were first published in them, and many other writers were given encouragement and the chance to develop. Carnell's magazines had to compete with a plethora of others: not only British reprints of such American magazines as *Astounding*, *Fantasy and Science Fiction*, and *Galaxy*, but also British magazines, such as *Authentic SF* and *Nebula* (the latter published in Scotland between 1952 and 1959). Carnell was led to republish American stories in his magazines, alongside British originals, partly for reasons of competition; he knew that his readers were well acquainted with American sf, and to a large extent regarded American sf as setting the standard. By the late

1950s, most British readers would regard only Clarke, Russell, and perhaps Wyndham as being worthy rivals to contemporary American sf writers; and it is perhaps significant that two out of that trio had their formative experience writing for the American pulps, and that in the 1950s the third, Clarke, was producing work that was accepted by both American and British readers as being among the best in the field.

Clarke and Wyndham are both good examples of the way in which British sf drew on, yet remained separate from, American sf during the 1950s. Clarke was well versed in the American tradition, yet was also steeped in the works of Wells and Stapledon. It was in *Childhood's End* (1953) that Clarke offered his response to Stapledon's vision of future human evolution, and, at the same time, to Wells's utopianism. No American writers had learned from Stapledon to imagine the future of humanity in terms of its death and its absorption into something greater and totally alien. The apocalyptic and visionary ending of *Childhood's End* is no doubt what has earned it the position in most polls since then as one of the top three of the 'Ten Greatest SF Novels of All Time'. But it is notable (though perplexing) that Clarke's novel carried this message on the copyright page: 'The opinions expressed in the book are not those of the author.' Clarke was prepared to follow up any possibility for the sake of a story (as we shall see when we look at 'The Nine Billion Names of God' in the next chapter). But it may be that he did not actually agree with what seems to be the overt message of *Childhood's End*: that without changing into something different, humanity would not reach the stars unaided. He believed, along with most American pulp writers, but in contrast to almost all British writers of 'scientific romance' between the wars, that humanity had a positive future, and that it lay in the exploration of space. *Childhood's End* also argued against Wells's utopianism, again in terms that would have been familiar to readers of American sf; a human utopia would be the road to stagnation and the death of the human will, because it would rule out challenge and the frontier spirit. Clarke's second visionary novel, *The City and the Stars* (1956, revised from earlier versions) had the same message: a perfect social structure and a total absence of want are meaningless without constant striving and new frontiers.

The Exploration of Space was the title of an award-winning non-fiction book that Clarke published in 1951, the most widely read of his many early forays into science (which included his celebrated proposal of 1946 to set up a world communications system based on satellites in geosynchronous orbits). But 'The Exploration of Space' has also been used as the title of a quartet of books which Clarke wrote in the early 1950s, which described the early years of space travel with the same realism and attention to detail that characterized the best of American sf: *Prelude to Space* and *The Sands of Mars* (1951), *Islands in the Sky* (1952), and *Earthlight* (1951, expanded 1956). Behind the rather wooden prose and characterization was a sincerity, a sense of excitement, and an optimism that owed much more to American sf than to British scientific romance.

The best-known novels of John Wyndham seem far from the American pulps. Wyndham, as John Beynon Harris, had been capable of adopting American pulp style in the 1930s, but during the 1950s he published novels which have been regarded as quintessentially British. His novels, which were not marketed as sf in Britain, attracted a large number of readers, who saw him as a respectable and direct descendant of the Wells of *The War of the Worlds*. Few knew that, as Harris, he was the author of crude space operas such as 'The Moon Devils', 'Exiles on Asperus', and the quaintly named 'The Third Vibrator'; and when he did publish straight space adventure, in *The Outward Urge* (1959), he felt constrained to add the name Lucas Parkes (another of his pseudonyms) to his own on the title-page, presumably not to alarm his wider British audience with the thought that he was capable of writing 'that crazy American space stuff' on his own. In his more popular novels, Wyndham, like Wells, frequently took the alien and placed it in the midst of a quiet, uncomprehending English bourgeois community. Aldiss dubbed him 'the master of the cosy catastrophe',[21] and he appeared to many (including those who put him on British school syllabuses) to be thoroughly 'safe'—again, not like those crazy American sf writers. But, as Rowland Wymer has convincingly argued,[22] Wyndham was actually a disturbingly subversive voice, concerned not so much with the standard British middle-class attitude which the characters adopt, but with the challenge presented to those attitudes by crisis. In crisis, the bourgeois façade usually crumbled; in the last resort, the survival of the species was much more important than the survival of polite civilization. As one of his characters says,

'There is no concept more fallacious than the sense of cosiness implied by "Mother Nature". Each species must strive to survive, and that it will do, by every means in its power, however foul—unless the instinct to survive is weakened by conflict with another instinct.'[23]

In *The Chrysalids* (1955; published in the USA as *Re-Birth*) Wyndham gives us his least British book. He depicts what had by 1955 become a standard post-holocaust community, living in North America, from which the mutations caused by latent radioactivity are savagely rooted out. Our sympathy is immediately captured by the young girl born with six toes and by the young male narrator, David, whose mutation has taken the form of telepathic powers. These are not just two powerless children. They represent a minority who are being persecuted by the majority in the name of religion; Christian fundamentalists have frequently been portrayed as villains by sf writers. At the end of the novel the boy is rescued by telepathic mutants who have set up a new society in 'Sealand' (New Zealand). He is carefully told that this society represents a new form of humanity, which will have to exterminate the old or be exterminated itself. David has already learned to kill in order to survive, and has already realized how inferior 'normal' people are. We know that in the end he will adopt the values of Sealand society, which are, arguably, as evil as those of the society from which he has fled. The novel subverts our expectations; in particular, it subverts the expectations of American pulp sf, by suggesting that the outsider and the misfit is not the hero, but the potential enemy. If in his earlier disaster novels, like *The Day of the Triffids*, Wyndham reran Wells (with a dash of social Darwinism), in *The Chrysalids* he was engaging in a dialogue with contemporary American sf. If he was prepared to enlarge his British audience by offering them updated Wells, he was also, as his numerous magazine short stories from the 1950s show, well able to converse also in the language of American sf.

There is one element in the growing domination of American forms of sf throughout the Western world in the 1950s that was able to have a direct impact upon many more people than ever sat down with an sf magazine: the Hollywood movie. There had been numerous sf films before the war, not only films of literary classics like *Frankenstein* (1910, 1931), *Dr Jekyll and Mr Hyde* (1920, 1941), and *Things to Come* (1936), and film classics like *King Kong* (1933), but also popular serials like *Flash Gordon* (1936), *Buck Rogers* (1939), and *Captain Marvel* (1941). The late 1940s produced little. But the 1950s saw an outpouring of sf films from Hollywood which was to have an impact on film studios in other countries. They also had a considerable impact (almost certainly for the worse) on the way in which people viewed sf. Few of them were sophisticated by the standards of the written sf of the day; most, indeed, went back to the worst of the pulps for their inspiration. There were notable exceptions, however: *Destination Moon* (1950), in whose script Robert A. Heinlein had a hand—a lonely attempt to portray, as realistically as possible, the first expeditions to the Moon—and *Forbidden Planet* (1956), a science-fictional reworking of *The Tempest*. Some of the most effective of the 1950s films played on the fears and anxieties of the contemporary world. *The Day the Earth Stood Still* (1951) warned of the dangers of nuclear war, while *Invasion of the Body Snatchers* (1956) was a complex film which can be interpreted as warning against either communism or McCarthyism, but is basically an allegory of the attack made on individualism by the pressures of conformity. In most cases, however, monsters from outer space, unlike the body snatchers in question, were simply that—monsters from outer space (or from the prehistoric past or from the radioactive desert); and, to the embarrassment and annoyance of sf fans who thought they were seeing their genre begin to emerge into literary respectability, most sf films of the 1950s were 'creature features'. Some of these monsters unleashed by science no doubt represented fears of science or of the bomb, but such fears were certainly disguised and trivialized by the context in which they were placed. There was *The Thing* (1951), which could, in addition, be accused of a drastic oversimplification of the John W. Campbell original (see above, p. 52); *The Beast from 20,000 Fathoms* (1953); *Them!* (1954); *The Monster that Challenged the World* (1957); and many others. Such films were seen all over the world, and through them, audiences became aware of some of the themes, images, and concerns of American pulp sf. Imitations came from some countries, including Britain and in particular Japan, where *Gojira* (1954) (Anglicized as Godzilla) started a spate of monster movies which would eventually outnumber their Hollywood competitors.

The relationship between the boom in Hollywood sf and the boom in written sf which also occurred in the early 1950s is a complex one. In most respects the two media were worlds apart, the attitudes of the average Hollywood sf film being diametrically opposed to those which predominated in the written medium. On the whole, written sf liked to believe that humanity, through science and rationality and by abandoning old social conventions (or re-establishing an imagined golden age), could build a better world; the films preached that there were things humanity should not dabble in, that the *status quo* should be defended against all attempts to change it, that emotion is more important than reason, and that the cold and essentially unwise scientist cannot be trusted. Written sf tended to think of the human species as being on the brink of a great new adventure in the frontier of outer space; Hollywood sf generally portrayed outer space as somewhere from which only evil could come. The flying saucer scare—the belief that humanity was being watched from outer space—had relatively little impact upon sf writers (see Chapter 4), but a tremendous effect upon the imagery in Hollywood movies.

Much more positive were the science-fictional images derived from comics, which spread to most parts of the world as effectively as the Hollywood film. Sf comics date back to *Buck Rogers in the Twenty-Fifth Century*, a strip which ran in American newspapers from 1929; it was a standard space opera setting, with death-rays, space rockets, and dastardly (in this case oriental) villains; it spawned innumerable imitators, notably *Flash Gordon* and *Brick Bradford*. By the late 1930s these comic strips were appearing in comic book form, and in 1938, in the first issue of one of these new comic books, *Action Comics*, Superman appeared. He too inspired imitators—Batman, Captain Marvel, Captain America—and the whole crew went to Europe with the American forces and became well established there, in the original and in translation. It was sf shorn of all sophistication, but with plenty of impact and with a huge range of visual images which helped familiarize a young readership with science-fictional ideas. Ironically, as far as British sf is concerned, the main impact of the American comic came in reaction to them. The Reverend Marcus Morris was determined to offer British children a healthy alternative to the American horror comics which were beginning to cross the Atlantic in the late 1940s; he founded the *Eagle*, a weekly comic which first appeared on 14 April 1950. Its first two pages then, and for several years to come, featured the clean-cut British space hero Dan Dare, with his (largely British) colleagues, including his commanding officer Sir Hubert Guest, his batman Digby, and Professor Jocelyn Peabody, the token woman and, interestingly, token intellectual at the same time. The strip was superbly drawn, by Frank Hampson, and very well thought out (so much so that its scientific adviser, Arthur C. Clarke, resigned after a brief stint, saying that his services were unnecessary), and it gave a whole generation of British boys (and those girls who found the companion publication *Girl* too tame) their first experience of sf, as well as a totally false impression that Britain was going to dominate the space race.

Sf films and sf comics may have attracted some people to sf literature, and together they may have played a part in the growing realization that sf was a significant cultural phenomenon. Both helped to confirm America's dominance in the field. Equally, both must have confirmed the prejudice against the genre already shared by most of those who presided over High Art, causing them to neglect the new talent that the sf publishing boom was bringing to the field.

The Publishing Boom of the 1950s

The sf boom in America during the 1950s was connected with a growth in sf readership, and that readership was inspired perhaps by worries about the future (for the cold war fostered paranoia of all kinds), encouraged by the higher standards and maturity of sf and also, perhaps, attracted to the literary form by its growing prominence in films and comic books. But the sf boom is clearly linked also to developments within publishing itself, most notably the growth of paperback publishing, which entailed the production of cheap books on a large scale, as well as the establishment of a distribution system which made them very widely available, and to economic and cultural developments, such as an increase in disposable income and a more self-conscious youth culture.

I have stressed how sf in the United States during the 1940s was almost entirely magazine-based. There were speciality presses, who produced hard-cover versions of magazine sf, but on a very small scale; after the appearance of two massive anthologies in 1946, *Adventures in Time and Space*, edited by Raymond J. Healy and J. Francis McComas (thirty-five stories, of which thirty-two came from *Astounding*) and Groff Conklin's *The Best of Science Fiction*, there was a gradual trickle of anthologies, again reprinting stories from magazines. But at the very end of the 1940s, a few commercial publishers (notably Simon and Schuster) began issuing sf in hardback, and even commissioning works that had not seen prior magazine publication. *Rocket Ship Galileo* (1947) was the first of a series of original juveniles written for Scribner's by Robert A. Heinlein (he produced one a year for twelve years); Harcourt Brace began publishing Andre Norton's juveniles in 1952. For the first time, gifted sf writers were producing well-crafted sf books for the younger reader, something which, in a very few years, must have helped to increase the readership for adult sf. Some of Heinlein's juveniles, such as *Red Planet* (1949) and *Farmer in the Sky* (1950), were among the best novels he wrote, introducing younger readers to the excitement of frontier life on the planets and to the challenge of different social structures and difficult moral dilemmas.

More significant than the slow growth of hardback sf in the United States, however, was the start of paperback sf lines and the huge (though temporary) boom in magazines. In 1952 former Futurian Donald A. Wollheim became an editor at Ace Books, and started paperback publishing: not just single novels, but also Ace Doubles—two novels, placed back to back (initially one full-length and one short novel) so that when you turned the book over and upside down, you were faced with a second 'front' cover. Among the writers whose first book publication was as one half of an Ace Double are Samuel R. Delany, Philip K. Dick, and Ursula K. Le Guin; Ace Doubles made a significant contribution to the field. In the same year Ian Ballantine set up Ballantine Books, a company which published some of the most important books of the decade, often using the then unknown tactic of simultaneous hardback and paperback editions. Ballantine also initiated the first paperback anthology series to be composed of original stories, *Star Science Fiction Stories*, edited by Frederik Pohl. Other American paperback houses, such as Signet and Pocket, began issuing sf books, and slightly later the trend was taken up in Britain, notably by Pan and Corgi. The increasing size of the market did, of course, attract a lot of dross, and some publishing houses specialized in the lower end of the market. In Britain, for instance, John Spencer and Company not only produced four different juvenile sf magazine titles in the early 1950s but, later in the decade, as Badger Books, began publishing scores of hastily written sf novels. Most of them were by Robert Lionel Fanthorpe, who produced them at the rate of one a weekend (at a remuneration of £25). He published them under his own name and under a host of splendid pseudonyms, notably partial anagrams such as Leo Brett, Bron Fane, Lionel Roberts, and Pel Torro.

The cutthroat competition and the problem of finding sufficient stories and, at the same time, readers, can be seen most obviously in the magazine sector. The 1940s ended with the creation of two significant new magazines, which we have already met in their European versions: *The Magazine of Fantasy and Science Fiction* (*F&SF*) and *Galaxy*. The former started in 1949 as a fantasy magazine; the phrase *and Science Fiction* was added only in 1950. It appeared monthly from September 1952. It published (as it still does) both fantasy and sf, as well as stories which defy categories and blur any possible distinction between the two genres. From the beginning it established a reputation for literary quality, thanks to the high standards of its editors (notably Anthony Boucher) and their willingness to publish authors who would never have been seen in *Astounding*: Raymond Chandler, Robert Graves, C. S. Lewis, André Maurois, and other well-known names. It attracted *Astounding* authors as well, and gave them much more liberty to write what they wanted than Campbell had ever done; the magazine had a much more eclectic feel than any other in the early 1950s. *Galaxy* was usually seen as occupying a middle ground between *Astounding* and *F&SF*: not so literary and experimental as *F&SF*, nor so ready 'to accept literary quality as a substitute for narrative excitement',[24] concentrating purely on sf, but not so hidebound and dominated by editorial obsessions as *Astounding* was becoming in the 1950s. *Galaxy* would publish satirical stories and stories that questioned social and moral conventions. Its reclusive and irascible editor H. L. Gold got the best from his authors, and could spot winners. Some of the best novels of the 1950s were serialized in *Galaxy*, including Isaac Asimov's *The Caves of Steel*, Robert A. Heinlein's *The Puppet Masters*, Frederik Pohl and C. M. Kornbluth's *The Space Merchants* (as *Gravy Planet*), and both *The Demolished Man* and *The Stars My Destination* by Alfred Bester; while among the classic short fiction appearing in the magazine was the novella forming the central part of Theodore Sturgeon's *More than Human* (1953).

F&SF and *Galaxy* offered *Astounding* some competition. But the real problem was that those three magazines were struggling to survive alongside an ever increasing number of other magazines. Three new sf magazines started in the United States in 1949; ten more in 1950, four in 1951, seven in 1952, and fourteen in 1953. Few of these magazines lasted more than a few issues, however, and some of the established titles like *Planet Stories* and *Thrilling Wonder* also disappeared at this time. The collapse of the major American magazine distributor, American News Company, was a major blow to the entire magazine market; so, probably, was the rise of television.[25] Only six magazines made it into the 1960s: the old titles *Amazing* and *Astounding/Analog*, together with *F&SF*, *Galaxy*, *Fantastic*, and *If*. But in the early 1950s there was for a time a massively increased market for writers, as well as opportunities for fledgling writers to establish themselves, writers who, by the end of the decade, were making more money from the ever expanding paperback market than from the magazines. The early 1950s, like the early 1940s, saw a major influx of new talent into the field. To pick out only some of the most important writers,[26] in 1950 came the first stories of Richard Matheson, Mack Reynolds, and Cordwainer Smith (the pseudonym of Paul Linebarger, an American political scientist and military adviser); in 1951, those of John Brunner, Harry Harrison, and Walter M. Miller; in 1952, Algis Budrys, Philip K. Dick, Philip José Farmer, Frank Herbert, and Robert Sheckley; in 1953, Brian W. Aldiss, Marion Zimmer Bradley, Anne McCaffrey, Kurt Vonnegut, jun., and James White; in 1955, Robert Silverberg; in 1956, J. G. Ballard and Harlan Ellison. Most of the writers who dominated Anglo-American (and world) sf until 1970 and beyond emerged from the magazine boom of the early 1950s.

Classic Themes

Sf mythology asserts that the golden age of American sf, beginning in 1938, lasted right through until the end of the 1940s. This was certainly the great age of *Astounding*, and it was clearly the period which saw American sf writers trying to produce better written works of speculation, which ranged more widely and thought more deeply than the standard sf pulp adventures. Many of the classic themes of sf were tackled by the writers of the 1940s. But there are good reasons for thinking of the 1950s as being the true classic era. In the 1950s ideas that had been introduced into sf writing in the 1930s and 1940s were explored in more detail, and often at greater length; because of the changed market, American sf was not so dominated by the short story, and there was more scope for novel-length treatment. There was a greater maturity in the writing; writers could build on the techniques developed by Heinlein and others in the 1940s. There was also still a freshness in the writing and an enthusiasm for the possibilities of the genre which already by the 1960s were beginning to diminish. (The revival of sf in the 1960s, generally labelled the 'new wave', was a response to, though it did not entirely dispel, the feeling that sf was becoming stale and was merely recycling old ideas.) Yet, by the 1950s, the genre had become sufficiently well established for authors to assume knowledge in their readership; situations did not have to be explained. Moreover, authors were content to write for this knowledgeable—but fairly restricted—readership, without undergoing the *Angst* of some writers of the 1960s who struggled to win the favour of the literary establishment. Writers in the 1950s denied themselves the chance of easily attracting novices to the field, perhaps, but they allowed themselves the luxury of knowing just what their readership knew and would like.

Donald A. Wollheim has argued that by the 1950s sf writers had managed unconsciously to create a consensus future history or cosmogony, with a pattern of premises which enabled experienced readers to situate themselves in the context of any new story very rapidly.[27] There is the initial exploration and colonization of the solar system, and perhaps the meeting with new alien races; the first flights to the stars, by generation-ship or by some faster-than-light gimmick, further meetings with aliens and the colonization of planets; there is the rise of the Galactic Empire, the Galactic Empire in full bloom, the exploration of the rest of the galaxy, and the decline and fall of the Galactic Empire; the interregnum, with worlds reverting to primitive conditions and the gradual loss of memory of the greatness of the past; and finally, the return of galactic civilization and the challenge to God, the end of the universe, and ultimate apocalypse. Much of this is first put together, or implied, in Asimov's 'Foundation' series, but the whole story emerges only after reading the work of many authors. By the 1950s the consensus was well known to readers; attempts by individual writers to add to it, or subvert it, were understood and appreciated as such.

One problem that critics have had with classic sf stems from their desire to find social relevance therein. What does this future history of the human species imply? What does it *mean*? It is quite clear that some writers have approached some of the classic themes with specific messages in mind. It is impossible not to connect the book-burning firemen of Ray Bradbury's *Fahrenheit 451* (1953) with the intellectual persecution of the McCarthy era; it is difficult not to see Asimov's *The Caves of Steel* (1954), with its robots who take ordinary people's jobs and even 'pass for human', as a comment upon relations between whites and blacks in America;[28] it is obvious that many of the nuclear holocaust and post-holocaust stories are warnings against the dangers of the contemporary situation. At the same time, however, it has to be recognized that for many writers, and readers, sf was an intellectual game, whose delights were to be discovered in the way in which variations were played upon classic themes, and how holes in the consensus cosmogony were plugged. As we shall see in the next chapter, sf was often self-referential, engaging in debate with other sf works, rather than directly with the world outside. And the pleasure often derives from the logical working out of an answer to the simple question 'What if . . . ?'

One classic theme in the sf of the late 1940s and 1950s—one very obvious 'What if . . . ?'—was 'What if there is nuclear war?' This clearly responded to the deep-seated worries of ordinary Americans and British, and the published fiction on this theme represents only a fraction of what was actually written. H. L. Gold, the editor of *Galaxy*, complained in 1952 that 'over 90% of stories submitted still nag away at atomic, hydrogen and bacteriological war, the post-atomic world, reversion to barbarism, mutant children killed because they have only ten toes and fingers instead of twelve . . . The temptation is strong to write: "Look, fellers, the end isn't here yet".'[29] Some of the most impressive contributions to the theme of the destruction of civilization in fact came from outside the sf field; George R. Stewart's *Earth Abides* (1949), Nevil Shute's *On the Beach* (1957), *Alas, Babylon* (1959) by Pat Frank (pseudonym of Harry Hart), and Mordecai Roshwald's *Level 7* (1959). The last three depict the actual events of nuclear war in horrifyingly plausible detail, two of them ending with the complete destruction of humanity, and *Alas, Babylon*, which describes the beginnings of the restoration of civilization, only some months after 'The Day', ends with the protagonist inuring himself to a thousand years of a new dark age. It is significant that sf writers have often been more interested in speculating about how disaster might cause the slow breakdown of society, rather than its total elimination, and that they often chose, very naturally, other forms of destruction than nuclear bombs. One thinks of Stewart's *Earth Abides*, in which plague causes the collapse of civilization, or Wyndham's *The Day of the Triffids* (1951), John Christopher's *The Death of Grass* (1956), or the whole series of disaster novels written by J. G. Ballard in the early 1960s, beginning with *The Wind from Nowhere* (1962). Most professional sf writers spent more time looking at the dark ages, the post-holocaust world, than at the event of a nuclear holocaust itself. Much more recently, in the so-called 'survivalist' novels of the 1980s, the holocaust has been seen as a useful cleansing exercise; according to them, only with the destruction of the corrupt Western world (in which far too much power has been given to feminists, homosexuals, liberals, and blacks) can the good honest values of the American Wild West be reborn. But in the 1950s, the post-holocaust novel was sometimes, much more interestingly, an evaluation of how societies decline into tribalism or barbarism (as in *Earth Abides*) or develop from barbarism to civilization. Walter M. Miller's *A Canticle for Leibowitz* (1959) shows three stages. In the first, monastic communities endeavour to preserve something of the past (as in the real Dark Ages after the fall of the Roman Empire), although they drastically misunderstand it, making the few relics of a pre-holocaust engineer called Leibowitz the focal point of a religious cult. In the second, a scholar recognizes that some of these relics actually consist of scientific papers which could make possible the rebirth of a science-based civilization. And in the third, the bombs begin to fall once more. In Leigh Brackett's *The Long Tomorrow* (1955), two boys are oppressed by the obscurantist fundamentalism of the Mennonites (who better to survive the holocaust than those who live today without modern technology?), and dream of returning to the scientific wonders of the past, a dream which inspires them to leave their home and seek the home of these scientists, the mythical Bartorstown. Again, there are no simplistic answers, however; as one of the scientists says at the end, 'You're forgetting we're fanatics too.'

Brackett's novel also belongs to another central category of classic sf, dubbed 'conceptual breakthrough' by Peter Nicholls.[30] Conceptual breakthrough mirrors what Thomas Kuhn has seen as the process by which one scientific paradigm gives way to another.[31] It is about acquiring knowledge of the world in such a way that one's view of the world changes radically. The reading of sf itself, of course, may involve conceptual breakthrough for an individual reader, but the development of an sf novel also frequently follows the transformation of the world-view of one or more characters. In Brackett's novel the two protagonists struggle against the anti-scientific faith of their elders, and come to see it as mistaken. In James Blish's 'Surface Tension' (1952) the microscopic protagonist manages to break through the surface of the puddle of water in which his race has always lived, to see the enormous airy world beyond. In Heinlein's 'Universe' and 'Common Sense' (*Astounding*, 1941, later fixed up as *Orphans of the Sky*, 1964), as well as in Brian Aldiss's *Non-Stop* (1958) and Harry Harrison's *Captive Universe* (1969), the central characters gradually come to realize that the tiny universe in which they were born is not the whole universe, but merely a huge spaceship, travelling at sub-light speed towards the distant stars. Such stories may be taken as allegories of scientific discovery or as allegories of the adolescent discovery of the complexities of the adult world, or they may be intended to make readers question the reality of their own perceptions. Many of the stories and novels of Philip K. Dick are about the impossibility of being certain about what constitutes reality. *Time Out of Joint* (1959), for instance, is apparently a tale about everyday life in the contemporary United States. The protagonist finds a picture of a young woman. The reader realizes that it is Marilyn Monroe, but no one in this fictional world recognizes her. Then the protagonist begins to have hallucinations that he is at the centre of the world and that everything is being organized to convince him of the reality of a wholly fake world; in the end he discovers that this is true, that he is living in 1998, not 1959, and that he has been provided with his artificial environment in order to stop him questioning his crucial military role. Conceptual breakthrough, for some sf writers, is closely related to paranoia.

Some post-holocaust novels are actually excuses for exploring our third classic theme: extra-sensory perception. Radiation can cause genetic mutation (another theme that fascinated writers in the 1950s), and why should not genetic mutation be benign as well as malign? Henry Kuttner's *Mutant* (1953) and John Wyndham's *The Chrysalids* are just two of those stories which are not so much about the post-nuclear holocaust world as, in the tradition of Van Vogt's *Slan*, about the ways in which ordinary people react to those who are different and/or superior, in this case those whose mutation has taken the form of telepathic power. Telepathy and other ESP powers formed the theme of some of the most significant novels of the 1950s, and the novels which are read today are only a small cross-section of the ESP stories to be found in the magazines. Campbell, in particular, was very anxious to demonstrate to his readers the potentialities of ESP, whose existence he believed to have been demonstrated by J. B. Rhine and other scientists. But the memorable stories in this category were written not by those who were trying to fit in with Campbell's assumptions, but by those who used ESP to investigate its possible effects upon society and the individual, and thus, perhaps, to shed light upon our own condition. Theodore Sturgeon's *More than Human* (1953) tells the story of a group of society's outcasts who discover that their mental powers bring them together into a single individual with tremendous mental potential; it is a powerful, although perhaps over-sentimental, tale, with Sturgeon's typical empathy with misfits and rage against 'normal' human insensitivity. It reads as well today as it did in 1953, which is true also of the two novels by Alfred Bester which, between them, form probably the most impressive monument to American sf in the 1950s: *The Demolished Man* (1953) and *Tiger! Tiger!* (UK, 1956; US: *The Stars My Destination*, 1957). These two novels, not linked in any way, look respectively at the ways in which telepathy and teleportation might change the way society operates; they do so in the course of fast-paced narratives, full of passion. In *The Demolished Man* Ben Reich, a wealthy industrialist and a non-telepath, tries to kill a rival: it is an exercise, both for him and for Bester, in how murder might be committed in a world in which telepaths—espers, but 'peepers' to normals—are numerous. Typographical tricks try to give us some idea of how telepaths might communicate with each other, and Bester gives us a convincing picture of a telepathic community living in an uneasy coexistence with 'normals'. In *The Stars My Destination*, another obsessed individual, Gully Foyle, seeks his enemy in a society in which 'jaunting', or teleportation—transportation by mental power alone—is commonplace. The problems of how society might cope with crime, privacy, and even ordinary economic affairs, given the existence of teleportation, is merely the backdrop to another thriller, oozing with inventiveness, colour, and pace.

Gully Foyle eventually learns to jaunt to the stars, not the usual method of space travel used in the 1950s. The exploration and conquest of space—the first necessary stage towards the consensual cosmogony—is, of course, a major theme in the sf of this period, as in all others. The success of the V2 rockets, and subsequently the slow beginnings of rocket technology in the United States (and in the former USSR, although until Sputnik in 1957 few Westerners believed the Soviet Union to have got very far), gave an impetus to serious thought about space travel, and the early 1950s are characterized by a number of novels which treat the first years of space travel with an attempt at great realism; Heinlein and Clarke are two of the most important writers in this area. But other areas of the space travel theme were explored in the 1950s. There is the common trope of the meeting between human and alien, particularly the so-called 'First Contact'. (This was the name of a celebrated 1945 story by Murray Leinster, which achieved the notable fate of being dissected and portrayed as an example of capitalist alienation in 'The Heart of the Serpent', a novella by the Soviet writer Ivan Yefremov.) Two different approaches to the theme are Hal Clement's *Mission of Gravity* (1954) and James Blish's *A Case of Conscience* (1958). The former looks on first contact as a scientific problem: how can human explorers open communication with an alien race that has evolved on a planet with several hundred times the gravity of Earth, and what would the psychology of such aliens be? Blish's scientist hero is very different: he is a Jesuit priest, and his problem is one of conscience. How should one deal with an alien race who seem to live a perfect, moral, Eden-like existence, and yet have no concept of God? Is it Eden, or a trap set for man by the Devil? The encounter with the alien, as with any encounter with the other, may often be used to hold up a distorting mirror to oneself and to humanity. In the 1950s that approach was most characteristically found in short stories, such as those written by Theodore Sturgeon and Philip José Farmer.

There are other classic themes which could be explored: the relationship between human being and machine (most characteristically between human being and robot) or time-travel or political and social satire (in which sf writers took Joseph McCarthy to task in ways that would have been impossible outside such an ignored genre). But touching on the themes of nuclear holocaust, conceptual breakthrough, ESP, space travel, and alien encounter should be enough to demonstrate some of the variety that existed within sf by 1960. In the thirty years since, few new themes have been added, although many variations have been worked on them. We have begun to discern the shape and content of modern sf. It is time now to see how it might be read.

3 Reading Science Fiction

SF and the Mainstream

Publishers try to create publishing categories; academics try to produce technically satisfying definitions; but it is ultimately the reader who decides what belongs to the genre. The reader—by which I mean the determined reader of sf, not the occasional or accidental reader—feels that sf has certain pleasures to offer which other kinds of literature normally do not; from a reader's point of view, the extent to which a particular book or story tries to supply, or succeeds in supplying, those pleasures determines whether it belongs to the genre or not. This chapter will look at what those pleasures are, and will also touch on some of the issues that this question of 'pleasure' raises. Why should the determined reader of sf often get very little pleasure out of reading what the sf world usually calls 'mainstream' or 'mundane' fiction (mimetic fiction concerned with this world as we experience it)? Why should the non-reader of sf frequently fail to discover any pleasures in reading sf at all? If there are a handful of sf readers who have little experience of reading outside the general area of sf and fantasy and who have ill-found general prejudices against 'the mainstream', there are very much larger numbers of readers of fiction (the majority) who have a very fixed notion that they will not enjoy sf and who therefore do not intend to try it.

To understand why this should be, we have to look again at some of the obvious differences between sf and 'the mainstream', and in particular at the different challenges they present to the reader. 'Mainstream' has, for some narrow-minded sf critics, meant anything from *Wuthering Heights* to *Valley of the Dolls*, but I propose to take the term 'mainstream' to be synonymous with 'the modern novel', 'the contemporary novel', the novel as taken seriously by the *Times Literary Supplement* and the *New York Review of Books*, rather than 'other' genre fiction, belonging to the categories of crime, horror, westerns, or the packaged best-seller.

We can immediately set up a number of oppositions; none of them are absolutes, but merely reflect generalities. Mainstream fiction generally takes human personalities or human relationships as its main subject-matter; sf is much more concerned with the world or environment that has been created in the fiction and with the interactions of people with that environment. The purpose of mainstream fiction is generally to express some perceptions about the human psyche; the purpose of sf is to speculate about the potentialities and possibilities of the human species and its place in the universe, either with serious extrapolative intent or playfully. Mainstream fiction normally takes the world of our own experience as its setting (hence the qualification 'mundane'); sf alters the world of our experience in minor or major ways. Mainstream fiction is usually set in the writer's present and in the writer's own geographical setting; sf is usually concerned with the future, and often does not situate the action on this planet. The readers of a mainstream text can assume they share a knowledge of the background to the narrative with the author. The readers of an sf text have to construct that background for themselves, reorganizing their assumptions and knowledge, reversing and distorting conventional structures and relationships, and drawing upon the reservoir of other fiction, in order to make sense of the text. A deliberately enigmatic sf writer like Gene Wolfe may offer readers an essential clue to the type of reality he is describing in just one word; but if readers are not sufficiently alert, they will not be able to work out the significance of what is happening at all.

Sf has often been regarded as escapist by its critics—that is, as failing to grapple with real concerns. We may leave aside the question of whether, from a reader's point of view, *all* fiction is escapist, since in practice it removes the reader's attention from his or her current surroundings and involvements. (Indeed, the taking-up of any reading material is a common delaying or displacing tactic.) Some sf is clearly exclusively intended as a form of entertainment (a less pejorative near-synonym for escapism), designed to fill an empty tract of time and to leave few lasting impressions. But many sf critics have argued—tendentiously and polemically, but plausibly none the less—that only in sf (*some* sf, that is) does fiction treat seriously the *real* problems of the present: over-population, mass unemployment, nuclear warfare, sexism, pollution, poverty, and, above all, some very basic questions which most mainstream fiction does not answer, such as 'Where does humanity go from here?' or even 'What are we all here for anyway?' Sf (like history, one might say) has often been more interested in the fate of humanity than the fate of humans. This brings us to a final opposition, which has been enough to damn sf as far as traditional literary criticism is concerned: mainstream fiction is generally concerned with the personalities of individuals and the development of character, whereas sf is often concerned more with the individual as representative of humanity as a whole than with that individual's particular quirks. Any form of literary criticism which privileges themes such as character development—that is, most traditional forms of literary criticism—is going to give most sf short shrift.

It is also not necessarily very helpful to treat sf as if it is just a metaphorical way of writing about the real world, which is the way mainstream literary critics have often approached it. Bruce Sterling is one modern sf writer who has reacted angrily to such an approach:

I resent it when my ideas, which I have gone to some pains to develop and explore, are dismissed as unconscious yearnings or a fun-house mirror reflection of the contemporary milieu. My writings about the future are not 'about the future' in a strict sense, but they are about my ideas of the future. They are not allegories.
  This question is part of an ongoing critical attempt to reduce sf to a sub-branch of mainstream literature: a sub-branch whose writers do not quite know what they are talking about.[1]

Sf writers and critics have often, not very successfully, tried to argue that the criteria used to judge sf works should be quite different from those which are normally used to judge works of literature; the debate at least illustrates the odd, if not isolated, position which sf occupies in the world of fiction.

An sf fan might provide simple answers to the double question of why sf attracts some people and why it repels others. Some people enjoy reading fiction that makes them think about these broader issues; others don't. Some people are future-oriented and think, or even worry, about the future of humanity; others don't (or would rather not). Some people do not turn their backs on the horrors and tremendous changes that await us in the twenty-first century and beyond; others do. Some people feel themselves to be in a world that is totally at the mercy of an infinite cosmos and unprotected by any divinity; others don't. Some people are fascinated by the thought of travel to the planets and the stars; others are not quite sure of the difference between the two. Sf fans are sometimes seen to express their perception of their place in the universe by wearing a T-shirt showing our galaxy from a distance of a few thousand light-years, with an arrow pointing to one corner and the caption 'You are here'; non-fans have some difficulty in understanding what that means. The astronaut Ed Mitchell said: 'You develop an instant global consciousness, a people orientation, an intense dissatisfaction with the state of the world and a compulsion to do something about it.'[2] It cost NASA several billion dollars and ten years of training to put him in space for this exercise in consciousness raising, which the average sf reader could have achieved with a couple of piles of paperbacks.

Looked at from the opposite angle, one can come to some equally simplistic characterizations of sf readers. They are stuck in an adolescent frame of mind that finds it difficult to come to terms with discussions of adult human relationships. They take refuge in power fantasies about super-heroes or people with strange secret powers such as telepathy. They prefer tales in which good and evil are portrayed in clear-cut terms and in which unhappy endings are the result of cosmic accident, not human weaknesses or failings. The typical sf reader is (or was) a bright adolescent male, who feels himself undervalued and excluded from structures of power (a 'nerd' shunned by girls and despised by the football team), and who takes refuge in fantasies which privilege those like him and promise them salvation.[3] He, and increasingly she, likes to be thought weird and exceptional, even if he or she is in many ways quite conventional. The thought of being exceptional as sf readers empowers them, just as, for women readers, reading of alternative futures in which women have escaped patriarchy, offers them real empowerment. Sf readers are often discontented with the world in which they live, for whatever reason, and find in sf some escape and some kind of vicarious satisfaction.

To the best of my knowledge, no psychologist has looked at the comparative psychology of those who are attracted to versus those who are repelled by sf. My own knowledge of sf readers and non-sf readers leads me to think that some or all the dichotomies suggested above are real, some of the time, but I shrink from making them any more than suggestions. Nor can I decide whether the particular attitudes of mind and ways of looking at the world which sf readers often *do* share are a result of immersion in sf from an early age or are a reason for that immersion.

Another type of explanation might be that sf readers are those who enjoy being jolted out of the ordinary—surprised, shocked, intrigued by the unreal or the surreal. Such jolts are not normally to be found in the 'mainstream', but can be found in any variant of the fantastic, from sf to horror. The real distinction, in other words, may be between those who are attracted by the fantastic, by imaginative and speculative variations on, and mutations of, the experienced world, and those who are repelled by all manifestations of the fantastic, whether sf or not. I have heard sf readers say that reading novels without the element of the fantastic is like eating food without salt or spices.

One should now perhaps put some of these generalizations into the past tense. Sf is itself much more diverse in the 1990s than it was in the 1950s or 1960s. Partly as a result of this diversity, the sf readership itself is much more varied also, with, on the one hand, many more female readers and, on the other, much more specialized reading habits; some sf readers, for instance, if we may call them that, restrict themselves entirely to spin-offs from the *Star Trek* television series. But the 1990s are different in other ways too. The days when mainstream fiction eschewed the fantastic—days which probably extended from the early Victorian period through to the 1970s—are now largely past. The categories, or the genres, are breaking down. Writers who do not consider themselves to be sf writers are writing novels which are very similar to sf works; writers brought up in the sf world are breaking into 'the mainstream', but producing work which betrays their background. And, more significantly, in the postmodernist world there has been a general reaction against the certainties of the mimetic novel; the postmodernist novel, in alliance with Latin American magical realism, frequently treats the world of experience in as cavalier and playful a way as any sf writer. Bruce Sterling has invented, or perceived, a new category resulting from this, which he nicknames 'the slipstream'. For him 'slipstream' includes such diverse novels as Peter Ackroyd's *Hawksmoor*, Isabel Allende's *House of Spirits*, Patrick Süskind's *Perfume*, and D. M. Thomas's *The White Hotel*.

It seems to me that the heart of slipstream is an attitude of peculiar aggression against 'reality'. These are fantasies of a kind, but not fantasies which are 'futuristic' or 'beyond the fields we know'. These books tend to sarcastically tear at the structure of 'everyday life'.

Some such books, the most 'mainstream' ones, are non-realistic literary fictions which avoid or ignore sf genre conventions. But hardcore slipstream has unique darker elements. Quite commonly these works don't make a lot of common sense, and what's more they often somehow imply that *nothing we know* makes 'a lot of sense' and perhaps even that *nothing ever could*.[4]

Sterling's category overlaps with postmodernism, but suggests also that postmodernism has a good deal in common with sf: indeed, some sf writers, like Philip K. Dick and J. G. Ballard, were writing postmodernist fiction long before the postmodernists.

An attempt at making a formal definition of sf which makes the links with the 'mainstream', and which thus also attempts to link sf to more 'respectable' literary traditions, has been made by the American critic Robert Scholes.[5] It is relevant to note that he places his discussion of sf ('structural fabulation') within the context of a polemic inspired by his vision of what was wrong with contemporary literature in 1975. Scholes argues that 'contemporary novelists and critics have lost faith in the ability of language to correspond with the non-verbal parts of life'.[6] Not only has realism failed, but fantasy has failed too; if reality always eludes language, then language cannot escape beyond reality—even fantasy offers us only another failed attempt to reflect reality. The future of fiction, he argues, lies in the fiction of the future: future-fiction avoids the problems of both realism and fantasy, and 'the imagination can function without self-deception as to its means and ends'.[7] And he points out that major contemporary novelists—he mentions Barth, Burgess, Durrell, Golding, Lessing, and Pynchon—were already, in the mid-1970s, moving to embrace the methods and concerns of sf.

Scholes divides fiction into two great categories, according to the relationship between the fiction and the world of experience. There are novels and romances; there is realism and fantasy. But one kind of romance, didactic romance, or *fabulation*, 'returns deliberately to confront reality', in the form of allegory, satire, fable, or parable. Sometimes this fabulation is concerned with religion—dogmatic fabulation—while sometimes it comes out of a more secular, humanistic, and open-ended tradition —as speculative fabulation. Dante's *Commedia* would be an example of the former, More's *Utopia* or Swift's *Gulliver's Travels* of the latter. Speculative fabulation changed its nature following the scientific discoveries of the nineteenth century, which extended the range of creation in space and time and put man into a different relationship with the natural world. In the twentieth century, science, philosophy, and linguistics have all challenged our certainties about our perception of the universe, making us 'free to speculate as never before'.[8] And so we come to the modern form of speculative fabulation: structural fabulation.

In works of structural fabulation the tradition of speculative fiction is modified by an awareness of the nature of the universe as a system of systems, a structure of structures, and the insights of the past century of science are accepted as fictional points of departure. Yet structural fabulation is neither scientific in its methods nor a substitute for actual science. It is a fictional exploration of human situations made perceptible by the implications of recent science.[9]

Scholes has to admit that not all of what passes for sf lives up to these noble aims (indeed, one might say, very little). Some sf is what Damon Knight called 'translations',[10] mere reworkings of traditional romance in science-fictional form: 'not structural fabulation but star dreck'.[11] Like the average thriller or airport best-seller, they provide sublimation or escapism, without any intellectual satisfaction.

But in the most admirable of structural fabulations, a radical discontinuity between the fictional world and our own provides both the means of narrative suspense and of speculation. In the perfect structural fabulation, idea and story are so wedded as to afford us simultaneously the greatest pleasures that fiction provides: sublimation and cognition.[12]

Scholes's attempt to place sf within the general categories of literature is useful, and his definition—'a fictional exploration of human situations made perceptible by the implications of recent science'—is suitably lacking in specificity. His attempt to excise the problematic 'science' from the label is also a laudable one, even if, in the two decades since his book was published, it is clear that he has failed to persuade enough people of the necessity for a new term. But even Scholes's definition is not so much a description as a prescription for a future development of future-fiction, which he sees as the possible saviour of contemporary fiction. He excludes a large number of texts generally accepted as sf, because they are 'not structural fabulation but star dreck'. It is clear that he does this in large part because of his intention to make sf seem respectable to his audience, originally a lecture audience at the University of Notre Dame, comprised largely, one suspects, of those brought up to believe that sf lies quite outside the margins of 'literature'. (At the very end he gives his readers a list of eleven sf books 'which I can personally vouch for as excellent'.)

In that final passage, however, he also emphasizes the 'pleasures of the text': it is the beginning of a definition of sf in relation to the specific pleasures that a reader can derive from it. It is to aspects of reader response that we must now turn to further our understanding of what sf is.

The Sense of Wonder

First, however, another definition, which will enable us to link the pleasures provided by sf with older, more traditional, literary pleasures. Brian Aldiss's definition, in *Billion Year Spree* (1972), is different in type from what we have encountered so far because, as he says, most previous definitions have failed through paying attention only to content, not form.

Science fiction is the search for a definition of mankind and his [*sic*] status in the universe which will stand in our advanced but confused state of knowledge (science), and is characteristically set in the Gothic or post-Gothic mode.[13]

Aldiss uses the word 'mode' deliberately; he sees sf as more than a publishing category or a genre. It is less easy to see precisely what he means by 'Gothic or post-Gothic'. The phrase is clearly linked to his conviction that Mary Shelley's *Frankenstein* is the first great—or the first—sf novel, and that sf is basically an offshoot of the Gothic novel. What sf shares with Gothic (and post-Gothic) is not a purpose, but a tone, an atmosphere, an approach to the relationship between mankind and the world. Aldiss clarifies:

In the Gothic mode, emphasis was placed on the distant and unearthly . . . Brooding landscapes, isolated castles, dismal old towns, and mysterious figures . . . carry us into an entranced world from which horrid revelations start. . . . Terror, mystery and that delightful horror which Burke connected with the sublime . . . may be discovered . . . in science fiction to this day.[14]

We have here a suggestion that sf is more about providing a particular kind of emotional fulfilment than, as Gernsback might have hoped, about inspiring us to invent a better kind of portable generator. And Aldiss is surely right to suggest that 'it would be as absurd to suggest that most SF writers were serious propagandists for the cause of science as that the author of *Romano Castle: or, The Horrors of the Forest* was a serious critic of the evils of the Inquisition—however much both sides may have considered themselves in earnest'.[15] The new romantic age, Aldiss said, had a passion for the inexplicable; this too is shared by many people today—including, one might add, many scientists.

The Romanian critic Cornel Robu has recently emphasized that 'terror, mystery and that delightful horror which Burke connected with the sublime' constitute an important element in much classic sf.[16] As he points out, only half jokingly, the words used by Edmund Burke to describe the sublime in the mid-eighteenth century are the very words adopted in the twentieth century for the titles of early sf magazines: *Amazing* and *Astonishing*. (One could add several other such titles to the list: *Astounding, Thrilling, Wonder*, and, of course, *Thrilling Wonder!*)

The feeling of the sublime is at once a feeling of displeasure, arising from the inadequacy of the imagination in the aesthetic estimation of magnitude to attain to its estimation by reason, and a simultaneously awakened pleasure arising from this very judgment of the inadequacy of the greatest faculty of sense being in accord with ideas of reason (Immanuel Kant, 1790).[17]

Burke too argued that it was magnitude, particularly magnitude in nature, which gave rise to these feelings. 'Infinity has a tendency to fill the mind with that sort of delightful horror which is the most genuine effect and truest test of the sublime.'[18] Mountainous scenery, vast deserts, grand thunderstorms, rivers in full flood, but above all, perhaps, the starry sky, all evoke that awe which is the essence of the Sublime: a feeling of helplessness and terror when humans realize their frailty and small size in the face of the might and magnitude of the universe. The literary tradition of the Sublime may go back to Longinus, in the ancient world, but it came to special prominence in the Romantic era. In the mind of most Romantics (as in the mind of most sf writers), there is no divinity to protect mankind from the universe; the Great Watchmaker, if he is there at all, is not concerned with individual human beings. The Sublime is a consequence of the liberation of humanity, by the Enlightenment, from the protection of revealed truth. The Gothic, Aldiss would argue, is the most realistic progenitor of sf, because of its historical context; it appealed to the human desire for awe and mystery in a world in which religion had largely been stripped of those qualities. With Mary Shelley's novel, the scientist Victor Frankenstein replaces the priest as the one who can probe the mysteries of human existence and open the door to wonder; it is fitting that, in Aldiss's formulation, Frankenstein stands at the threshold of sf itself.

That the concept of the Sublime, a major aesthetic criterion of the Romantic era, has a close connection with the pleasures derived from reading sf has long been recognized by readers and critics, even if that word has seldom been used. The phrase that *has* been used, and which to a large extent corresponds, is 'Sense of Wonder' (sometimes jocularly or cynically abbreviated as 'sensawunda'). The very first collection of sf criticism was Damon Knight's *In Search of Wonder* (1956). For many sf readers, that search for wonder—the search for another fix of the sublime that they first experienced at the age of 14—is what drives them to continue reading. Sf editor David Hartwell has expressed it very well in his *Age of Wonders*:

A sense of wonder, awe at the vastness of space and time, is at the root of the excitement of science fiction. Any child who has looked up at the stars at night and thought about how far away they are, how there is no end or outer edge to this place, this universe—any child who has felt the thrill of fear and excitement at such thoughts stands a very good chance of becoming a science fiction reader.

To say that science fiction is in essence a religious literature is an overstatement, but one that contains truth. SF is a uniquely modern incarnation of an ancient tradition: the tale of wonder. Tales of miracles, tales of great powers and consequences beyond the experience of people in your neighborhood, tales of the gods who inhabit other worlds and sometimes descend to visit ours, tales of humans travelling to the abode of the gods, tales of the uncanny: all exist now as science fiction.

Science fiction's appeal lies in its combination of the rational, the believable, with the miraculous. It is an appeal to the sense of wonder.[19]

Sf, in this description, is not only a modern reincarnation of the Gothic, as Aldiss suggests, but a modern version of much older forms of literature: the mythological tale, medieval hagiography, the traveller's tale, and, above all, perhaps, the medieval romance. These are not themselves in any sense sf, but Hartwell suggests, surely rightly, that they appeal to *some* of the same needs and emotions that sf satisfies. It is of interest historically that Hartwell links sf closely with religion; if the appeal of sf is in a combination of the rational and the miraculous, then we ought to think about the ways in which sf fulfils a role once fulfilled by religion in an age in which for many the power of traditional religion has disappeared totally. Even if sf can create dogma—we shall see in Chapter 4 how it played a fundamental role in the creation of the Church of Scientology and how various semi-religious flying saucer cults draw their inspiration from sf—in general sf has been against the dogma of revealed religion. If it draws on the traditional myths of the established religions of the present or past, whether Christian or Buddhist or pagan, it generally does so tongue in cheek. Yet, in doing so, it can create a rival sense of wonder, which acts almost as a replacement religion: a religion for those deprived of all traditional certainties in the wake of Darwin, Einstein, Planck, Gödel, and Heisenberg.

As an example, consider the well-known fable by Arthur C. Clarke, 'The Nine Billion Names of God'.[20] A computer is installed by Western technicians in a Tibetan lamasery; its task is to speed up the compilation of all the possible names of God. This, the monks believe, is what the human race was created for, and on its completion the Earth, and perhaps all creation, will come to an end. The technicians do their job, with some condescension, and flee back to civilization.

> 'Wonder if the computer's finished its run. It was due about now.'
> Chuck didn't reply, so George swung round in his saddle. He could just see Chuck's face, a white oval turned toward the sky.
> 'Look,' whispered Chuck, and George lifted his eyes to heaven. (There is always a last time for everything.)
> Overhead, without any fuss, the stars were going out.

At one level, this story may be primarily an ironical comment on two totally incompatible dogmas. The computer scientist wonders at the folly of the lama; the true folly 'is the scientist's who, both because of his religious skepticism and his economic cynicism, hastens the end of the universe'.[21] But I do not believe that Clarke was writing a fable to point out the folly of scientific rationalism. He was inciting sf readers with a basic knowledge of science, for whom the tale was written, to exercise their imagination. How would God cause the stars to go out together, as seen from Earth, when in fact their light has been travelling for very different lengths of time? The light of some of the visible stars has taken several hundred years to reach us; the light of even the nearest (except for the sun) took some four years to reach Earth. Is Clarke telling us that the Earth is the centre of the universe, and has been created to allow for the experiment of the creation of humanity? For the visible stars to go out together, God would have had to foreknow, in Shakespeare's day or considerably earlier, exactly when the computer program was going to finish, so that he could begin winding up the universe as viewed from Earth. Or did God deliberately provide the evidence which would mislead scientists into thinking that the universe was very much larger than it actually is? Either the punch line is merely playful, or it implies a devious or jesting God. It would be rash to say what Clarke's purpose was. But what this reader (at the age of 13 or 14) learned from the story was the unimaginable size of the universe and the implausibility of some of the traditional human images of God. An almost religious sense of awe (or wonder) was created in me, as I tried to perceive the immensity of the universe, and contemplate the possibility of the non-existence of God.

Reading Strategies

One of the problems for the non-sf reader approaching an sf book is that a different style of reading is involved from that encountered in most 'mainstream' fiction. We can approach this question by looking at the definition of sf proposed by Darko Suvin. 'SF is a literary genre whose necessary and sufficient conditions are the presence and interaction of estrangement and cognition, and whose main formal device is an imaginative alternative to the author's empirical experience.'[22]

Suvin is a Canadian critic who was brought up within the European tradition (he studied first at Zagreb), and he links sf to the European utopian tradition; not only is sf sometimes specifically within that tradition, but both sf and utopia share these two features—estrangement and cognition. *Estrangement*, espoused as a principle by the Russian formalists and then by Bertolt Brecht, arouses the interest of readers by presenting them with something jarringly different from their experience. For the formalists or Brecht it is a mere device, but for sf it is the main distinguishing framework. Estrangement is offered by the fairy-tale and other literary genres as well; but sf is distinguished also by *cognition*, the process of acquiring knowledge and of reason. 'It sees the norms of any age, including emphatically its own, as unique, changeable, and therefore subject to a cognitive view,'[23] unlike, for instance, the myth or the fairy-tale, which offer absolutes, not enquiry. 'Cognition' is, in fact, frequently the main subject of sf: the investigation, for instance, of possible social systems or new forms of science. 'A cognitive— in most cases strictly scientific—element becomes a measure of aesthetic quality, of the specific pleasure to be sought in SF.'[24] As implied here, 'cognition' is more inclusive than 'science', and while his 'literature of cognitive estrangement' is never going to be acceptable as a term in the way that 'science fiction' has been, it is certainly more apposite and descriptive.

Suvin also introduces another useful term: the *novum*. 'SF is distinguished by the narrative dominance or hegemony of a fictional "novum" (novelty, innovation) validated by cognitive logic.'[25] A novum is a deliberately introduced change made to the world as experienced by author and reader, but a change based upon scientific or other logic; it is such a significant part of sf that frequently the novum determines the subsequent narrative. This observation by Suvin to some extent merely puts into impeccably correct critical language the long-observed phenomenon that a classic sf story frequently originates with a question beginning 'What if . . . ?' arising in the author's mind. What if a handful of people survived a nuclear holocaust? What if humanity came across alien intelligence on Mars? What if men were wiped out by a gender-specific virus? What if Hitler had won the war or the Roman Empire had never fallen? What if a time-traveller kidnapped Jesus the night before the crucifixion? Or even, as a throw-away line in a novel,[26] what if God's corpse was discovered in deep space? As Suvin noted, most *novums* (the correct plural, *nova*, would only confuse astronomers) create a new historical situation, different from the one that we know. In consequence, sf is usually just as much about *history* as it is about *science*. Sf writers have to construct new histories, of our own world or of others, in order to set their novum (or novums) in context and discuss its (or their) impact upon individuals or society as a whole—that is, to discuss the historical impact of the novum.

Suvin's definition allows the critic to make clear distinctions between what is sf and what is not. Indeed, in his own *Victorian Science Fiction in the UK* (1983) Suvin does just that, in a rigorous way, compiling his list on the basis of a new definition, and helpfully including a list of 'Two Hundred Victorian Books that should be Excluded from S-F Bibliographies'. The definition is: 'SF is distinguished by the narrative dominance of a fictional novelty (novum, innovation) validated both by being continuous with a body of already existing cognitions and by being a "mental experiment" based on cognitive logic.'[27] As an example of how this works, we may take the lost race tale, such as Rider Haggard's *She*.[28] Potentially such a story is going to answer an interesting 'What if . . . ?' question: what if a civilization develops totally separately from the rest of the known world? What would it be like? An interesting novum, such as a new political and/or social system (as in Thomas More's *Utopia*), could easily be introduced, and if such a novum is dominant in the narrative, then that story may well be sf. But in the great majority of cases the Victorian lost race novel imagines only feudal, slave-owning, or tribal societies, with pre-modern technological systems; none of these constitutes a novum in Suvin's terms. One can compare this with Edward Bulwer-Lytton's *The Coming Race* (1871), where the lost race, under the surface of the Earth, is distinguished by a very different kind of social structure from anything on the surface, determined in large part by their taming of *vril*, a powerful electromagnetic life-force (the origin of the Victorian adman's creation 'Bovril'); this is classic sf.

Another distinction made by Suvin which is significant, given the past history of definitions of sf, is between science fiction and 'science fantasy'. The latter is a term used originally by H. G. Wells, but in more recent years it has come to mean a mingling of science fiction and fantasy: sf with the rigour removed. Suvin cites nineteenth-century examples such as Marie Corelli's *A Romance of Two Worlds* (1886), in which a young woman learns of the existence of pure spirits inhabiting other planets, who can be reached in a trance state. More significant as a test case, however, and published in the same year is Robert Louis Stevenson's *Strange Case of Dr Jekyll and Mr Hyde*. Suvin argues that although the change from Jekyll to Hyde comes about via a chemical concoction, Jekyll eventually changes without the chemical. Suvin talks of 'this unclear oscillation between science and fantasy, where science is used for a partial justification or added alibi for that part of the readership that would no longer be disposed to swallow a straightforward fantasy or moral allegory', and concludes that it is 'an early example of "science fantasy", with its force not stemming from any cognitive logic, but rather from the anguish of Jekyll over his loss of control and from the impact of the underlying moral allegory'.[29]

Others have tried to distinguish between 'science fiction' and 'science fantasy'. Suvin himself cites with approval the strictures of James Blish on the growing popularity in the 1960s of 'science fantasy', 'the kind of yarn in which nobody is supposed to care about gross scientific errors and inconsistencies because they are covered over with great gobs of color and rhetoric'.[30] Blish was complaining about Brian W. Aldiss's 'Hothouse' stories, in which Aldiss conjures up an exotic and poetic picture of an Earth in the far future and of the Moon stationary above the Earth and linked to it by the webs of giant spider-like beings ('ballistically the idea is utter nonsense,' said Blish). One problem with such strictures, and in general with attempts to exile 'science fantasy' (or even 'fantasy') beyond the bounds of 'science fiction' proper, is that ideas about what is or is not 'utter nonsense' scientifically vary from individual to individual, and cannot be anything other than subjective. The most obvious examples are faster-than-light travel and travel through time; both are dismissed by many scientists as 'utter nonsense', yet both feature in the stories of many sf writers (including Blish), partly on the grounds that scientists today *may* be wrong, but partly because such devices allow sf writers to explore situations and possibilities that would otherwise be denied them.

The purpose of definitions is to create boundaries: to exclude whatever is deemed to be outside the category. Suvin's definitions do their work admirably, but fall victim to the problem that has affected most of the definitions that we have looked at in the previous chapters: that they are prescriptive rather than descriptive. Or, to put it another way, the definition may encompass most sf, particularly the more self-conscious and ambitious sf (I am trying desperately to avoid using the word 'good'), but may arbitrarily exclude other works that are normally recognized as sf.

Suvin's formula 'the literature of cognitive estrangement' has much to offer us, however, particularly if we regard it as a definition of the *core* of what is sf and do not use it over rigidly to include or exclude. John Clute has objected that sf is rarely concerned with estrangement: indeed, that it 'seeks to create the exact opposite of estrangement ... [making] the incredible seem plausible and familiar'. Nicholls and Stableford comment that this disagreement is in essence a reflection of two very different approaches to sf, which they characterize as satire and romance.[31] The satirical approach (which Suvin favours) sees sf as intended primarily to comment on our own world, 'through metaphor and extrapolation'; estrangement is an important device for concentrating the reader's mind on differences between the fictional and real worlds. But much sf is romance— that is, in this context, a game—whose object is to create alternative realities, and often to domesticate them and render them plausible by making them familiar. As my comments on Vance's 'The Moon Moth' suggest (pp. 125 ff. below), I do not see these two approaches as incompatible; rather, they are different ways of achieving the same result. 'Making the incredible seem plausible and familiar' is in fact a method of estrangement: the incredible becomes familiar, and in the process the ways and customs of our own world begin to seem strange.

The emphasis on novums is useful in our attempt to look at the specific strategies to employ in reading sf. As Tom Shippey has put it: ' "Estrangement" . . . means recognising the novum; "cognition" means evaluating it, trying to make sense of it. You need both to read science fiction. Some people are willing to do neither.'[32] We do not meet novums in most 'mainstream' fiction. I may read a novel set in a world which is somewhat obscure and alien to me—in a Guatemalan village or a Los Angeles suburb, say—but I can use my general knowledge of the world to understand what is happening, and if I do not immediately understand what is happening (if I stumble across a word in Spanish or some Californian slang), then I use the context in order to establish what it means. I trust the author as an observer of the world; I add the fact which I have just acquired by deduction or inference to my accumulated knowledge of the world.

Of all the non-sf genres, only historical fiction presents readers, and authors, with problems which resemble those of sf. Authors are describing the real world, but not one directly experienced by either the authors or their readers. Authors have to reconstruct their worlds—Victorian London or eleventh-century Byzantium or even Palaeolithic Africa—not only from their own readings in history and archaeology, but also from their own imaginations. The amount of background detail they need to provide for the benefit of the reader will depend partly on the authors' judgement as to the familiarity of the period to the general public; for many readers, Victorian London is almost as familiar (through chronological proximity and accumulation of reading experience) as our own time, while eleventh-century Byzantium requires a substantial filling in of background and local colour, some of which, at least, must come from the author's own imagination. Novels of prehistory, however, require so much speculation—based on modern sciences such as anthropology and archaeology—that they closely resemble sf. The author has to reconstruct almost all the details of the fictional world, and to present that information as naturally and clearly as possible to the readers. It is no accident at all that a number of novels of prehistoric life have been written by sf writers, and sometimes even packaged as sf or fantasy. If much sf is actually historical fiction—historical fiction of the future—then it becomes perfectly possible to classify prehistoric fiction as sf. Kim Stanley Robinson concludes: 'Considering the impenetrable barriers placed between us and the prehistoric past, and the future, and alternative courses of history, it is possible to revise the "historical" definition of science fiction a final time, and say that *science fiction concerns itself with the history that we cannot know*.'[33]

An important difference between historical fiction and sf, however, is that the rules of historical fiction require that history be presented as far as possible as it actually happened. There is an unwritten contract between writer and reader which reassures the reader that the writer is dealing with something that happened, or could have happened, in the world in which he or she lives, even if it is his or her world a century or more ago. It is *real*. A historical novel becomes a way of learning about history without the pain of having to plough through an actual history book; indeed, Jean Plaidy has probably taught far more people what they know about Tudor England than Sir John Neale or Sir Geoffrey Elton. The unwritten rules of sf, on the other hand, require that the world written about is *not* that of the reader: there is something wrong, somewhere; there is a novum lurking under the bed, waiting to pounce and to disconcert.

One of the most disconcerting forms of sf, particularly for the reader of historical fiction, is the alternative history. This fictional form may be set in the past, like historical fiction, or the present—that is, in the late twentieth century—but in a present that is subtly, or not so subtly, distorted by some difference in the past. The assumption is that history is the result of an almost infinite series of accidents and choices, and at almost any point could have gone in a different direction. The classic image is that of John Barr, in Jack Williamson's sf novel *The Legion of Time* (1938, revised 1952), standing in a field; if he picks up a magnet, rather than a stone, the history of the galaxy will be transformed. Sf writers have come to call these decisive moments 'Jonbar points'; they range from the non-arrival of the comet which caused the extinction of the dinosaurs (Harry Harrison's *West of Eden*, 1984) to the non-occurrence of the Protestant Reformation (Kingsley Amis's *The Alteration*, 1976; Keith Roberts's *Pavane*, 1968) or the defeat of the Allies in the Second World War (many examples, but the classic is Philip K. Dick's *The Man in the High Castle*, 1962).[34] Much of the pleasure derived from reading these works lies in determining where the Jonbar point lies, and in enjoying the way in which the author has worked out the fictional world, and, in some cases, dealt with the characters that the alternative world shares with ours. (In Amis's *The Alteration*, Sartre and Himmler have both become cardinals; in William Gibson's and Bruce Sterling's *The Difference Engine* (1990), Byron has become Prime Minister.)

Whatever the sf setting, the author has to be able to present the necessary information to the readers so that they can determine what the novums are and how to evaluate them. It is possible—and used to be common in the nineteenth century and later—for characters in the novel to lecture each other about their own world: this is the most straightforward, and crudest, method of 'infodump', as used, for instance, by Hugo Gernsback:

And then, the scientist in him to the front: 'Tell me all about this new tube. Busy with my own work I have not followed its progress closely enough to know all its details.'

'It has been most interesting work,' said James 212B 422, 'and we regard it as quite an achievement in electrical engineering. The new tube runs in a straight line between New York and Brest, France. If the tube were to run straight along the bottom of the ocean the distance between the two points would be from 3,600 to 3,700 miles due to the curvature of the earth. For this reason the tube was pushed *straight through the earth*, thereby making the distance only 3,470 miles. You will understand it better by examining this chart . . .'[35]

Other methods involve providing a historical introduction (traditionally italicized) or interspersing the narrative with fictional documents from the period: letters, newspapers, advertisements. It has come to be accepted, however, that part of the sf writer's art is to introduce the reader to the background by means of clues inserted in the text. The decoding and assessment of these clues can be a major part of the pleasure provided by the work; indeed, *without* that decoding and assessment, in a process of careful reading, it may be impossible to understand the text at all.

A classic instance of this decoding is provided by the first page of Robert A. Heinlein's *Beyond This Horizon* (serialized in *Astounding* in 1942, book 1948). After a brief italicized comment to the effect that there was no more poverty, disease, or war and that 'all of them should have been happy'—a comment that immediately alerts the reader to the presence of a failed utopia—we shift to a discussion between an economist and his friend Felix in the former's office at the Department of Finance. There are just three hints as to the characteristics of this futuristic setting (which now have to be assessed historically, in the light of what we know about America in 1942): Felix gets to the office via a slideway—a moving strip of floor, known in our present (in airports, for instance), but not in 1942; he gets into the office by punching in a code combination— common now, but not in 1942—and waiting for a face check; and when he passed security, 'the door dilated'.

And no discussion. Just 'the door dilated'. I read across it, and was two lines down before I realised what the image had been, what the words had called forth. A *dilating* door. It didn't open, it *irized*! Dear God, now I knew I was in a future world.

Thus Harlan Ellison's reaction, as quoted by Samuel R. Delany.[36] Delany himself comments that 'the door dilated' is meaningless as naturalistic fiction or as fantasy: 'as sf—as an event that hasn't happened, yet still must be interpreted in terms of the physically explainable—it is quite as wondrous as Ellison feels it.' It is a classic novum. Delany himself offers a sly homage to it in his *Stars in My Pocket Like Grains of Sand* (1984):

The door deliquesced.
Cool against my thigh, chest, and face mist from the sill-trough blew

back as I lifted my foot over the—'Hey, don't step in that!' . . . You're supposed to step *over*. You yell at little kids for getting their feet wet in the door trough. I laughed. 'Look . . .' as I stepped over.

The blue liquid, behind us now, began to foam; the foam rose, climbing at the jambs faster than in the middle; and darkening, and shutting out light as the door's semicrystals effloresced.[37]

Such hints of future technology are major elements of estrangement, and in a sense they are meant to remain estranging; to explain exactly how they work (with diagrams, as Gernsback would have done) would be to make them familiar, to destroy the sense of wonder.

Readers approaching an sf book have to read it rather like someone who is reading a traditional whodunit. They have to keep their eyes open all the time for significant clues; they have to act the Poirot, deducing the world from the hints and clues left by the author. They have to evaluate these clues, and, to do it properly, even have to do it historically. (Is this technological commonplace intended to be a novum? Was it a commonplace when the author wrote?) But sf authors do not usually gather all their readers together in the library at the end of the book, in order to explain what all the clues meant and fit them together into a logically compelling narrative. Sf readers can never relax the overdrive of the imagination; they must try to evaluate the clues in their context, in the knowledge that they may otherwise never find out what is happening. In William Gibson's *Neuromancer* (1984), for example, the clues come thick and fast, and much faster than the answers.

Like a student in a class a little too hard, the reader finds the language being spoken always just a bit beyond comprehension, though never incomprehensible . . . In Van Vogt, to invoke one of the first masters of the technique, we usually know when we do not know what is being talked about. Gibson puts us in a much more nervous position: we usually have the anxiety that we have missed an explanation somewhere earlier. One thematic effect of the device is to imply that the reader has never grasped more than an edge of the whole reality. Such an anxiety is different from that which the characters themselves feel: they do not know some plots, but they are completely at home in the technology.[38]

We shall return to this question of anxiety. But, continuing to explore the question of the flow of information to the reader, let us take, as an example, the first page of a well-known sf book:

A beginning is the time for taking the most delicate care that the balances are correct. This every sister of the Bene Gesserit knows. To begin your study of the life of Muad'Dib, then take care that you first place him in his time: born in the 57th year of the Padishah Emperor, Shaddam IV. And take the most special care that you locate Muad'Dib in his place: the planet Arrakis. Do not be deceived by the fact that he was born on Caladan and lived his first fifteen years there. Arrakis, the planet known as Dune, is for ever his place.

—from 'Manual of Muad'Dib' by the Princess Irulan

In the week before their departure to Arrauis, when all the final scurrying about had reached a nearly unbearable frenzy, an old crone came to visit the mother of the boy, Paul.

It was a warm night at Castle Caradan, and the ancient pile of stone that had served the Atreides family as home for twenty-six generations bore that cooled-sweat feeling it acquired before a change in the weather.

The old woman was let in by the side door down the vaulted passage by Paul's room and she was allowed a moment to peer in at him where he lay in his bed.

By the half-light of a suspensor lamp, dimmed and hanging near the floor, the awakened boy could see a bulky female shape at his door, standing one step ahead of his mother. The old woman was a witch shadow—hair like matted spiderwebs, hooded 'round darkness of features, eyes like glittering jewels.

'Is he not small for his age, Jessica?' the old woman asked. Her voice wheezed and twanged like an untuned baliset.

Paul's mother answered in her soft contralto: 'The Atreides are known to start late getting their growth, Your Reverence.'

'So I've heard, so I've heard,' wheezed the old woman. 'Yet he's already fifteen.'

'Yes, Your Reverence.'

'He's awake and listening to us,' said the old woman. 'Sly little rascal.' She chuckled. 'But royalty has need of slyness. And if he's really the Kwisatz Haderach ... well ...'

Within the shadows of his bed, Paul held his eyes to mere slits. Two bird-bright ovals—the eyes of the old woman—seemed to expand and glow as they stared into his.

'Sleep well, you sly little rascal,' said the old woman. 'Tomorrow you'll need all your faculties to meet my gom jabbar.'

And she was gone, pushing his mother out, closing the door with a solid thump.

Paul lay awake wondering: *What is a gom jabbar?*[39]

And so will we. (Even if we have by now realized that there is a glossary at the back of the book—which is Frank Herbert's *Dune* (1965)—in the British paperback edition that we are using, 'gom jabbar' has been subtly placed out of alphabetical order, so that we won't immediately find it.)

The information in this passage is conveyed in two ways: via quotations from a document and via the narrative. The document as epigraph is a common device. Two of the best-known exponents are Isaac Asimov, who uses extracts from the *Encyclopedia Galactica* in his 'Foundation' series, and Jack Vance, who not only quotes from various future authors—such as Unspiek, Baron Bodissey—but even quotes extracts from reviews of their works (and offers further information in parodic academic footnotes). We learn from the Princess Irulan of the existence of an educated sisterhood, the Bene Gesserit; of the existence of an emperor, who clearly rules over several, if not many, planets; and of the importance of Muad'Dib, born on Caladan, who departed for the planet of Arrakis, or Dune, at the age of 15. When the narrative proper begins on Caladan, and with the immediate appearance of a 15-year-old boy, Paul, we realize that the book is going to be about Paul's life on Arrakis. The fact that the text tells us that he is about to depart for Arrauis, not Arrakis, causes momentary worry (one has to be open to every eventuality in sf), but recalling that proof-reading of fiction in paperback is highly erratic, we assume (correctly) that Arrauis = Arrakis. (Sf is much more information-dense than other forms of fiction, because it is constructing a world that does not necessarily have any relationship to the world which we have experienced; so every word may count.) The alert reader will realize from the Princess Irulan that we are in a world of space travel, and hence

high technology (although the suspensor lamp is the only
direct evidence of technological sophistication), and that this
appears to be in some conflict with the setting of the story: an
emperor, a princess, a stone castle, an old woman who looks
like a witch. But Princess Irulan makes it clear, too, that
Muad'Dib is a legendary figure; the passage tells us not only
that Paul is Muad'Dib, but that he will be Kwisatz Haderach.
Whatever that is, it sounds important. Paul ultimately becomes a figure of myth; perhaps for that reason his childhood
is steeped in images drawn from myth and fairy-tale. Or is it
that the aristocracy want to buttress their power by reference
to antiquity—castles that remain in the family for twenty-six
generations and names which recall the names of ancient Earth
(presuming we are in the far future), and even the name of a
family, the Atreides, celebrated in pre-Christian Greek mythology? We don't know everything, yet; nor does Paul. We are
going to learn about this world not just through the narrative,
but through the eyes of an adolescent as he learns about his
own world: a common, but effective, device. In fact, within a
page or two we do learn who or what the Kwisatz Haderach is
(unlike in David Lynch's overblown and overcut epic film of
Dune, in which the first, and last, reference is when Paul's
little sister, near the end, pipes up 'He *is* the Kwisatz Haderach',
to the amusement and total incomprehension of cinema
audiences).

An experienced sf reader, of course, is not necessarily worried by the appearance of inexplicable names; they give depth
and historico-cultural resonance to an alien world. One of the
most celebrated examples of the deliberately inexplicable is the
last sentence of A. E. Van Vogt's *The Weapon Makers* (1943;
book 1946): 'This much we have learned: here is the race that
shall rule the sevagram.' We have had no mention of the
sevagram before. If readers knew that it was the name of the
ashram recently founded by Gandhi, it was clearly meant to do
much more than remind them of the Indian leader; in the context, it stirs 'images in the reader's mind of the broadest conceivable vistas. It would appear to mean at least this galaxy,
maybe other galaxies, perhaps even the entire multiverse.'[40] One

word, at the very end of a novel, can set the imagination reeling and trigger the sense of wonder.

Uncertainties of interpretation, too, are part of the pleasures of reading sf.

The science fiction reader, of course, *likes* this feeling of unpredictability. It creates intense curiosity, as well as the pleasure of working out, in the long run, the logic underlying the author's decisions, vocabulary and invented world. It is a powerful stimulus to the exercise of 'cognition', of putting unknown data into some sort of mental holding tank, to see if and when they do start to fit together, and what happens when they do. Yet this experience is in a sense a deeply 'anxious' one.[41]

That anxiety can be almost too much for those not fully initiated into sf, as the (slipstream) novelist Robert Irwin has recently expressed well in a review of *Winterlong* by Elizabeth Hands:

A hundred pages into this first novel by Elizabeth Hands, I was still suffering the sort of panic attacks that I (and other people who do not read much science fiction) invariably get when tackling books in the genre. Who are the aardmen? Who are the lazars? What is an Ascendance and who are the Ascendants? Why are people so afraid of falling roses? How come all the empaths seem to be autistic? Where and when is the City of Trees? And (the big question) was I ever going to have a firm grip on what makes the world of Winterlong tick? Winterlong is so very different from, say, Kingsmarkham and the world of Inspector Wexford, as conjured up by Ruth Rendell. The recognisable landscape of the Wexford novels has powers to soothe: the familiar police station, the Italian restaurant across the road, the used-car dealer, the housing estate, and so on. However convoluted and nasty the Rendell plot may be, one still knows exactly where to buy a pizza or a used car. Science fiction writers, on the other hand, prefer to tell their readers to get lost, and it is the landscape in which the readers get lost that poses some of the nastiest challenges. It is not just the body on the library floor which is in question; it is the library itself and the nature and function of libraries in a world where all the familiar parameters are missing. The environment itself is the horrific riddle; it may even be the product of some unguessed-at crime.[42]

The reader has to function to some extent like the reader of a detective story; but the resolution of the reading turns out very differently in the two genres. There is no tidy summing up, no comforting closure at the end; instead, there is the satisfaction for the reader of having decoded a part of the author's imaginary universe. The difficulties may account for the way in which the necessity to decode repels many readers; it may also explain why those who are attracted to it are usually captured young, in their teens or earlier. Children and adolescents spend much of their time trying to decode the weird and alien world in which they live; decoding sf is no different for them, and indeed, working on an understanding of a deliberately coded work such as an sf novel may actually assist them in learning to understand the meaning of the culturally and unconsciously coded world of a mimetic novel, or, indeed, of 'real life'.

Three Tales

We can look more closely at some of the pleasures of reading sf through a study of three very different sf short stories.

Consistently at, or near, the top of readers' (and writers') polls for the best sf short story ever written is Isaac Asimov's 'Nightfall'; whether or not we *agree* with that ranking, it is clear that if we *understand* it, we may get closer to the appeal of sf.[43]

As is well known, the theme of 'Nightfall' was proposed to Asimov by his editor, John W. Campbell:

He had come across a quotation from . . . Emerson: 'If the stars should appear one night in a thousand years, how would men believe and adore; and preserve for many generations the remembrance of the city of God . . .'

Campbell asked me to read it and said, 'What do you think would happen, Asimov, if men were to see the stars for the first time in a thousand years?'

I thought, and drew a blank. I said, 'I don't know.'

Campbell said, 'I think they would go mad. I want you to write a story about that.'[44]

The story as published begins with that quotation from Emerson. We immediately join a conversation between an angry astronomer, Aton 77, and an importunate young reporter, Theremon 762. We do not know what the argument is about until the second page (except, of course, that Emerson and Campbell's own blurb in the original publication have alerted us):

He stared moodily out at the skyline where Gamma, the brightest of the planet's six suns, was setting. It had already faded and yellowed into the horizon mists, and Aton knew that he would never see it again as a sane man.

We now know we are on another planet, and soon we learn the problem. Normally at least one of the planet's six suns is always in the sky, and no one on Lagash experiences true darkness. But astronomers who have learned about gravitation and orbital mechanics have worked out that once every 2,049 years, when five of the suns are below the horizon, the sixth is eclipsed. Putting this information together with archaeological evidence about the periodical destruction of civilization, roughly every 2,000 years, and with evidence about the psychological inability of people on Lagash to cope with darkness, a group of scientists has concluded that their civilization, too, is facing destruction. Their cities will be burnt by people who seek fire in order to avoid the horrifying darkness. There are legends preserved by religious fanatics (the Cultists) that mysterious objects called Stars appear in the sky during the darkness. Scientists speculate that perhaps there are a couple of dozen other suns in the universe, whose light normally never penetrates the intense daylight of Lagash. And the scientists, trusting in their reason, are convinced that they can preserve their sanity, since they have the rational explanation for these events, and they believe that in the Hideout they have established they can protect the achievements of their time, so that civilization can be rebuilt once the crisis has passed.

All this information is conveyed, as the eclipse itself draws closer, via conversation, among the scientists who have elected to witness the action rather than seal themselves in safety in the Hideout. The feeling of claustrophobia and panic increases as the light grows dimmer. Finally, the Stars appear:

Not Earth's feeble thirty-six hundred Stars visible to the eye—Lagash was in the center of a giant cluster. Thirty thousand mighty suns shone down in a soul-searing splendor that was more frighteningly cold in its awful indifference than the bitter wind that shivered across the cold, horribly bleak world . . .

Someone clawed at the torch, and it fell and snuffed out. In the instant, the awful splendor of the indifferent Stars leaped nearer to them.

On the horizon outside the window, in the direction of Saro City, a crimson glow began growing, strengthening in brightness, that was not the glow of a sun.

The long night had come again.

That is the end of the story, and an ambiguous one: we know that Saro City is burning, as predicted, and we are left feeling pessimistic about the fate of the nearby scientists. But we do not know whether the Hideout is going to be successful in breaking the endless cycle of destruction and rebirth. This ambiguity has rarely been noted. Some critics have seen the end of the story as presaging the end of civilization, as had always happened before—'The long night had come *again*'— while others have seen it as the triumph of reason, and thus, presumably, assume the survival of those in the Hideout.[45]

There are all kinds of problems with the story, apart from the wooden, banal quality of much of Asimov's dialogue. (The inhabitants of Lagash, in their speech and most of their behaviour, seem little different from inhabitants of New York in about 1941; but that may even be an advantage, for, as Wells said, one oddity per story is quite enough.) There is the lapse at the beginning of the section quoted above, the jarring mention of Earth, when Earth had not been mentioned before and indeed, as far as the inhabitants of Lagash were concerned, was quite literally inconceivable: an authorial intrusion that a skilled sf writer would have avoided, one might think. In fact, Asimov's autobiography tells us that the whole poetic paragraph was added by Campbell, to Asimov's intense annoyance, because Asimov did not want to write 'poetically', and saw the gratuitous mention of Earth as a 'serious literary flaw'.[46] But Asimov has to take responsibility for the problems of plausibility. Did the people of Lagash *never* experience darkness? Would a civilization really be wiped out by madness caused by a short-lived eclipse that 'lasts well over half a day so that no spot on the planet escapes its effects'? Above all, what is the psychological problem: is it the darkness, or is it the starlight that shone from 30,000 stars in 'soul-searing splendor' and 'its awful indifference'? It is possibly both the darkness *and* the starlight which drive people insane; as the reporter Theremon goes mad, he blames 'the Dark and the Cold and the Doom', but when one of the astromers goes mad, he cries 'Stars—all the Stars—we didn't know at all . . .'. Nevertheless, Asimov seems to be having his cake and eating it here, a result, perhaps, of producing a story to the specifications laid down by Campbell rather than according to his own wishes. Asimov usually celebrates rationality, rather than this pessimistic view of the human mind (if Lagashans are human) poised on a knife-edge between sanity and insanity.

Why, then, the story's popularity, and its status as the 'classic' sf short story? First of all, it intrigues simply on the level of a pure 'What if . . . ?' story. It proceeds in a manner not unlike Wells's 'The Country of the Blind', which, through rational explanation, subverts the common idea that 'in the country of the blind the one-eyed man is king' (apart from anything else, the blind function much better in the dark than the sighted do). Emerson's idea seems reasonable, on the face of it, but is it true? Secondly, there is the story's sweep: this is no earth-bound vignette, but a mini-saga that sets us on an unknown planet, in a distant star cluster, at the end of a millennia-long historical cycle, and at a potentially significant moment, when that cycle might be broken for ever. (The ambiguity of the ending may also contribute to its popularity, in that generations of readers have subconsciously chosen their own ending, optimistic or pessimistic, to suit their own preferences.) And thirdly, there is the ambiguous role of science. At one level we have a scientific revolution: astronomy, archaeology, and psychology have come together to explain the entire course of Lagashan history. Yet these rational scientists ignore the warnings of the Cultists about the soul-destroying properties of the Stars; their imagination stretches only to postulating a few other suns in their pocket universe (eight light-years across), and they pour scorn on the

Cultist idea of a million stars ('There just isn't any space in the universe you could put a million suns—unless they touch one another'). The story sets up the idea that scientists can control human destiny, and ends by posing in stark terms the truth that Asimov, among many other sf writers, holds to: that this universe is indifferent to humans, is uncontrollable and ultimately unknowable by either scientists or priests, and is more vast and mysterious than the human mind can imagine. The shiver of Burke's 'delightful terror' which the reader experiences as the 30,000 suns reveal themselves is a pure expression of the classic 'sense of wonder'.

The second story reveals a very different aspect of the appeal of science fiction: it is Jack Vance's 'The Moon Moth'.[47] It is a fairly straightforward detective story: a consular official, Edwer Thissell, is ordered to apprehend a notorious criminal, Haxo Angmark, who has just landed on the planet Sirene. Unfortunately, the criminal is able to blend in well with the local inhabitants, for he knows their customs, and Thissell is himself still learning. The story tells how Thissell applies logic to the (literal) unmasking of the villain.

The essence of Sirene culture is the concept of *strakh*, or personal prestige. A citizen can go into a shop and take whatever corresponds to his *strakh* (*his*: we are told nothing about the position of women in this society). There is no money, and no one would dream of exceeding his own personal level of prestige. An individual's *strakh* can best be assessed by examining the particular type of mask he wears: is it that of a Sea-Dragon Conqueror or a Forest Goblin or what? The individual's place in society is expressed in the anonymity bestowed by a mask; and anyone who went out in public unmasked would be executed immediately for such an act of gross indecency. The levels of status are also expressed in music, for all communication is formalized as music, and must be sung to the accompaniment of one of the small collection of portable instruments that a citizen of Sirene wears about his person. Poor Thissell makes mistake after mistake, like his predecessor, who, 'Masked as a Tavern Bravo . . . had accosted a girl beribboned for the Equinoctial Attitudes for which he had been instantly beheaded by a Red Demiurge, a Sun Sprite and a Magic Hornet'. Thissell at first unwittingly risks his life by appearing without a mask; he then chooses a Sea-Dragon Conqueror mask, vastly in excess of his *strakh*; and when he has finally been given his inoffensive, humble Moon Moth mask, he manages to upset several people by addressing them to a musical accompaniment inappropriate to their social status. Rolver, another outsider, is his mentor and teacher. Here he tells him how inappropriate his Sea-Dragon Conqueror mask is:

'You couldn't even walk around Fan in that regalia you're sporting now. Somebody wearing a Fire-Snake or a Thunder Goblin mask would step up to you. He'd play his *krodatsch*, and if you failed to challenge his audacity with a passage on the *skaranyi*, a devilish instrument like a baby bagpipe, he'd play his *hymerkin*—the instrument we use with the slaves. That's the ultimate expression of contempt. Or he might ring his duelling-gong and attack you then and there.'

'I had no idea that people here were quite so irascible,' said Thissell in a subdued voice.

Rolver shrugged and swung open the massive steel door into his office. 'Certain acts may not be committed even on the Concourse at Polypolis without incurring criticism.'

'Yes, that's quite true,' said Thissell.

Thissell eventually finds his man, by analysing the frequency with which different masks are worn by the various suspects, and, by what Sirenians regard as an act of supreme bravery, he brings Angmark to his death and wins for himself a Sea-Dragon Conqueror mask.

Vance, better than all modern sf writers, shows the links between modern sf and the early traveller's tale. His 'General Culture' stories and novels present an immense range of exotic cultures and societies, described with an unfailing delight in the bizarre, a dry, droll wit, and a deft use of ironic and even baroque language. (The stiff, mannered dialogue is a splendid estranging device, making the speech appear like a rather unidiomatic translation from a foreign language.) The delight the reader takes in 'The Moon Moth' has little to do with the plot (though the traditional whodunit form is better treated here than by most sf writers—as John Holbrook Vance, the author has also written award-winning detective novels); nor is science ever important in Vance—except the so-called soft sciences of anthropology, sociology, or linguistics. Yet cognitive estrangement is a major element in 'The Moon Moth' and the rest of Vance's planetary travelogues, and a major part of their charm. Exotic and superficially illogical human behaviour is shown to be perfectly reasonable and normal, and we can become so accustomed to it that we begin to question our own norms; the alien is domesticated, and thus we are estranged from our own reality. Rolver himself has become so totally acclimatized to Sirene that he dreads going back home. '"Back to the world of faces," shuddered Rolver. "Faces! Everywhere pallid, fish-eyed faces. Mouths like pulp, noses knotted and punctured; flat, flabby faces. I don't think I could stand it after living here."' Vance's reiterated message is that human nature is not a given fact, but is, instead, determined by environment, history, and culture. No one social structure or mode of behaviour can be considered 'normal'; in an infinite universe there are an infinite number of possibilities—and all are equally valid. It is a subversive, liberating, and exhilarating doctrine, and was particularly so when it first appeared in the 1950s; and that, together with Vance's wit and style, accounts for much of his wide popularity among sf readers.

The third story is 'Light of Other Days', by the Northern Irish writer Bob Shaw.[48] As Silverberg has noted, 'This small, quiet, well-nigh perfect short story shows just how much science fiction can accomplish within a span of three or four thousand words.'[49] It starts: 'Leaving the village behind, we followed the heady sweeps of the road up into a land of slow glass.' The married couple see rows of windows standing on the hillside, facing the view: farms of glass. We learn that their marriage is at the point of collapse, because of the impending arrival of an unwanted child. They turn off the road at a whim to visit one of the glass farms. They see a middle-aged man, Hagan, sitting outside the house; through a window can be seen what they take to be his young wife, with a small boy in her arms. Through the conversation with the man, and in the reflections of the narrator, we finally learn about 'slow glass', a relatively recent scientific discovery. Slow glass is highly opaque, but it absorbs and retains the light that falls on it. The light penetrates to the other side of the glass only a year or ten years later; the time depends on the thickness of the glass. Once the light comes through, the viewer sees whatever the window has absorbed. These Scottish glass farms sell a year or more's worth of a view of a Scottish valley to city-dwellers; what the purchasers see through their window is indistinguishable from what they would have seen through the window of a Scottish cottage. The narrator (the husband) decides to buy; Hagan goes off to unclip a pane from the hillside. The couple take shelter from the rain under the eaves of the cottage, and the young woman inside takes no notice of them. The narrator's wife goes into the cottage to leave inside a rug that is getting soaked; the couple see that the interior is a junk-heap, bearing little resemblance to what they had seen through the window from outside. The narrator explains to his shaken wife: 'Slow glass works both ways. Light passes out of a house as well as in.' Hagan's explanation comes as the end of the story:

'It wasn't my fault. A hit-and-run driver got them both, down on the Oban road six years ago. My boy was only seven when it happened. I'm entitled to keep something.'

I nodded wordlessly and moved down the path, holding my wife close to me, treasuring the feel of her arms locked around me. At the bend I looked back through the rain and saw Hagan sitting with squared shoulders on the wall where we had first seen him.

He was looking at the house, but I was unable to tell if there was anyone at the window.

In some ways this is little different from a classic tale by H. G. Wells. An invention is introduced (Suvin's novum), and so is one small telling result of the effect of this invention on one aspect of human life. A scientific explanation for slow glass is given, just detailed enough to be plausible. The invention is introduced alongside a presentation of a marriage in crisis; the revelation of the tragedy of the slow glass farmer's life serves to solve some, at least, of the problems of that couple's marriage. Hagan's grief has been cushioned by the existence of slow glass (but with the knowledge that one day soon, if the glass in his window is of ten-year thickness, the image of his wife and child will disappear for ever); their own marital problems and the life of their future child are thus put into perspective. The story follows all the precepts that Heinlein stipulated in 1947 (see above, p. 59); above all, it is concerned with *human* problems, not abstract technical ones. But it also introduces a note of poetry that makes it thoroughly memorable, in the marvellous first line which brings us 'along heady sweeps of the road up into a land of slow glass' and in the husband's comment about light passing out of a house as well as in. Almost the greatest value of the story, however, is in what it leaves out. That mention of 'slow glass' in the first line is not explained until nearly a third of the way through the story; the reader's imagination is already working overtime to explain the mystery. And once we understand what slow glass does, we are given few hints as to how it has affected the world. Like many other great sf stories, it incites the readers' imagination (even their sense of wonder), and urges them to participate by trying to fill in the rest of the details of the new world which must have been produced by slow glass. A writer of the Gernsback school might well have produced a story which attempted to list them all, thereby stifling the imagination of the reader. Bob Shaw certainly thought of some of the other possibilities (he described them in the novel *Other Days, Other Eyes*, 1972). But in this story he restricted himself to the production of one fine vignette, and the reader is left intrigued, wondering, entranced—not sated or bored.

4 The SF Community

The Growth of Fandom

Sf fandom is a subculture which had its origins in the United States, but is now to be found in most developed countries throughout the world. Since the late 1920s sf fandom—the body of enthusiastic and committed readers of sf—has had an appreciable and unique, if unmeasurable, impact upon the evolution of sf, influencing writers, producing the genre's historians, bibliographers, and many of its best critics, and, above all, producing many of the writers themselves. There is no branch of literature where the contact between reader and writer has been so close, and the interaction so strong, over so long a time. Fandom is what has helped American sf attain its individual voice; American fan culture has been imitated in other parts of the world, alongside American sf itself. For better or worse, it has helped to mould the sf culture of today.

The origins of sf fandom, as Sam Moskowitz has argued,[1] go back to the days before sf had gained its name. Editors of general fiction magazines before 1926 noted the considerable enthusiasm among their readership for 'different stories', and as soon as Gernsback started *Amazing Stories*, he was 'overwhelmed by the tremendous amount of mail we receive from—shall we call them "Scientifiction Fans"?—who seem to be pretty well oriented in this sort of literature'.[2] *Amazing Stories* and *Amazing Stories Quarterly* assisted these isolated enthusiasts to come together into the beginnings of an organized fandom. Gernsback established a 'Discussions' section in the January 1927 issue of *Amazing*, and began publishing readers' addresses so that they could get in touch with each other. By 1929 a number of science correspondence clubs had been founded in various parts of the

United States, and some of them started producing their own magazines, like the *Planet* in New York (1930) and *Cosmology* on the West Coast. Gernsback declared himself very ready to publish addresses of clubs and reports on their progress, but insisted (in an editorial in the Summer 1929 issue of *Amazing Stories Quarterly*) that it was up to readers to organize their own clubs. A few years later he changed his mind, beginning to see the commercial possibilities of playing a rather more active role. In 1934 he used his editorials in *Wonder Stories* to create the Science Fiction League, which would soon have chapters in the major cities and regions. The first overseas chapter of the SFL was formed in Leeds, in Yorkshire (1935), followed shortly afterwards by the Nuneaton (Warwickshire) chapter and then by chapters in Melbourne and Sydney. The League did not last long (although its emblem is still used by First Fandom, those individuals who became fans in the 1930s and whose enthusiasm has continued into the 1990s), but several of the chapters evolved into local sf societies with long histories in front of them. Fans met for discussions. They began collecting sf books and magazines, the foundation of collections that would sometimes, thirty or forty years later, be larger than those in all but a very few of the world's public or university libraries (a slogan still to be seen on fans' T-shirts is 'The one who dies with the most books wins'). They corresponded furiously. They wrote endless letters of praise or forthright condemnation to the professional magazines. They published their own fan magazines (later, 'fanzines'). They began developing their own jargon; sometimes they 'gafiated' (left fandom, to 'get-away-from-it-all'), but many of them continued their 'fanac' ('fannish activity') for many years, content to aspire to 'fiawol' ('fandom-is-a-way-of-life'), although some secretly admitted to 'fijagh' ('fandom-is-just-a-goddam-hobby'). Above all, or so it seems today, they quarrelled. Sam Moskowitz's history of early fandom, *The Immortal Storm* (1954), details the course of some of these epic storms in a teacup (one of which has been mentioned above, on p. 64). His book has been called 'an extraordinary and outstanding (if quite unintentional) study in small-group dynamics', while James Gunn commented that it has been said that it 'may be the only book . . . in which World War II comes as an anticlimax'.[3]

The Science Fiction League was an attempt to put fandom on a national, or even international, basis, although its first result was the foundation of local groups, such as the Philadelphia Science Fiction Society, the Los Angeles Science Fantasy Society, and, unforgettably, the San Francisco society that took its name from the *Barnaby* comic strip: the Elves, Gnomes and Little Men's Science Fiction Chowder and Marching Society. National fandom really got under way when these local groups began meeting one another. Fan mythology has remembered the bus trip in 1937, when a group of New York fans went to meet sf fans in Philadelphia, as the symbolic beginning of greater things: the beginning of the endless round of fan conventions that had evolved by the 1980s and 1990s to such an extent that, for example, there were sixteen nationally advertised conventions taking place in North America during the month of October 1992. But if this Philadelphia meeting *was* the first American sf convention, America was forestalled in any bid to have had the world's first sf convention. That was held on 3 January 1937 in Leeds, when a number of British fans gathered together from various parts of the country, including Arthur C. Clarke, Walter Gillings (editor of a serious fanzine and subsequently of Britain's first sf magazine, *Tales of Wonder*), E. J. Carnell (later editor of the fanzine *Novae Terrae* and then of the long-lasting British sf magazine *New Worlds*), and Mike Rosenblum, the Leeds fan from whose fanzine, the *Futurian* (1938–40), the celebrated New York fan group (see pp. 64 and 138) took its name.

Two years later Sam Moskowitz organized the self-styled first World Science Fiction Convention in New York (see above, p. 64). The following year, in 1940, the World SF Convention was held in Chicago, and several of what remain traditional features of major conventions made their appearance: songs were sung—old tunes, with new science-fictional words (a genre much later to be known as 'filksong'); mock weapon-fights took place in hotel corridors; crowded hotel room parties went on until early morning, and a banquet was organized; there was even a masquerade, at which fans and writers dressed up as their favourite sf characters (a regular feature ever since, and an ideal occasion for the media to find photo opportunities which they can use to ridicule the event and the genre.) There was a guest of honour, E. E. 'Doc' Smith, whose speech must have delighted the assembled fans, and not only because Smith, by now a veteran writer, counted himself as one of them, saying:

The casual reader does not understand science fiction, does not have sufficient imagination of depth or breadth of vision to grasp it, and hence does not like it. What brings us together and underlies this convention is a fundamental unity of mind. We are imaginative, with a tempered analytical imaginativeness which fairy tales will not satisfy. We are critical. We are fastidious. We have a mental grasp and scope which do not find sufficient substance in stereotypes, in the cut and dried. Science fiction fans form a group unparalleled in history, in our close-knit though informal organisation, in our strong likes and dislikes, in our partisanships and our loyalties. The necessity of possessing what I may call the science-fantasy mind does now and probably always will limit our number to a very small fraction of the total population. In these personal meetings, there is a depth of satisfaction, a height of fellowship which no-one who has never experienced it can even partially understand.[4]

The World SF conventions have been annual since 1939, apart from the years 1942 to 1945. The 'World' suffix was a totally grandiose claim, of course, akin to the 'World Series' in baseball; the World SF conventions (worldcons) in fact remained in North America until 1957, when the venue was London; thereafter the worldcon visited London again (1965), Heidelberg (1970), Melbourne (1975 and 1985), Brighton (1979 and 1987), and The Hague (1990), but otherwise stayed in North America. The growing internationalization of the world conventions has mirrored developments in fandom itself; but even more striking has been the growing size of the attendance at these conventions. New York in 1939 (subsequently named Nycon I) attracted 200 fans; Loncon I in 1957 drew 268 (not much fewer than most worldcons in the USA during the 1950s); Conspiracy in Brighton in 1987 drew 5,300; and Noreascon III in Boston in 1989 attracted 7,700. The scale of the worldcons, and of the national and regional conventions too, changed drastically during the 1970s; so did the scale and the style of fandom, as we shall see in the final section of this chapter.

In the beginning, through the 1940s and beyond, fandom was small. There were only a few hundred active fans in the United States in the 1930s and 1940s, and only a few dozen in Britain and Australia. As Smith's speech suggests, those few regarded themselves as an élite, the vanguard in a movement which was virtually religious in nature. The feeling is perhaps best expressed not in the relatively measured tones of 'Doc' Smith, but in the words of fans themselves. In 1935 the 16-year-old fan David A. Kyle (who, at the Chicago convention five years later, appeared as Ming the Merciless, Flash Gordon's arch-enemy, and won the masquerade competition) answered the Science Fiction League's question 'Why do you read science fiction?' thus:

The common people of the world have been noted for their obsolete views concerning the advancement of science; despite persuasion, they will not swallow anything that is beyond their infinitesimal brains. But science fiction changes that—the sheer power of magnificence that will leave the reader vainly wondering what he is on this wee tiny Earth. The force of science-fiction can never be equalled by any other type of story. When I finish a science-fiction yarn, I feel overwhelmed with thoughts that surge in my brain. Can it ever be true? Will such things ever come to pass? The glorious heights that the reader soars to make one realize why there are such active fans. Science-fiction makes one think—to ponder on the whole universe. Is it a wonder that science-fiction is an opiate?—to feel that exuberant thrill course through your body; to feel your sense rise and your pulse beat stronger. Ah, deep is the love . . . Science is stupendous. The huge thoughts that we humans try to understand, to analyze, are great. Science-fiction has the ability to grasp me and to whirl me up—up—up into the realms that dominate the cosmos. A fiction that gives fact, food for thought, and yet contains exciting adventure, is indeed a marvellous fiction. It is a fiction that is intelligent and that educates, not toward the bad or immoral things, but for the future advancement of the people of the world. Why do I read science-fiction? Ah! Feeble are the words to express such a great subject![5]

Sf fans banded together not so much because they enjoyed reading sf, but rather because they had a particular sweeping vision of the place of humanity in the universe and of the tremendous potential which the future offered, which set them apart, they felt, from the humdrum world of the ordinary people around them. They were passionately committed to a technocratic approach to the world's problems. Like Gernsback, they thought that sf had an educational mission which was at the forefront of the progress of society towards a better world. Sf fans were the missionaries, and if at times they might refer to the infinitesimal brains of non-sf readers, at other times they certainly believed that it was their duty to proselytize and to win some of those brains over.

It is not difficult to extend the analogy suggested in the last sentence, and to see sf and sf fandom as fulfilling many of the functions of a religion. Few sf fans are notably religious in the traditional sense. For most of them the discoveries of science and the realization of the immensity of the universe have destroyed any illusion that the traditional Judaeo-Christian God is looking after the world; when God and the Bible appear in sf, it is usually for satirical purposes. But science itself, and the awesome prospects of time and space which it reveals, offered the sf fan the 'sense of wonder' as a substitute for those feelings of sublimity, awe, and mystery which can be found at the heart of most religions. The near-religious experience when wonder is encountered is something that the fan feels less and less frequently, as his or her senses become jaded; but the search for further experiences often keeps the fan reading. (Older fans have always complained that sf is no longer as good as it used to be; whereas it is rather that the sense of wonder becomes dulled with repetition.) Fandom, like religion, also provides a sense of community, in the coming together of like-minded people (not infrequently after long travel, as in a medieval pilgrimage) and in communication by letter and by fanzine. That sense of community is fostered by the feeling that fans possess a truth which is denied to outsiders (although disagreement over the finer points of the truth can lead to the declaration of heresy and the onset of sectarian warfare); it is also bolstered by the sense of persecution engendered by the mockery and disdain of 'mundanes' (non-fans) for fannish activities and for sf itself. It is not surprising that Van Vogt's *Slan* (1940), with its telepathic slans, superior to *Homo sapiens* and persecuted by them, should have appealed so much to sf fans; it gave its name to Slan Shack, a fannish commune founded in 1943 in Battle Creek, Michigan (with the inscription 'Civilization' set up above the front entrance), and to fanzines such as *Slantasy* and *Slant*. Like many slans, fans wanted to take over the world: to persuade people of the educative and mind-expanding properties of sf and to help to move the world faster in the direction of what they perceived as scientific progress. It is worth adding too that sf readers tend to find their own answers to the traditional questions that religion is supposed to answer. Christian leaflets commonly picture faces in a crowd asking questions like 'What am I here for?', 'What is the world coming to?', and 'What is the point of it all?' If those are the questions which religions try to answer, then sf supplies responses too: in order, 'To survive, and to achieve'; 'Read sf and find out'; and 'Why on earth do you presume to think there has to be a point to it all?'

Fans had side interests, of course, apart from the promotion of sf. In pre-war days, fandom tended to overlap with groups interested in scientific experimentation and particularly with rocketry. To continue the religious analogy, the fannish version of the Promised Land was outer space. The experiments of Goddard and the German Interplanetary Society during the 1920s and 1930s inspired numerous fans: for example, Arthur C. Clarke, experimenting as a teenager with home-made rockets in his parents' Somerset garden, and later combining fandom and sf writing with his secretaryship of the British Interplanetary Society (founded in 1933).

Other fannish activities were more directed to sf itself. In the 1940s, almost no hardback sf was published by the main American publishing companies; this was left to small-scale speciality houses founded by fans. In 1946 Lloyd A. Eshbach founded Fantasy Press, which published such authors as John W. Campbell and E. E. Smith and, in 1947, the first book about modern sf. David Kyle and Martin Greenberg started Gnome Press in 1948, and gave first publication to Asimov's 'Foundation' books; during that year Shasta, founded by three Chicago fans, published *The Checklist of Fantastic Literature*, the first of the fundamental sf and fantasy bibliographies produced by Everett F. Bleiler (the most recent was published in 1990).

It was indeed from the fannish community, and not from academia, that the first scholarly study and criticism of sf emerged. Some of the early fanzines, notably Claire P. Beck's *Science Fiction Critic* (1935–8), themselves published serious and informed criticism. One of the best-known pieces of early criticism, later named 'Cosmic Jerrybuilder', was written by an ex-Futurian and writer, Damon Knight, for the fanzine *Destiny's Child*; it was a relentlessly thorough demolition of *The World of Ā*, by the then revered Van Vogt, contradicting Campbell's claim that it was a 'once-in-a-decade' classic by arguing that it was 'one of the worst allegedly-adult science fiction stories ever published'. Knight's collected reviews, published in 1956 by Advent (another Chicago-based fan publishing house), formed the first book of criticism of contemporary sf, a milestone in the evolution of the serious evaluation of the genre, and an important lesson to fan reviewers of the then prevalent 'gosh-wow' school of criticism. Although prone to 'gosh-wowwery' itself, the pioneering work on the early history of American sf and fandom by Sam Moskowitz also deserves to be mentioned. In addition, fans laid the foundations for future academic work in other ways, with the compilation of important reference and bibliographical works. Most notable of these, apart from Bleiler's *Checklist*, was probably Donald B. Day's *Index to the Science Fiction Magazines, 1926–1950* (1st edition, 1952), but the early work of the Australian fan Donald H. Tuck (*A Handbook of Science Fiction and Fantasy*, 1954) was also important.

The Community of Writers

There is little doubt, however, that the most significant contribution of fandom to sf was the production of writers. A high proportion of active sf fans aspire to be published writers of sf; and a high proportion of published writers of sf have emerged from fandom.

I have already mentioned the early group of New York fans called the Futurians. This relatively small group at the end of the 1930s included people who subsequently became some of the most important writers and editors in the field: Isaac Asimov, James Blish, Damon Knight, Cyril Kornbluth, Judith Merril, Frederik Pohl, and Donald A. Wollheim. British fandom of the late 1930s also produced some of the most significant writers of the 1940s and 1950s, including Arthur C. Clarke, William F. Temple, and Sam Youd (who writes as John Christopher).

The fannish urge to write frequently took the form of self-publication: the production of a fanzine, duplicated as well as finances and contemporary technology would allow, and frequently written largely by the editor. Many major sf authors first saw publication in the pages of fanzines, and often in those that they themselves edited.[6] James Blish began publishing the *Planeteer* in 1934, when he was 14. Ray Bradbury began *Futuria Fantasia* in 1939, persuading people such as Heinlein and Kuttner to write for him. Robert A. Lowndes, a Futurian, a writer, and later a prolific editor, began with his fanzine *Le Vombiteur*. Algis Budrys, probably better known as a critic than a writer today, began by publishing *Slantasy*, at the age of 15. Frederik Pohl was 16 when he launched *Mind of Man*. Robert Silverberg edited *Space Ship*; Marion Zimmer Bradley edited *Mazrab*; Harlan Ellison edited *Science Fantasy Bulletin*; Gregory Benford, with his brother Jim, edited the long-lived fanzine *Void*. It was probably between 1935 and 1965 that this phenomenon was most prominent; this was the period when the production of a fanzine was the archetypal fannish activity.

If would-be writers did not gain their experience writing for their own fanzines, then they could write for others. Fanzines provided an ideal opportunity for honing writing skills and a relatively private forum for receiving criticism. Walt Willis, for instance, was a Belfast fan whose fanzines *Slant* (1948–53) and *Hyphen* (1952–65) were reckoned to be among the best of their kind, partly because of his own humorous prose; but it is notable also that James White and Bob Shaw, two of the only three sf writers to have come from Northern Ireland, were able to publish much of their early writing in Willis's fanzines.

Nearly all writers of sf have been readers of sf from an early age. It is important to consider how the experience of fandom might change their attitude towards the writing of sf; but in many ways, from the point of view of the development of the genre of sf, early exposure to sf was just as important as membership of the fannish community. A young reader learns a great deal about the expectations of the genre, about the standard themes and viewpoints, and about the kinds of plots and dilemmas which are exciting and intriguing. The early experience of reading sf, essential though it has been in the education of sf writers, may thus impose serious limitations, by implanting restricted views of the nature of sf and of its read-ership. Not a few professional writers have achieved success by writing basically what would have appealed to their adolescent selves. If that adolescent reader then manages to learn about and contact fandom—not necessarily easy to do for the average young reader—then the situation may grow worse. Fandom will introduce the reader to knowledge of the traditions and the classics of the field; it will enforce an internal view of those traditions. It may well also impose the idea that the most im-portant thing for a would-be writer is to be original; but originality, for most fans, means generating original ideas, not original in terms of the nature of fiction or narrative, but as regards novum, plot-line, story gimmick, exotic planet, or col-ourful alien. Fan critics have established originality—or, better, novelty—as one of the greatest challenges to the writer (and, as the weight of the accumulated fiction of the past grows and grows, one of the most difficult to fulfil), and have also, on the whole, been severe on anyone who has attempted to be 'original' by emulating the literary techniques of the 'mainstream' writer.

The effects of fandom upon writers are mixed, therefore. On the one hand, writers will encounter their readers, in large and unusually articulate numbers. Through frequent meetings with enthusiastic readers, at club meetings or conventions, writers of sf can have a much clearer idea of the kind of reader they are writing for than most writers have; most 'mainstream' novelists hardly ever meet the 'ordinary' reader. In one sense, of course, fans are not 'ordinary' readers of sf. Fans form only a minute percentage of the total readership of an Isaac Asimov or an Arthur C. Clarke novel; they are the 'fanatic' minority, who are in a position to meet the authors they read. They tend to be voracious readers both inside and outside the field, and are frequently highly informed readers as well. Many have encyclopaedic memories for science-fictional trivia, and may remember writers' work somewhat better than the writers do themselves; they may well be prepared to discuss it, at length, and not necessarily favourably. Fans are frequently bright, iconoclastic, and knowledgeable: ideal sounding-boards for new ideas and stimuli for further thought about plot or fictional environment. But there is another side to the question. Fans provide a degree of adulation which writers may find very flattering, and which offers encouragement to writers simply to produce more of the same. Fans, as much as publishers, encourage authors to write yet more stories or novels set in the same universe and to produce the endless series which, from the 1970s, have become more and more a part of the sf publishing scene; many sf readers like meeting the same characters again, while many genuinely enjoy seeing the author explore further the possibilities of his or her imagined universe. Fans, while mouthing the received wisdom about the importance of originality/ novelty, may deter writers from venturing into new territory. They may well, however, offer them ideas and suggestions about future stories; critics and historians of sf are unlikely ever to know the extent to which individual works of sf are in fact the result of unconscious collaboration between writer and fan, the eventual outcome of a long conversation with a group of fans in a convention bar in the small hours of the morning.

Because of fandom, there have always been close connections between writers and readers; the connections between writers and other writers are also very important, and again exist to a much greater extent within sf than elsewhere in the writing world. Writers are frequently close friends, and often have been since their early days in fandom. Writers who are not close friends see each other relatively frequently at conventions and, increasingly, academic conferences.

There are also more formal occasions for writers to exchange ideas. Over the history of sf, sf writers have not infrequently been editors of magazines, and thereby have had an opportunity to provide an input (welcome or otherwise) into the published work of other writers. Sf writers seem more prone to collaboration than writers of other types of fiction. Collaborations, which in the past probably took place in smoke-filled rooms, are as likely now to be done by exchanging floppy disks or by writing over the computer network or by fax. They have produced some classic sf: the partnership between Frederik Pohl and C. M. Kornbluth is the most famous, while that between husband-and-wife team Henry Kuttner and C. L. Moore is the most difficult for posterity to disentangle. More recently there have been Larry Niven and Jerry Pournelle, Frederik Pohl and Jack Williamson, William Gibson and Bruce Sterling, and Terry Pratchett and Neil Gaiman. Nowadays, collaborations have even become posthumous, or much delayed. Thus Robert Silverberg has written a novella which looks at C. L. Moore's story 'Vintage Season' (1946) from a different character viewpoint; Silverberg has also written a novel which forms a sequel to Isaac Asimov's short story 'Nightfall' (published as *Nightfall*, by Asimov and Silverberg, 1990); while *Beyond the Fall of Night*, as by Arthur C. Clarke and Gregory Benford (1990), was in fact Clarke's *Against the Fall of Night* (1948) with a sequel by Benford.

This type of collaboration—participating in an author's fictional creation—is the 'shared-world' phenomenon. This is by no means restricted to sf; for instance, writers (some of them sf writers) have for a long time written stories and novels set in Conan Doyle's world of 221B Baker Street. But the 1980s saw a boom, and many would say a plague, in this type of writing within the sf field. The world that Isaac Asimov created in *The Caves of Steel* (1954) was packaged by Byron Preiss and became the basis of the *Isaac Asimov Presents Robot City* series, to which several authors contributed. Marion Zimmer Bradley has herself edited several volumes of stories written by various authors, all set in her own Darkover world. Several volumes of short stories have been published filling in some of the background to the conflicts between men and the alien kzin in Larry Niven's

'Known Space' series. Isaac Asimov has justified such operations, saying that

> sharing literary universes is as old as literature [cf. the worlds of Homer, or of King Arthur], that it has always permeated modern science fiction writing, and that properly done, it enables old relics like myself to help other people, particularly young writers. I don't think that's so bad.[7]

Asimov conceals the fact that sharing universes in a strict sense is a fairly recent, and highly commercial, development; but he also highlights another aspect of the community of sf writers not so far touched on. Established sf writers have often been extremely helpful and encouraging to younger writers, seeing them not as potential rivals, but as younger members of the extended family of sf.

The community of sf writers has been strengthened in other ways during the last few decades, in the context of the teaching of the craft of sf writing. A key word is Milford. In 1956 the first annual science fiction writers' conference was held at Milford, Pennsylvania, where the leading light was the writer and critic Damon Knight. One had to be a published writer to participate, but editors also attended, and consequently there were accusations over the years of favouritism, élitism, and of the existence of a 'Milford mafia'; but it achieved considerable affection among its devotees. When one of its founders, James Blish, moved to England, he created, in 1972, its British equivalent, at a little seaside resort favoured only by its name: Milford-on-Sea, Hampshire.

In 1967 Robin Scott Wilson, a published writer, came to Milford, Pennsylvania. He was also a professor of English, and he brought from Milford the idea of a six-week summer school for would-be sf writers. The first of these was held at his own Clarion University, in Clarion, Pennsylvania (1968); in 1971 'Clarion West' was founded at the University of Washington in Seattle, and 'Clarion East' moved out of Clarion[8] and in 1972 settled in East Lansing, at Michigan State University. East Lansing and Seattle still host the Clarion workshops, and between them, over the last twenty years, they have trained several hundred aspiring writers. A considerable proportion of

American sf writers under 45 are alumni of Clarion; the six weeks of producing short stories to order for the ferocious scrutiny of fellow students and teachers has helped to give those alumni a great sense of camaraderie (similar to that produced by prisoner-of-war camps). Denunciations of a 'Clarion mafia' ring rather more true than did those of a Milford mafia.

It has also been alleged that one of the results of the Clarion workshops has been a change in the nature of American sf. It has coincided with, but not necessarily created, the change in the origin of American sf writers. In the 1930s and 1940s the majority of sf writers were trained as scientists or engineers, or had gone straight from high school into one of the professions. From the 1960s onwards, the majority of American sf writers had read English, literary concerns taking precedence over scientific ones. There is also the so-called Clarion credo: an emphasis on rounded characterization, clear expression, a strong internal logic, a narrative driven by a situation of conflict—all of which, it is alleged, result in formulaic writing in which the *point* of sf writing, to communicate the archetypal science-fictional idea, is lost.[9]

Another offshoot of Milford has been even more significant in bolstering the sf writer's sense of community: the Science Fiction Writers of America (SFWA). It was founded in 1965, and the first president was Damon Knight, convinced by his Milford gatherings of the need for some permanent organization of sf writers, not just for exchanging information, but also for helping writers deal with publishers and agents. 'Science fiction' has always been interpreted very broadly (and in 1992 fantasy was officially added to the title of the organization). The same broad interpretation applies to 'of America'; foreign nationality is no bar, and SFWA has effectively become an international writers' union. The utility of belonging to the SFWA is, however, much more obvious if, as a writer, one is intending or hoping to penetrate the US market; here the advice and contacts provided by the SFWA can be useful.

One attempt to broaden the international appeal of the SFWA was a serious mistake, at least in terms of the publicity it received and the deep divisions it revealed within the community of writers. This was the so-called Lem affair. The Polish sf writer Stanisław Lem was invited in 1973, by the SFWA executive, to be an honorary member. In 1975 one of Lem's articles highly critical of American sf was published in the United States and republished in the *SFWA Forum*. He argued that in literary terms the sf most prized in the United States was rubbish—and worse: it was a 'cultural cancer'.

Most science fiction is to authentic scientific, philosophical, or theological knowledge as pornography is to love.

To me pornography is not evocative of erotic stimulation but of gynecology and anatomy, which I once studied. Similarly science fiction does not convey to me the fate of man strapped in his own devices but rather removes itself from human concerns through deceptive ballyhoo. I have nothing against entertainment, even if it is nonsense. But idiocy that passes itself off as Faustian mythology is a cultural cancer.[10]

The end of the article implies that Lem is, in fact, against entertainment. He quotes Frederik Pohl's advice in an *SFWA Bulletin*—'Think of Heinlein's warning—we are competing for our readers' beer money'—and argues that 'honest literature can never conform to external pressures or exigencies'.

Of course it is embarrassing to learn that publishers still pay 2 cents a word—the same as in 1946—while books have doubled in price during the same period, along with the salaries of editors, printers, and all others on the production end with the exception of authors. These data I have gathered from the SFWA Bulletins. Unfortunately a bad standard of living is no excuse for bad literature.

Lem has never allowed truth as he sees it to take second place to tact. Members called for his immediate expulsion from the SFWA. It was felt that he had dishonoured sf, and the fact that he was a foreigner and a Communist was an unspoken, but ever present, factor. A solution was found: it was argued that he (and, before him, Tolkien) had been eligible for ordinary membership, and hence should be removed from honorary membership—for non-payment of dues. (Ursula Le Guin commented: 'Tolkien has not been expelled yet, possibly because he is dead.'[11]) Of those members of the SFWA who responded to a poll, 15 per cent argued for an apology to be made to Lem,

15 per cent abstained, and 70 per cent voted for his expulsion. The affair caused a great deal of bad feeling and a number of resignations. It was a reminder, if one was needed, that sf writers do not always see eye to eye. But it also demonstrated with what strength of feeling sf writers defended their craft and their community from what was seen as external attack. Lem's criticisms were highly plausible, and hit them at a vulnerable point, even though his assault on the deadening effects on art of the capitalist system do not actually make much sense for the majority of members of the SFWA, who do not make their living from writing. Sf writers, and the academic critics who were becoming more and more numerous in the 1970s, were still spending a great deal of energy attempting to justify sf in terms of its literary quality, and Lem's attack from his inside position as an sf writer seemed to many to be the work of a traitor.

Another long-running and almost continuous controversy indulged in by the SFWA also speaks volumes for the sf community. In 1965 it was decided that the SFWA should sponsor annual awards for the best sf novel (over 40,000 words), novella (17,500–40,000 words), novelette (7,500–17,500 words), and short story (under 7,500 words); these would be called the Nebula awards. In theory, since they would be awarded according to the judgement of fellow writers, the Nebulas should go to a different type of work than the Hugo awards. The latter, named after Hugo Gernsback, first given in 1953 and still the main awards in the sf field, were awarded on the basis of votes cast by the fans registered for each year's worldcon. In practice, Nebulas and Hugos go to the same type of works, or, indeed, the same works, and there have been frequent accusations that the Nebulas are given to those with the most friends and/or the best political skills. Even though the number of votes cast in either case is not large, 'Hugo-Winner' or 'Nebula-Winner' printed on the cover of a book still increases sales, and it is well worth the publisher's time and money to target individual SFWA members on behalf of a particular book. The award-winning novels and stories do, nevertheless, give the historian a good idea of those works which these two sections of the sf community regarded as the best in a particular year; the awards annually affirm the literary ideals and values of the whole sf community. The winners generally belong to the group of writers content to be categorized as sf writers, and are almost invariably American; one has to look to more recently established awards, like the Arthur C. Clarke Award, decided by a small panel of 'experts', to find awards being given to 'outsiders', to writers such as Margaret Atwood and Marge Piercy.[12]

The SFWA, an abbreviation which since 1992 has denoted the Science Fiction *and Fantasy* Writers of America, forms the core of the sf community. Full membership is theoretically gained only by selling three short stories or one full-length novel to a 'professional' market in the United States (that is, for short stories, to magazines with a circulation of more than 12,000). It has two journals, the *SFWA Bulletin*, which is available to the public, and the *SFWA Forum*, which (theoretically) is not; the *Forum* is where the more bitter of the internal wrangles generally take place. But an even more obvious expression of the professional sf community than either of these SFWA publications—because it is more public—is the monthly magazine called *Locus: The Newspaper of the Science Fiction Field*. Published by Charles N. Brown, in Oakland, California, for over twenty-five years, it is here that sf writers, publishers, and editors can learn of the latest publishing deal, read reviews of the latest fiction, see photographs of their friends and colleagues, and hear their gossip—the finishing of their latest novel, their change of agent, their change of marriage partner. Like the SFWA itself, it interprets sf very broadly, by including fantasy, and horror to some extent. If one wants to understand the sf industry, a year's subscription to *Locus* is as good a way of doing it as anything else.

One final aspect of the sf community to mention here (and to touch on again in the final chapter, p. 198) is, in literary terms, perhaps the most interesting of all: recursiveness. Writers may, and often do, signal their membership of the sf community by making reference to the sf tradition within their fiction itself. The term 'Tuckerism' (after Wilson Tucker) is used of references to actual members of the community, fans or writers, in the course of a fiction: mere in-jokes. A number of the characters in James Blish's *Black Easter* (1968), for instance, have the names and personalities of other sf writers. True recursiveness is the borrowing of elements—plots, characters, planetary environments, technological gizmos—from other sf writers, or indeed from oneself. In Robert A. Heinlein's late novels, for instance (notably in '*The Number of the Beast*—'), one meets many characters from Heinlein's earlier fiction, as well as characters from other novels. In some cases apparent self-referentiality merely reflects the fact that the future will be aware of the sf writers of the twentieth century; thus Kim Stanley Robinson, in *Red Mars* (1992), calls the communities at the two ends of his sky-hook space elevator Clarke and Sheffield, after the two writers who, independently of each other, in 1979, simultaneously produced the 'first' novel to feature a space elevator. But in most cases sf writers make references to other works of sf to establish themselves in the tradition of genre sf and their place in Wollheim's consensus future (see above, p. 88). In a broader sense, sf writers from within the community are indulging in intertextuality on a massive scale; we shall look at some examples of this in the final chapter. Sf authors' texts refer, often quite obliquely to dozens or hundreds of other texts which they and their readers will have read. They may make reference to other works to debate them or criticize them. They may be simply borrowing icons or images from other works, which nevertheless will have the intended effect of setting up resonances with the rest of the field. Whatever the reason, the effect is to make it clear to their readers that they are members of the community.[13]

Beyond the Fringe

Another community exists alongside, and overlaps and interacts with, the sf community. It is often called 'the lunatic fringe'. Brian Aldiss has written of the special purgatory reserved for sf authors:

They have to endure conversations with people who assume automatically that they believe, as do their interrogators, in Flying Saucers and telepathy and Atlantis and the Bermuda Triangle and God as astronaut and acupuncture and macrobiotic foods and pyramids that sharpen razor blades.[14]

Most sf writers, and many sf readers, are sceptics and professional agnostics, who have a reasonable amount of knowledge of, and hence little respect for, such views. At the same time, there is also a strong tendency among sf readers (and some writers) to react with almost as much annoyance to the apparent dogmatism and conservatism of scientists as to the irrationality of the unconventional and the pseudo-scientific. Scientists have often been proved wrong by the arrival of new, radical ideas; sf readers often enjoy thinking of themselves as the standard-bearers of those new ideas. A cool observer like Martin Gardner expressed the problem pungently when, in the early 1950s, he wrote about one of John W. Campbell's pseudo-scientific editorials in *Astounding*:

How far from accurate is the stereotype of the science-fiction fan as a bright, well-informed scientifically literate fellow. Judging by the number of Campbell's readers who are impressed by this nonsense, the average fan may well be a chap in his teens, with a smattering of scientific knowledge culled mostly from science fiction, enormously gullible, with a strong bent towards occultism, no understanding of scientific method, and a basic insecurity for which he compensates by fantasies of scientific power.[15]

Like it or not, the strong connection between sf and what we may call the 'pseudo-sciences' still persists. Sf has unwittingly given birth to a number of cult beliefs which have been accepted by an audience wider than the sf audience; sf's greatest impact on the twentieth-century world may be indirectly communicated by those people who present science-fictional ideas as fact.

The unpalatable truth is that sf presented as fact reaches a far wider audience than sf published as fiction. The classic example is that of Whitley Strieber, an sf and fantasy author who succeeded in achieving enormous financial success as a writer only when his book *Communion* (1987) was published as autobiography. It told of his abduction by aliens in a flying saucer, dwelling, as many such abduction accounts have done,

on the intimate examination inflicted on him by the aliens.[16]
Strieber swears that his account is genuine; his experiences are
indeed echoed by others—abductees who have not had a career
as professional sf writers, but who have indeed accepted what
one might describe as a science-fictional view of the world. The
flying saucer cult is one of the corners of the field of pseudo-
science which owes a great deal to the permeation of our culture
by science-fictional ideas.

There are problems with the term 'pseudo-science', of course.
It arrogantly assumes that the science in question is 'wrong'
and not, as its protagonists declare, years ahead of its time.
Pseudo-scientists themselves make much of the fact that some
great names of establishment science were themselves derided
or even suppressed in their day, Galileo being their hero. But
'pseudo-science' is not just wrong science, science that has been
rejected or not yet proved by acceptable scientific means; it is
'science' that depends on intuition and emotional response rather
than scientific method. Its adherents are normally totally convinced of their beliefs. Their beliefs are held to even more firmly
under the pressure of rational argument, which only convinces
them that conventional scientists are involved in a conspiracy
to conceal the truth from the world. The conspiracy theory is
widespread among pseudo-scientists and their followers; and
the increasing complexity of science and its remoteness from
ordinary people, as well as the increasing domination of science
and technology—to the point where it threatens humanity itself—are undoubtedly major factors in the growing popularity
of the pseudo-sciences in the industrialized world. Pseudo-
sciences can offer simplicity; a return to, or a substitute for,
traditional religious values; and a possible salvation from nuclear
war (via flying saucer saviours); they can even offer that
comforting feeling of being a persecuted, but superior and
morally right, minority. The similarities with sf fandom itself
are notable.

Sf authors exhibit a complex attitude towards pseudo-science.
Occasionally they have viewed it with undisguised glee and,
without believing a word of it, have constructed stories set in
a pseudo-scientific locale: examples would be Barrington J.

Bayley's 'Me and My Antronoscope', which adopts the splendid idea adhered to by some pseudo-scientific cults that we all live inside a bubble of air in a universe largely made of solid rock, and Philip José Farmer's 'Sail On! Sail On!', in which Columbus sails over the edge of a flat earth.[17] But sometimes the question of belief is more difficult to resolve. There have been a number of sf writers heavily influenced by that ambiguous patron saint of pseudo-scientists, Charles Fort. Fort, who died in 1932, spent his last twenty-six years in libraries, researching oddities: rains of blood or frogs, unexplained disappearances, prodigies of all kinds. His findings were published in four books, one of which, at least, by being serialized in *Astounding*, reached a considerable sf readership. His explanations were bizarre. Red-tinged rain, he suggested, might be produced by a haemorrhage in the living being that forms the sky, or perhaps by a huge invisible being hanging in space which has been injured by another. Why do stars twinkle? Stars are holes in the sky, and the sky is made of a gelatinous substance which wobbles, producing the twinkle effect. Fort, actually, had a highly developed sense of humour (rare among real pseudo-scientists), and he took none of his ideas very seriously; all he shared with pseudo-scientists was a desire to make people distrust the pronouncements of conventional scientists. But he did have a wide influence among sf writers. The English writer Eric Frank Russell is the most notable example; he once declared that his three favourite authors were 'Charles Fort, Charles Fort and Charles Fort', and that each of them was 'the greatest genius sf ever had'.[18] Russell certainly used Fort's suggestions (notably that human beings were the property of aliens) as a source of plot inspiration, but not necessarily as a source for genuine explanations of the universe. Annoyance at what were perceived to be the closed minds of scientists and at their reluctance to involve themselves in the investigation of, for instance, psychic phenomena often caused sf writers to follow up Fortean ideas in the 1940s and 1950s; like Fort, they campaigned against the closed mind, whether of the scientist or of the pseudo-scientist.

Psychic phenomena—telepathy, psychokinesis, precognition—were a regular area for science-fictional discussion, particularly

under the influence of John W. Campbell, jun., who believed in
ESP (or psi) and in the efficacy of pseudo-scientific gadgets for
measuring or amplifying those powers, like the Dean machine
and the Hieronymus machine. The mid-1950s was the first great
age of ESP stories, including some of the best novels in the
field, like Alfred Bester's *The Demolished Man* (1953) and
Theodore Sturgeon's *More than Human* (1953). But the mid-
1950s were also the period when Professor J. B. Rhine was busy
publicizing his apparently successful ESP experiments at Duke
University, which made ESP, for a brief period, scientifically
respectable; sf authors were only doing what some of them saw
as their job—presenting to the public the results and possible
consequences of the latest scientific research. The next brief
revival of ESP came in the 1970s, in the wake of renewed interest in the mystic and the occult, but also alongside the re-
appearance of well-known scientists, such as John Taylor, who
were prepared to give credence to the claims of Uri Geller and
his spoon-bending followers. ESP again, very briefly, brushed
the margins of scientific respectability. Thus ESP is not quite
like those other pseudo-sciences that I am dealing with: it
plays at the frontiers of known science, and does not confront
them head on; and although it no doubt panders to the wish-
fulfilment fantasies of readers, it has not become the focus of
a popular cult. That is one of the distinguishing features of the
great pseudo-sciences, which has been neatly expressed by Isaac
Asimov's corollary to Clarke's law. Arthur C. Clarke advanced
the proposition that 'when a distinguished but elderly scientist
states that something is possible, he is almost certainly right.
When he states that something is impossible, he is very probably wrong.' Asimov's corollary ran: 'When, however, the lay
public rallies around an idea that is denounced by distinguished
but elderly scientists and supports that idea with great fervour
and emotion—the distinguished but elderly scientists are then,
after all, probably right.'[19] Asimov was thinking of Immanuel
Velikovsky's theories that biblical events could be explained by
close encounters with the planet Venus and other bodies,
theories which became deeply rooted in popular awareness only
after being denounced by scientists of all kinds (who should

have had the good sense to ignore him, as biblical scholars seem to have done).

The most obvious example of a pseudo-scientific cult with the closest links to sf is that connected with flying saucers, or unidentified flying objects (UFOs). Ufology can be a proper science; there are serious scientists who investigate the possible scientific, sociological, or psychological explanations for UFO sightings. But it is also a pseudo-science; some who purport to study UFOs scientifically have constructed a system of beliefs which contradicts the beliefs of conventional scientists and familiarly regards such scientists as conspiring against the truth. The semantics associated with the acronym UFO themselves conspire in that direction. 'Do you *believe* in UFOs?' is a question which means 'Do you believe in flying saucers, piloted by beings from beyond this world?' and not 'Do you believe that there are aerial or astronomical phenomena which are at present imperfectly understood?' In fact, the phrase 'flying object' immediately prejudges the issue, since we do not think of the planet Venus or unusual cloud conditions or electrical phenomena—all common and possible explanations of UFOs—as either flying, or indeed objects.

The phrase 'flying saucer' was born in the summer of 1947. It was not long before explanations of these phenomena—soon seen over large parts of the world—were drawn out of the clichés of sf. The most popular and lasting is that they are the spacecraft of a wise race which watches over humanity and hopes to avert the disasters which threaten Earth. For the United States in particular, fear of communism and fear of the atom bomb both played a role in the flying saucer hysteria of the first cold war era; this could be seen a secular science-fictional version of a belief in the coming of the Messiah.

Sf writers were, initially, perfectly happy to jump on the UFO bandwagon, and a host of stories appeared in the late 1940s and early 1950s in sf magazines, which extended the range of UFO mythology and introduced ideas which were immediately seized by the UFO fraternity—a fraternity which seems to have overlapped with the sf-reading community quite extensively at the time. UFOs fitted neatly with some contemporary sf obsessions, notably those associated with Richard S. Shaver. Shaver was a Philadelphia welder who published a number of 'articles' in *Amazing* from March 1945 onwards, which he claimed were genuine visions or memories of the super-races, Titans and Atlans, who lived in Lemuria in the distant past, but who had left Earth to the inferior humans because of harmful radiation coming from the Sun. Some of these supermen had stayed behind and degenerated into evil beings who, from their underground laboratories, created most of humanity's evils; those who escaped now kept a benevolent watch upon the world. The Shaver stories dramatically increased readership for *Amazing*; the magazine was overcome with Shaver mania, which culminated in the special Shaver issue of June 1947. That was the very month that the Idaho businessman Kenneth Arnold saw saucers in the sky over the Rockies and began UFO mania. The Shaver mythology rapidly assimilated UFOs and, to the consternation of authors and readers who took sf seriously, *Amazing*'s editor Raymond Palmer began to devote himself more and more to the flying saucer cult. He founded the occult magazine *Fate*, and then a new sf magazine called *Other Worlds*, which, by 1957, had become *Flying Saucers from Other Worlds*.

The origins of Shaver's ideas are fairly clear; not only had he read sf widely, but he had also certainly absorbed some of the ideas of Madame Blavatsky, the founder of theosophy in the later nineteenth century, who had written widely (and imaginatively) on the lost races of Atlantis and Lemuria. Her vanished continents have made frequent appearances in sf, and recur in many pseudo-scientific and occult variants, sometimes in a very science-fictional guise. The educationalist Rudolf Steiner, for instance, made clairvoyant contact with Atlantis, and discovered it to have airships and many of the trappings of a superior technological civilization—this was a commonplace in the sf of the 1930s and 1940s. By the time Kenneth Arnold saw his flying saucers, there was a whole array of beliefs in place to explain what he had seen.

These explanations were greeted with a mixture of amusement and annoyance by sf writers at the time. Many sf readers undoubtedly fell for the flying saucer craze initially; after all, wasn't contact with aliens exactly what they had been waiting for? But subsequent developments convinced most of them otherwise, particularly the well-publicized claims of George Adamski and others in the early 1950s that they had actually met the pilots of UFOs. Anyone who had read a modicum of sf and thus imbibed some basic astronomical and astronautical facts could only have greeted Adamski and his kind with laughter; Adamski's *Flying Saucers Have Landed* (1953) had to be published as non-fiction, for it was so full of clichés and scientific ignorance that even Raymond Palmer would have been unlikely to take it as sf. The first flying saucer religion emerged in 1954, when George King received the message that he was to be the earthly spokesman for the benevolent Interplanetary Parliament, and as a result founded the Aetherius Society. Sf writers and editors became more and more wary of the theme, to the extent that flying saucers could no longer appear on the covers of books or magazines, lest they offend the sf reader and mistakenly attract the UFO believer. Some major novels of the early 1950s, such as Clarke's *Childhood's End* (1953), drew on the UFO mythos; by the early 1960s an sf writer could do so only in a tongue-in-cheek manner, as Fritz Leiber did in *The Wanderer* (1964), which offers an affectionate look at a group of UFO believers of different types: pseudo-scientific, mystic, and prophetic. More recent sf versions of the UFO have been even more complex, such as Ian Watson's elaboration of the Jungian explanation for UFOs in *Miracle Visitors* (1978) or Steven Spielberg's film *Close Encounters of the Third Kind* (1977), which Thomas M. Disch has convincingly analysed as a conscious allegory of religious experience.[20] Flying saucer enthusiasts continue to draw on sf imagery. For instance, Andrija Puharich, the biographer of Uri Geller, has managed to contact 'the Nine', the committee who control the universe (one might have guessed it was run by committee!), via a medium in Poona, India. It was revealed that their appointed agents on Earth were to be Puharich and Geller. Messages from the Nine appeared mysteriously in 1972, on a tape recorder that was not even plugged in. Mass landings of UFOs will soon take place, they announced, 'but the landings might be invisible'. (They were.)[21]

The most successful of those who have presented the sf mythos as truth have been Erich von Däniken and L. Ron Hubbard. Erich von Däniken is one of the most successful authors of all time, with over fifty million copies of his books published, in most Terran languages, beginning with *Chariots of the Gods?* (1968). His sincerity has been questioned, in part because a great deal of what he writes reads so much like self-parody that it often seems consciously witty. In a *Playboy* interview of 1974 he admitted: 'in some parts I mean what I say seriously, in other ways I want to make people laugh.'[22] Those who treat him seriously—those who believe every word, or those who become academically outraged—have the wrong approach. After all, he even quotes sf novels as authorities in the bibliographies of some of his later books.

The von Däniken technique has been described by one reviewer as 'an old cosmic recipe: simply *ad astra*, mix feverishly, and half bake'.[23] The plot is simple. At some time or times in the past, beings from other worlds have visited Earth. They have left memories of themselves in ancient legends and religions (gods were really alien visitors), and they have left mementoes of themselves not only in the art of prehistoric and primitive man, but in monuments such as (inevitably) the pyramids. *Homo sapiens* does not deserve the distinguishing adjective: almost anything original in human civilization or even in human imagination has in fact been supplied by beings from outer space. Most of the obsessions of the occultists and pseudoscientists have been included—Egypt, Atlantis, Stonehenge, the Kabbalah, Madame Blavatsky's *Book of Dzyan*—and he adds Easter Island, the Nazca Plain symbols from Peru, Ezekiel's fiery chariot (a spaceship, according to him), and leaves it to his English imitators to add the inevitable ley lines and Glastonbury. He is depressingly unimaginative and ill-informed when it comes to the 'Great Mysteries'. How could huge blocks of stone be manœuvred into place to build the Great Pyramid, save by occult or extraterrestrial force, particularly when the Egyptians did not know how to make rope? (He ignores archaeological discoveries of Egyptian rope, and the well-known tomb paintings of massive statues, far larger than the building blocks of the pyramids, being dragged along by slaves, helped by ropes and sledges.) He is also depressingly unoriginal. So many of his ideas, if not all of them, had already been put forward, usually quite unseriously, by sf writers. The role of superior alien beings in the development of human history has had a long life in sf. The related motif of the seeding of man on earth by aliens has become the ultimate sf cliché, above all in the so-called Shaggy God variant (where the two space travellers who crashland on an unpopulated planet turn out to be called Adam and Eve): this is still reputed frequently to find its way from would-be writers to editor's desks, and thence into the wastepaper basket. It is no doubt comforting to those who believe that the traditional mythologies have no place in the modern world to imagine that, out there, there are planets inhabited by folk like us, and even to imagine that they maintain a benevolent watch over us (from their flying saucers). The advantage of this space-age religion is that the Bible need not be abandoned; all that needs to be done is to reinterpret it, in a perfectly literal but science-fictional sense.

Von Däniken is not the only author to have achieved bestseller status with such ideas, nor was he the first: Immanuel Velikovsky's *Worlds in Collision* (1950) had already reinterpreted Old Testament history in terms of catastrophes brought about by near-collision with a comet (eventually moving into solar orbit as the planet Venus), which, among other things, parted the Red Sea and deposited edible hydrocarbons (manna) from its tail into the desert for the waiting Hebrews. Such ideas, derided by scientists and sf writers alike (von Däniken's severest critics have been sf writers John Sladek and John Brunner[24]), have had great influence throughout the world in the last two decades. Those unskilled in separating fact from fiction (let alone biblical criticism) have clearly found that they provided a satisfying explanation of the inexplicable world in which they find themselves. Research conducted among 13-year-old boys in British public schools in 1983 showed that the idea that Jesus Christ may have been an alien from another planet was taken seriously by many boys; quite a number believed that Ezekiel and Christ had both ascended to the heavens in a spaceship.

One pupil had written, 'I think God is a scientist, and we are his experiments', a theory that would have delighted Charles Fort![25]

For sf religion in its most developed form—with clergy, hymn singing, and churches—one need look no further than L. Ron Hubbard, an immensely prolific writer of sf and other fiction in the 1940s. Sf editor Sam Merwin recalled that 'he was exceedingly anxious to hit big money—he used to say that the best way to do it would be to start a cult'; someone else remembered him in a group gathered around John W. Campbell's kitchen table, saying, 'I'd like to start a religion. That's where the money is.'[26] By 1950 he had invented the 'science' of dianetics (see above, p. 71) which so captured the imagination of John W. Campbell and numerous sf readers. Dianetics was a method of bringing an individual to a state of mental health without using the detested methods of modern psychoanalysis; the terminology was in part drawn from the then infant science of computing. When all the harmful engrams (memories of past traumatic experiences) had been erased from the patient's memory banks by a process of auditing—later compared to the confession procedures of Christianity—that person became a 'Clear'; the IQ was raised, the health improved beyond credibility, and there was full control of bodily processes (teeth could be regrown) and of the mind. The links between dianetics and sf stories about people with super-powers—indeed, Hubbard's own sf stories of supermen—are obvious; there are numerous stories written during the 1930s and 1940s which concern the development of superhuman mental powers, involving either intelligence or ESP. Hubbard had problems finding enough people who could be plausibly presented as 'clears'; he sought to explain this, for the benefit of initiates, and in 1952 published *The History of Man*, an elaborate science-fictional frame for his burgeoning cult. Engrams could be acquired by an individual not only at any time from conception onwards, but during any previous incarnation; auditors must listen to an individual's memories of all past lives, going all the way back to the simple organisms of the Precambrian era. (Many harmful engrams arose at the clam stage.) Once all possible engrams had been audited, the total Clear was 'an Operating Thetan'. The Thetans are the masters of the universe: omnipotent and immortal beings, who created worlds for a hobby. But, billions of years ago, they had begun to find this boring (Hubbard, who had created worlds throughout the 1940s, at a hack writer's rates, no doubt sympathized). To relieve their boredom, Thetans voluntarily denied themselves some of their powers, and began to live in the universe they had created for themselves. When doing so, they became enmeshed with the material universe, and forgot their previous existence. They passed from one being to another, leaving their host shortly before death and reporting to an implant station on Mars while waiting to pick up another body. By now, of course, they were inhabiting human beings rather than clams. Hubbard's methods could help people make contact with their Thetan 'souls', and thus with immortal and potentially omnipotent beings. Auditing to this depth was a long process, of course; Hubbard did not have to produce an Operating Thetan on the spot.[27]

The move in 1952 from vague theories about engrams to a scientific certainty involving the past history of the universe mirrored the move that year from dianetics (the Dianetics Institute in Wichita was in financial trouble) to scientology. The story of Hubbard and scientology is well known, and mostly remote from the sf world (although throughout he had his personal admirers among both writers and fans). Scientology became the Church of Scientology in 1954; by 1959 it had prospered enough for him to buy, from the Maharajah of Jaipur, the Saint Hill estate in East Grinstead, Sussex. This remained his headquarters until the later 1960s, when he founded the Sea Organization, and began lengthy cruises around the world. This move did not completely avoid the constant investigations for fraud or income tax evasion which had plagued him since scientology began. In 1980 he went into complete seclusion. Some thought that he was dead; his son tried to obtain a legal injunction declaring him dead. In 1986 he did actually die, in California, and that, perhaps, is where he had been all along. By then Hubbard himself was irrelevant; the sf religion of scientology was in other hands, and was a multi-million-dollar operation.

During his last years, Hubbard again entered the world of sf. His first sf novel for over thirty years, *Battlefield Earth* (1982), became a best-seller, thanks partly to massive promotion by the Hubbard organization. *Mission Earth*, a ten-volume serial (Hubbard called it a 'dekalogy'), published by the scientologists' own publishing house (Bridge in the USA, New Era in the UK) ranged over a similar array of Hubbard targets (psycho-analysts, liberals, feminists), and was similarly violent, insensitive, and amoral. It sold very well—but, one suspects, more to scientologists than to sf readers. Alongside this attempt to rehabilitate Hubbard as a writer was the attempt to promote Hubbard as a benefactor of sf. Since 1984 the Hubbard organization has spent quite a lot of money on 'Writers of the Future', a contest with cash prizes and ensured publication, for new writers of sf; it has more recently been joined by 'Artists of the Future', for sf artists. Various well-known sf writers, such as Algis Budrys, Gregory Benford, Jack Williamson, and others, were enrolled to act as judges for the contest and to lend their respectable names to the Hubbard enterprise. This promotion came to the attention of a wide group of people at the World SF Convention in Brighton in 1987. The organizers had allowed New Era Publications to sponsor the convention booklet, which thus appeared with the clenched fist logo from Hubbard's *Mission Earth* series on its cover, and had also per-mitted Algis Budrys to make a speech at the opening ceremony which included considerable praise for the late Hubbard and much publicity for Hubbard's 'Writers of the Future'. New Era succeeded in giving some people the impression that the scientologists were sponsoring the entire convention. Prolonged booing and hissing greeted the announcement of Hubbard's name as a nominee for a Hugo Award, and subsequently there was much controversy among fans and writers, and, apparently, a realization on the part of New Era and Bridge that such open efforts to gain respectability for the Hubbard name were counter-productive.

Fandom Today

The sf community can be defined in a number of ways. Clearly those who borrow an sf book from the public library every now and then, or who occasionally buy an sf paperback on the strength of the author or the cover, are not part of that community. Those who read widely and intelligently, who recognize the authors they like, and have some awareness of the breadth of the field, are unintentionally part of an sf community, in the sense that they probably understand the way the genre's conventions operate and they may even share in the general belief systems adhered to by sf writers, even if they do not actually take part in any communal sf activities. Only a few of these readers become fans: those whose love of the genre makes it their major hobby, and impels them to join with other fans in fannish activities, whether simply meeting in local groups to talk about sf or publishing their own fiction or book reviews or attending sf conventions. Sf writers, editors, and publishers form the core of the sf community; they also admit (though perhaps on sufferance) those other people who make their living from sf, such as critics and academics. But fans have been the life-blood of the community, if only by providing the time and the energy to enable the sf community to get together, on the printed page or in the hotel meeting room.

Fandom today is distinguished from the fandom of the 1960s and earlier by its size, its diversity, and the prominence of media fandom as opposed to 'print fandom'. Fandom is no longer a small-scale enterprise, undertaken by people who are in general accord with regard to their interests and aims. No longer is there a basic canon of texts and lore which fans have in common, and the sense of mission has evaporated. In large part this is due to the enormous diversity and size of the sf publishing industry itself; since the 1960s it has not been possible for individual readers to keep up with the bulk of what was being published in the English language. (The old fannish spirit may be more alive in those countries where publishing is still restricted, where only a small core of Anglo-American sf has been translated, and where fandom is a relatively recent development: Bulgaria or Brazil, for instance.) But there has also been a tendency for the activity of some fans to concentrate not on the entire sf field, but on some aspect of it. Thus, there are fanzines and conventions which concentrate not on the work of Marion Zimmer Bradley as a whole, but specifically on Darkover (the world about which Bradley has written in many of her books). Most particularly, however, there has been fan activity based on a number of sf television series; there are *Doctor Who* fans, on both sides of the Atlantic, and fans of *The Prisoner*, the surreal British sf mystery which ran for seventeen episodes in 1967. But there is one television series which has created a fan industry which puts all others into the shade: *Star Trek*.

NBC started broadcasting *Star Trek* in September 1966. The first series achieved no great critical acclaim, except within the sf community. Harlan Ellison, along with a number of other professional writers, spearheaded a letter-writing campaign to save the series in December 1966. A second season began in 1967; again by December there were rumours of cancellation, and this time fans ensured that a flood of letters—more than a hundred thousand—reached NBC. The third series went ahead in 1968, but there was no renewal. Seventy-eight episodes, plus a pilot, were broadcast in all. It was not long before those episodes were syndicated across the United States, and sold all over the world; they have been rerun ever since. The typical *Star Trek* fan today owns all of them on video (legitimately or otherwise), and knows them by heart. Novels set in the *Star Trek* universe, featuring the same characters, began to appear; a TV cartoon series ran for a time; the series of full-length movies began in 1979; and the original cast began to move visibly towards retirement age. *Star Trek: The Next Generation* began in 1987, providing a whole new array of characters, and has transmitted many more episodes than the original; although some say that it is often better than the old version, it seems to have been received with mixed feelings by a fan audience, of all ages, still wedded to 'Classic Trek'. In 1993 a third *Star Trek* series, *Star Trek: Deep Space Nine*, began transmission.

Organized *Star Trek* fandom began with the letter-writing campaign of the winter of 1967–8. The first *Star Trek* convention was organized in New York in 1972, by a group of fans who expected a few hundred people: 3,000 attended. A further letter-writing campaign took place in 1976. After receiving some 400,000 letters, Washington agreed to the naming of the first of NASA's space shuttles after *Star Trek*'s *USS Enterprise*. By the late 1980s *Star Trek* conventions, in the United Kingdom as well as the United States, had become frequent, and well attended; but they were often organized as commercial operations. The fans—Trekkers or Trekkies—are consumers much more than traditional sf fans are. Similarly, *Starlog*, originally a fanzine dedicated to *Star Trek*, has now become a professional magazine (and broadened itself to cover media sf as a whole). *Star Trek* fans have become a commercial market, targeted by those selling books, signed portraits of the stars, Space Fleet costumes in which to parade at convention time, models of the characters or of the space hardware, and so on. There is some overlap between *Star Trek* fans and fans of other brands of media sf, and *Star Trek* fandom draws a certain amount from the traditions of sf fandom; but sf fans and *Star Trek* fans are effectively two different communities, with very different agendas.

What is the appeal of *Star Trek*? It is obvious that, as with any long-running series with an unchanging cast of main characters, viewers become fascinated by the characters. The interrelationship between Captain Kirk (played by William Shatner) and Mr Spock, the pointy-eared Vulcan alien (Leonard Nimoy), is central to the appeal of the series; they are two well-defined and attractive characters, with human failings and alien mysteries, whose strong emotional bond is usually suppressed, or understated by the use of irony and humour. Kirk and Spock alone may account for a hitherto unknown phenomenon in the history of fandom: the fact that the majority of *Trek* fans were, and are, women. (It was the discovery, very early on, that many women found Spock fascinating that led to the decision not to drop him from the series—because of a fear that Americans would find his 'devil's ears' upsetting—but instead to 'promote' him in Kirk's team from number four to number one.[28]) The appeal of *Star Trek* to women had considerable importance for the growth of a role for women in sf, as writers and readers, during the 1970s and 1980s. *Star Trek* almost certainly introduced more women to sf than did the slow emergence of feminist sf, which occurred at the same time as the growth of *Trek* fandom, in the first half of the 1970s.

As sf, *Star Trek* was usually unremarkable. It tended to use sf clichés and to repeat itself, and only occasionally (though not only in the episodes written by professional sf writers, like Harlan Ellison, Norman Spinrad, and Theodore Sturgeon) did it achieve any sort of originality. But it incorporated some of the finer points of the American sf of the past and of the liberal wing of American politics in the 1960s. The crew of the *Enterprise* is multiracial; the episode "Plato's Stepchildren" even includes American network television's first interracial kiss, between Kirk and Lieutenant Uhura. (Bigots can take heart; they were forced into this unpleasantness by evil beings who have the power of mind control.) Crew members are dedicated to the 'Prime Directive', which forbids interference in other people's cultures. Above all, *Star Trek* shows that humanity can improve, that society can change, and that there is a final frontier to be crossed and conquered. *Star Trek* embodies, in unadulterated form, the optimism in humanity and faith in progress which was so characteristic of American sf up to the 1960s.

The commercialization of *Star Trek* has not destroyed the amateur activities of its fans; indeed, it may have stimulated it. There are numerous fanzines devoted to the series, and hundreds of amateur novels, with limited circulation, have been written. One of the strangest branches of *Star Trek* fans are the 'slashers', writers and connoisseurs of the amateur writing known as K/S fiction. The 'K' and 'S' stand for Kirk and Spock; the slash designates the sexual relationship between them (like the amateur S/H fiction which concerns itself with an imagined sexual relationship between Starsky and Hutch). Romantic, erotic, or pornographic fiction concerned with Kirk and Spock seems to be almost entirely produced by heterosexual women, and has caused a certain amount of perplexed comment from cultural critics. The *Star Trek* universe gestures towards gender equality (there are women on the bridge of the *Enterprise*), but in a half-hearted way; if a strong-minded woman appears, she is generally evil. It has been argued that female *Trek* fans can imagine a sexual relationship between strong, good characters, and between equals, only by projecting it upon Kirk and Spock. It has been suggested that K/S fiction portrays the pair as androgynous; but it seems that their maleness is emphasized, yet not their gayness. Even their sexual intercourse is portrayed in terms which resemble heterosexual intercourse, yet without either partner being dominant. In this manner K/S fans can identify with either Kirk or Spock, and their relationship can be seen in the context of the liberal utopia of the *Star Trek* universe. This is summarized by the fans' adoption of the acronym IDIC, which expresses Vulcan philosophy—'Infinite Diversity in Infinite Combination'. Even the love between Kirk and Spock has something futuristic and utopian about it: the Vulcan mind-meld allows them to become emotionally much closer than any pair of human lovers, male or female. Their love has problems, however, thanks to Spock's alien biology. The creator of *Star Trek*, Gene Roddenberry, has reported the comment of 'the real Kirk': 'I would dislike being thought of as so foolish that I would select a love partner who came into sexual heat only once every seven years.'[29]

There are general sf conventions which welcome all the many varieties of fandom; but just as common now are the specialist conventions: conventions for Trekkies (a nudist *Star Trek* convention was reported in 1992), for fantasy fans, for fans of Douglas Adams's *Hitch Hiker* series, for fans of filking (sf folk-singing), for sf film fans. There are even conventions specifically for written sf (excluding media fans)—and conventions for people who organize conventions.

All these, as has been said, are recent developments. But also recent, and even more interesting in cultural terms, is the development of sf conventioneering on the American model over much of the world. There are conventions all over Western Europe, in Brazil, in Japan, and in many parts of the former Communist world. Who, a few years ago, could have imagined that in August 1990, 150 Russians would gather near the Siberian town of Krasnoyarsk, for a week of Hobbit Games, role-playing Tolkien's *Lord of the Rings*? or that a group of Moscow fans would set up barricades at the time of the abortive coup in 1991 under the banner 'Frodo is with us'?[30] Or that in July 1992 a week-long 'sf creation camp' would be held along the banks of the Danube, on an island in the Danube, and on ships moored in the Danube, near Cernavoda in Romania?[31] Recent reports of East European conventions suggest that many of the elements of a traditional American convention have been transported overseas. Volgacon (held in Volgograd in September 1991) attracted some 300 fans and fifty or more writers, editors, and publishers. Book dealers set up their wares wherever they could find space, and there were sessions at which American sf authors signed copies of their books; this occurred only two years after most Western sf authors were known only through illegally circulated samizdat translations.[32] At Lituanicon, in Kaunas, in June 1992, many of the institutions of the Anglo-American convention could be found. There were hotel room parties, like the one thrown by Boris Sidyuk, editor of the English-language Ukrainian fanzine *Chernobilization*. There was a fancy dress competition, with three categories (Lithuanian mythology, aliens, and film and book characters). There was an art show, an auction, role-playing games, a film show, and drinking. The representatives of Swedish fandom at the convention presented the editors of *Kaukas*, the first professional Lithuanian sf magazine, with a second-hand computer. The computerized world of American sf fandom in the 1990s (with innumerable sf bulletin boards on Internet and highly professional desktop-published fanzines) has yet to come to Eastern Europe. On the other hand, Lithuanian fandom has moved beyond the established capitalist countries in succeeding to attract commercial sponsorship to pay for the hotel rooms of foreign visitors.[33] The reciprocal arrangements for East European visitors to Western conventions are much less formal, but are impressive in another way. At the worldcon at the Hague in 1990, scores of East European fans arrived, with hardly any money at all. Western fans staffed a welfare desk, collecting funds to pay for their food and lodging. The feeling of community among sf fans, at its best, transcends national and political divisions.

The present state of sf fandom directly mirrors the developments in sf which I examine in the next chapter. Sf in the English-speaking world is really no longer one genre, but a set of sub-genres, each with its own protocols and its own loyal readers. Print-based sf is no longer dominant; sf film and sf TV have large groups of devotees (and, of course, reach a very much wider audience than would ever read an sf book). There are some in America who belong to organizations dedicated to promoting space exploration and colonization, but far fewer fans are interested in the space programme or see technology as the saviour of the human condition than would have been the case twenty or thirty years ago. The sense of sf's mission, which Gernsback and Campbell promoted, has gone. The fragmentation of sf and of sf fandom could be related to the fragmentation of culture at large, the replacement of widespread values and loyalties by smaller, more specialized subcultures, which some see as the most typical feature of postmodern or postmodernist culture. But I wish to end with Eastern Europe where, for a very long time, sf had often been used as an expression of subversive attitudes towards the régime and of alternative approaches to the orthodox future, for there, sf fandom, though small, still has the vitality and a sense of shared purpose that, thirty years ago, could have been found in Britain or the United States.

5 From New Wave to Cyberpunk and Beyond, 1960–1993

The New Wave

Historians of sf seem to agree that the 'classic years' of English-language sf were the 1940s and 1950s. Writers like Asimov, Bester, Bradbury, Clarke, Heinlein, Sturgeon, and numerous others produced some of their finest work, and set the agenda for what still constitute the core concerns and themes of sf. By the early 1960s, however, there were some writers and readers who felt that these themes were played out, that sf was becoming too inward-looking, and was losing its excitement and relevance. This reaction, generally termed the 'New Wave', was in part a generational change. Most of the 'classic' writers had begun writing before the Second World War, and were reaching middle age by the early 1960s; the writers of the so-called New Wave were mostly born during or after the war, and were not only reacting against the sf writers of the past, but playing their part in the general youth revolution of the 1960s which had such profound effects upon Western culture. It is no accident that the New Wave began in Britain at the time of the Beatles, and took off in the United States at the time of the hippies— both, therefore, at a time of cultural innovation and generational shake-up—nor that the classic anthologies were called *England Swings SF* (1968, edited by Judith Merril) and *Dangerous Visions* (1967, edited by Harlan Ellison).

In April 1963 Michael Moorcock contributed a guest editorial to John Carnell's *New Worlds*, Britain's leading sf magazine, which effectively announced the onset of the New Wave.

Science fiction has gone to hell and Kingsley Amis is mapping it.[1] The fans shout that s-f isn't what it was (which is true) and critics are treating it seriously at last (which is kind) . . .

Let's have a quick look at what a lot of science fiction lacks. Briefly, these are some of the qualities I miss on the whole—passion, subtlety, irony, original characterization, original and good style, a sense of involvement in human affairs, colour, density, depth and, on the whole, real feeling from the writer ...

Let us hope that there will always be writers only capable of helping us escape from the ordinary world for a few hours—on the other hand there will always be writers who will want to do more than this, who will want to appeal to *all* the reader's senses, to strip away as much illusion as possible, to show things as they really are and to do so masterfully, with passion and craftsmanship. This is the science fiction writer I am interested in—but as yet he hardly exists.

There are signs, however, that he is beginning to come into existence—that adult writers are beginning to write adult stories and that the day of the boy-author writing boys' stories got up to look like grown-ups' stories will soon be over once and for all ...[2]

He mentions four writers as particularly promising: J. G. Ballard (whose *The Drowned World* was reviewed in the same issue of *New Worlds*), E. C. Tubb, Brian Aldiss, and John Brunner. The first three had been given their first chances, and much of their more substantial publication thereafter, in Carnell's magazines. Although Carnell was quite a conservative editor, he was also someone who had his own ambitions for the genre, and was prepared to encourage innovation. Not only did he publish the early Ballard stories, but he also serialized a number of American novels which would probably have escaped Moorcock's censures and which in a sense looked forward to the New Wave—notably Philip K. Dick's *Time Out of Joint* (1959), the first of his great novels to question the nature of our own reality, and Theodore Sturgeon's *Venus Plus X* (1960), which, some ten years before Ursula Le Guin's *The Left Hand of Darkness*, imagined a society of hermaphrodites whose social harmony and lack of aggression made them superior to ourselves.

Moorcock soon had a chance to put his ideas into effect. Carnell's three sf magazines had been slowly declining in sales, largely because of the growing paperback boom. In 1964 Carnell relinquished *New Worlds* and *Science Fantasy*, and recommended Michael Moorcock as new editor of the former. Moorcock's editorial control lasted, through several financial crises, from 1964 to 1969. The last issue of the magazine was effectively number 200, in 1970; but the name stumbled on, intermittently and in various guises, until 1979 (and Gollancz revived the name in 1992). Under Moorcock the magazine constituted the cutting edge of Anglo-American sf. For the first time, stories published in a British magazine began to win the major sf awards in the United States: Moorcock's own 'Behold, the Man' (1966), a controversial story in which the crucified Christ turns out to have been a twentieth-century time-traveller, and two stories by American writers, Samuel R. Delany's 'Time Considered as a Helix of Semi-Precious Stones' (1968) and Harlan Ellison's 'A Boy and his Dog' (1969). Moorcock gathered around himself a group of talented British writers—like Barrington J. Bayley and David I. Masson—but also recruited a new generation of American writers, such as Samuel R. Delany, Thomas M. Disch, and John Sladek, all of whom came to London to live, to share in the excitement of those years. Other American writers were published in *New Worlds*, notably Harlan Ellison, whose publishing career had begun in the 1950s, but whose classic stories, in the late 1960s, were very much in the New Wave mould, and Norman Spinrad, whose *Bug Jack Barron* was serialized in *New Worlds* in 1967–8 (leading directly to the banning of the magazine by the leading newsagent, W. H. Smith, because of its violence and profanity).

Moorcock was determined to breathe new life into British sf, to break with the old science-fictional clichés, and to put sf on a par with 'mainstream' literature. His writers were inspired by the avant-garde writers of the previous decade; the fringe sf of William Burroughs, like *The Naked Lunch* (1959), *The Ticket that Exploded* (1962), and *Nova Express* (1964), was particularly influential. There was also a rejection of many of the sf themes of the past. As Ballard had written in Carnell's *New Worlds*, in another early manifesto for the New Wave:

Science fiction should turn its back on space, on interstellar travel, extra-terrestrial life forms, galactic wars and the overlap of these ideas that spreads across the margins of nine-tenths of magazine s-f. Great writer though he was, I'm convinced that H. G. Wells has had a disastrous influence on the subsequent course of science fiction . . .

Similarly, I think, science fiction must jettison its present narrative forms and plots . . .

The biggest developments of the immediate future will take place, not on the Moon or Mars, but on Earth, and it is *inner* space, not outer, that needs to be explored. The only truly alien planet is Earth.[3]

Ballard claims that devices such as time-travel and telepathy hinder, rather than assist, the writer's imagination, and urges writers to move away from the physical sciences that have dominated sf and turn towards the biological sciences, which will provide room for imaginative exploration of the human condition; that is the task of the writer, not the exploration of the universe. 'Accuracy, that last refuge of the unimaginative, doesn't matter a hoot.'[4]

'Inner space' was a term which had been invented in 1953, by J. B. Priestley, and been applied by him to the stories of Ray Bradbury (someone who even in the heyday of Campbellian sf didn't himself give a hoot for scientific accuracy).[5] Now 'inner space' became the watchword of the British New Wave and the shibboleth by which one recognized those who had abandoned Gernsback and Campbell. Sf should no longer be an exploration of the possibilities for humanity and science in the future or an educational introduction to aspects of science wrapped in the sugar coating of plot and adventure. Sf should not be an exploration of a hypothetical external reality, because objective reality is, in the post-Heisenberg world (and in the world of Timothy Leary and mind-altering drugs), a dubious concept. (One suspects that the advocates of 'inner space' also felt that the playfulness of the exploration of hypothetical external realities was not a serious enough concern for literature.) Sf should be a means to explore our own subjective perceptions of the universe and our fellow human beings. If a 'cosmonaut of inner space', as Ballard termed himself, has aims which are not unlike those of the serious writer, then the method he employs is very different. Sf writers could learn from the surrealists (whom Ballard greatly admired) to juxtapose the realistic and the totally unexpected and fantastic, in order to force the reader to perceive humanity afresh and from a different angle; sf writers could learn from Jung to explore images and icons, not just to understand the personal unconscious better, but also to investigate the collective unconscious. The landscapes which Ballard created in his various attempts to destroy the world—*The Drowned World* (1962), *The Burning World*, otherwise known as *The Drought* (1964), and *The Crystal World* (1966), or the decaying artists' resort of the far future in *Vermilion Sands* (short stories from the 1960s, collected in book form in 1971)—were all landscapes of the mind, whose psychological effects on the protagonists were almost secondary to their psychological effects on the readers.

The American perception of the typical British New Wave story, shared by many British readers, was described by Christopher Priest:

The writing would be obscure to one degree or another. There would be experiments with the actual prose: with grammar, with viewpoint, with typography. There would be reference to all sorts of eclectic sources: philosophy, rock music, newspaper articles, medicine, politics, automobile specifications, etc. There would be a 'downbeat' or tragic resolution to many stories, if any resolution at all. There would frequently be explicit descriptions of sexual activity, and obscenities were freely used.[6]

J. G. Ballard's 'You: Coma: Marilyn Monroe' might stand as a typical example.[7] It is one of his 'condensed novels', in which Ballard explored the 'media landscape'—modern icons like Marilyn Monroe or Kennedy ('The Assassination of John Fitzgerald Kennedy Considered as a Downhill Motor Race') or Reagan ('Why I Want to Fuck Ronald Reagan')—in a series of related or apparently unrelated snapshots, focusing on a mysterious sleeping woman and a character called Coma, set on a typical Ballardian landscape of a deserted beach. Here is one section:

The Persistence of the Beach. The white flanks of the dunes reminded him of the endless promenades of Karen Novotny's body—dioramas of flesh and hillock; the broad avenues of the thighs, piazzas of pelvis and abdomen, the closed arcades of the womb. This terracing of Karen's body in the landscape of the beach in some way diminished the identity of the young woman asleep in her apartment. He walked among the displaced contours of her pectoral girdle. What time could be read off the slopes and inclines of this inorganic musculature, the drifting planes of its face?

If this extract is not typical, it at least represents some of the problems that the New Wave had in coming to terms with sf, and vice versa. Ballard's clinical descriptions resemble the physical descriptions of the universe to be found in traditional sf, and yet they have totally other, metaphorical intent. Some other *New Worlds* writers use science-fictional and scientific language and imagery to describe perfectly 'ordinary' scenes of life, and by doing so produce altered perceptions of reality in the reader. Probably the best instance of this is Pamela Zoline's fine story 'The Heat Death of the Universe', in which the daily chores of a housewife and her mental collapse are seen in terms of entropy and the inevitable decay of matter from order into chaos.[8] 'But is this sf?' readers asked. 'Is this readable? ... Is this even comprehensible?' Other contributions to *New Worlds* were much more accessible, like the stories written by Moorcock and other writers about Jerry Cornelius, the amoral chameleon-like anti-hero of the Swinging Sixties. But even these proved too much for many sf readers, so far removed were they from the normal concerns and approaches of sf writers.

Brian Aldiss, one of Carnell's most respected young authors, was a supporter of Moorcock's *New Worlds* during its times of financial peril, and in such novels as the highly experimental *Report on Probability A* (1968; although it was largely finished by 1960) and the stories of a drug-drenched Europe collected as *Barefoot in the Head* (1969) seems to have embraced the New Wave ideals. But Aldiss, like many sf readers and writers at the time, had his doubts about where they were heading. In 1966 he wrote to Judith Merril:

It's great to be even a splash in a new wave. But even the newest wave gets cast upon the shore. One feature of this particular wave (which I suspect to be a journalistic invention of yours and Mike Moorcock's, ultimately of no service to any writers willy-nilly involved ...) is a strong tendency to abolish plot. Plot, I mean, in the grander sense of structure ... I feel I am no part of the New Wave; I was here before 'em, and by God I mean to be here after they've gone (still writing bloody science fiction)![9]

Aldiss refused to be characterized as New Wave, and, indeed, several of the writers associated with *New Worlds* were unhappy with the label 'New Wave'; it was imposed on them by outsiders, like the writer Christopher Priest or the anthologist Judith Merril. Their unhappiness was in part, as Priest has explained, because those who used the term were trying to create a *product*, thinking of New Wave as a new sub-genre of sf; while Moorcock and those closely associated with him were concerned with the *process* of trying to rethink the whole nature of speculative fiction (the preferred expansion of 'sf').

The traditional idiom of sf speculates about technology, about man's aspirations, about the future, about inventiveness, and so forth. Is it not possible that similar speculation can be made, in fictional form, about other aspects of man's experience? Why can science fiction not explore the inner world of emotion, of neurosis, of sexual desire, of boredom? Can it not describe transitory experiences like drug-trips, or the appreciation of music, or defecation, or the act of writing itself?[10]

This was not an agenda that was greeted with enthusiasm by American writers or editors, who still thought of sf as being more about entertainment than experiment. There were exceptions: Damon Knight's *Orbit*, an anthology series for original stories, began in 1966, and often contained material that would never have been accepted by any magazine editor apart from Moorcock himself. Samuel R. Delany and Marilyn Hacker founded another original-anthology series, *Quark* (1970); it was even more experimental, but only lasted for four issues.

When the American New Wave did emerge, it was very different in nature from the British version. It did not reject the pulp tradition of genre sf, but, rather, endeavoured to improve on it. It did not abandon the traditional sf icons and venues—spaceships, robots, exotic planets—but it did inject a new interest in style, psychological complexity, and interest in character, as well as some topics that were at least conventionally regarded as taboo. Even if Philip José Farmer had started publishing stories about sex with aliens back in 1952, many sf editors felt that their responsibilities towards a teenage readership prevented them from moving too far in that direction. Harlan Ellison's massive anthology *Dangerous Visions* (1967) was a deliberate attempt to break taboos, and has often been seen as a milestone. Sex was indeed the main taboo, including miscegenation and incest (the latter treated in Theodore Sturgeon's splendidly named story 'If All Men Were Brothers, Would You Let One Marry Your Sister?').

The American New Wave consisted mostly of writers who had already started to establish themselves, even as early as the 1950s, but who in the mid- to late 1960s started writing more mature and more literary fiction. The most startling example was Robert Silverberg, who had been an extremely prolific writer of routine sf in the 1950s, and who in the late 1960s suddenly began producing some of the most interesting works in modern American sf: *Thorns* (1967), *The Masks of Time* (1968), *A Time of Changes* (1971), *Tower of Glass* (1971), *Dying Inside* (1972), the classic novel of telepathy, and several others. Harlan Ellison, too, had begun his writing career in the 1950s, but came to prominence at the same time as his *Dangerous Visions* anthology, with a series of award-winning stories, told in his striking emotive and angry style—which is suggested by the equally striking titles: ' "Repent, Harlequin!" Said the Ticktockman' (1965), 'I Have No Mouth and I Must Scream' (1968), and 'The Beast that Shouted Love at the Heart of the World' (1968). Most typically his stories were about alienation and the struggle between the individual and the all-destroying machine/God/society. 'I Have No Mouth and I Must Scream' described the great computer which has taken over the world and preserved the lives of just five individuals, whom it tortures endlessly in revenge for its own meaningless existence. ' "Repent, Harlequin!" said the Ticktockman' is about the tyranny of time in our industrial society.

YOU CANNOT VOTE UNLESS YOU APPEAR AT 8:45 A.M.
'I don't care if the script is *good*. I need it Thursday!'
CHECK-OUT TIME IS 2:00 P.M.
'You got here late. The job's taken. Sorry.'
YOUR SALARY HAS BEEN DOCKED FOR TWENTY MINUTES TIME LOST.
'God, what time is it, I've gotta run!'
    And so it goes. And so it goes. And so it goes. And so it goes goes

goes goes goes tick tock tick tock tick tock and one day we no longer let time serve us, we serve time and we are slaves of the schedule, worshippers of the sun's passing, bound into a life predicated on restrictions because the system will not function if we do not keep the schedule tight.[11]

The Ticktockman was responsible for 'turning off' those workers who were consistently late; the Harlequin tried, ineffectually, to rebel.

The two other main writers of the American New Wave, Roger Zelazny and Samuel R. Delany, were more recent entrants to the field, both publishing their first sf in 1962, but again getting into their stride with some of the best fiction of their career in the years 1965 to 1968. Their achievements, too, were readily recognized by the sf community, with Hugos or Nebulas going to Zelazny's 'The Doors of his Face, the Lamps of his Mouth' (1965), *This Immortal* (1966), and 'He who Shapes' (1966) and to Delany's *Babel-17* (1966), *The Einstein Intersection* (1967), 'Aye and Gomorrah' (1967), and 'Time Considered as a Helix of Semi-Precious Stones' (1969). Zelazny has never again written as well as he did in the 1960s; but Delany has continued to evolve, and to use in his work exhilarating concepts which few other sf writers have tackled. *Babel-17*, for instance, reflects Noam Chomsky's linguistic theories (as did *The Embedding* (1973), by the British writer Ian Watson); later, Delany was to write works reflecting on semiotics and poststructuralism.

The furore raised by the New Wave on both sides of the Atlantic, between those writers and readers who saw such experimentation as the only way forward and those traditionalists who regarded it as a betrayal of the very spirit of sf, abated early in the 1970s. If what traditional sf readers regarded as its excesses died away (in particular, the dominance of stylistic device and experimentation over narrative form and what Peter Nicholls called 'its sometimes miasmic gloom'[12]), some of the positive results remained: a more profound awareness of the political and moral complexities of the world, a more sophisticated and self-conscious literary approach, and a more realistically pessimistic attitude to human nature and the ability of technology to improve the human condition. But one must distinguish between what was happening on the two sides of the Atlantic. The American New Wave was, on the whole, quite unlike the British. The latter was effectively a group of people associated with a magazine that had a particular programme (even if it had a dozen ways of realizing it), whereas even those American writers who gathered in London at the time, like Delany, Disch, and Sladek, were individualists pursuing their *own* ends, not those of Ballard or Moorcock. As a 'movement', the American New Wave was even less real than the British; it was no more than a concatenation of talent flourishing at the same time and bringing new ideas and new standards to the writing of sf. The British New Wave had few lasting effects, even in Britain; the American New Wave ushered in a great expansion of the field and of its readership. No doubt the writers did not achieve this success on their own. It may be noted, for instance, that this burst of originality occurred at almost exactly the same time as the three seasons of *Star Trek*, which certainly contributed to the expansion of sf's readership. Whether or not much of this boom can be attributed to the American New Wave, it is clear that the rise in literary and imaginative standards associated with the late 1960s contributed a great deal to some of the most original writers of the 1970s, including John Crowley, Joe Haldeman, Ursula Le Guin, James Tiptree, jun., and John Varley.

New Directions in the 1970s

If some of the new writers of the 1970s were New Wave in all but name, the older traditions did not die away; the 1970s saw the beginning of a divergence of values, or the creation of new sub-genres, which have helped to create the tremendous variety and fragmentation in recent sf. The home of the traditionalist was *Analog* (formerly *Astounding*), still edited, until his death in 1971, by John W. Campbell, and thereafter edited (until 1978) by Ben Bova. Under Bova's direction, some New Wave writers, or old writers who had adopted some of the New Wave themes, began to publish in *Analog*. It is difficult to imagine Campbell publishing Frederik Pohl's 'The Gold at the Starbow's End', for instance, as Bova did in March 1972.[13] In this story the crew of a spaceship are sent to the stars; over the ten years of solitary introspection and study, they become geniuses and near-gods. At the very end they return: 'the great golden ships from Alpha-Aleph landed and disgorged their bright, terrible crewmen to clean up the Earth—just in time.' Traditional *Analog* readers were not amused. Letters in the July edition complain about the mathematics and the over-use 'of the presently "in" thing—drugs, sex, *I Ching*, etc.'; though a letter in August complained about the immorality which John Campbell would never have permitted, and then went on to make it clear that he was referring not to the sex, drugs, or politics but to the illogical use of mathematics. The politics were the stumbling-block for other readers:

The prime objection to the story is its basic philosophy of man—the ideal man is loving, compassionate, nonaggressive and nonviolent. Man got where he is today because he has the useful and good characteristics of bias, prejudice, aggression, and vengeance.[14]

Indeed, the same issue of *Analog* in which Pohl's 'The Gold at the Starbow's End' appeared had a story which established the conventional *Analog* wisdom concerning man's animal nature: Larry Niven's 'Cloak of Anarchy'.[15] Niven was the most successful of the American authors of the late 1960s who turned their backs on the New Wave to produce traditional sf, relying heavily on scientific extrapolation, and doing it all in a new, lively, assured manner. Like Heinlein, Niven developed a future history and a whole universe, but filled, unlike Heinlein's, with colourful and suitably exotic aliens: the extinct thrint, the pak, the bandersnatchi, the puppeteers, and the kzin. His 'Tales of Known Space', in short or long form, won Hugo awards in 1967, 1971, 1972, and 1975. His politics, like those of Heinlein and many writers of what was becoming known as 'hard sf', were to the right of most of the New Wave writers. 'Cloak of Anarchy' imagined a Californian park in which any behaviour was allowed except violence to other people; the violent were immediately stunned by one of the many floating copseyes. Somebody wanting total freedom from authority smuggled in an electronic gadget to short-circuit all the copseyes. The result: violence, rape, the disappearance of all the niceties of civilized behaviour. 'I was wrong. Anarchy isn't stable. It comes apart too easily.' Man is not by nature non-violent; the difference between left-wing anarchists and right-wing libertarians is that the latter argue that only the threat of violence preserves civilization.

Niven was a writer of 'hard sf', the main sub-genre which was defining itself in opposition to the New Wave. Traditionalists regarded the latter as having abandoned the sf interest in technology, physics, and space exploration in favour of the soft sciences like psychology and sociology or of pure literary experimentation; the writers of 'hard sf' were preserving the core and essence of what sf was about. *Analog* was, and remains today, the main refuge for hard sf, where scientific formulae can still be used in stories, and where fiction is often written by practising scientists or engineers rather than, as was becoming more and more common everywhere else, by writers who majored in English. Devotees of hard sf would mumble into their beers at conventions that sf was going to the dogs: not only was sf falling into the hands of people who didn't understand science, but more and more of them were women, and more and more of the imaginative literature that was being published was fantasy and not sf at all.

The rise of women's sf and the rise of fantasy were, indeed, two of the most important developments of the 1970s, and they were developments which are still being worked out in the 1990s.

Fantasy, first of all. The borderline between fantasy and sf is one that has been endlessly debated. The only thing that can be said for certain is that each person who tries to describe it will do so differently. A true devotee of hard sf might well say, at least to earn a debating point, that in our present state of scientific knowledge both faster-than-light travel and time-travel can be regarded as scientifically impossible, and thus in the realm of fantasy. Another, with rather more justification, perhaps, might say that telepathy is fantasy. It is possible to exclude considerable portions of the sf canon if one applies the criterion of 'scientific plausibility'. And the distinction between the two is blurred still more if the fantasy is being written, as it often has been, by writers of sf, who will often, playfully, treat magic with rigorous logic, effectively making it an alternative science. Alternatively, sf writers have been tempted to rationalize—to explain in scientific terms—aspects of the world of fantasy: vampires, werewolves, ghosts, unicorns, dragons, and magic itself. And, as Arthur C. Clarke has said (in a phrase endlessly repeated), 'Any sufficiently advanced technology is indistinguishable from magic.'

Although the hard sf fan did, and still does, bemoan the increasing dominance of fantasy, the two genres are in fact extremely closely linked, and have been since the earliest days of genre sf. Campbell himself, whose *Astounding* was the home of hard sf, also edited *Unknown*, devoted to fantasy, and the same authors would frequently write for both magazines. This has been just as true in the years since the rise of 'adult fantasy', from the end of the 1960s; many, perhaps most, sf authors have turned their hand on occasion to fantasy. Sf readers may have their preferences, but they are often prepared to enjoy fantasy. Readers occasionally complain in the letter columns of *Isaac Asimov's Science Fiction Magazine* (founded in 1977) about the fantasy that is published there; yet they, or other readers, quite happily buy *The Magazine of Fantasy and Science Fiction* or read *Locus: The Newspaper of the Science Fiction Field*, which unapologetically includes fantasy within its brief. As we have seen, the terminology of some European traditions makes no distinction between the two genres, like the Italian *fantascienza* or the Russian *nauchnaia fantastika*.[16]

The origins of modern fantasy go back, ultimately, to Graeco-Roman mythology, to medieval romance, and to the Gothic, and fantasy had a respectable literary reputation in the early twentieth century. But the more direct origins of the modern fantasy tradition, and sf itself, are with the American pulps of the 1920s and 1930s. In *Weird Tales*, above all in the 1930s, appeared Robert E. Howard's tales of Conan the Barbarian, the epitome of the genre labelled 'sword-and-sorcery' by Fritz Leiber in 1960—narratives set in a primitive world reminiscent of those in early European history, where magic works, where there are powerful gods, but where mindless barbarians with large swords and even larger pectorals always seem to come out on top. *Weird Tales* also published C. L. Moore's Jirel of Joiry stories, the first to feature a sword-and-sorcery heroine, and H. P. Lovecraft's tales of the Cthulhu mythos, full of eldritch terrors and nameless horrors (which nevertheless have a science-fictional rationale). In *Unknown*, in the early 1940s, were to be found Fritz Leiber's first stories about Fafhrd and the Gray Mouser, the best known, and certainly the most witty and intelligent, of all sword-and-sorcery series, which Leiber was still writing at the time of his death in 1992. Leiber was also an exponent of 'contemporary fantasy' or 'urban fantasy', another major strand in modern fantasy, in which the fantasy elements are realized in our own world, rather than in the imagined one of sword-and-sorcery. His *Conjure Wife* (1943; book publication, 1953), about witchcraft in a modern American setting, is the classic example.

If modern fantasy has its roots in the same sort of world as American sf, it is undoubtedly true that the modern fantasy publishing boom has its roots in Oxford, in a donnish study and a back room in the Eagle and Child pub. Professor J. R. R. Tolkien published *The Hobbit* in 1937 and *The Lord of the Rings*, the adult trilogy set in the same imaginary world, in 1954–5. At that time his books achieved considerable critical acclaim, an even greater amount of bemusement, and a small band of devotees. It was the simultaneous publication of *The Lord of the Rings* by two American paperback houses in 1965 that set off the fantasy boom. By 1968 three million copies of the paperback trilogy had been sold in the United States, and by 1980 sales world-wide had topped eight million.[17] Nigel Walmsley, from whom those figures are taken, has plausibly linked Tolkien's success among American youth in the years 1965 to 1968 to a particular phase in American history, when youth culture rejected politics and the rat race and sought an alternative world, through drugs, living in hippy communes, or the imagination. *The Lord of the Rings*, a product of philological enthusiasm and donnish whimsy,[18] bizarrely became the bible of the counter-culture.

What Tolkien had done was what many sf writers before and since have done: he created a world of his own, which resonates with our own world, but contains its own extraordinary depth of traditions, history, and languages. It was situated in a mythical past, rather than on another planet; but its appeal was very similar to that of the sf blockbuster which came out in the same year as the paperback version of *The Lord of the Rings*: Frank Herbert's *Dune*. Tolkien's world, with its limited technology, its wizards, and its warrior cultures, might be labelled 'heroic fantasy' or, better, 'high fantasy', and its popularity encouraged the reprinting of the Conan books and other 'classics' of earlier heroic fantasy or sword-and-sorcery. In 1969 Lin Carter began an 'Adult Fantasy' series for Ballantine Books, which brought writers of much more literary significance (such as Lord Dunsany and James Branch Cabell) back into print. Since 1965 Carter had been joining the bandwagon by writing a series of low-grade Conan imitations, featuring the warrior Thongor. The fantasy boom was well under way by 1970; it may have reached its peak in the late 1980s. It was a sign of the times that in 1971 Fritz Leiber's new Fafhrd and the Gray Mouser story, 'Ill Met in Lankhmar', won the Hugo award for the best sf novella. It is worth remarking that in 1974 Gary Gygax and Dave Arendson published *Dungeons and Dragons*, the first fantasy role-playing game, and that at roughly the same time the fantasy computer game *Adventure* was created, the progenitor of numerous other text and, eventually, text-and-graphic computer games. The kind of imaginative youngsters who, ten years earlier, would have been reading sf, were by the end of the 1970s acting out their own fantasy narratives with their friends and, by the end of the 1980s, playing them out on their own, on screen.

Despite appearances, the growth of modern fantasy has considerable relevance to a study of sf. There was a heavy overlap between the categories of sf reader and fantasy reader, as well as between sf writer and fantasy writer; the traditionalists were right in bemoaning the way in which the fantasy boom was diverting attention away from the 'real' core of sf. The appeal of fantasy also led to a great expansion of a type of sf with a strong fantasy flavour. Good examples include Poul

Anderson's novelettes 'The Queen of Air and Darkness' (1971) and 'Goat Song' (1972), both of which won both Hugo and Nebula awards. But what I want to look at in closer detail are the two series which established their authors, Marion Zimmer Bradley and Anne McCaffrey. Both these writers had begun their series earlier than the 1970s: Bradley in 1958 and McCaffrey in 1967. But they achieved their great popularity in the early 1970s, riding on the crest of the fantasy wave.

Neither Bradley's 'Darkover' series nor McCaffrey's 'Pern' series is fantasy. Both are what have been called planetary romances; that is, they are novels whose main focus is the exotic nature of a planetary culture, created by humans in an indeterminate distant future.[19] Darkover and Pern are planets that have been colonized from Earth; although both series include novels which relate the earliest settlement (*Darkover Landfall*, 1972; *Dragonsdawn*, 1988), they concentrate on the period when those human settlers had devised their own new planetary culture. Bradley emphasizes the differences by imagining, late in the chronological sequence, the arrival of a new wave of settlers from Earth, from a technological culture much like our own. Like many planetary romances (the Barsoom novels of Edgar Rice Burroughs, for instance), the trappings of this planetary culture are very similar to those of heroic fantasy. The level of technology is low; the structure of society is semi-feudal; the sword is a common weapon. McCaffrey's trump card is the dragon: a flying creature bred from the local fauna of Pern, and used as a means of transport. It is an alien creature with some kind of scientific rationale; but it is, of course—along with wizards, elves, and unicorns—one of the most familiar icons of high fantasy. McCaffrey's dragon-riders are in telepathic communication with their dragons (who are intelligent creatures); this stems, McCaffrey once admitted, from a wish that she could communicate with her horses. There is telepathy on Darkover too, and indeed in some of the Darkover novels (those early in the chronological sequence) telepathy is one of the few science-fictional devices; most of the novels are content to study different cultures, in the manner of a fantasy writer, most notably *The Shattered Chain* (1976) and *Thendara House* (1983), which describe a cult of warrior women, the Renunciates or Free Amazons.

Although a somewhat awkward and dubious feminism enters Bradley's works, notably in the Renunciate books, Darkover and Pern are usually not treated as part of the rise of women's sf during the 1970s. But they were more widely read than many feminist sf novels, and are probably responsible for attracting more women to sf than anything apart from *Star Trek*. There were a number of factors which, around 1970, were traditionally thought to keep the number of female readers to quite a small proportion of the whole sf readership. Most notable, of course, is the almost total absence of believable female characters in the bulk of earlier sf with which female readers could identify; Ursula K. Le Guin has admitted that she initially found it very difficult to depict complex female characters in her sf, because of the absence of literary role models.[20] There was also the normal concentration on the hardware, the technology, and the grand sweep of human history, at the expense of serious investigation of human relationships, and 'that's what girls are into isn't it? relationships not rocketships.'[21] Fantasy has often been more concerned with moral dilemmas and individual people, rather than the problem-solving and social development of sf. Sf resembling fantasy, or vice versa, was perhaps much more approachable for women than genre sf, and indeed more approachable for the reader of either gender who was not familiar with the conventions of the sf genre. The conventions of fantasy, unlike those of sf, are the conventions of fairy-tale; they are embedded in our culture, rather than in opposition to it.[22]

Studies of women's sf, such as Sarah Lefanu's *In the Chinks of the World Machine* (1988), however, have tended to concentrate on the avowedly feminist writers who emerged at the time, as a direct outcome of the Women's Movement of the late 1960s: Joanna Russ, Suzy McKee Charnas, and Alice Sheldon (and Ursula Le Guin, although Le Guin's commitment to feminism was belated). The potential for a feminist sf was already apparent in the long history of feminist utopian writing, of which the most interesting example is Charlotte Perkins

Gilman's *Herland* (1915), and also in feminist writing itself. The last chapter of Shulamith Firestone's *The Dialectic of Sex: The Case for Feminist Revolution* (1970), for instance, suggested a whole catalogue of social and biological changes which ought to take place, allowing the freeing of women from the tyranny of reproduction, for instance, which had obvious potential for sf writers. Such was the tyranny of publishing categories that when overtly feminist sf books did emerge, they did not readily find publishers. Joanna Russ's *The Female Man* eventually appeared in 1975, but she had been searching for a publisher for several years. In Britain it was only the foundation of the sf line of the Women's Press, in 1985, that allowed a number of important works of feminist sf to come into print. Because of where they were published, they did not necessarily reach a wide sf audience, but they probably did increase the readership of sf among women.

In retrospect, the publication of Joanna Russ's first novel, *Picnic on Paradise*, in 1968, was significant. Although it did not make any obvious political points, it did offer the field Alyx, one of the very first strong female characters, independent, resourceful, and tough: the model of many to follow, from both male and female writers, in the succeeding twenty-five years. Russ's 1972 short story 'When it Changed', a much more deliberately feminist work, won the Nebula Award.[23] The story starts with the narrator being driven along a road by the narrator's wife, with their 12-year-old eldest daughter asleep in the back seat.

Some day soon, like all of them, she will disappear for weeks on end to come back grimy and proud, having knifed her first cougar or shot her first bear, dragging some abominably dangerous beastie behind her, which I shall never forgive for what it might have done to my daughter.

We learn a little more about the narrator, a 34-year-old fighter of three duels. But not until two or three pages later do we realize for certain that the narrator is female too. Earth men have just arrived on Whileaway, the first to be seen since the plague had wiped them out 600 years earlier. The story economically and powerfully contrasts the two women with the four arrogant, sniggering, uncomprehending males, and the narrator at the end remembers the long cry of pain to be found in her ancestors' journals, and wonders if the men can be kept out of Whileaway.

A rather different Whileaway is to be seen in *The Female Man* (1975); its utopian all-female society is contrasted with three others through the four characters in the novel: Joanna (from our world), Janet (from Whileaway), Jeannine (from a socially backward world in which the Second World War never happened), and Jael (from a future world in which men and women are at war). The constant cutting from one of these characters to another—they all really represent different versions or potentialities of the same person—is often confusing, and the narrative thread is difficult to discern. But the book contains some of the most sharply observed comic writing in sf. Sf has rarely been so effectively used to argue about our own condition, and rarely been written with such wit and anger.

The Female Man was circulated in typescript among Russ's friends for a couple of years before publication; Ursula K. Le Guin and Samuel R. Delany were two of the writers who read it.[24] Le Guin had written sf novels and short stories in the 1960s, and had won both Hugo and Nebula awards for *The Left Hand of Darkness* (1969). This was a 'thought-experiment' to see how a society could function without fixed gender; people were primarily neuter, but could become either male or female at the peak of their sexual cycle. Le Guin was blamed for a generally male-oriented approach to this, a charge she eventually came to accept.[25] The novel is nevertheless one of the very first serious analyses of gender to be attempted in sf (or, given the nature of the thought-experiment, anywhere else). Le Guin's *The Dispossessed: An Ambiguous Utopia* (1974) (which also won Hugo and Nebula awards), if written after she had read *The Female Man*, betrayed little sign of it; the ambiguous utopia of Anarres is indeed the result of the political philosophy of a woman, Odo, but a woman inspired by anarchism rather than feminism. Lip-service is paid to sexual equality, but we do not really see it in action. However, the book remains one of the most powerful pieces of political sf ever written; at the same time it contains one of the most convincing accounts of the work of a theoretical physicist—Shevek, the man who made the instantaneous communication device of Le Guin's earlier novels, the ansible, a practical possibility. Modern sf has few utopian novels: it is intriguing, not accidental, that the three most significant were all written in interaction with each other and within a short space of time. The most successful purely as a utopian novel, perhaps, and in some senses the most feminist, is the third, its subtitle echoing Le Guin's: Samuel R. Delany's *Triton: An Ambiguous Heterotopia* (1976). Delany was perhaps particularly conscious, as a black and a gay, of the power of traditional utopias to repress minorities in the name of an ideal, and his utopia was about tolerance, about the ability for totally differing life-styles and sexualities to coexist.

The most important of the feminist writers of the 1970s, however, and surely the most powerful short-story writer, was James Tiptree, jun. 'The Women Men Don't See' (1973) utilized a classic sf cliché—women being taken away in a flying saucer—but the sting in the tail is that, rather than being abducted, the two women actually hitch a lift. They see life with aliens as no different from what they are used to, living in a man's world: 'We survive by ones and twos in the chinks of your world-machine . . . I'm used to aliens.' Robert Silverberg commented that this was 'a profoundly feminist story told in an entirely masculine manner', and a few pages earlier in his introduction to the collection which included this story he remarked: 'It has been suggested that Tiptree is female, a theory that I find absurd, for there is to me something ineluctably masculine about Tiptree's writing.'[26] It was not just the writing, however, but the life-style. Silverberg noted how Tiptree in a letter had admitted to having worked in a Pentagon basement during the war and to having subsequently 'batted around the jungly parts of the globe'. Those interested in the difference between 'masculine' and 'feminine' writing (like Le Guin and Silverberg himself) were delighted (or embarrassed) to find, in 1977, that Tiptree was actually Alice Sheldon, and that therefore Tiptree was also the feminist sf writer Raccoona Sheldon.

Most of Tiptree's stories offer a bleak vision of life. The very first story in her first collection, *Ten Thousand Light Years from Home* (1973), gave readers a glimpse of the power of her story-telling, but also its despair in the face of human self-deception and lust. 'And I Awoke and Found Me Here on the Cold Hill's Side' (1971) takes its title from a line in Keats's 'La Belle Dame sans merci', which is about how a fairy deprives a knight of the power to love ordinary humanity. In Tiptree's story, human beings who hang around spaceports have become infatuated and sexually enslaved to the exotic aliens from other worlds. Earth is swapping rare resources for alien status symbols, the equivalent of glass beads or Mickey Mouse watches; humans are fulfilling their inbred passion to impregnate the stranger, and yet get nothing in return, save the loss of their souls. 'Now we've met aliens we can't screw, and we're about to die trying.' The narrator, a reporter, listens, but does not understand: at the end he suddenly sees two sleek scarlet shapes: 'My first real aliens! I snapped the recorder shut and ran to squeeze in behind them.'[27]

Even those stories which offer some humour do not carry encouraging messages. 'Houston, Houston, Do You Read?' (1976) is the story of three male astronauts who find themselves time-warped into the future, into a world where men, and indeed most women, have died out. When they first realize their situation—like the men who land on Russ's Whileaway in 'When It Changed'—they fantasize about their future role. ' "Two million hot little cunts down there, waiting for old Buddy. Gawd. . . ." ' But Tiptree can envisage no solution. Two of the men are killed, and the third and last is handed a drug. The story ends:

'Tell me, what do you call yourselves? Women's World? Liberation? Amazonia?'

'Why, we call ourselves human beings.' Her eyes twinkle absently at him, go back to the bullet marks. 'Humanity, mankind.' She shrugs. 'The human race.'

The drink tastes cool going down, something like peace and freedom, he thinks. Or death.[28]

Tiptree's four collections of stories between 1973 and 1981[29] contain some of the most powerful stories in the genre, and had a considerable impact upon the field. She wrote two novels, and more stories in the 1980s, in which death figured prominently. Ill health prevented her output being what it had been in the 1970s, however. In 1987 she shot her husband, who was terminally ill, and then turned the gun on herself.

If Tiptree won the respect of sf readers, it was Ursula Le Guin who won the respect of non-sf critics. Perhaps partly because of her own academic connections, as well as her sheer literacy and intelligence, Le Guin became one of that small band of living sf writers which the steadily growing community of sf academics was keen to promote to the outside world. There had been sf courses taught, particularly in the United States, since the early 1950s, but the number of university teachers thinking of themselves primarily as sf academics grew massively in the late 1960s and early 1970s. Most sf academics were still very intent on proving to their colleagues (usually in departments of English) that their subject was a respectable one, and the authors studied tended to be carefully selected. Le Guin was in; Gernsback was never mentioned.

There had been just one academic journal devoted to sf before 1970: *Extrapolation*, launched by Thomas D. Clareson in 1959. In 1970 the Science Fiction Research Association was founded in America; in 1971 the Science Fiction Foundation was created in Britain, and based at the North-East London Polytechnic; in 1972 the SFF began a journal, *Foundation: The Review of Science Fiction*; and in the following year the third journal was founded, *Science-Fiction Studies*, initially at Indiana State University, soon to achieve a reputation as the most academic of the three (and sometimes the most obscure). *Extrapolation* and *Science-Fiction Studies* did much to encourage the development of sf studies as an academic discipline in North America; *Foundation* did not have the same effect in Britain, where sf (except in its more 'respectable' guises of utopian or dystopian fiction) is rarely taught at university level. It is in fact one of the strengths of *Foundation* that many of its contributors—especially its reviewers—are not academics but practising sf writers.

The impact that British sf made upon the world sf scene in the 1960s did not last long, and few of the British writers associated with *New Worlds* continued writing into the 1970s. But the 1970s were by no means unimportant for British sf. One writer who had published just one story in *New Worlds*, Ian Watson, published six highly intelligent and complex novels in the 1970s, exploring the themes of perception and communication. Writers such as Michael Coney, Richard Cowper, and Bob Shaw produced what posterity may regard as their best work. And John Brunner transformed himself, Silverberg-like (see p. 174), from a competent, prolific, but routine writer of sf into the author of some of the most painstaking dystopic extrapolations into the near-future of any modern sf author. *Stand on Zanzibar* (1968) was the first, and most important: a detailed picture of a near-future world reeling under the strains of overpopulation. Brunner subsequently turned to other targets, equally successfully: *The Jagged Orbit* (1969) examined the military-industrial complex; *The Sheep Look Up* (1972) was an utterly convincing warning about the dangers of pollution; and in *The Shockwave Rider* (1975), which described a world in the grips of the computer explosion, he invented the concept of computer viruses and worms.[30]

Only three novels by British authors have ever won either a Hugo or a Nebula award (Brian Aldiss's *Hothouse* (1962; US: *The Long Afternoon of Earth*) was a fixed-up novel but won a short-fiction Hugo). One was *Stand on Zanzibar* (Hugo in 1969), and the other two were by Arthur C. Clarke: *Rendezvous with Rama* (1973) and *The Fountains of Paradise* (1979), both of which received the Hugo and the Nebula. Clarke's great periods of production were in the early 1950s and the 1970s; his role as co-author of the film *2001* (1968) had given him a great deal of publicity, and in the early 1970s the most lucrative book contract yet offered to an sf writer by an American publisher gave a boost to his fictional productivity. *Rendezvous with Rama* is the classic study of the Big Dumb Object, something calculated to give the fan a jolt of 'sense of wonder'.[31] In this case the BDO was an enormous alien artefact, *Rama*, which travelled into the solar system and out of it again, mysteriously and pointlessly. The exploration team whose adventures the book relates is hardly wiser at the end than at the beginning: indeed, a large part of the success of the book lies in the way it creates mystery and emphasizes the difficulty, or impossibility, of humans ever understanding alien cultures. Clarke's other award-winner of the 1970s was the novella 'A Meeting with Medusa' (Nebula, 1972), about the discovery of life in the atmosphere of Jupiter. *The Fountains of Paradise* was more successful than either in purely literary terms (though without the distinct sense of wonder produced by the other two); the oriental background was effectively sketched (Clarke had become a resident of Sri Lanka in 1956), and the story of the construction of a sky-hook space elevator was, like his 'Exploration of Space' series in the early 1950s, a convincing study of current technology working at its theoretical limits. Brunner and Clarke both successfully broke into the huge American market. That, for non-American authors, was becoming increasingly important for their economic survival as sf writers. British and Australian authors could make it in America, though with great difficulty; it was virtually impossible (and had been so since the origins of American sf) for sf writers who had published originally in a foreign language. Only Stanisław Lem and the Russian writing brothers Boris and Arkady Strugatski made some impression on the Anglo-American market, both to some extent helped by the films made of their work by Andrei Tarkowski: *Solaris* (1971, based on Lem's novel of 1961) and *Stalker* (1979, based on the Strugatskis' novel of 1972).

The 1970s offered feminism, fantasy, the consolidation of the advances made by the New Wave, the continuation of old themes under new guises, and the emergence of sf on the fringes of academia. But really the most important aspect of the late 1960s and early 1970s was that sf for the first time invaded the entire cultural milieu of the Western world. The Apollo Moon landings between 1969 and 1972 accustomed the public to the science-fictional nature of the world they lived in, and even caught the attention of the media for a short time. It is said that an American TV channel missed the high drama of the Apollo 13 mission because it was running an sf movie; fiction made more compelling viewing than real life.[32] Audiences had, at any rate, seen it all before. Stanley Kubrick's film *2001* (1968), based on Arthur C. Clarke's 'The Sentinel', did as much as Apollo to make space flight both real and even banal; unlike Apollo, the film also stressed its mystical and transcendental potential. Its prolonged psychedelic journey sequence was the best-known cinematic representation of the mystic aspirations of the drug culture of the late 1960s.

During the late 1960s sf entered the public domain as part of popular culture. This can best be seen in rock music.[33] The Californian group Jefferson Airplane had lyrics referring to Heinlein and to John Wyndham; their successor Jefferson Starship's album *Blows Against the Empire* (1970) is a rock symphony which incorporates a classic sf theme: the hijacking of a spaceship by a group of rebels from a fascist United States and their search for salvation in the stars. In the late 1960s Pink Floyd 'Set the Controls for the Heart of the Sun', while Jimi Hendrix sang 'Third Stone from the Sun'; David Bowie's 'Space Oddity' (1969), about the astronaut Major Tom, was actually used as theme music during the TV coverage of the first Moon landing. In the early 1970s, Bowie's 'Ziggy Stardust' persona was an sf creation, notably in the album *The Rise and Fall of Ziggy Stardust and the Spiders from Mars* (1972). Michael Moorcock had his own group, Deep Fix, but is better known for his association with the band Hawkwind, whose lyrics transformed stories by Zelazny, Bradbury, and others. In the 1950s, sf writers had frequently been influenced by jazz; from the late 1960s, not only do sf writers make frequent reference to rock, but rock musicians return the compliment.

The public, throughout the Western world, was also attracted in very large numbers to sf in the cinema. Some of the biggest blockbusters of the 1970s were sf films: above all, George Lucas's *Star Wars* (1977), Steven Spielberg's *Close Encounters of the Third Kind* (1977), and Ridley Scott's *Alien* (1979), but also such homages to the past as *Superman—the Movie* (1978) and *Star Trek—the Motion Picture* (1979). *Star Wars*, with its sophisticated special effects and non-stop action, was the most perfect version of 1930s space opera to be filmed up to that date. Sf fans may have winced at the way in which the X-wing ships weaved and manœuvred like Second World War fighters, in total defiance of the laws of inertia, or at the explosions which resounded though the vacuum of space; others were uneasy at the implied racism and fascism of the final victory ceremony; yet more cringed at the unbearably cute robots R2D2 and C3P0; but few failed to be captivated by the stunning visuals and by the essential innocence of it all. A younger generation, unaware of its wholesale plundering of sf traditions and earlier non-sf movies, was entranced. Ultimately, manufacturers of *Star Wars* toys benefited from the craze much more than did publishers of written sf. In the 1980s the type of marketing campaigns associated with *Star Wars* were frequently linked to cartoon programmes which were little more than lengthy advertisements designed to persuade children to bully their parents into buying the toys: *Transformers* and *Teenage Mutant Ninja Turtles* were the commercial descendants of *Star Wars*. By the 1980s, sf was to dominate the imagery of pre-teen toys, as it did that of the teenagers' computer games.

The films by Spielberg and Scott were much more mature, or at least aimed at a more mature audience. *Close Encounters* related the obsession of a technician who sees a number of UFOs, and is drawn, along with others, to a mysteriously shaped mountain in Wyoming; there an immense alien mother-ship lands, disgorging some humans who had been missing for decades (who had nevertheless not aged) and then taking the hero up with them into space. It was a confusing and somewhat simplistic film, but one that, in its final sequences, elicits the familiar 'sense of wonder' better than almost any other. Like Spielberg's *E. T. The Extra-Terrestrial*, it has strong religious overtones, and might be taken as an allegory of religious yearning; like *E. T.*, it introduced the idea of the alien as benevolent, all-powerful, and even god-like. The alien need not be threatening, and can even offer salvation. Those old-time sf readers upset by such saccharine wishful thinking (*Close Encounters* had 'Wishing Upon a Star' as its theme song) could take comfort in Scott's *Alien*. The alien is suitably loathsome, whether clamped on John Hurt's face, bursting forth from his stomach in larval form, or, vastly grown, picking off the crew members of *Nostromo* one by one until it meets its match in Ripley (Sigourney Weaver), one of the very small number of redoubtable female characters in sf cinema. At one level *Alien* is no more than a horror film, 'a gigantic "Boo!", set in outer space'.[34] Yet it is also one of the few sf films since *2001* to have taken real care with the milieu of outer space, and to give an impression of how ordinary working people might actually operate in such an environment.[35] The underlying conflict, which is not settled by Ripley, is not between human and alien, but between the human crew of *Nostromo* and the exploitative multinational company for which they work; the company is much more interested in the commercial potential of this alien creature than in the safety of its workers. In its characterization of a future in which the individual struggles to escape from the tyranny of the multinational, *Alien* prefigures the cyberpunks of the 1980s.

Cyberpunk and its Aftermath

In the current critical literature, the 1980s appear to be overshadowed by a new New Wave, labelled 'cyberpunk'. It responded to the changing icons of the time, and appealed, or aimed to appeal, to a new generation of sf readers: 'cyber' from 'cybernetics', the study of systems in machines and animals, and 'punk' from 1970s rock terminology, meaning young, aggressive, alienated, anti-Establishment.

Eighties tech sticks to the skin, responds to the touch: the personal computer, the Sony Walkman, the portable telephone, the soft contact lens.

Certain central themes spring up repeatedly in cyberpunk. The theme of body invasion: prosthetic limbs, implanted circuitry, cosmetic surgery, genetic alteration. The even more powerful theme of mind invasion: brain-computer interfaces, artificial intelligence, neurochemistry—

techniques radically redefining the nature of humanity, the nature of the self . . .

The cyberpunks, being hybrids themselves, are fascinated by inter-zones: the areas where, in the words of William Gibson, 'the street finds its own uses for things.' Rolling, irrepressible street graffiti from that classic industrial artifact, the spray can. The subversive potential of the home printer and the photocopier. Scratch music, whose ghetto innovators turn the phonograph itself into an instrument, producing an archetypal Eighties music where funk meets the Burroughs cut-up method . . .

Cyberpunk work is marked by its visionary intensity . . . Like J. G. Ballard—an idolized role model to many cyberpunks—they often use an unblinking, almost clinical objectivity . . .

With this intensity of vision comes strong imaginative concentration. Cyberpunk is widely known for its telling use of detail, its carefully constructed intricacy, its willingness to carry extrapolation into the fabric of daily life. It favors 'crammed' prose: rapid, dizzying bursts of novel information, sensory overload that submerges the reader in the literary equivalent of the hard-rock 'wall-of-sound'.[36]

This description of cyberpunk gains in significance, if it loses in objectivity, when it is understood that it comes from the word processor of Bruce Sterling, the first spokesman and publicist for cyberpunk, a cyberpunk sf writer himself, and a close friend of the effective inventor of the movement (sometimes 'The Movement'), William Gibson. These words, published in 1986, were not so much a description of a movement as an attempt to create one. The noise sent out by adherents of the new fashion was always rather more than the actual achievement.

What is interesting about this manifesto, however, and about the fiction that emerged from it was that, unlike any previous movement in sf, cyberpunk was about a particular vision of the future. It was the 1980s, exaggerated, and not usually ex-trapolated beyond the twenty-first century. It was urban, run down, yet using the technology of the 1980s with as much in-souciance as we use the technology of the 1940s. It is dominated by multinationals, and Japan is the big economic power. Satellites and space stations are sometimes as much part of the cyberpunk world as the world of Arthur C. Clarke; yet, like the cities, they are run-down, seedy slums, as far removed from the sanitized stainless steel of the *2001* space station as possible. Cyberpunk authors wrote, to a large extent, within a 'shared world' (see above, p. 141); they wrote to a recipe:

One cup *film noir*, one cup Bester, two tablespoons *Blade Runner*, one tablespoon James Bond, a dash of Delany, 'several thousand micrograms' (for those who don't speak cyberpunk, a half gram) of Dexadrine; mix thoroughly, cover in a thick layer of Reagenesque hype and Ramboesque aggressiveness. Bake at full heat for three years, then let simmer. Serves two good writers and several hangers-on.[37]

The two good writers singled out here by Kim Stanley Robinson are presumably William Gibson and Bruce Sterling. Cyberpunk arose with William Gibson's *Neuromancer* (1984); most discussion of cyberpunk since has tended, soon or later, to devolve into a discussion of *Neuromancer*, which remains its classic text. Its opening, like that of *Dune* (discussed above, p. 118), is a challenge to the reader to reconstruct the world from the clues:

The sky above the port was the color of television, tuned to a dead channel.
 'It's not like I'm using,' Case heard someone say, as he shouldered his way through the crowd round the door of the Chat. 'It's like my body's developed this massive drug deficiency.' It was a Sprawl voice and a Sprawl joke. The Chatsubo was a bar for professional expatriates; you could drink there for a week and never hear two words in Japanese.
 Ratz was tending bar, his prosthetic arm jerking monotonously as he filled a tray of glasses with draft Kirin. He saw Case and smiled, his teeth a webwork of East European steel and brown decay . . . In an age of affordable beauty, there was something heraldic about his lack of it. The antique arm whined as he reached for another mug.

Drugs, prosthetics, brand-names, cosmetic surgery, a cosmopolitan yet Japanese setting; a few pages later we learn that Case was a 'cowboy', who had been on a 'permanent adrenaline high, a byproduct of youth and proficiency, jacked into a custom cyberspace deck that projected his disembodied consciousness into the consensual hallucination that was the matrix'.[38] Case is the future embodiment of that 1980s phenomenon; the computer hacker. When he physically jacks himself into his deck, he enters cyberspace, a landscape (akin to virtual reality) inhabited by computer programs and simulacra created by artificial intelligences. Case's world, like our own, is underpinned by an all-encompassing but hidden electronic world of connections and data, which can be explored and exploited by those with the ability to enter it, like Case himself. One of the most striking images in the book, illustrating how the electronic world connects with and controls the physical world, comes when one of the artificial intelligences, Wintermute, tries to contact him:

> There were cigarettes in the gift shop, but he didn't relish talking with Armitage or Riviera. He left the lobby and located a vending console in a narrow alcove, at the end of a rank of pay phones.
>
> He fumbled through a pocketful of lirasi, slotting the small dull alloy coins one after another, vaguely amused by the anachronism of the process. The phone nearest him rang.
>
> Automatically he picked it up.
>
> 'Yeah?'
>
> Faint harmonics, tiny audible voices rattling across some orbital link, and then a sound like wind.
>
> 'Hello, Case.'
>
> A fifty-lirasi coin fell from his hand, bounced, and rolled out of sight across Hilton carpeting.
>
> 'Wintermute, Case. It's time to talk.'
>
> It was a chip voice.
>
> 'Don't you want to talk, Case?'
>
> He hung up.
>
> On his way back to the lobby, his cigarettes forgotten, he had to walk the length of the ranked phones. Each rang in turn, but only once, as he passed.[39]

Neuromancer had its progenitors, of course. The most obvious one was Ridley Scott's film *Blade Runner* (1982), which, for all its faults as a film (and as a version of Philip K. Dick's much more subtle novel *Do Androids Dream of Electric Sheep?*, 1968), was a stunning visual expression of the cyberpunk world. Los Angeles in the film had a largely oriental population, and the neon advertisements showed oriental faces; it had high-tech traffic alongside bicycles, futuristic buildings alongside decaying slums, glamour alongside squalor. The story involved a cop's search for androids or replicants: machines virtually indistinguishable from men, the ultimate in the typical cyberpunk fascination with the meshing of human and machine. Few sf films have been made with such minute attention to the creation of a near-future world, and to a darkly realistic one, rather than the bright-plastic-and-chrome futures of many sf films (and books). William Gibson, who was writing *Neuromancer* when the film came to his town, left the cinema after thirty minutes: 'It looked so much like the inside of my head.'[40]

Literary progenitors of cyberpunk include the novels of Philip K. Dick himself, the stories of John Varley (after Tiptree perhaps the strongest new short-story writer of the 1970s), and, indeed, John Brunner's *The Shockwave Rider* (1975). It is not the progenitors who have puzzled some critics of cyberpunk, so much as its actual writers. In an effort to increase the scale of The Movement, all kinds of contemporary sf writers were claimed to be cyberpunk. Greg Bear, for instance, the most prolific and interesting of the hard sf writers of the 1980s, has been claimed to write cyberpunk, because in novels such as *Blood Music* (1985) he envisaged the evolution of humanity into something different and superior ('a *Childhood's End* for the 1980s', trumpeted the blurb), and because he uses concepts such as artificial intelligence, virtual reality, and so on. But Bear illustrates the artificiality of the whole cyberpunk movement. In reality, cyberpunk writers were doing what sf writers had traditionally always done, and were doing it in a way which showed that they were not revolutionary (as the British New Wave had been) but thoroughly embedded in sf traditions. Much of their work, indeed, is a dialogue with traditional sf.

In 'The Gernsback Continuum' Gibson explored the way in which the imagery of Gernsback-era sf flowed into the real America of the 1930s, where the first generation of industrial designers created 'a series of elaborate props for playing at living in the future'. Frank Lloyd Wright's Johnson's Wax building came straight off the cover of *Amazing Stories*: 'The employees of Johnson's Wax must have felt as though they were walking into one of [Frank R.] Paul's spray-paint pulp utopias.' The protagonist of Gibson's story, a professional photographer, begins a project shooting some of these relics from the 1930s: 'factory buildings . . . came across with a kind of sinister totalitarian dignity, like the stadiums Albert Speer built for Hitler . . . During the high point [of this age] they put Ming the Merciless in charge of designing California gas stations. Favoring the architecture of his native Mongo, he cruised up and down the coast erecting raygun emplacements in white stucco.' In the end the photographer hallucinates a vision of this alternative 1980s: a vast city of skyscrapers, the air above it thick with futuristic aircraft, a 'dream Tucson thrown up out of the collective yearning of an era', its inhabitants smug, happy, and utterly content with themselves—and white, blond, and probably blue-eyed. 'It had all the sinister fruitiness of Hitler Youth propaganda.' Back in the 'human near-dystopia we live in', he remarks, in response to a newspaper seller's 'Hell of a world we live in, huh? . . . But it could be worse, huh?': 'That's right. Or even worse, it could be perfect.'[41]

The dialogue with traditions in cyberpunk is part of the fresh look at many of the assumptions of sf which writers have been making since the 1960s. But from the 1980s the dialogue has become much more explicit and open. Tom Shippey notes that Bruce Sterling's *Schismatrix* (1985)

begins with the Arthur Clarke motif of an ultra-light aircraft wheeling in the sky of a low-gravity hollowed-out asteroid; but of course, with Sterling the ultra-light crashes, just as his spaceships have roaches, his hydroponics all go sour, and his aging space people are all clogged with dirt. Such jabs are all aimed at making readers drop their ballast of (science-fictional) cultural assumptions, to float free (balloon images recur in Sterling) into the larger space of qualified reality.[42]

Cyberpunks, like other sf writers, extrapolated from current trends into the near-future; and although their future often looks black, it is actually suffused with hope and optimism about the potentialities of science for the radical improvement of the human condition. What makes the group look radical is that they have accepted what would have been anathema to previous generations of sf writers, but seemed only natural to young American writers in the mid-1980s: that America was not going to retain its world dominance for ever; that the conquest of space was not the solution to humanity's problems; that the energy crisis, the poverty of the Third World, famine, pollution, and environmental destruction had no simple ready-made answers or technological fixes. The explosion of the space shuttle *Challenger*, on 28 January 1986, was more than the symbolic end of the science-fictional dream.

Cyberpunk was thus a response to a crisis in sf that had become apparent by the 1980s: a growing divergence between the traditional sf images of the future and the increasingly depressing reality. As John Brunner put it:

> Science fiction used to be the most optimistic form of literature, apart from inspirational propaganda. That too has been taken away. I no longer believe in our glorious future among the stars. Too many of us are behaving too stupidly down here on Earth for those worn visions to be any longer credible. In consequence I don't write a lot of science fiction nowadays.
>
> I find I'm mostly writing horror.[43]

Even though sf writers know that they are not in the business of prediction, they take great care to extrapolate plausible futures. This is why many avoid the near-future, or 'solve' the problems of the present by having a historical rupture between our present and their narrative time: a nuclear war, a plague, a comet strike, or whatever. When David Brin, a hard sf writer who gained great popularity in the 1980s, came to write of the twenty-first century in his massive *Earth* (1990) he felt he had to include an odd preface:

> As writers go, I suppose I'm known as a bit of an optimist, so it seems only natural that this novel projects a future where there's a little more wisdom than folly . . . maybe a bit more hope than despair.
>
> In fact, it's about the most encouraging tomorrow I can imagine right now.
>
> What a sobering thought.

Brin, a scientist and a thorough researcher, knows all the problems that are likely to be afflicting Earth in the middle of the next century, and in his novel inflicts a few more; the effect is starkly realistic, which makes an even greater contrast with the implausible sf gimmick which actually saves the planet at the end and which suggests that in fact Brin, too, has no solutions.

It is undoubtedly ironic that just at the time when most sf writers were having serious doubts about the ability of technology to solve social and political problems, a group of Californian sf writers led by Larry Niven and Jerry Pournelle were instrumental (or so they claim) in starting the process of lobbying and persuading which led President Reagan to launch the Strategic Defence Initiative, popularly known as 'Star Wars': the idea of protecting the so-called Free World from attack by an umbrella of satellite-based anti-missile weapons.[44] It is a science-fictional idea which goes back a long way in the literature. In financial terms it has cost more than any other sf idea: in the ten years from its launch in March 1983, $32 billion has been spent, and very little of it to any effect.[45] Changed political and economic circumstances and the weight of hostile scientific opinion meant that it was inevitable that President Clinton would in 1993 announce the demise of this sf quick-fix gimmick.

The novels and short stories from that handful of writers which it is legitimate to label 'cyberpunk' do not, at least, resort to the sf gimmick, and if they offer no solutions, they do suggest where humanity is going. The solution for other sf writers in the 1980s was to ignore the problems of the twentieth or twenty-first century by fleeing to the far future, or to give up on the possibility of solution by writing about catastrophe, environmental or otherwise. An example of the latter would be the Australian sf writer George Turner's *The Sea and Summer* (1987; US: *Drowning Towers*), which showed the collapse of civilization in Melbourne as global warming caused the ocean gradually to engulf the city. A much more extreme example might be the exceptionally popular series by Douglas Adams, *The Hitch Hiker's Guide to the Galaxy* (published in book form, 1979–93), which solved the problem of the popular dislike of sf by treating all its themes satirically, and which avoided any solution to Earth's problems by underlining the essential pointlessness of human existence and destroying the whole planet in the first volume, to make way for an interstellar bypass or freeway.

The opposite approach, fleeing to the far future, offered great artistic possibilities, if only in the creation of one of the greatest modern works of the sf imagination, Gene Wolfe's four-volume *The Book of the New Sun*: *The Shadow of the Torturer* (1980), *The Claw of the Conciliator* (1981), *The Sword of the Lictor* (1982), and *The Citadel of the Autarch* (1983). This is really one immense novel, given a sequel in 1987 with *The Urth of the New Sun*. It is set on Earth

eons hence, a world so impacted with the relics of humanity's long residence that archaeology and geology have become, in a way, the same science: that of plumbing the body of the planet for messages which have become inextricably intermingled over the innumerable years.[46]

The story tells of Severian, an apprentice torturer and a man (he tells us himself) with a perfect memory (but less than total openness), who travels across the world in search of his destiny as the future Autarch. Wolfe is allusive and elusive; part of the pleasure of reading Wolfe is trying to discover, from the clues scattered by this playfully misleading writer, the truth of Severian's world and Severian's destiny, while part of it is the recognition of the innumerable reworkings of myth, of religious tradition, and of genre sf cliché. This huge novel is an immensely complex work, which leads to the type of sf which was to become more and more common in the 1980s and into the 1990s: the sf work whose theme and area of exploration is not so much the physical or historical universe as the texture and meaning of sf itself. This is the sign of the maturity of a genre, perhaps, or of its decadence.

Current Trends in SF

Sf writers, as well as historians, know that prediction is a fruitless exercise. It is impossible, at the moment of writing, to determine what the future holds for sf, and difficult to determine which current trends are significant and which are merely ephemeral. The publishing industry in the United States and the United Kingdom, hit by recession, take-overs, and reorganization, is still in a state of flux. Sf in Eastern Europe, which flourished in the last years of communism as one of the few semi-legitimate outlets for protest, now suffers from massive paper shortages and hyper-inflation. The easing of restrictions there has meant the publication of some Western authors for the first time, although in most cases without payment of any royalties to those authors; but it has not been good news for indigenous authors. In the rest of the world indigenous authors still struggle, and publishers' lists are still dominated by translations of Anglo-American work. In the United States and the United Kingdom, fantasy, particularly fantasy aimed at the adolescent market, continues its 1980s trend of outselling most sf: lists of the best-selling genre books in the United States mostly consist of the latest books in various fantasy series, and if sf figures at all, it is either sf by a best-selling author, such as Orson Scott Card or Isaac Asimov (whose new 'Foundation' novels were among the big publishing successes of the 1980s), or the latest *Star Trek* novel. Figures from a leading bookseller in Britain in 1993 indicate that 14 per cent of fiction sales are sales of sf and fantasy (as opposed to, say, 7 per cent for crime fiction), but that the 14 per cent breaks down into 70 per cent fantasy and 30 per cent sf. A second bookseller reports a similar finding: that 10 per cent of all fiction sold is fantasy, and that 10 per cent of all fantasy sold is by Terry Pratchett.[47]

There have been predictions, mostly by sf writers, that fantasy may be on the decline; they have also suggested that horror, which also boomed in the 1980s, had peaked by the early 1990s. The horror writer Stephen King (whose first book, which was sf, was rejected by editor Donald A. Wollheim) became the best-selling author in history by the early 1990s, with some eighty million books in print; but perhaps his many imitators are running out of steam. Sf writers have also predicted recently that sf was at last on the verge of being accepted by literary critics; this has been predicted for over thirty years now, without showing signs of becoming true. These current predictions are based largely on the way in which some 'mainstream' writers (the 'slipstream' writers, as Sterling has called them: see above, p. 100) share with sf and fantasy writers a delight in reshaping the world so that it differs from the world of our own experience. Some critics have seen this as typical of the postmodernist novel, and have suggested that postmodernism owes a good deal to the sf model (just as sf itself is now borrowing from postmodernism). Brian McHale suggests that:

Science fiction is to postmodernism what detective fiction was to modernism: it is the ontological genre *par excellence* (as the detective story is the epistemological genre *par excellence*), and so serves as a source of materials and models for postmodernist writers (including William Burroughs, Kurt Vonnegut, Italo Calvino, Pynchon, even Beckett and Nabokov).[48]

Postmodernism, says McHale, has ontology as its dominant, whereas modernism had epistemology. The latter was concerned primarily with the nature of knowledge, whereas the former, like sf, tackles the nature of existence. Sf writers and post-modernist writers, he suggests, approached the problem from quite different angles—he looks at the work of Philip K. Dick in the 1960s, and Philip José Farmer in the 1970s—but more recently they have converged, and they now share more and more in terms of concerns and themes. Some sf writers are going to be reassured by this project to provide a common ground between themselves and the current avant-garde, but it is not clear that many non-sf readers are going to be attracted to the genre on these grounds. *The Feast of the Khroobles* still taints the field (see above, p. 2), for all that books such as Samuel R. Delany's *Stars in My Pocket Like Grains of Sand* (1984), John Crowley's *Aegypt* (1987), or Gene Wolfe's *The Book of the New Sun* (1980–7), are comparable in complexity and quality to those produced by most postmodernists.

As has been said before, Anglo-American sf in the 1990s is too varied to make any predictions about where it is heading. In commercial terms the trends are probably distorted by the effects of the recession of the early 1990s. In numbers of new titles, 1992 figures for the United States show a decline from the all-time peaks of 1990 and 1991: 239 new sf novels published, dropping from 308. New fantasy novels dropped from 301 to 278; new horror novels stood at 165, a decline from the all-time high of 182 in 1988.[49] The trend has been similar in the United Kingdom, and the proportions between genres have been similar too: figures for 1992 show that the number of new sf novels was 84, a 35 per cent drop from the 1989 figure of 130; the number of new fantasy novels was down to 109, from 137 in 1989; and the number of new horror novels stood at 52, 10 fewer than in 1991.[50] In the United Kingdom the number of reprints roughly equalled the number of original issues, a more healthy state than in the United States (in that reprints are more profitable than originals), where originals far outnumber reprints. Book distribution systems are also very different in the two countries, in a way which favours the British author; the shelf-life of paperbacks is much shorter in the United States, and a high proportion of a print run is destroyed to make room for the next month's issues.

Most American magazines have also been having problems in the early 1990s, although some specialist fiction magazines continue to survive, including *Aboriginal*, *Amazing*, *Analog*, *Asimov's*, and *Fantasy and Science Fiction*. Only *Analog* and *Asimov's* have sales of more than 70,000 per month, both down from peaks of more than 100,000 in the early 1980s. In the United Kingdom the one steady sf magazine, *Interzone*, under the editorship of David Pringle, went monthly in May 1990, and seems to be flourishing, with a readership of some 10,000 per month.

Perhaps the main sign of health in any field, however, is not in commercial terms, but in terms of talent. In both North America and Britain new writers are coming into the field, and in the early 1990s are producing interesting and indeed exciting work (mostly in English, though one must not forget the relatively recent efflorescence of French Canadian sf). In the United Kingdom many of the newer writers have been associated with *Interzone*, and started their writing careers there with short fiction before moving to book publication; one might single out Steve Baxter, Keith Brooke, Eric Brown, Molly Brown, and Nicola Griffith. The Northern Irish writer Ian McDonald was an exception, establishing himself in the United States, in *Asimov's* and in Bantam Books, before being published in the United Kingdom. *Interzone* also published some of the important early work of the Canadian writer Geoff Ryman (now resident in the UK) and the Australian Greg Egan. In the United States it is probably rather more common for writers to begin publishing with novels, but the magazines still offer themselves as nurseries for new writers, as they have done ever since the 1920s. (The difference is that because there are so many more would-be writers of sf than in the 1920s or 1930s, the average age of writers at first publication is considerably higher now than it used to be, and the literary maturity correspondingly greater.) The most consistently interesting of the American magazines, *Isaac Asimov's Science Fiction Magazine*, under the editorship of Gardner Dozois since 1986, has always encouraged the careers of promising new writers (at present, Alexander Jablokov, Geoffrey A. Landis, R. Garcia y Robertson, and Mary Rosenblum), while continuing to publish writers it encouraged in the 1980s, such as James Patrick Kelly, John Kessel, Kim Stanley Robinson, Lucius Shepard, Michael Swanwick, and Connie Willis. (*Asimov's* also published in 1992 several new stories by the 85-year-old L. Sprague de Camp, who had published his first story in *Astounding* in 1937.) Although British writers such as Gwyneth Jones, Ian McDonald, and Ian Watson have appeared in *Asimov's* and other American magazines, it is probably true to say that *Interzone* publishes more American writers than American magazines publish British writers. The dominance of American sf is still considerable; rather more significant, however, is the fact that American editors believe, perhaps rightly, that American readers do not readily take to foreign writers. British writers are frequently criticized for being too British; those few British writers who are succeeding in the American market in the 1990s are those who can best hide their Britishness, as Eric Frank Russell did in the 1940s or John Brunner in the late 1960s. The American writer Orson Scott Card, in a review of George Turner's *Brain Child* (1991), notes that Turner is so Australocentric that 'he never registers even the faintest surprise that such astonishing scientific achievements would take place in Australia', and that America seems hardly to exist for him.

I also realized that this is *precisely* how most American science fiction for many decades has seemed to non-US readers. It is simply taken for granted that anything that matters in the world of the future will be American. So it's a deliciously sharp experience to read a novel that seems to have exactly that level of naive arrogance, only centred in a different country.[51]

Clearly, many American readers do not want to share that deliciously sharp experience.

Sf still flourishes in a variety of sub-genres. There has been a vogue for alternative histories since the late 1980s, with anthologies about how the world might be if Hitler had won, or with alternative versions of the careers of American presidents. There is the sub-genre of 'steampunk', of which William Gibson and Bruce Sterling's *The Difference Engine* (1990) is the best example: fantasy or sf stories set in an alternative version of Victorian London. (This is, of course, best done by American writers, publishing wisdom runs, as British proponents tend to be too British.) There has been a growing sub-genre of military sf. And sf still persists in thinking seriously about the future, and about itself.

As an example of the different approaches which coexist, I will end by taking a number of recent examples of novels set on Mars. Mars has had all kinds of different treatments, from Edgar Rice Burroughs's romantic land of warriors and lost princesses to Ray Bradbury's nostalgic images of Midwest American culture coexisting with the ghosts of past Martian civilizations to the hard sf of the 1950s, by Clarke and Heinlein, describing the nuts and bolts of the future colonization of the planet. The inspiration for the six recent novels set on Mars has been, it would seem, either a desire to revisit some of the haunts of past sf or else the 1990 announcement by President Bush of the long-term plan to send men (or even women) to Mars by 2019. With *Mars* (1992), Ben Bova, an American writer of hard sf, wrote an account of that first international expedition, contrasting the difficulties of the mission itself, its interpersonal rivalries and hostile conditions in space and on Mars (radiation from solar flares, a dust storm), with the political problems and rivalries on Earth. Kim Stanley Robinson's *Red Mars* (1992) is an account of the second mission, and the beginning of the project to terraform the planet, to remake it in Earth's image, suitable for colonization. He too contrasts the difficulties of the mission itself, its interpersonal rivalries and hostile conditions in space and on Mars (radiation from solar flares, a dust storm), with the political problems and rivalries on Earth. It is more apocalyptic than Bova's and at the same time much more radical politically, as befits someone who wrote *Pacific Edge* (1990), by far the most interesting utopian novel since Delany's *Triton* (1976). Both authors do their research, and both novels are genuine attempts to understand what the problems of Mars exploration will actually be; but both are fully aware of the many earlier attempts by sf writers to cover the same problem. It is impossible to deny that Terry Bisson's *Voyage to the Red Planet* (1990) is much more fun. This is not sf as extrapolation, but sf as satire. The United States Government has privatized most of its functions; NASA is a Disney subsidiary; the first Mars mission is financed by a movie mogul, who sends the spaceship *Mary Poppins* off to Mars with two astronaut heroes, two Hollywood stars, and a cameraman. Bisson takes his science almost as seriously as Bova and Robinson, but he plays the politics for laughs, and has plenty of in-jokes for sf readers. Even more upfront about their confrontation with the sf tradition are three novels by British writers: Ian McDonald's *Desolation Road* (1988), Paul J. McAuley's *Red Dust* (1993), and Colin Greenland's *Harm's Way* (1993). McDonald revisits Ray Bradbury's Mars, and infuses it with the spirit of Gabriel García Marquez's *One Hundred Years of Solitude* (1967), the classic novel of South American magic realism; it is a gloriously evocative and poignant novel. McAuley borrows from an even wider set of sf tropes and icons. *Red Dust* is set 500 years in the future, in a Mars under Chinese control, but with numerous echoes of the American Wild West: we have cyberspace, virtual reality, nano-technology, wonder drugs, and a reincarnation of Elvis Presley. Greenland's *Harm's Way*, on the other hand, takes us to a Mars in a splendidly Dickensian alternative future, in which the British Empire has colonized Mars in its space-travelling sailing ships, and established an uneasy relationship with the ferocious flying Martians, the 'angels'. The ideal reader for both these 1993 novels, as for so much modern sf, is the reader steeped in the sf of the past; the uninitiated will revel in the surface texture, but may never penetrate beneath it.

Sf has become part of the modern idiom, infusing our language, our media culture, and our children's world of play with its images and its concepts. But sf as a literary medium is also still engaged with developments in modern science and technology; it still offers serious speculation about the future; it is still a place for satire. It now acknowledges and interacts with a century-long tradition of sf writing, enriching and broadening it and preparing it for whatever awaits it in the next millennium. Since the history of sf teaches us, among other things, the follies of prediction, here the story must end.

Notes

Preface

1. Gene Wolfe, *The Shadow of the Torturer* (1980), which is the first volume of *The Book of the New Sun*, quoted from Arrow edn. (London, 1981), 49, 52.

Introduction

1. Reprinted in Robert Short, *The Gospel from Outer Space* (New York, 1983), 16.
2. Frank Cioffi, in *Formula Fiction? An Anatomy of American Science Fiction, 1930–1940* (Westport, Conn., 1982); Farah Mendlesohn in her current doctoral research at the University of York.
3. Samuel R. Delany, *The Jewel-Hinged Jaw: Notes on the Language of Science Fiction* (New York, 1978; cited in 1978 rev. paperback edn.), p. 9.
4. Quoted by Brian M. Stableford, 'William Wilson's Prospectus for Science Fiction: 1851', *Foundation*, 10 (June 1976), 6–12, at 9–10.
5. First pointed out by Gary Westfahl, ' "An Idea of Significant Import": Hugo Gernsback's Theory of Science Fiction', *Foundation*, 48 (Spring 1990), 26–50, at 47.
6. Quoted in ibid. 37.
7. See Brian M. Stableford, *Scientific Romance in Britain, 1890–1950* (London, 1985), 5–7; Sam Moskowitz, *Explorers of the Infinite: Shapers of Science Fiction*, 2nd edn. (Westport, Conn., 1974), 314–22.
8. David Lewis, 'Japanese SF', in Neil Barron (ed.), *Anatomy of Wonder: A Critical Guide to Science Fiction*, 3rd edn. (New York and London, 1987), 474.
9. Darko Suvin, *Metamorphoses of Science Fiction: On the Politics and History of a Literary Genre* (New Haven, Conn., and London, 1979), p. viii.

Chapter 1: The Development of a Genre, 1895–1940

1. Figures derived from Everett F. Bleiler, *Science-Fiction: The Early Years* (Kent, Oh., 1990), 926. All works referred to in this section were first published in 1895 unless otherwise stated.

2. Stableford, *Scientific Romance*, 34–8.

3. Listed in Philip Babcock Gove, *The Imaginary Voyage in Prose Fiction* (New York, 1941).

4. Indexed by Bleiler, *Science Fiction*, 896–8.

5. The quotation is from Jean Chesneaux, *The Political and Social Ideas of Jules Verne* (London, 1972), 37; the argument, which depends on a rather narrow view of sf, from Arthur B. Evans, 'Science Fiction vs. Scientific Fiction in France: From Jules Verne to J.-H. Rosny Aîné', *Science-Fiction Studies*, 44 (Mar. 1988), 1–11.

6. See Michael J. Crowe, *The Extraterrestrial Life Debate, 1750–1900. The Idea of a Plurality of Worlds from Kant to Lowell* (Cambridge, 1986).

7. W. Warren Wagar, *Terminal Visions: The Literature of Last Things* (Bloomington, Ind., 1982), 16.

8. Quoted and trans. in Paul K. Alkon, *Origins of Futuristic Fiction* (Athens, Ga., and London, 1987), 8.

9. An extensive bibliography is given in the excellent study by I. F. Clarke, *Voices Prophesying War, 1763–1984* (Oxford, 1966), from which much of this information comes.

10. See E. James, '1886: Past Views of Ireland's Future', *Foundation*, 36 (Summer 1986), 21–31.

11. Published in Isaac Asimov (ed.), *Future Days: A Nineteenth-Century Vision of the Year 2000* (New York, 1986).

12. See the account in Moskowitz, *Explorers of the Infinite*, ch. 7; and Bleiler, *Science Fiction*, 549–62.

13. *The Frank Reade Library* was republished in facsimile by Garland, New York, ed. E. F. Bleiler, between 1979 and 1986.

14. Moskowitz, *Explorers of the Infinite*, 120.

15. Bleiler, *Science-Fiction*, 549.

16. John Clute, in John Clute and Peter Nicholls (eds.), *The Encyclopedia of Science Fiction* (London, 1993), 368.

17. A point made to me by Eric S. Rabkin.

18. Neil Harris, *Humbug: The Art of P. T. Barnum* (Chicago, 1973), 79. I should like to thank my colleague Chris Clark for drawing my attention to this.

19. Essay reprinted in Robert Philmus and David Y. Hughes (eds.),

H. G. Wells: Early Writings in Science and Science Fiction (Berkeley, Calif., 1975), 22–31; quotation from 30–1.

20. Cited in Frank McConnell, *The Science Fiction of H. G. Wells* (Oxford, 1981), 8.

21. Both passages from the Epilogue, cited from H. G. Wells, *Selected Short Stories* (Harmondsworth, 1958), 83.

22. Ibid. 76–8.

23. Quoted in Elaine Showalter, *Sexual Anarchy: Gender and Culture at the Fin de Siècle* (London, 1992), 63.

24. Quoted in ibid. 88.

25. Darko Suvin, *Victorian Science Fiction in the UK: The Discourses of Knowledge and of Power* (Boston, 1983), 125.

26. Stableford, *Scientific Romance*, 149.

27. The story is related by Bates in Alva Rogers, *A Requiem for Astounding* (Chicago, 1964), pp. ix–x.

28. In Barron (ed.), *Anatomy of Wonder*, 443. The chapters on the various national sf traditions in this book are a prime source for what follows in this section.

29. Huxley, quoted in by far the best account of the book, in Krishan Kumar, *Utopia and Anti-Utopia in Modern Times* (Oxford, 1987), ch. 7, at p. 225.

30. In the preface to his *Seven Famous Novels* (New York, 1934), quoted by Alexei and Cory Panshin, *The World Beyond the Hill: Science Fiction and the Quest for Transcendence* (Los Angeles, 1989), 236.

31. For these encomia, see Leslie Fiedler, *Olaf Stapledon: A Man Divided* (Oxford, 1983), 5–6.

32. See ibid. 42.

33. Brian Aldiss, with David Wingrove, *Trillion Year Spree: The History of Science Fiction*, rev. edn. (London, 1988), 204–5.

34. Peter Nicholls (ed.), *Explorations of the Marvellous: The Science and the Fiction in Science Fiction*, 2nd edn. (London, 1978), 149.

35. In Marshall B. Tymn and Mike Ashley (eds.), *Science Fiction, Fantasy, and Weird Fiction Magazines* (Westport, Conn., 1985), 63.

36. 'Forgetfulness', *Astounding*, June 1937, repr. in, e.g., John W. Campbell, *Cloak of Aesir* (New York, 1972), 15–46; 'Who Goes There?', *Astounding*, Aug. 1938, repr. in, e.g., John W. Campbell, *The Thing* (London, 1966), 11–75.

37. I follow here the analysis by Panshin and Panshin, *World Beyond the Hill*, 272–6.

38. On this see Sam Moskowitz, 'The Origins of Science Fiction

Fandom: A Reconstruction', *Foundation*, 48 (Spring 1990), 5–25.

39. Here I draw on G. Westfahl in *Foundation*, 48 (Spring 1990), 26–50.

Chapter 2: The Victory of American SF, 1940–1960

1. The speech opened the science debate at the Labour Party's annual Conference at Scarborough in 1963. It is printed in Harold Wilson, *Purpose in Politics: Selected Speeches* (London, 1964), 15.
2. See G. Westfahl, ' "Dictatorial, Authoritarian, Uncooperative": The Case against John W. Campbell, Jr.', *Foundation*, 56 (Autumn 1992), 36–61.
3. I draw here on the discussion by G. Westfahl in ' "A Convenient Analog System": John W. Campbell Jr.'s Theory of Science Fiction', *Foundation*, 54 (Spring 1992), 52–70.
4. Introduction to Campbell, *Who Goes There?* (Chicago, 1948), 5.
5. Introduction to Campbell, *Analog 1* (Garden City, NY, 1963), p. xv.
6. Quoted by Panshin and Panshin, *World Beyond the Hill*, 376: probably the best accounts of the writers who made up the Campbell revolution.
7. In Lloyd A. Eshbach (ed.), *Of Worlds Beyond* (Reading, Pa., 1947), cited from London, 1965, reprint, pp. 13–20.
8. Ibid. 17–18.
9. Ibid. 19.
10. Introduction to Edmund Crispin (ed.), *Best SF: Science Fiction Stories* (London, 1958), 9.
11. Kingsley Amis, *New Maps of Hell* (London, 1960), quoted from 1963 Four Square edn., 14.
12. Foreword to M. A. DeFord, *Elsewhere, Elsewhen, Elsehow*, quoted by Aldiss with Wingrove, *Trillion Year Spree*, 30.
13. Delany, in *Jewel-Hinged Jaw*, 135.
14. In what follows in this section I acknowledge my debt to three excellent studies by Albert I. Berger: '*Analog Science Fiction/ Science Fact*', in Tymn and Ashley (eds.), *Science Fiction*, 61–88; 'Theories of History and Social Order in *Astounding Science Fiction*, 1934–55', *Science-Fiction Studies*, 44 (Mar. 1988), 12–35; and 'Towards a Science of the Nuclear Mind: Science-Fiction Origins of Dianetics', *Science-Fiction Studies*, 48 (July 1989), 123–44.
15. Berger, 'Theories', 25.

16. H. Bruce Franklin, 'Don't Look Where We're Going: The Vision of the Future in Science-Fiction Films, 1970–1982', *Science-Fiction Studies*, 29 (1983), 72; repr. in Annette Kuhn (ed.), *Alien Zone: Cultural Theory and Contemporary Science Fiction Cinema* (London, 1990).
17. Figures from Gianni Montanari, in Barron (ed.), *Anatomy of Wonder*, 506.
18. See H. Heidtmann, 'A Survey of Science Fiction in the German Democratic Republic', *Science-Fiction Studies*, 17 (Mar. 1979), 92–9.
19. Published on the cover of *Foundation*, 41 (Winter 1987).
20. In Peter Nicholls (ed.), *The Encyclopedia of Science Fiction: An Illustrated A to Z* (London, 1979), 511.
21. Aldiss with Wingrove, *Trillion Year Spree*, 315.
22. Rowland Wymer, 'How "Safe" is John Wyndham? A Closer Look at his Work, with Particular Reference to *The Chrysalids*', *Foundation*, 55 (Summer 1992), 25–36.
23. Wyndham, *The Midwich Cuckoos* (Harmondsworth, 1960), 112–13.
24. James Gunn, *Alternate Worlds: The Illustrated History of Science Fiction* (Englewood Cliffs, NJ, 1975), 216.
25. See Frederik Pohl, 'The Publishing of Science Fiction', in Reginald Bretnor (ed.), *Science Fiction, Today and Tomorrow* (Baltimore, 1974), 30–1.
26. Relying on Gunn's lists, *Alternate Worlds*, 212.
27. Donald A. Wollheim, *The Universe Makers: Science Fiction Today* (London, 1972), 42–4, quoted by Gunn, *Alternate Worlds*, 225–6.
28. On this see E. James, 'Yellow, Black, Metal and Tentacled: The Race Question in American Science Fiction', in Philip John Davies (ed.), *Science Fiction, Social Conflict and War* (Manchester, 1990), 26–49.
29. H. L. Gold, editorial in *Galaxy Science Fiction*, 3 (Jan. 1952), quoted by Paul A. Carter, *The Creation of Tomorrow: Fifty Years of Magazine Science Fiction* (New York, 1977), 230.
30. See the entry in Nicholls (ed.), *Encyclopedia of Science Fiction*, 134–6.
31. Thomas Kuhn, *The Structure of Scientific Revolutions* (Chicago, 1962).

Chapter 3: Reading Science Fiction

1. Bruce Sterling, interviewed by Andy Robertson and David Pringle, *Interzone*, 15 (Spring 1986), 12.

2. Ed Mitchell, quoted in Bretnor (ed.), *Science Fiction*, 198.

3. On all this, see Thomas M. Disch, 'The Embarrassments of Science Fiction', in Nicholls (ed.), *Explorations of the Marvellous*, 139–55.

4. Sterling, 'Catscan', *Science Fiction Eye*, 1/5 (July 1989), 77–80, at 78; he has a 'Slipstream List' on 79.

5. Notably in Robert Scholes, *Structural Fabulation: An Essay on Fiction of the Future* (Notre Dame, Ind., 1975).

6. Ibid. 3.

7. Ibid. 18.

8. Ibid. 38.

9. Ibid. 41–2.

10. Discussed by James Blish, in William Atheling, jun. (pseudonym for Blish), *More Issues at Hand* (Chicago, 1970), 110–13.

11. Scholes, *Structural Fabulation*, 43.

12. Ibid. 44.

13. Quoted from the updating of this book, with David Wingrove, as *Trillion Year Spree*, 2nd edn., 30; the wording is slightly different. 'Man and his status' has become 'mankind and his status' (a small improvement) and 'Gothic or post-Gothic mould' has become 'Gothic or post-Gothic mode'.

14. Ibid. 42–4.

15. Ibid. 43.

16. Cornel Robu, 'A Key to Science Fiction: The Sublime', *Foundation*, 42 (Spring 1988), 21–37.

17. Kant, quoted by Robu, ibid. 25, from *The Critique of Judgement* (1790).

18. Edmund Burke, 'On the Sublime and Beautiful' (1756), quoted by Robu, ibid. 22.

19. David Hartwell, *Age of Wonders: Exploring the World of Science Fiction* (New York, 1984), 42.

20. Published in Frederik Pohl (ed.), *Star Science Fiction Stories* (New York, 1953), and collected many times, as in Clarke, *The Other Side of the Sky* (New York, 1958), and E. Crispin (ed.), *Best SF Two* (London, 1956), and R. Silverberg (ed.), *The Science Fiction Hall of Fame*, vol. 1 (New York, 1970).

21. John Huntington, *Rationalizing Genius: Ideological Strategies in the Classic American Science Fiction Short Story* (New Brunswick, NJ, and London, 1989), 151.

22. Suvin, *Metamorphoses of Science Fiction*, 7–8.

23. Ibid. 7.

24. Ibid. 13.

25. Ibid. 63.
26. Philip K. Dick, *Our Friends from Frolix 8* (1970), Panther edn. (London, 1976), 125.
27. Suvin, *Victorian Science Fiction*, 86.
28. Discussed in ibid. 94–5.
29. Ibid. 94.
30. Atheling, *More Issues at Hand*, 98–9.
31. For the comments of Clute, Nicholls, and Stableford, see 'Definitions of SF', in Nicholls (ed.), *Encyclopedia of Science Fiction*, 159–61.
32. Tom Shippey, 'Learning to Read Science Fiction', in Shippey (ed.), *Fictional Space: Essays on Contemporary Science Fiction* (Oxford, 1991), 13.
33. Kim Stanley Robinson, 'Notes for an Essay on Cecelia Holland', *Foundation*, 40 (Summer 1987), 60: an interesting discussion of the one recent historical novelist who has also written sf.
34. On this, see G. B. Chamberlain, 'Allohistory in Science Fiction', and B. C. Hacker and G. B. Chamberlain, 'Pasts That Might Have Been, II: A Revised Bibliography of Alternative History', both in C. G. Waugh and M. H. Greenberg (eds.), *Alternative Histories: Eleven Stories of the World as It Might Have Been* (New York, 1986), 281–300, 301–63.
35. Hugo Gernsback, *Ralph 124C 41+* (1911–12, book 1925), quoted from the UK paperback edn. (Kemsley, 1952), 45–6; the chart in question is reproduced on p. 46.
36. In Delany, *Jewel-Hinged Jaw*, 34.
37. Delany, *Stars in My Pocket Like Grains of Sand* (1984), quoted from UK paperback edn. (London, 1986), 304.
38. J. Huntington, in Shippey (ed.), *Fictional Space*, 70.
39. Text taken from 1st British paperback edn. of Frank Herbert's *Dune* (London, 1968), 9–10.
40. Comment from Panshin and Panshin, *World Beyond the Hill*, 586.
41. Shippey, 'Learning to Read', 17.
42. Robert Irwin, *Foundation*, 55 (Summer 1992), 116–17.
43. 'Nightfall' was first published in *Astounding*, Sept. 1941, and subsequently much anthologized: e.g. in Raymond J. Healy and J. Francis McComas, *Adventures in Time and Space* (New York, 1946; repr. 1975), 378–411, and Silverberg (ed.), *Science Fiction Hall of Fame*, i. 112–43. 'I don't even consider it the best I've written': I. Asimov, *In Memory Yet Green: The Autobiography of Isaac Asimov, 1920–1954* (New York, 1979), 296.
44. Asimov, *In Memory Yet Green*, 295.

45. For a discussion of this, see Huntington, *Rationalizing Genius*, 145–51. For what it is worth, the novel version and continuation of the story, published as Isaac Asimov and Robert Silverberg, *Nightfall* (New York, 1990), assumes the survival of the Hideout.

46. Asimov, *In Memory Yet Green*, 313. This point is discussed in J. Huntington, ' "Not Earth's Feeble Stars": Thoughts on John W. Campbell, Jr.'s Editorship', in G. E. Slusser, G. Westfahl, and E. S. Rabkin (eds.), *Science Fiction and Market Realities* (University of Georgia Press, forthcoming). For the intrusion of editorial and commercial decisions into the criticism of sf, see the illuminating pamphlet by Algis Budrys, *Non-Literary Influences on Science Fiction: An Essay* (Polk City, Ia., 1983).

47. 'The Moon Moth' was first published in *Galaxy*, 87 (Aug. 1961), and republished in Vance collections such as *The Best of Jack Vance* (New York, 1976) and *Green Magic* (San Francisco, 1979), and in B. Bova (ed.), *The Science Fiction Hall of Fame*, vol. IIB (New York, 1973).

48. 'Light of Other Days' was originally published in *Analog*, Aug. 1966, and has been republished several times, as part of Shaw's 'fix-up' *Other Days, Other Eyes* (London, 1972) and, e.g., in R. Silverberg (ed.), *Robert Silverberg's Worlds of Wonder* (London, 1988), 329–35.

49. Silverberg, *Worlds of Wonder*, 335.

Chapter 4: The SF Community

1. Moskowitz, 'Origins of Science Fiction Fandom'.

2. Gernsback, editorial for 3rd issue of *Amazing*, June 1926, quoted by Moskowitz, ibid. 18.

3. Harry Warner, jun., *All Our Yesterdays: An Informal History of Science Fiction Fandom in the Forties* (Chicago, 1969), 54; Gunn, *Alternate Worlds*, 183.

4. Warner, 96.

5. Published in *Wonder Stories*, May 1935, p. 1517, and quoted here from Brian M. Stableford, *The Sociology of Science Fiction* (San Bernardino, Calif., 1987), 73.

6. Here I rely entirely on Sam Moskowitz, 'From Fanzines to Fame: SF Figures who Began as Fan Editors', *Foundation*, 45 (Spring 1989), 5–23.

7. Asimov, editorial, *Isaac Asimov's Science Fiction Magazine*, Aug. 1990, p. 8.

8. See Damon Knight's comments in *Isaac Asimov's Science Fiction Magazine*, Mar. 1990, p. 21.

9. On this, see, e.g., Richard Grant, 'The Exile's Paradigm', *Science Fiction Eye*, 6 (Feb. 1990), 41–51, and, against, Lucius Shepard, 'Who is Richard Grant and Why is He Saying Such Dreadful Things about Clarion?', *Science Fiction Eye*, 7 (Aug. 1990), 69–73. Lucius Shepard's experiences at Clarion in 1980 are recalled in 'How I Spent My Summer Vacation: A Student Perspective on Clarion', *Isaac Asimov's Science Fiction Magazine*, Feb. 1985, pp. 30–42.

10. Lem's article is reprinted, along with much other documentation on the affair, in *Science-Fiction Studies*, 12 (vol. 4, pt. 2) (July 1977), 126–44.

11. Ursula K. Le Guin, letter to *Science-Fiction Studies*, 11 (vol. 4, pt. 1) (Mar. 1977), 100.

12. For a list of the winners, see under 'Arthur C. Clarke Award', 'Hugo' and 'Nebula', in Clute and Nicholls (eds.), *Encyclopedia of Science Fiction*. In fact there was considerable disquiet in British sf circles in 1993 when the award went to Marge Piercy, an 'outsider', for her novel *Body of Glass* (US: *He, She, and It*).

13. Damien Broderick has some very interesting things to say in relation to this in 'Reading SF as a Mega-Text', *New York Review of Science Fiction*, 47 (July 1992), 1–11.

14. Brian W. Aldiss, *This World and Nearer Ones* (London, 1979), 12.

15. Quoted in Nicholls (ed.), *Encyclopedia of Science Fiction*, under 'Pseudo-science'.

16. On Strieber, see B. Wignall's interview in *Interzone*, 40 (Oct. 1990), 31–3, and two articles by Thomas M. Disch in *Interzone*, 25 (Sept.–Oct. 1988), 25–9, and 29 (May–June 1989), 44–6.

17. See Barrington J. Bayley, *The Knights of the Limits* (London, 1978). The Farmer story can be found in D. Knight (ed.), *A Century of Science Fiction* (New York, 1962), and James E. Gunn (ed.), *The Road to Science Fiction #3* (New York, 1979).

18. Quoted by Peter Roberts in the entry on Fort in Nicholls (ed.), *Encyclopedia of Science Fiction*.

19. Arthur C. Clarke, 'Asimov's Corollary', in K. Frazier (ed.), *Paranormal Borderlands of Science* (Buffalo, NY, 1981), 223–32.

20. Thomas M. Disch, 'A Closer Look at Close Encounters', *Foundation*, 15 (Jan. 1979), 50–3.

21. See A. Puharich, *Uri: The Original and Authorised Biography of Uri Geller* (London, 1974), 183.

22. T. Ferris, 'Playboy Interview: Erich von Däniken', *Playboy*, Aug. 1974.

23. Quoted in Ronald D. Story, 'Von Däniken's Golden Gods', in Frazier (ed.), *Paranormal Borderlands*, 318.
24. See John Sladek, *The New Apocrypha: A Guide to Strange Sciences and Occult Beliefs* (London, 1974); John Brunner, 'Science Fiction and the Larger Lunacy', in Nicholls (ed.), *Explorations of the Marvellous*, 75–104.
25. Reported in the *Guardian*, 29 Mar. 1983.
26. Interview with Sam Merwin, reported in Russell Miller, *Bare-Faced Messiah: The True Story of L. Ron Hubbard* (London, 1988), 172; Lloyd Eshbach's memory reported in Hubbard's obituary, *Locus*, 302 (Mar. 1986), 54.
27. Much of this is derived from Christopher Evans's excellent *Cults of Unreason* (London, 1973); but see also Miller, *Bare-Faced Messiah*.
28. S. E. Whitfield and G. Roddenberry, *The Making of Star Trek* (New York, 1968), 129.
29. Quoted in Constance Penley, 'Brownian Motion: Women, Tactics and Technology', in C. Penley and A. Ross, *Technoculture* (Minneapolis, 1991), 135–61, at n. 2; her 'Feminism, Psychoanalysis and the Study of Popular Culture', in L. Grossberg et al. (eds.), *Cultural Studies* (New York, 1992), 479–500, also deals with K/S. I am most grateful to Professor Penley for supplying me with copies of these articles.
30. For Hobbit Games, see *Shards of Babel: The European SF Newsletter* (published by Roeloff Goudriaan in Rijswijk), 37 (July 1992), 10; for Frodo, see Serge V. Berezhnoj, 'The Long Hot Summer of Russian Fandom', *Locus*, 372 (Jan. 1992), 42.
31. Bridget Wilkinson, in *Shards of Babel*, 38 (Oct. 1992), 4–5.
32. See Christopher Stasheff's report in *Locus*, 371 (Dec. 1991), 48.
33. The report by Ahrvid Engholm is in *Shards of Babel*, 38 (Oct. 1992), 5.

Chapter 5: From New Wave to Cyberpunk and Beyond, 1960–1993

1. A reference to Amis's *New Maps of Hell*, the most influential early critical study of sf.
2. Michael Moorcock, guest editorial, *New Worlds*, 129 (Apr. 1963), 2 and 123.
3. J. G. Ballard, 'Which Way to Inner Space?', *New Worlds*, 118 (May 1962), 117.

4. Ibid.
5. Noted by Colin Greenland, in his essential history of the New Wave: *The Entropy Exhibition: Michael Moorcock and the British 'New Wave' in Science Fiction* (London, 1983), 52.
6. Christopher Priest, 'New Wave', in R. Holdstock (ed.), *Encyclopedia of Science Fiction* (London, 1978), 170.
7. Published in *New Worlds*, 163 (June 1966), and repr. in, e.g., J. Merril (ed.), *The Best of Sci-Fi*, vol. 12 (London, 1970), 274–8.
8. *New Worlds*, 173 (July 1967), 32–9; most recently repr. in P. Zoline, *Busy About the Tree of Life* (London, 1988), 50–65.
9. Quoted in Greenland, *Entropy Exhibition*, 69.
10. Priest, 'New Wave', 170.
11. Quoted from H. Ellison, *All the Sounds of Fear* (London, 1973), 135–6.
12. In Clute and Nicholls (eds.), *Encyclopedia of Science Fiction*, 862.
13. Reprinted in F. Pohl, *The Gold at the Starbow's End*, a 1972 collection; expanded into novel form in *Starburst* (1982).
14. John H. Gault, writing to *Analog*, July 1972, p. 169.
15. Repr. several times, including in T. Shippey (ed.), *The Oxford Book of Science Fiction Stories* (Oxford, 1992), 400–19.
16. For a discussion of this, which nevertheless comes to make distinctions, see Peter Nicholls, 'Fantasy', in Clute and Nicholls (eds.), *Encyclopedia of Science Fiction*, 407–11.
17. See Nigel Walmsley, 'Tolkien and the '60s', in R. Giddings (ed.), *J. R. R. Tolkien: This Far Land* (London, 1983), 73.
18. T. S. Shippey's *The Road to Middle Earth* (London, 1982), by far the best book on *The Lord of the Rings*, has the unique advantage of being by an Old English scholar, who alone can fully appreciate what Tolkien was trying to do.
19. See John Clute for a discussion of that sub-genre, in Clute and Nicholls (eds.), *Encyclopedia of Science Fiction*, 934–6.
20. Ursula K. Le Guin, *The Language of the Night, Essays on Fantasy and Science Fiction*, rev. edn. (London, 1989), 119.
21. Gwyneth Jones, in Maxim Jakubowski and Edward James (eds.), *The Profession of Science Fiction: SF Writers on their Craft and Ideas* (London, 1992), 169.
22. This is an over-simplification, of course, as it does not apply to all sf; there are fairy-tale elements, e.g., in *Star Wars*. See Eric S. Rabkin, 'Fairy Tales and Science Fiction', in George E. Slusser et al. (eds.), *Bridges to Science Fiction* (Carbondale, Ill., 1980), 78–90.
23. First published in H. Ellison (ed.), *Again, Dangerous Visions* (New

York, 1972), and here quoted from I. Asimov (ed.), *Nebula Award Stories*, vol. 8 (London, 1975), 117–25.

24. Tom Moylan, *Demand the Impossible: Science Fiction and the Utopian Imagination* (New York and London, 1986), 57.

25. See Le Guin's 'Is Gender Necessary?' (1976) and her further thoughts, 'Redux', in *idem, Language of the Night*, 135–47.

26. R. Silverberg, introduction to James Tiptree, jun., *Warm Worlds and Otherwise* (New York, 1975), p. xii.

27. James Tiptree, jun., *Ten Thousand Light-Years from Home* (1975), quoted from the Pan edn. (London, 1978), 17.

28. Quoted from the collected version, Tiptree, *Star Songs of an Old Primate* (New York, 1978), 225–6.

29. The fourth, in addition to the three cited above, is *Out of the Everywhere and Other Extraordinary Visions* (1981).

30. Brunner has offered some recent comment on his 'predictions' in 'Sometime in the Recent Future . . .', *New Scientist*, 10 Apr. 1993, pp. 28–31.

31. The phrase 'Big Dumb Object' seems to have been first used in Roz Kaveney's knowledgeable and perceptive survey 'Science Fiction in the 1970s', *Foundation*, 22 (June 1981), 5–35.

32. Mentioned in Tim Radford, 'Down to Earth with a Bump', *Guardian*, 16 Apr. 1993, supplement, 2.

33. By far the best introduction is the section on music, by various authors, in Clute and Nicholls (eds.), *Encyclopedia of Science Fiction*, 840–6.

34. Phil Hardy, *The Encyclopedia of Science Fiction Movies*, rev. edn. (London, 1986), 346.

35. An article on the problems of interpersonal stress in space travel uses stills from *Alien* to make its point: Ian Mundell, 'Stop the Rocket, I Want to Get Off', *New Scientist*, 17 Apr. 1993, p. 35.

36. From Sterling's preface to B. Sterling (ed.), *Mirrorshades: The Cyberpunk Anthology* (1986), quoted from Paladin edn. (London, 1988), pp. xi–xiii.

37. Kim Stanley Robinson, in the special cyberpunk issue of *Mississippi Review*, 47/8 (1988), 51.

38. Gibson, *Neuromancer* (London, 1986), 12.

39. Ibid. 121.

40. Quoted from L. Olsen, *William Gibson*, Starmont Reader's Guide, 58 (Mercer Island, Wash., 1992), 8.

41. Gibson, 'The Gernsback Continuum', first pub. in T. Carr (ed.), *Universe*, vol. 11 (1981), and cited from Gibson, *Burning Chrome* (London, 1988), 37–50.

42. T. Shippey, 'Semiotic Ghosts and Ghostliness in the Work of Bruce Sterling', in G. Slusser and T. Shippey (eds.), *Fiction 2000: Cyberpunk and the Future of Narrative* (Athens, Ga., 1992), 218–19.

43. Brunner, 'Sometime', 31.

44. H. Bruce Franklin, *War Stars: The Superweapon and the American Imagination* (New York, 1988).

45. See the special 'Star Wars' issue of *New Scientist*, 20 Mar. 1993.

46. The words of John Clute (in Clute and Nicholls (eds.), *Encyclopedia of Science Fiction*, 1339), the most perceptive of Wolfe's critics. See also several essays in Clute, *Strokes: Essays and Reviews 1966–1986* (Seattle, 1988).

47. The booksellers in question are W. H. Smith and Dillons; the figures are reported in Jo-Ann Goodman, 'In Defence of Fantasy', *The Independent on Sunday*, 25 July 1993, *The Sunday Review*, pp. 32–3.

48. Brian McHale, *Postmodernist Fiction* (London, 1987), 16.

49. Figures from *Locus*, 385 (Feb. 1993), 41.

50. Figures from *Locus*, 387 (Apr. 1993), 64.

51. Card, *Magazine of Fantasy and Science Fiction*, Feb. 1993, p. 23.

Bibliography

Chronological List of Selected Science Fiction

The emphasis in this bibliography of recommended reading (recommended, that is, to give determined readers a sense of the history and variety of sf) is on English-language material and on books (novels, collections, anthologies). A high proportion of the short fiction listed is that chosen by the Science Fiction Writers of America as the best of the genre. Their choices were published in 1970 and 1973 as the *Science Fiction Hall of Fame*, (SFHF), volumes I and II respectively; the paperbacks were published as I (1971) and IIA and IIB (1974); but all of them have been anthologized and collected several times (often in author collections entitled *The Best of—*, which are not listed here). Short stories with *Oxford* after them are to be found in Tom Shippey (ed.), *The Oxford Book of Science Fiction Stories* (Oxford, 1992).

A linked collection, common especially in the 1950s, is a book which collects stories published separately in magazines but which concern the same characters or series of events; if a conscious effort is made to stitch these together into something resembling a novel, it is traditionally called a 'fix-up'. An asterisk following a title indicates that it is the first in a series; sometimes the name of the series appears in parentheses; sometimes it is a series of anthologies. An H or an N indicates that the item was winner of a Hugo or a Nebula award.

1895   H. G. Wells, *The Time Machine* (UK) (SFHF IIA)
1896   H. G. Wells, *The Island of Dr Moreau* (UK)
1898   H. G. Wells, *The War of the Worlds* (UK)
1899   H. G. Wells, *When the Sleeper Wakes* (UK)
1901   H. G. Wells, *The First Men in the Moon* (UK)
1905   Rudyard Kipling, 'With the Night Mail', in J. Brunner (ed.),
           The Science Fiction of Rudyard Kipling (1992) (UK)
1907   Jack London, *The Iron Heel* (US)
1909   E. M. Forster, 'The Machine Stops' (UK) (SFHF IIB)
1911   J. D. Beresford, *The Hampdenshire Wonder* (UK)
           Hugo Gernsback, *Ralph 124C 41+* (book 1925) (US)

1912 Garrett P. Serviss, *The Second Deluge* (US)
1914 George Allan England, *Darkness and Dawn* (US)
1915 Charlotte Perkins Gilman, *Herland* (US)
     Jack London, 'The Scarlet Plague', in R. S. Powers (ed.), *The Science Fiction of Jack London* (1975) (US)
1917 Edgar Rice Burroughs, *A Princess of Mars* (US) * (John Carter of Mars, Barsoom)
1918 Edward Shanks, *The People of the Ruins* (UK)
1920 Karel Čapek, *R.U.R.: A Fantastic Melodrama* (Czechoslovakia)
     David Lindsay, *A Voyage to Arcturus* (UK)
     Konstantin Tsiolkowsky, *Beyond the Planet Earth* (USSR)
1922 Edgar Rice Burroughs, *At the Earth's Core* (US) * (Pellucidar)
     Ray Cummings, *The Girl in the Golden Atom* (US)
1923 Edgar Rice Burroughs, *Pellucidar* (US) *
     E. V. Odle, *The Clockwork Man* (UK)
     H. G. Wells, *Men Like Gods* (UK)
1924 Yevgeny Zamyatin, *We* (USSR)
1925 J.-H. Rosny aîné, *Navigators of the Infinite* (Belgium/France)
1926 Thea von Harbou, *Metropolis* (Germany)
1927 H. G. Wells, *The Short Stories of H. G. Wells* (UK)
     S. Fowler Wright, *Deluge* (UK)
1928 Philip Francis Nowlan, 'Armageddon 2419 A.D.' (book 1962) (US)
     E. E. Smith, *The Skylark of Space* (book 1946) (US) * (Skylark)
     Jack Williamson, 'The Metal Man' (US) (*Oxford*)
1930 John W. Campbell, jun., 'The Black Star Passes' (book 1953) (US)
     Olaf Stapledon, *Last and First Men* (UK)
1931 André Maurois, *The Weigher of Souls* (France)
1932 Aldous Huxley, *Brave New World* (UK)
1933 Nat Shachner, 'Ancestral Voices' (US)
     Philip Wylie and Edwin Balmer, *When Worlds Collide* (US)
1934 John W. Campbell, jun. (as Don A. Stuart), 'Twilight' (US) (SFHF I)
     John Gloag, *Winter's Youth* (UK)
     Alun Llewellyn, *The Strange Invaders* (UK)
     Stanley G. Weinbaum, 'A Martian Odyssey' (US) (SFHF I)
1935 Joseph O'Neill, *Land under England* (UK)
     Olaf Stapledon, *Odd John* (UK)
1936 H. P. Lovecraft, 'At the Mountains of Madness' (book 1964) (US)

1937 John W. Campbell, jun. (as Don A. Stuart), 'Forgetfulness' (US)
Katherine Burdekin, (as Murray Constantine), *Swastika Night* (UK)
E. E. Smith, 'Galactic Patrol' (US) * (Lensman)
Olaf Stapledon, *Star Maker* (UK)

1938 John W. Campbell, jun. (as Don A. Stuart), 'Who Goes There?' (US) (SFHF IIA)
Lester del Rey, 'Helen O'Loy' (US) (SFHF I)
C. S. Lewis, *Out of the Silent Planet* (UK) *
Jack Williamson, *The Legion of Time* (book 1952) (US)

1939 Eric Frank Russell, *Sinister Barrier* (UK)
A. E. Van Vogt, 'Black Destroyer' (US)

1940 Robert A. Heinlein, 'The Roads Must Roll' (US) (SFHF I)
L. Ron Hubbard, *Final Blackout* (book 1948) (US)
A. E. Van Vogt, *Slan* (book 1946) (US)

1941 Isaac Asimov, 'Nightfall' (US) (SFHF I)
Robert A. Heinlein, 'Universe' (US) (SFHF IIA)
—— (as Anson MacDonald), 'By His Bootstraps' (US) (SFHF IIA)
Theodore Sturgeon, 'Microcosmic God' (US) (SFHF I)

1942 Isaac Asimov, 'Foundation' (book 1951) (US) *
Robert A. Heinlein, *Beyond This Horizon* (book 1948) (US)

1943 Henry Kuttner and C. L. Moore (as Lewis Padgett), 'Mimsy Were the Borogroves' (US) (SFHF I)

1944 Olaf Stapledon, *Sirius* (UK)

1945 Murray Leinster, 'First Contact' (US) (SFHF I)
A. E. Van Vogt, *The World of Null-A* (book 1948) (US)

1946 Groff Conklin (ed.), *The Best of Science Fiction* (anthology) (US)
Raymond J. Healy and J. Francis McComas (eds.), *Adventures in Time and Space* (anthology) (US)
C. L. Moore (as Lawrence O'Donnell), 'Vintage Season' (US) (SFHF IIA)

1947 Robert A. Heinlein, *Rocket Ship Galileo* (US)

1948 Judith Merril, 'That Only a Mother' (US) (SFHF I)

1949 Everett Bleiler and T. E. Dikty (eds.), *The Best Science Fiction Stories* (anthology) (US) *
Robert A. Heinlein, *Red Planet* (US)
George Orwell, *Nineteen Eighty-Four* (UK)
George R. Stewart, *Earth Abides* (US)
Jack Williamson, *The Humanoids* (US)

1950 Isaac Asimov, *I, Robot* (linked collection) (US)

Ray Bradbury, *The Martian Chronicles* (linked collection) (US)

Jack Vance, *The Dying Earth* (linked collection) (US)

A. E. Van Vogt, *The Voyage of the Space Beagle* (fix-up) (US)

1951 Isaac Asimov, *Foundation* (fix-up) (US) *

Ray Bradbury, *The Illustrated Man* (loosely linked collection, including 'The Veldt') (US)

Robert A. Heinlein, *The Puppet Masters* (US)

John Wyndham, *The Day of the Triffids* (UK)

1952 James Blish, 'Surface Tension' (US) (SFHF I)

Clifford D. Simak, *City* (linked collection) (US)

Bernard Wolfe, *Limbo* (US)

1953 Alfred Bester, *The Demolished Man* (US) H

Ray Bradbury, *Fahrenheit 451* (US)

—— *The Golden Apples of the Sun* (collection, including 'A Sound of Thunder') (US)

Arthur C. Clarke, *Childhood's End* (UK)

—— *Expedition to Earth* (collection, including 'The Sentinel') (UK)

Charles Harness, *The Paradox Men* (US)

Frederik Pohl and C. M. Kornbluth, *The Space Merchants* (US)

Frederik Pohl (ed.), *Star Science Fiction Stories* (anthology) (US) *

Theodore Sturgeon, *E Pluribus Unicorn* (collection) (US)

—— *More than Human* (US)

1954 Poul Anderson, *Brain Wave* (US)

Isaac Asimov, *The Caves of Steel* (US)

Fredric Brown, *Angels and Spaceships* (collection) (US)

Hal Clement, *Mission of Gravity* (US)

Tom Godwin, 'The Cold Equations' (US) (SFHF I)

1955 James Blish, *Earthmen, Come Home* (fix-up) (US) * (Cities in Flight)

Leigh Brackett, *The Long Tomorrow* (US)

Edmund Crispin (ed.), *Best SF* (anthology) (UK) *

Eric Frank Russell, *Men, Martians and Machines* (linked collection) (UK)

William Tenn, *Of All Possible Worlds* (collection) (US)

John Wyndham, *The Chrysalids* (UK) (US: *Re-Birth*)

1956 Alfred Bester, *Tiger! Tiger!* (UK) (US: *The Stars My Destination*, 1957)

John Christopher, *The Death of Grass* (UK) (US: *No Blade of Grass*)

Arthur C. Clarke, *The City and the Stars* (UK)

Robert A. Heinlein, *Double Star* (US) H

Judith Merril (ed.), *The Year's Greatest Science-Fiction and Fantasy* (anthology) (US) *

1957   Robert Sheckley, *Pilgrimage to Earth* (collection) (US)

1958   Brian W. Aldiss, *Non-Stop* (UK) (US: *Starship*)

James Blish, *A Case of Conscience* (US) H

Arthur C. Clarke, *The Other Side of the Sky* (collection, including 'The Nine Billion Names of God' and 'The Star') (UK)

Ivan Antonovich Yefremov, *Andromeda* (USSR)

1959   Philip K. Dick, *Time Out of Joint* (US)

Robert A. Heinlein, *Starship Troopers* (US) H

Daniel Keyes, 'Flowers for Algernon' (US) (SFHF I) H

Jack Vance, *The Languages of Pao* (US)

Kurt Vonnegut, jun., *The Sirens of Titan* (US)

1960   Algis Budrys, *Rogue Moon* (US)

Philip José Farmer, *Strange Relations* (linked collection) (US)

Walter M. Miller, jun., *A Canticle for Leibowitz* (fix-up) (US) H

Theodore Sturgeon, *Venus Plus X* (US)

1961   Philip José Farmer, *The Lovers* (US)

Daniel F. Galouye, *Dark Universe* (US)

Harry Harrison, *The Stainless Steel Rat* (US) *

Robert A. Heinlein, *Stranger in a Strange Land* (US) H

Zenna Henderson, *Pilgrimage: The Book of the People* (linked collection) (US)

Jack Vance, 'The Moon Moth' (US) (SFHF IIB)

1962   Brian W. Aldiss, *The Long Afternoon of Earth* (fix-up) (US) (UK: *Hothouse*) H

Isaac Asimov (ed.), *The Hugo Winners* (anthology) (US) *

J. G. Ballard, *The Drowned World* (UK)

Philip K. Dick, *The Man in the High Castle* (US) H

Cordwainer Smith, 'The Ballad of Lost C'Mell' (US) (*Oxford*)

Jack Vance, 'The Dragon Masters' (US) H

James White, *Hospital Station* (UK) * (Sector General)

1963   Clifford D. Simak, *Way Station* (US) H

1964   Philip K. Dick, *Martian Time-Slip* (US)

Fritz Leiber, *The Wanderer* (US) H

1965   Harlan Ellison, ' "Repent, Harlequin!" said the Ticktockman' (US) H, N

Frank Herbert, *Dune* (US) * H, N
Donald A. Wollheim and Terry Carr (eds.), *The World's Best Science Fiction: 1965* (anthology) (US) *

1966 Samuel R. Delany, *Babel-17* (US) N
Harry Harrison, *Make Room! Make Room!* (US)
Robert A. Heinlein, *The Moon is a Harsh Mistress* (US) H
Damon Knight (ed.), *Nebula Award Stories 1965* (anthology series with different editors) (US) (UK: *Nebula Award Stories 1*) *
—— (ed.), *Orbit 1* (annual original anthology) (US) *
Roger Zelazny, *This Immortal* (US)

1967 Harlan Ellison (ed.), *Dangerous Visions* (anthology) (US)
Robert A. Heinlein, *The Past Through Tomorrow: Future History Series* (definitive collection) (US)
Michael Moorcock, 'Behold the Man' (UK) (book 1969) N

1968 Brian W. Aldiss and Harry Harrison (eds.), *Best SF: 1967* (anthology) (US) (UK: *The Year's Best Science Fiction No. 1*)*
John Brunner, *Stand on Zanzibar* (UK) H
Arthur C. Clarke, *2001: A Space Odyssey* (UK, Sri Lanka)
Philip K. Dick, *Do Androids Dream of Electric Sheep?* (US)
Thomas M. Disch, *Camp Concentration* (US)
Stanisław Lem, *Solaris* (Poland)
Anne McCaffrey, *Dragonflight* (US) * (Pern)
Judith Merril (ed.), *England Swings SF* (anthology) (US)
Michael Moorcock, *The Final Programme* (UK) * (Cornelius Chronicles)
Larry Niven, *Neutron Star* (collection including 'Neutron Star', H) (US)
Keith Roberts, *Pavane* (UK)

1969 Brian W. Aldiss, *Barefoot in the Head* (UK)
Harlan Ellison, 'A Boy and his Dog' (US) N
Ursula K. Le Guin, *The Left Hand of Darkness* (US) H, N
Norman Spinrad, *Bug Jack Barron* (US)

1970 J. G. Ballard, *The Atrocity Exhibition* (collection) (UK) (US: *Love and Napalm: Export U.S.A.*)
Larry Niven, *Ringworld* (US) H, N
Robert Silverberg, *Downward to the Earth* (US)
—— (ed.), *The Science Fiction Hall of Fame,* vol. 1 (anthology) (US)

1971 J. G. Ballard, *Vermilion Sands* (linked collection) (UK)
Terry Carr (ed.), *Universe 1* (annual original anthology) (US) *

Samuel R. Delany, *Driftglass* (collection including 'Time Considered as a Helix of Semi-Precious Stones', H, N) (US)

Philip José Farmer, *To Your Scattered Bodies Go* (US) * (Riverworld) H

Robert Silverberg, *A Time of Changes* (US) N

—— *The World Inside* (US)

Roger Zelazny, *The Doors of His Face, The Lamps of His Mouth* (collection including title-story, N) (US)

1972   Isaac Asimov, *The Gods Themselves* (US) H, N

John Brunner, *The Sheep Look Up* (UK)

Harlan Ellison (ed.), *Again, Dangerous Visions* (anthology, including Ursula K. Le Guin, 'The Word for World is Forest', H, and Joanna Russ, 'When It Changed', N) (US)

Barry Malzberg, *Beyond Apollo* (US)

Larry Niven, 'Cloak of Anarchy' (US) (*Oxford*)

Frederik Pohl, 'The Gold at the Starbow's End' (book: *Starburst*, 1982) (US)

Bob Shaw, *Other Days, Other Eyes* (fix-up) (UK)

Robert Silverberg, *Dying Inside* (US)

Norman Spinrad, *The Iron Dream* (US)

Arkadi and Boris Strugatsky, *Roadside Picnic* (USSR)

1973   Ben Bova (ed.), *The Science Fiction Hall of Fame,* vols. IIA and IIB (anthology) (US)

Arthur C. Clarke, *Rendezvous with Rama* (UK, Sri Lanka) H, N

Norman Spinrad, 'A Thing of Beauty' (US) (*Oxford*)

James Tiptree, jun., *Ten Thousand Light Years from Home* (collection including 'And I Awoke and Found Me Here on the Cold Hill's Side') (US)

Ian Watson, *The Embedding* (UK)

1974   Isaac Asimov, *Before the Golden Age* (historical anthology) (US)

Suzy McKee Charnas, *Walk to the End of the World* (US)

Ursula K. Le Guin, *The Dispossessed* (US) H, N

Larry Niven and Jerry Pournelle, *The Mote in God's Eye* (US)

1975   Michael G. Coney, *Hello Summer, Goodbye* (UK)

Harlan Ellison, *Deathbird Stories* (collection including 'Pretty Maggie Moneyeyes' and 'Shattered like a Glass Goblin') (US)

Joe Haldeman, *The Forever War* (US) H, N

M. John Harrison, *The Centauri Device* (UK)

Ursula K. Le Guin, *The Wind's Twelve Quarters* (collection including 'Vaster than Empires and More Slow' and 'Nine Lives') (US)

Joanna Russ, *The Female Man* (US)
Pamela Sargent (ed.), *Women of Wonder: SF Stories by Women About Women* (anthology) (US) *
James Tiptree, jun., *Warm Worlds and Otherwise* (collection including 'The Women Men Don't See' and 'Love is the Plan, the Plan is Death') (US)
1976 Isaac Asimov, 'The Bicentennial Man' (US) H, N
Samuel R. Delany, *Triton* (US)
Marge Piercy, *Woman on the Edge of Time* (US)
Frederik Pohl, *Man Plus* (US) N
1977 Frederik Pohl, *Gateway* (US) * H, N
1978 Barrington J. Bayley, *The Knights of the Limits* (collection including 'Me and My Antronoscope') (UK)
Richard Cowper, *The Road to Corlay* (UK) *
James Tiptree, jun., *Star Songs of an Old Primate* (collection including 'Houston, Houston, Do You Read?', H, N) (US)
George Turner, *Beloved Son* (Australia) *
John Varley, *The Persistence of Vision* (collection including 'The Persistence of Vision', H, N) (US) (UK: *In the Hall of the Martian Kings*)
Ian Watson, *Miracle Visitors* (UK)
1979 Douglas Adams, *The Hitch-Hiker's Guide to the Galaxy* (UK)*
Isaac Asimov and Martin Greenberg (eds.), *Isaac Asimov Presents the Great Science Fiction Stories. Vol. 1: 1939)* (historical anthology) (US) *
Michael Bishop, *Transfigurations* (US)
Arthur C. Clarke, *The Fountains of Paradise* (UK, Sri Lanka) H, N
John Crowley, *Engine Summer* (US)
Stephen King, *The Dead Zone* (US)
Doris Lessing, *Shikasta* (UK) *
Robert Silverberg, *Lord Valentine's Castle* (US) *
Brian Stableford, *The Walking Shadow* (UK)
Kurt Vonnegut, jun., *Slaughterhouse-Five* (US)
Ian Watson, *The Very Slow Time Machine* (collection) (UK)
1980 Gregory Benford, *Timescape* (US) N
Damien Broderick, *The Dreaming Dragons* (Australia)
C. J. Cherryh, *Serpent's Reach* (US)
Russell Hoban, *Riddley Walker* (US, UK)
Gene Wolfe, *The Island of Doctor Death and Other Stories* (collection including 'The Island of Doctor Death and Other Stories' and 'The Death of Doctor Island', N) (US)

—— *The Shadow of the Torturer* (US) * (The Book of the New Sun)

1981   C. J. Cherryh, *Downbelow Station* (US) H
Philip José Farmer, *The Unreasoning Mask* (US)
Larry Niven and Jerry Pournelle, *Oath of Fealty* (US)
James Tiptree, jun., *Out of the Everywhere and Other Extraordinary Visions* (collection including 'The Screwfly Solution', N (*Oxford*), and 'With Delicate Mad Hands') (US)

1982   Brian W. Aldiss, *Helliconia Spring* (UK) * (Helliconia)
William Gibson, 'Burning Chrome' (US) (*Oxford*)
Donald Kingsbury, *Courtship Rite* (US) (UK: *Geta*)

1983   David Brin, *Startide Rising* (US) H, N
Michael G. Coney, *The Celestial Steam Locomotive* (UK, Canada)
Mary Gentle, *Golden Witchbreed* (UK) *
Norman Spinrad, *The Void Captain's Tale* (US)

1984   Octavia E. Butler, 'Blood Child' (US) H, N
C. J. Cherryh, *Voyager in Night* (US)
Samuel R. Delany, *Stars in My Pocket Like Grains of Sand* (US)
Gardner Dozois (ed.), *The Year's Best Science Fiction: First Annual Collection* (anthology) (US) *
Suzette Haden Elgin, *Native Tongue* (US) *
William Gibson, *Neuromancer* (US) * H
John Varley, 'PRESS ENTER ■' (US) H, N
Ian Watson, *The Book of the River* (UK) *

1985   Margaret Atwood, *The Handmaid's Tale* (Canada)
Greg Bear, *Blood Music* (US)
Algis Budrys (ed.), *L. Ron Hubbard Presents the Writers of the Future* (original anthology) (US) *
Orson Scott Card, *Ender's Game* (US) * H, N
Robert Silverberg, 'Sailing to Byzantium' (US) N
Bruce Sterling, *Schismatrix* (US)

1986   Orson Scott Card, *Speaker for the Dead* (US) H, N
Gwyneth Jones, *Escape Plans* (UK)
Frank Miller, *The Dark Knight Returns* (graphic novel) (US)
Pamela Sargent, *The Shore of Women* (US)
Bob Shaw, *The Ragged Astronauts* (UK) *
Joan Slonczewski, *A Door into Ocean* (US)

1987   Iain M. Banks, *Consider Phlebas* (UK) *
Octavia E. Butler, *Dawn: Xenogenesis I* (US) *
Judith Moffett, *Pennterra* (US)

Alan Moore and Dave Gibbons, *Watchmen* (graphic novel) (UK)
Pat Murphy, 'Rachel in Love' (US) N
Kim Stanley Robinson, 'The Blind Geometer' (US) N
Lucius Shepard, *Life during Wartime* (US)
George Turner, *The Sea and Summer* (Australia) (US: *Drowning Towers*)

1988 Ian McDonald, *Desolation Road* (UK)
Brian Stableford, *The Empire of Fear* (UK)
Sheri S. Tepper, *The Gate to Woman's Country* (US)

1989 Ian McDonald, *Out on Blue Six* (UK)
Pat Murphy, *The City, Not Long After* (US)
Geoff Ryman, *The Child Garden* (UK, Canada)
Dan Simmons, *Hyperion* (forms one novel, *Hyperion Cantos*, with *The Fall of Hyperion*, 1990) (US) H
Sheri S. Tepper, *Grass* (US)

1990 Terry Bisson, *Voyage to the Red Planet* (US)
David Brin, *Earth: A Novel* (US)
William Gibson and Bruce Sterling, *The Difference Engine* (US)
Colin Greenland, *Take Back Plenty* (UK)
Joe Haldeman, 'The Hemingway Hoax' (US) N
Kim Stanley Robinson, *Pacific Edge* (US)

1991 Stephen Baxter, *Raft* (UK)
Brian Stableford, *Sexual Chemistry: Sardonic Tales of the Genetic Revolution* (collection) (UK)

1992 Ben Bova, *Mars* (US)
Nancy Kress, 'Beggars in Spain' (US) H
Kim Stanley Robinson, *Red Mars* (US) *
Tom Shippey (ed.), *The Oxford Book of Science Fiction Stories* (historical anthology) (UK)
Vernor Vinge, *A Fire upon the Deep* (US)
Walter Jon Williams, *Aristoi* (US)

1993 Colin Greenland, *Harm's Way* (UK)
Paul J. McAuley, *Red Dust* (UK)

Major English-Language Science Fiction Magazines

Amazing Stories (Various minor title changes after 1958) (US) 1926–present day
Astounding/Analog (*Astounding Stories*, 1930–8; *Astounding Science-Fiction*, 1938–60 (hyphen dropped in 1946); *Analog Science Fact–Science Fiction*, 1961–5; *Analog Science Fiction–Science Fact*, 1965–present) (British reprint, 1939–63) (US) 1930–present day

Fantastic (*Fantastic Science Fiction, Fantastic Science Fiction Stories*, etc.) (US) 1952–80

Galaxy (*Galaxy Science Fiction, Galaxy Magazine*, etc.) (US) 1950–80

If (US) 1952–74

Interzone (UK) 1982–present

Isaac Asimov's Science Fiction Magazine (*Asimov's Science Fiction*, from 1992) (US) 1977–present

Magazine of Fantasy and Science Fiction (US) 1949–present

New Worlds (UK) 1946–71

Planet Stories (US) 1939–55

Science Fantasy (UK) 1950–66

Startling Stories (US) 1939–55

Wonder Stories (*Science Wonder Stories*, 1929–30; *Wonder Stories*, 1930–6; *Thrilling Wonder Stories*, 1936–55) (US) 1929–55

Reference Works with Some Annotations

Barron, Neil (ed.), *Anatomy of Wonder: A Critical Guide to Science Fiction*, 3rd edn. (New York and London, 1987). Essential bibliographical and other information on English-language and other sf, together with a great deal of useful material for researchers in the field.

Bleiler, Everett F., *The Checklist of Science-Fiction and Supernatural Fiction* (Glen Rock, NJ, 1978).

—— *Science Fiction: The Early Years. A Full Description of more than 3,000 Science Fiction Stories from Earliest Times to the Appearance of the Genre Magazines in 1930* (Kent, Oh., 1990).

—— (ed.), *Science Fiction Writers. Critical Studies of the Major Authors from the Early Nineteenth Century to the Present Day* (New York, 1982).

Brown, Charles N., and Contento, William G. (eds.), *Science Fiction in Print—1985: A Comprehensive Bibliography of Books and Short Fiction Published in the English Language* (Oakland, Calif., 1986). First of an annual series, subsequently called *Science Fiction, Fantasy, and Horror*, and in 1990 extended backwards to 1984.

Clareson, Thomas D., *Science Fiction in America, 1870s–1930s. An Annotated Bibliography of Primary Sources* (Westport, Conn., 1984).

Clute, John, and Nicholls, Peter (eds.), *The Encyclopedia of Science Fiction* (London, 1993). By far the best single reference work, containing important primary critical work as well as much bibliographical and other data.

Contento, William G., *Index to Science Fiction Anthologies and Collec-*

tions (Boston, 1978). A second volume, published in 1984, covers 1977–83.

Currey, Lloyd W. (ed.), *Science Fiction and Fantasy Authors: A Bibliography of First Printings of their Fiction and Selected Nonfiction* (Boston, 1979).

Day, Donald B., *Index to the Science Fiction Magazines, 1926–1950*, rev. edn. (Boston, 1982).

Gunn, James (ed.), *The New Encyclopedia of Science Fiction* (New York, 1988).

Hardy, Phil, *The Encyclopedia of Science Fiction Movies*, rev. edn. (London, 1986).

Magill, Frank N. (ed.), *Survey of Science Fiction Literature* (5 vols., Englewood Cliffs, NJ, 1979).

—— with Tymn, Marshall B. (eds.), *Survey of Science Fiction Literature. Bibliographical Supplement* (Englewood Cliffs, NJ, 1982).

Reginald, R., *Science Fiction and Fantasy Literature: A Checklist, 1700–1974, with Contemporary Science Fiction Authors II* (2 vols., Detroit, 1979).

Tuck, Donald H. (ed.), *The Encyclopedia of Science Fiction and Fantasy*. Vol. 1: *Who's Who, A–L* (Chicago, 1974); Vol. 2: *Who's Who, M–Z* (Chicago, 1978); Vol. 3: *Miscellaneous* (Chicago, 1982).

Tymn, Marshall B., and Ashley, Mike (eds.), *Science Fiction, Fantasy, and Weird Magazines* (Westport, Conn., 1985).

Watson, Noelle, and Schellinger, Paul E. (eds.), *Twentieth-Century Science-Fiction Writers*, 3rd edn. (Chicago and London, 1991). Bibliographies, critical assessments, and autobiographical pieces by many writers.

Wolfe, Gary K., *Critical Terms for Science Fiction and Fantasy: A Glossary and Guide to Scholarship* (Westport, Conn., 1986).

Secondary Works (Excluding Studies of Individual Authors)

Aldiss, Brian W., and Harrison, Harry (eds.), *Hell's Cartographers: Some Personal Histories of Science Fiction Writers* (London, 1975).

—— with Wingrove, David, *Trillion Year Spree; The History of Science Fiction* (London, 1986).

Amis, Kingsley, *New Maps of Hell* (London, 1961).

Armitt, Lucie (ed.), *Where No Man Has Gone Before: Women and Science Fiction* (London, 1991).

Bainbridge, William S., *Dimensions of Science Fiction* (Cambridge, Mass., 1986). Sociological study of sf fans.

Barr, Marleen S., *Alien to Femininity: Speculative Fiction and Feminist Theory* (Westport, Conn., 1987).
—— *Feminist Fabulation: Space/Postmodern Fiction* (Iowa City, Ia., 1992).
—— (ed.), *Future Females: A Critical Anthology* (Bowling Green, Oh., 1981).
Blish, James (as William Atheling, jun.), *The Issue at Hand* (Chicago, 1964).
—— (as William Atheling, jun.), *More Issues at Hand* (Chicago, 1970).
Bretnor, Reginald (ed.), *Science Fiction, Today and Tomorrow* (Baltimore, 1974).
—— (ed.), *Modern Science Fiction: Its Meaning and its Future*, 2nd edn. (Chicago, 1979).
Carter, Paul A., *The Creation of Tomorrow: Fifty Years of Magazine Science Fiction* (New York, 1977).
Cioffi, Frank, *Formula Fiction? An Anatomy of American Science Fiction, 1930–1940* (Westport, Conn., 1982).
Clareson, T. D., *Some Kind of Paradise: The Emergence of American Science Fiction* (Westport, Conn., 1985).
Clarke, I. F., *The Pattern of Expectation, 1644–2001* (London, 1979).
—— *Voices Prophesying War, 1763–1984* (London, 1966).
Davies, Philip John (ed.), *Science Fiction, Social Conflict and War* (Manchester, 1990).
Delany, Samuel R., *The Jewel-Hinged Jaw: Notes on the Language of Science Fiction* (New York, 1977).
Del Rey, Lester, *The World of Science Fiction, 1927–1976: The History of a Subculture* (New York, 1980).
Dowling, David, *Fictions of Nuclear Disaster* (London, 1987).
Franklin, H. Bruce, *War Stars: The Superweapon and the American Imagination* (New York, 1988).
—— (ed.), *Future Perfect: American Science Fiction of the Nineteenth Century* (New York, 1966).
Garnett, Rhys, and Ellis, R. J. (eds.), *Science Fiction Roots and Branches: Contemporary Critical Approaches* (London, 1990).
Greenland, Colin, *The Entropy Exhibition: Michael Moorcock and the British 'New Wave' in Science Fiction* (London, 1983).
Gunn, James, *Alternate Worlds: The Illustrated History of Science Fiction* (Englewood Cliffs, NJ, 1975).
—— *Inside Science Fiction: Essays on Fantastic Literature* (San Bernardino, Calif., 1992).
Hartwell, David, *Age of Wonders: Exploring the World of Science Fiction* (New York, 1984).

Huntington, John, *Rationalizing Genius: Ideological Strategies in the Classic American Science Fiction Short Story* (New Brunswick, NJ, and London, 1989).

Jakubowski, Maxim, and James, Edward (eds.), *The Profession of Science Fiction: SF Writers on their Craft and Ideas* (London, 1992).

Ketterer, David, *New Worlds for Old: The Apocalyptic Imagination, Science Fiction and American Literature* (Bloomington, Ind., 1974).

Knight, Damon, *In Search of Wonder*, 2nd edn. (Chicago, 1967).

Kuhn, Annette (ed.), *Alien Zone: Cultural Theory and Contemporary Science Fiction Cinema* (London, 1990).

Lefanu, Sarah, *In the Chinks of the World Machine: Feminism and Science Fiction* (London, 1988) (US: *Science Fiction and Feminism*).

Le Guin, Ursula K., *The Language of the Night: Essays on Fantasy and Science Fiction*, rev. edn. (London, 1989).

Lem, Stanisław, *Microworlds: Writings on Science Fiction and Fantasy* (San Diego, 1984).

Lundwall, Sam J., *Science Fiction: An Illustrated History* (New York, 1978).

McGuire, Patrick J., *Red Stars: Political Aspects of Soviet Science Fiction* (Ann Arbor, Mich., 1985).

Malzberg, Barry, *The Engines of the Night: Science Fiction in the Eighties* (New York, 1982).

Manlove, C. N., *Science Fiction: Ten Explorations* (London, 1986).

Meyers, Walter E., *Aliens and Linguists: Language Study and Science Fiction* (Athens, Ga., 1980).

Moskowitz, Sam, *Explorers of the Infinite: Shapers of Science Fiction*, 2nd edn. (Westport, Conn., 1974).

—— *The Immortal Storm: A History of Science Fiction Fandom*, 2nd edn. (Westport, Conn., 1974).

—— *Science Fiction by Gaslight. A History and Anthology of Science Fiction in the Popular Magazines, 1891–1911*, 2nd edn. (Westport, Conn., 1974).

—— *Seekers of Tomorrow: Masters of Modern Science Fiction*, 2nd edn. (Westport, Conn., 1974).

Moylan, Tom, *Demand the Impossible: Science Fiction and the Utopian Imagination* (New York and London, 1986).

Nicholls, Peter, *Fantastic Cinema: An Illustrated Survey* (London, 1984).

—— (ed.), *The Encyclopedia of Science Fiction: An Illustrated A to Z* (London, 1979) (US: *The Science Fiction Encyclopedia*, 1979).

—— (ed.), *Explorations of the Marvellous: The Science and the Fiction in Science Fiction*, 2nd edn. (London, 1978).

—— (ed.), *The Science in Science Fiction* (London, 1982).

Panshin, Alexei, and Panshin, Cory, *SF in Dimension: A Book of Explorations*, 2nd rev. edn. (Chicago, 1980).

—— and —— *The World Beyond the Hill: Science Fiction and the Quest for Transcendence* (Los Angeles, 1989).

Parrinder, Patrick, *Science Fiction: Its Criticism and Teaching* (London and New York, 1980).

—— (ed.), *Science Fiction: A Critical Guide* (London, 1979).

Pierce, J. J., *Foundations of Science Fiction: A Study in Imagination and Evolution* (Westport, Conn., 1987).

—— *Great Themes of Science Fiction: A Study in Imagination and Evolution* (Westport, Conn., 1987).

—— *When Worlds Collide: A Study in Imagination and Evolution* (Westport, Conn., 1989).

Platt, Charles, *Dream Makers*, Vol. II: *The Uncommon Men and Women who Write Science Fiction* (New York, 1983).

—— *Who Writes Science Fiction?* (London, 1980).

Pringle, David, *Modern Fantasy: The Hundred Best Novels. An English Language Selection, 1949–1987* (London, 1987).

—— *Science Fiction: The 100 Best Novels. An English Language Selection, 1948–1984* (London, 1985).

Rogers, Alva, *A Requiem for Astounding* (Chicago, 1964).

Rose, Mark, *Alien Encounters: Anatomy of Science Fiction* (Cambridge, Mass., 1981).

—— (ed.), *Science Fiction: A Collection of Critical Essays* (Englewood Cliffs, NJ, 1976).

Scholes, Robert, *Structural Fabulation: An Essay on Fiction of the Future* (Notre Dame, Ind., 1975).

—— and Rabkin, Eric S., *Science Fiction: History—Science—Vision* (New York, 1977).

Shippey, Tom (ed.), *Fictional Space: Essays on Contemporary Science Fiction* (Oxford, 1991).

Slusser, George E., and Shippey, Tom (eds.), *Fiction 2000: Cyberpunk and the Future of Narrative* (Athens, Ga., 1992).

Stableford, Brian M., *Scientific Romance in Britain, 1890–1950* (London, 1985).

—— *The Sociology of Science Fiction* (San Bernardino, Calif., 1987).

Suvin, Darko, *Metamorphoses of Science Fiction: On the Poetics and History of a Literary Genre* (New Haven, Conn., and London, 1979).

—— *Victorian Science Fiction in the UK: The Discourses of Knowledge and of Power* (Boston, 1983).

Wagar, W. Warren, *Terminal Visions: The Literature of Last Things* (Bloomington, Ind., 1982).

Warner, Harry, jun., *All Our Yesterdays: An Informal History of Science Fiction Fandom in the Forties* (Chicago, 1969).

Warrick, Patricia S., *The Cybernetic Imagination in Science Fiction* (Cambridge, Mass., 1980).

Wolfe, Gary K., *The Known and the Unknown: The Iconography of Science Fiction* (Kent, Oh., 1979).

Wollheim, Donald A., *The Universe Makers: Science Fiction Today* (New York, 1971; London, 1972).

Wuckel, Dieter, and Cassiday, Bruce, *The Illustrated History of Science Fiction* (Leipzig, 1989).

Index

OXFORD

MORE OXFORD PAPERBACKS

This book is just one of nearly 1000 Oxford Paper-backs currently in print. If you would like details of other Oxford Paperbacks, including titles in the World's Classics, Oxford Reference, Oxford Books, OPUS, Past Masters, Oxford Authors, and Oxford Shakespeare series, please write to:

UK and Europe: Oxford Paperbacks Publicity Manager, Arts and Reference Publicity Department, Oxford University Press, Walton Street, Oxford OX2 6DP.

Customers in UK and Europe will find Oxford Paperbacks available in all good bookshops. But in case of difficulty please send orders to the Cash-with-Order Department, Oxford University Press Distribution Services, Saxon Way West, Corby, Northants NN18 9ES. Tel: 0536 741519; Fax: 0536 746337. Please send a cheque for the total cost of the books, plus £1.75 postage and packing for orders under £20; £2.75 for orders over £20. Customers outside the UK should add 10% of the cost of the books for postage and packing.

USA: Oxford Paperbacks Marketing Manager, Oxford University Press, Inc., 200 Madison Avenue, New York, N.Y. 10016.

Canada: Trade Department, Oxford University Press, 70 Wynford Drive, Don Mills, Ontario M3C 1J9.

Australia: Trade Marketing Manager, Oxford University Press, G.P.O. Box 2784Y, Melbourne 3001, Victoria.

South Africa: Oxford University Press, P.O. Box 1141, Cape Town 8000.

POPULAR SCIENCE FROM
OXFORD PAPERBACKS

THE SELFISH GENE

Second Edition

Richard Dawkins

Our genes made us. We animals exist for their preservation and are nothing more than their throwaway survival machines. The world of the selfish gene is one of savage competition, ruthless exploitation, and deceit. But what of the acts of apparent altruism found in nature—the bees who commit suicide when they sting to protect the hive, or the birds who risk their lives to warn the flock of an approaching hawk? Do they contravene the fundamental law of gene selfishness? By no means: Dawkins shows that the selfish gene is also the subtle gene. And he holds out the hope that our species—alone on earth—has the power to rebel against the designs of the selfish gene. This book is a call to arms. It is both manual and manifesto, and it grips like a thriller.

The Selfish Gene, Richard Dawkins's brilliant first book and still his most famous, is an international bestseller in thirteen languages. For this greatly expanded edition, endnotes have been added, giving fascinating reflections on the original text, and there are two major new chapters.

'learned, witty, and very well written . . . exhilaratingly good.' Sir Peter Medawar, *Spectator*

'Who should read this book? Everyone interested in the universe and their place in it.' Jeffrey R. Baylis, *Animal Behaviour*

'the sort of popular science writing that makes the reader feel like a genius' *New York Times*

POPULAR SCIENCE FROM
OXFORD PAPERBACKS

THE AGES OF GAIA

A Biography of Our Living Earth

James Lovelock

In his first book, *Gaia: A New Look at Life on Earth*, James Lovelock proposed a startling new theory of life. Previously it was accepted that plants and animals evolve on, but are distinct from, an inanimate planet. Gaia maintained that the Earth, its rocks, oceans, and atmosphere, and all living things are part of one great organism, evolving over the vast span of geological time. Much scientific work has since confirmed Lovelock's ideas.

In *The Ages of Gaia*, Lovelock elaborates the basis of a new and unified view of the earth and life sciences, discussing recent scientific developments in detail: the greenhouse effect, acid rain, the depletion of the ozone layer and the effects of ultraviolet radiation, the emission of CFCs, and nuclear power. He demonstrates the geophysical interaction of atmosphere, oceans, climate, and the Earth's crust, regulated comfortably for life by living organisms using the energy of the sun.

'Open the cover and bathe in great draughts of air that excitingly argue the case that "the earth is alive".' David Bellamy, *Observer*

'Lovelock deserves to be described as a genius.' *New Scientist*

PHILOSOPHY IN OXFORD PAPERBACKS
THE GREAT PHILOSOPHERS
Bryan Magee

Beginning with the death of Socrates in 399, and following the story through the centuries to recent figures such as Bertrand Russell and Wittgenstein, Bryan Magee and fifteen contemporary writers and philosophers provide an accessible and exciting introduction to Western philosophy and its greatest thinkers.

Bryan Magee in conversation with:

A. J. Ayer	John Passmore
Michael Ayers	Anthony Quinton
Miles Burnyeat	John Searle
Frederick Copleston	Peter Singer
Hubert Dreyfus	J. P. Stern
Anthony Kenny	Geoffrey Warnock
Sidney Morgenbesser	Bernard Williams
Martha Nussbaum	

'Magee is to be congratulated . . . anyone who sees the programmes or reads the book will be left in no danger of believing philosophical thinking is un-practical and uninteresting.' Ronald Hayman, *Times Educational Supplement*

'one of the liveliest, fast-paced introductions to philosophy, ancient and modern that one could wish for' *Universe*

OXFORD POETRY LIBRARY
WILLIAM WORDSWORTH
Edited by Stephen Gill and Duncan Wu

Wordsworth was one of the most illustrious of the Romantic poets. In this selection generous extracts are given from his important work *The Prelude*, together with many of his shorter poems. The reader will find classics such as *Tintern Abbey*, *Westminster Bridge* and 'I wandered lonely as a cloud' well represented. Notes and introduction are provided by Wordsworth's biographer, Stephen Gill, and Duncan Wu.

WORLD'S CLASSICS SHAKESPEARE

'not simply a better text but a new conception of Shakespeare. This is a major achievement of twentieth-century scholarship.' Times Literary Supplement

Hamlet
Macbeth
The Merchant of Venice
As You Like It
Henry IV Part I
Henry V
Measure for Measure
The Tempest
Much Ado About Nothing
All's Well that Ends Well
Love's Labours Lost
The Merry Wives of Windsor
The Taming of the Shrew
Titus Andronicus
Troilus & Cressida
The Two Noble Kinsmen
King John
Julius Caesar
Coriolanus
Anthony & Cleopatra

Oxford Reference

The Oxford Reference series offers authoritative and up-to-date reference books in paperback across a wide range of topics.

OXFORD REFERENCE

THE CONCISE OXFORD COMPANION TO ENGLISH LITERATURE

*Edited by Margaret Drabble and
Jenny Stringer*

Based on the immensely popular fifth edition of the
Oxford Companion to English Literature this is an
indispensable, compact guide to the central matter
of English literature.

There are more than 5,000 entries on the lives
and works of authors, poets, playwrights, essayists,
philosophers, and historians; plot summaries of
novels and plays; literary movements; fictional
characters; legends; theatres; periodicals; and much
more.

The book's sharpened focus on the English literature of the British Isles makes it especially convenient to use, but there is still generous coverage of
the literature of other countries and of other disci-
plines which have influenced or been influenced by
English literature.

From reviews of *The Oxford Companion to
English Literature*:

'a book which one turns to with constant pleasure
. . . a book with much style and little prejudice' Iain
Gilchrist, *TLS*

'it is quite difficult to imagine, in this genre, a more
useful publication' Frank Kermode, *London Review of Books*

'incarnates a living sense of tradition . . . sensitive
not to fashion merely but to the spirit of the age'
Christopher Ricks, *Sunday Times*